Stars for Night & Shadow

by

Ruquayya Sajjida

First edition paperback ISBN: 978-1-7379465-2-6

KDP Paperback edition published February 2024.

Edited by Ruquayya Sajjida
Layout by Ruquayya Sajjida
Interior illustration of Kalysma by Patricia Pérez (patop.art)
Map by Michael J. Patrick (Fiverr)
Cover art by winda_chu (Fiverr)

100,574 approximate words

Poetry and songs and other writings are author's own work, although outside works/musical artists may be referenced.

An imprint of Blacke Books
Louisville, KY, United States of America
All fonts are free for commercial use. All rights reserved.

ADULT DARK ROMANTIC SCIENCE-FANTASY

Blacke Books
Indie Publishing

STARS FOR NIGHT

& SHADOW

To all the unsung heroes of my generation—you have cracks, but you are by no means broken.

Trigger Warning!

Hello, my lovelies!

Thank you for picking up this book! I'm sorry if the content is too graphic for some, so I thought I'd add some trigger warnings at the beginning to help some in case they're on the fence about purchasing this:

Strong language

Reference to suicide

References to sexual assault

Physical abuse

Verbal abuse

Slavery

Violence

Murder

Explicit [consensual] sex

Among other things.

If this sounds like something that may bother you, please don't read this. I'm sorry if it's a lot or triggers some readers. Therefore, if you think it possibly could, DO NOT READ!

Things to look out for when reading...

-The fetishization of BIPOC men/women

-The racism amongst the top tier, even within our own black communities

-Self-hatred after being taught that you are "other"

-The impossibility of gaining your freedom "legally" when in bondage

-Trauma of racial oppression

-Two-facedness of some black liberators, who usually aren't even black

-The willingness to do what is needed to gain freedom

-The use of blackness to identify self-worth (or lack thereof)

-Racism amongst northerners (and their denial of it)

-Black spirituality

-Not being able to figure out where we're from

-Many stories about God(s), but most have been tampered with

-Needing God to cope with real life struggles

-Mental health within the black community

-Unwillingness to get help

-Sexualization, manipulation and abuse of our women by our own men

-Willingness to "roll over" and conform when under pressure from oppressors or even people within our community

-Shame/repression/over-selling of sexuality (esp. after sexual abuse)

-Finding worth in the wrong things

-Corruption of self after gaining money

-Prostitution (i.e., fuck for rent) for money, status, or leverage

-Inability to leave once ensnared in organization or other relationships

-Mental health of BIPOC

-BLACK EXCELLENCE!

Dear Reader,

If you decided to stick around, thank you. I hope that you can find this story entertaining. When I wrote it, I wrote it as a means to understand my own struggles with depression, C-PTSD, and racism. I'm not sure how successful the former will be, but I do want to say that if you experienced some of the things that my character went through in this book, whether as a victim of abuse or a person of color, (which really, if you're the later, you're the former) you contain strength beyond measure. You are more than your story—you are a survivor. And yes, even though sometimes abuse doesn't make us stronger in the beginning, and may leave us feeling broken or defeated, it does give us some pretty neat scars, and a story that may one day save the lives of others.

So don't give in just because something happened to you. Don't listen to the vicious lies your abuser tries to feed you. You are loved, beautiful and strong.

You are a survivor.

I'm planning on this being part of a four-book series known as The Glass Quartet. If you can handle book one, then you can most likely handle the next three, although I can't guarantee your durability. Only you can gauge that.

Just so you know, this story is supposed to be the creation of a villain. She goes from an antihero to a full-fledged villain throughout this series, slowly at first, but more rapidly as time progresses. This means that I, as the author, will have to make difficult choices, and that you as a reader will be put through hell. You will be witnessing, to put it bluntly, a fall from grace.

It's not meant to be inspiring or to show a pure spirit that beats all odds, but rather a person with a tainted soul, who finds that since they cannot be the heroine everyone needs, she will be the villain who saves herself. It's a tough decision but I thoroughly enjoy characters that are not totally one-dimensional. The first book is more of an origin story if anything else, will books two thru four are more of the story continued on once the premise has been set up. I'll try to make it worth it and I know that I'll lose many friends along the way, but how can I say that I've truly lived if I don't draw out every emotion in others?

I promise, my intention is not to hurt anyone, dear reader, but rather to understand humanity and myself as an individual; I hope you can understand that and don't hold it against me too much.

Thank you for picking up my book and thank you to all the people that helped me get here and put up with my daily ramblings, especially my dear friend, Julie, and my permanent beta-reader, Donna K. I can't believe I'm finally sending my baby out into the real world!

Please pay attention to the trigger warnings!

And thank you, dear reader, for your time and your resilience.

I often thought drowning would be
A particularly painful way to go.
Limbs weighted down and
Lungs dragging in the undertow.

And I thought that fire would be
Especially cruel for one such as me,
With bones turned to ash
And face twisted in agony.

But when faced with death,
Either of hellfire or of the sea,
It seems befitting to say
Both would bring me glee.

Drown.
Burn.
Un-hinder me if you will.
Lose me not,
But let me go still.

—*Drown or Burn?* by Ruquayya Sajjida

"Hail the Goddess that yanked the sun from the sky, just as the Immortals yanked us as little babes from our mother's tit to be sold at auction. Hail the Goddess who buried our powers deep within the Earth, who sheltered us from raging winds, who calmed us when our cries were loud. Hail the Goddess who blessed us with many faces so that we sink into the brush, blend in with the sand, paddle through the swamp and hunt in the snowy tundra. She who has buried our strength in the Earth. She who has warmed planets in the space between her thighs and held stars in her grasp. She is the beginning, the end, the holder of the One Light and the protector of the Many. Thank you for these Gifts that we have been made with, for we are the Few. May you always prosper, even if your womb is barren, for your days shall continue if our path is before us, from the Earth to the Great Beyond. By magic we are bound and from split blood we shall refrain. Under the stars, we praise, we worship, and we remain."

--The Revenant, C

Preface: Part One

Her Design

The old Gods and Goddess communed in their Trinity.

"Gather round, Daughter, Son, Kalysma, Cato, children of nightly wanderers and bloodlust. What shall have ye for your born day?"

The Son, Cato, wanting to be a great ruler like His Father, said, "I shall have the sun, for long days of battle and life."

To his favorite, Father beamed. "And you, my Daughter?"

She pondered for a good long while to us, but was only a blink for them. "A different kind of light. Stars for night and shadow. To feed the hollow souls who gander at the moon and ponder, 'Why not I, love?'"

We are the stars and all that envelope it.

We are different, new, and our tale is tragic.

For we are love.

Preface: Part Two

The First of Us

Dear Sir, Madam or Xe,

It is said that the Good Mother Kalysma was the First of Us, thrown from the Creator's Garden once her husband, Blithe, was driven mad by his jealousy. All her inherent offspring were cursed to wander the Zuora, denied the Hand that Fed and silent to Her calls. We were cursed to look like monsters and were quickly enslaved on Zuora by the Creator's chosen children: **the Immortals**. *Our Mother Kalysma found her way into another dimension where she could mourn her beloved. And she welcomed all who would follow Her.*

She left us the One Light, now known as the North Star, which would guide those chosen into the afterlife. It is said that She handpicks each of Her offspring from those born on this forgotten planet, gifting us with special abilities to aid us in this accursed life. And no Gifted can ignore Her call forever, finding ourselves drawn to Her bosom like a moth to a flame. **They** *say that suffering makes one pure—but we all know that this is a lie force-fed to the Gifted to keep us in line. And we Gifted have suffered for hundreds of years, slaving away for the Immortals,* ostracized and hunted by the Mortals, and loved by none.

But I believe that we are here for another reason: to conquer.

For too long, we were shamed for our looks. For too long, we were beaten, raped and enslaved at the hands of the Immortals. The Rebellion offers you a chance to fight back and take the Zuora for your own. You didn't really think we were born to suffer, did you?

Don't you want to be free in this life, too?

If you have received this letter, it is because you share a vision and a likeness with the Gifted. You want to see us prosper and multiply. And don't let anyone tell you that you are misguided.

We have been **chosen**.

We are not soldiers for Immortal Armies. We are not slaves. We are spies, mercenaries, warriors. If you want to take your name back—take your life and soul back—then bring this letter to the rock in the field just north of the Maeoran harbor—you know the one. I'll see you there.

Sincerely, Valentina Guadalupe Garcia

P.S. Present this password at the door. This will be the key to your entry. Good luck.

From tyranny we ran

To the underground.

Loud is our cause

Though we make no sound.

The Good Mother, we worship

And do condemn

The Great Father

For what he did to them.

Chapter One

Sacrifice

BOOM! BOOM! BOOM!

"Five minutes to place your bets!"

Master stroked one chalk-white finger along my cheek. A thousand blessings from a thousand stars kept me in line, kept me from challenging the man that could undoubtedly beat me with just a flick of the wrist—that and the humiliation of past defeats. I dug my fingernails into my palms, forming little crescent moons in my skin.

"I will miss you, my love."

I ground my teeth, barely choking out the words. Goddess, I could hardly summon them! "As will I."

"I will have Valentina cook you up some sweets when we get home—" I knew there was a but, "—but only if you win."

"I always win."

"Yes, yes. How could I forget, *aimé?*"

Boom! Boom! Boom!

The drums shook the very planet.

"The time to place bets is almost at a close! I repeat—Immortals, place your bets before the showdown begins!"

Jacques glanced around, his eyes skimming the one thing Maeora had plenty to give its people—sand, sand and more sand—underneath our feet, mixed with water and mud to make the walls, hardened to make the now-invisible glass dome that surrounded the magic-and-technology-controlled arena. Two Gifted men stood guard at the lip of the dugout, their skin the green, brown and deeper-brown of desert snakes, their eyes two yellow pools with slits, their otherness outwardly marking them as my kin, yet I knew that in a way, they were no more my brothers than the furry, fanged wolf-men of Amoria. That went the same for the jaguars of Espanza and the Mortals of Sidra. I frowned.

There are no more gators at home, in the Southern Isles…why is that?

The Goddess was silent.

I looked back to my Master, a sheen of glistening hellfire coming to his eyes before they returned to me; he was always tense before a fight. And it would be my duty to later relieve that tension. He fully faced me and nodded once, signaling that it was time.

Jacques had seen my true form a thousand times, but my otherness never ceased to bother him, just as *his* distress never seemed to stop bothering *me*. He steeled his shoulders, preparing himself.

Letting my Glamour slip away like a veil showed the monster beneath.

My bones slid throughout my skin, popping and grinding as they shifted to reform in a way that was no longer painful, but familiar. My almond-brown body took on armored scutes, my eyelids doubled, the outer pair blinking back to front, my slit pupil of my emerald-green eyes ready to see through the murkiest of waters. My teeth sharpened to rows of jagged, snaggle-toothed fangs set to devour whole worlds. My true nature was revealed even without my Gift being displayed: I was not human, but a monster, a creature known as a Gifted.

My Gift, the mark of all descendants of the Barren One, the Good Mother, the Maker of all Strife, was rising beneath my skin, begging to be released. The electricity within me writhed, alive. My skin was hot from anticipation and wet from the dip in the swamp I took an hour ago—my own way of relieving tension. The breeze from the overhead ventilation worked to cool my skin, causing a chill to race down my spine. I licked away a bead of salty water from my upper lip.

I was infinite. Not just I, but the thousands of Gifted who walked the Zuora. Like our Goddess Kalysma, who we revered and loathed all at once, our apartness lived on forever.

"Entering from this side...is the illustrious Marve of the Faux Empire!" an automated voice boomed from the loudspeakers. *"Come now, great champion Marve! Come and give us your offering!"*

I stepped into the arena and faced the shouting masses. Glancing into the stands, I saw Master nod. Pumping a fist in the air, a crazed grin overtook my face, *and the crowd went nuts!* Dunes of sand rose around me, pockets littered here and there, meant either for hiding or for creatures to emerge. The artificial sun shone

7

brighter here; a woman in the stands waved a fan in front of her face.

Imagine it: piles of creatures wearing the skin of humans, slathered with sweat, stacked on top of one another, squirming and writhing with life as they waited for my death. Only they weren't human at all: they were monsters, eternal living beings known as the Immortals. They saw the killing of my kind as sport, as primitive and daring as the people in the fabled Roman arenas that inspired these tremendous showdowns. Animals, the whole lot of them.

"Entering from this side..." the voice droned. *"...a slave-girl that has not earned a name yet. Will she triumph this day, spilling blood for the beauteous Immortals? Enter, slave-girl!"*

She resisted for only a moment, but there was a flare of bright, fleshy pink in her eyes—the light of her liege's magic—and she came, drawn forward by the will of her Master.

First, a plethora of dark-as-night shadows swirling around her feet reached my eyes, before I was to hear them hissing and singing sweet nothings as she took her final step. We sized each other up, looking for any sign of weakness. I knew how I looked—the frazzled red hair that I inherited from my mother, which was the only thing that kept me from looking like a total beast, and the frail bag-of-bones slanted features. With her ivory skin, flashing blue eyes and tumbling blonde hair, it was obvious that she had more Mortal ancestry than Gifted, but the thick hair on her legs suggested a possibly Amorian ancestry mixed in with her Sidran roots.

"This is what they send me to kill?" the girl cried, flinging a bony arm towards the stands. "I could snap her neck like a twig!"

8

Most of the crowd roared in laughter, their voices rumbling the ground like earthquakes. But a few looked to me. They'd seen me fight—they grew up on stories about Gifted like me. My surprise drowned out my offense. Electricity crackled just beneath my skin, again crying out, *Release me!*

I reached past skin, past blood, past bone, past sinew, past my heart and into my soul. On cue, there was the hastened awakening of my raging, sinister side—the side that drew directly on the magic imbedded in my genetic code.

"Now!" The automated voice took on an excited human zeal. *"SACRIFICE!"*

Charging, my storm not only guided me but assisted me. Her shadows became more frenzied the closer I got. They sang to me, calling for the darkness in my heart, wanting me to give in…

"Dark and evil, wrong and chaotic you are," one shadow wisped, its voice hot like a kindling flame.

"Let us fester, let us grow, let us eat, let us know," said another, sounding like a child demanding a fistful of sweets.

"Let us devour your filthy heart," said the last, its voice heavy like the planet we stood upon.

Stopping mere inches from her, my hand automatically pushed forward. It glowed with an unearthly purplish light as my Gift warmed my skin, making it bubble like water. Electricity spazzed its way across the arena. The girl dropped to the sand and dodged with a roll.

She lifted her hands. A pair of red eyes blinked back at me as the shadows curled tighter around their lady-liege. Still, they whispered to me, calling to the evil within. I'd had enough of their senseless chatter. She dug her heels into the ground and charged with a sword made of pure darkness in her hand.

I charged forward…and slipped over a long, thick root, crashing down into one of the pits in a none-too-graceful fashion.

"No!" she cursed aboveground.

A shadow cast over me and across the wall, spindly and wrong. Pretending to panic for a moment, I glanced around. The air was chilly here, a place where the sun did not touch…an even more accursed monster's dwelling. I refrained from rolling my eyes when I met the beast's gaze.

"Is…?" I said in lowered voice, "Is that who I think it is?"

A woman crouched before me, the same freckles on my face spread across her alabaster white skin. Her hair fell around her head in crimson waves, like the ocean when the sky bled like a gushing wound; the First Days of the Immortals Wars, when the Gifted extinguished the sun. She lifted her head, lifted it like the red sun as it was hefted into the sky, breathy sobs wrenching from her throat, her face obscured by her flaming locks. For a moment, my heart went out to her, my eyes finding sameness in the plank of her waist, of the gaunt of her arms.

"Mar?"

The Fabic (the language spoken in the Southern Isles and Sidra) word for Mom. It had no extension. *Da* was the meaningful word for Dad, *Danri* its extension for Father.

I yearned for the days of my past, her fingers coiling through my hair as she worked it into elaborate braids, her own red hair bound up in a ponytail that was

10

commonly worn in the largest of the Southern Isles. My father had been her opposite, with coffee bean-black skin that was easier to come by on the smaller Isles. Both had appeared totally human, physically unmarked in the way my appearance had been—their curse hidden only until they lost control…until the magic became too strong and spilled over, pouring from their fingertips and into the world.

Or at least it had—

Until they died.

"Don't you love me? Don't you miss me?"

The anger at the familiar demon's mistake pooled in my stomach, warming me from the inside out. "We both know you are not my mother."

The sobbing stopped. I saw what I hadn't seen before—what was hidden by the darkness: she reached up, her hands gnarled and wrinkled with the bones in them going in every direction. She pushed the hair away so that it was no longer covering her face. I recoiled. Her eyes were two gaping holes, blood running down her face. She flicked one long, serpentine tongue across her lips, sweeping the droplets into her waiting mouth. Instinctually, those lips peeled back to expose two rows of sharp teeth.

I waited for a camera to catch my good side before smirking at her: "So, we meet aga—"

But she had no patience.

The light sliced across her bottom half, showing scales many shades of green, from the pale green of a fig to the partial green of a leaf to the deep, dazzling green of an emerald. The darkest green, which was at the tip of her tail, matched my *real*

11

mother's eyes, and from it protruded a long, thin needle about five inches in length and one inch across.

Her tail swished back and forth as she slinked forward, faster than most, but not fast enough to alarm me. I stood there, used to the antics of the Weeper, a demon created by the makers of these matches. This was just an intimidation tactic—it would need to get its acid into my bloodstream to subdue me.

Fun fact: the Weeper could disguise itself as anyone from an enemy's past— but not its hands or its bottom half—*that's* why it waited in the shadows.

Her long tail flicked behind her as she wrapped her hands around my midsection. That needle gleamed 'menacingly'—but I knew from past matches that she was the weakest of the monsters that called these arenas home. It was all too easy to maneuver out of her weak, disfigured grip.

We grappled for only a moment. Her hands made their way across my body, seeking purchase. But they found none. She extended her tail and held it just above the throbbing vein at my throat. Quick as a dart, my own hand shot out and grabbed her tail before plunging it into one of her eye sockets.

Her screech was deafening.

And unbelievably satisfying.

Using those few fatal moments against her was easy: I reached up and grabbed hold of a long root just outside the hole—the same root that made me fall in—and hoisted myself out. As the sun fell through the area where I just was, the demon clawed at me, trying to wrench me back into its fathomless prison. The sunlight hit her body. She screamed like the cowardly serpent she was, slithering away from the light.

"Finally decided to join us, eh?"

I was engulfed in darkness. It was the blinding, suffocating, damningly claustrophobic kind. As soon as it surrounded me, there was the realization that this match could not be drawn out like most. Hearing a laugh skitter by and three pairs of red eyes circling me, I turned. My paranoid mind mistook the shadows for long, broken hands. My mind danced with their whispers.

A flash of tumbling blonde locks passed me, then the sight of blue eyes, not yet hardened with the ice of endless battles. And I grinned a mad grin.

I lunged the same way the Weeper had, grabbing a fistful of her hair. The darkness dissolved and then I was in the arena again, the crowd silent, the air still. Yanking the slave-girl's head back then forward, my other fist shot forward like a rocket. I felt a sharp pain in my knuckle, but I was prepared for it. A bruise began to form on the back of my hand as I wrenched her closer to the ground. The last lick of darkness evaporated as she cried out.

I was already panting in exertion when I charged up a lightning bolt. That familiar storm sizzled beneath my skin. There wasn't much time left before my powers gave out. I latched onto her. She wrenched back, but without nearly enough strength to break my grip, a scream untangling itself from her throat and reverberating throughout the arena. The final voltage ramped through me. Electricity crawled over her skin like a spider.

There was an audible pop as her head whipped at an unnatural angle. The tendons in her neck jutted out like the pop-ups of a child's picture book. As if she were gargling water, the sound of her last choking breaths filled the space between us. I'll never forget that sound: it was not quite a gasp, but not nearly a wheeze either. Her body convulsed in a seizure. Then she went still, foam dripping from the side of her mouth.

The cheering had already begun. I tried to see it as a good thing. At least she had a taste of glory in her last few moments. I twisted, separating our bodies, then I stood and smiled at the smoke rising from her form.

"We have a winner!"

I turned.

The golden coins twinkled in the sun as Master pocketed his winnings. The dead woman's face briefly flashed across the screen. I should earn two more drachmas from this battle, which was exactly one more than what I need. I felt my mask crack and give way as I grinned. I felt excitement at the thought of leaving this place behind.

A stout, chubby man waddled into the arena, flanked by two black boys about five years my junior, which put them in their mid-teens. The man's hair and mustache were brown streaked through with stressing grey flyaway strands. As my master slinked forward to take his hand, Jacques addressed him as Grayson. The other Master, who was probably leagues younger than my own liege, turned to me. He nodded gruffly before kicking out a foot.

The body of the woman nudged to one side, her blonde hair sticking up around her head like a halo, and Grayson gruffly harrumphed, "Foolish Natalia. If only she'd fought harder."

14

"Yes, well," Jacques smirked, "we can't all be winners, can we?"

One of the boys waited for Grayson's nod before throwing a match onto the corpse. As the flames rose into the sky, I felt my chest inflate. At least she would reach the stars, where her ancestors danced with the moon.

Under my breath, I whispered the mantra that every Gifted said when one of our own passed, a gift for her sacrifice: "By magic we are bound and by blood we remain. Among the stars you shall lay."

My Master eyed me, his face blank, unreadable. I wondered if he would punish me for the religious custom as he had before—but he didn't. Reaching into the pouch he had just pocketed, he grabbed two golden coins. I tried not to eye his movements too intensely.

"You did well."

"Thank you, Master."

He held the coins out. Not snatching them too quickly was a tremendous feat. I grabbed his hand and dipped my head in, kissing it briefly. My fingers pressed onto the ice-cold flesh of his palm, taking the coins.

But instead of letting go, he held my clenched fist. Our eyes locked. There was a hungry look in his eyes as he watched me, devouring me as much as assessing me. I held my hand steady, refusing to let it shake as I slid the coins into my back pocket. I thanked him again.

He waved a hand. "Try not to eat too many sweets when we get home. I can't have you crashing from a sugar high tomorrow."

"Of course, Master."

15

But that hunger remained. I trembled, mentally praying that he found some humanity, and let me go without tainting me. He loved my innocence almost as much as he desired to press night-black into its seafoam-white.

And that made him dangerous.

Chapter Two

Roses in the Water

Seven windows glowed like the tips of candles. Vines crept along the edges of the grand porch steps. A cedar door seemed to stare down at me, its gaze sharp and imposing. The house was painted a deep cobalt blue with lighter blue accents. Tall, gangly limbs of trees rose into the air around it, while diseased hands of black ferns and thorny roses reached out from their shadows as if to grab me, the forest creeping along its edges. It was buried in a part of Sidra not too far from my childhood home, constructed by slaves who were now dead, in a time when my Master was more patient, but also more vulnerable. He had intended this to be the home for his now ex-lover and himself to share.

But that was a dead dream—cold, beautiful, and unobtainable, just like the man who ordered its construction.

"Get a bath ready," he bid me, a gleam in his eyes.

My heart hammered in fear. My head swam with images, images that refused to stay buried without a fight. My stomach swam with nausea, my body swaying as if I were a ship on choppy waters.

"Yes, sir."

Kneeling, not needing to count, my fingers skimmed the roses in the garden. The sting of the thorns' bites did not dissuade me. I plucked twenty-two rose petals, beginning the ritual as he watched me in satisfaction.

I opened the door, bowing my head, gaze lowered to the ground. A pair of feet glided past me into the house. I entered after him. The other two slaves were kneeling on the floor, their eyes downcast as well. A smile graced the oldest one's lips, one that couldn't be placed in sanity's realm.

My body quickly flitted through the long, narrow hallway, past a room with glass cases where antiques were kept, to the bathroom. Afforded no more than a glance at the porcelain sink with heavy gold, faceted knobs, went to the black claw-footed, open-faced tub. Turning on the faucet mechanically, I tried not to think of what came next, trying not to let fear take a complete hold on me. After a while, my fear dulled to background noise. I ran the water as he liked it—scalding hot.

There was an audible *swish* of clothes dropping to the floor. I tensed. He moved past me, lowering his slender, pale, naked body into the water. Sitting near the tub, my hand drooped in the water, my purposely numb mind unable to register that my hand was burning until he murmured something. I yanked it out of the water and moved to stand.

"The roses?" he reminded me.

I picked up the petals, nearly forgotten.

Every time I ran him a bath, twenty-two rose petals were to be placed into the water. This daily ritual was a tribute to the only divine he knew—the Immortals—and the age at which they left their mortality behind and became impervious to everything: twenty-two. The Weeper must have gotten to me today—not good.

"Well?" he prompted, raising a brow.

I picked up the shampoo that doubled as a body wash, reached out, and began with his hair. The wash was imported from Amoria, a country just north of here, that held winter nearly year-round and was known for its lavish soaps, thick oils, and frothy healing concoctions. It would be summer there now, but only until the biting winds and clumpy snow packed in. His eyes closed as my nails scraped his scalp; he hummed in satisfaction. I massaged his scalp for only a moment, wanting to get it over with. Then I picked up a sponge and lathered it with the same liquid soap.

He smirked.

This was his favorite part.

I dipped my hand into the water, dragging it across his back. He leaned into the touch. Pressing a bit harder, I scraped his skin. He hissed, but did not stop me. Moving higher, I got his neck, and then I maneuvered my arm around to cover the expanse of his ivory-white chest. The sponge caressed his nipples; they hardened in the air.

"You little tease," he groaned.

This brought me no joy, no excitement. He loved it though. One day this wouldn't be enough.

He wanted more than to possess my touch, more than to own my mouth, more than to steal my air—to invade the deepest parts of me. But that wasn't what made me pause. It was a sudden, random thought that was far, far worse.

Even though I believed that he would honor our bargain of me going free once I procured two-hundred-and-fifty drachmas, a blind panic was ever present. Had I truly saved enough to buy freedom for both Tiara and I?

My hand was frozen on his chest.

He breathed out two impatient, solitary words: "Do it."

So, my hand crept through the water like a snake, inching towards him like a damned thing.

I reached him.

"Slower," he commanded. "It's been a long day."

Chapter Three

Spy

Master let me sleep in the next day.

In the shower, it took three scrubbings before the thick sand from yesterday finally came off to reveal the freckled, brown skin beneath. The cold also woke me. When I pulled out of my sleepy haze, I reminded myself to put on the correct face.

If the Rebellion ever wins this war, I thought, *I will wear my true face until the end of my days…*

I brushed my teeth before throwing on a pair of khakis and a white button-up shirt. Avoided looking in the mirror. And reassured myself that I was not a *whore* as he liked to call me, since we all had our duties to fulfill.

Walking down the hall brought me past the dining room table and the front door across from it. My feet turned me deeper into the hall. Stacked before me, from floor to ceiling, were a duo of mahogany cabinets that stretched across the length of the room. Tiara was already there, shakily cleaning a set of sake cups. I remembered the first week when she arrived here, when Master beat her so badly that he caused permanent brain damage: not only was her balance affected, but her speech as well. That was the day that I decided to free us both.

Tiara cleaned the mansion with me in record time. I sang as we worked, Tiara smiling and humming along. Her short, tight dress looked wrong on her form, but she wore it with pride. With her hair braided down her back and her white teeth standing out against her dark skin, she shone with an innocent beauty that only a child could possess. She didn't have an Armored State—the skin some Gifted were born into—so she didn't have to hide who she was. It'd be lying to say I wasn't a little jealous.

I thought of the scales and jagged teeth that I readily hid and frowned. The words died in my throat. Tiara kept humming into the next line of the song. Of course, it wasn't her fault. She couldn't help that she was naturally beautiful.

"I have a sweet treat in my room," I whispered nudging her, "will you go get it for me?"

Her eyes twinkled. She took off running.

I imagined her as a blue jay flitting through the halls, t twittering a song of freedom in learned ignorance and self-inflicted blindness. *Fly, blind bird, fly.* I smiled back at her when she returned. Without a second thought, I broke it in two. I moved to eat mine, but noticed her staring at me with wide eyes, crumbs on her mouth, her half nowhere in sight. I rolled my eyes.

"Now where did yours go, little one?" I whispered, fake-frowning at her.

"P-p-please, Marve?"

I forked it over.

22

"Mm, mm, mm!" she hummed, smacking her lips.

And then she started telling me about what she saw in the city the day before. She told me of two women (one of them with a prominent scar,) who wore purple bandanas and stole swiftly and quietly. One of them got caught stealing and left her bandana trying to get away.

This was a good opportunity to teach her about the real world; she'd need this when we were on our own. "Do you remember anything distinct about them?"

"Well..." Tiara poked out a lip, her face screwing tight as she thought. "The one that left her bandana—the one with the scar—she had a tattoo!"

"Remember them," I warned, "and stay far away."

"Aye, cap'n!"

I laughed, feeling more at ease in those few moments than I had in many days.

The loquacious girl was the only one of us that got to leave the house regularly, since she was trusted not to run away. The envy wasn't because she could leave, but *why* she could leave: she was happy with this life. And I would never let that part of her be snuffed out by the Ring of Death.

I set down the cups just as Tiara reached for the crown of a long-forgotten queen. I plucked it from her fingers and sat it upon her head. She giggled and twirled around in a circle. For a moment, what she saw was clear to me: a princess that refused to be broken and a merciful king. A sudden sadness crept upon me, settling upon my head like a dark cloud.

I took the crown, scrubbed it so that no trace of her was left upon it, and placed it back in its glass prison. There was no room for princesses nor queens here—just a god and his fearful subjects. Sensing my dark mood, Tiara bumped my hip. I smiled for her sake and went back to my job. The sooner we finished, the better.

"What else did you see with your knowing eyes—" I asked Tiara, finally bumping her hip back. "Any cute fellas?"

"Ooh, I saw an I-m-m-mortal with skin that looked like real g-g-gold. He was *so* pretty!" She smiled wistfully. "He even gave me a drachma!"

I grinned down at her. "You must've stolen it from him, you little devil!"

"Or m-m-maybe I f-f-fought him for it!" she cried back cutely, making fake jabs with her tough little fists.

I stumbled back, clutching my sides in mock horror. "Whoa, watch out! We've got a Champion on the loose!"

Shouting reached me. There was a crash, the woosh of flames, the zing of a blade being freed, and a firm voice yelling one word: *"NO!"*

I shuddered. For a moment, the magic flicked off in my fear. I was flickering between my two states before I was finally able to grab hold of myself enough to settle into my glamour form. I sharply commanded Tiara to stay put before down the hallway.

My Master, Jacques Faux, leaned on the counter with a knife in his hand. His usually paper-white skin was tinged black around the knife, eons darker than the crimson blood running down the blade; his skin was tinted black not from an egregious illness, but from the demon-blood that coursed through his veins. The usually russet-colored cook, who was now a pale brown that almost matched my own skin, stood in

24

the center of the room, clutching her right arm. Blood ran down her arm in a steady flow, which was twisted at an odd angle, and just behind her, smoke rose into the air. Jacques moved for her again, but I got to her first. I raised my hands in self-defense, hoping to curb his anger.

After all, he'd already taken her eye a year ago—next was her life.

"What happened?"

Master's jaw flexed as a vein in his temple throbbed. His usually impassive mouth was now curved in a disgusted sneer. There was a crimson fleck of blood on his stark white shirt front. He impatiently tugged at it and I knew that someone would have to clean it before he had an all-out meltdown. It was safe to say that he was pissed.

I tensed as he whirled on me.

"She's a Rebel spy!"

My entire body was rigid, a startled gasp tumbling from my lips. The Rebels were legends—not just in Sidra but across the continent. They fought to free the Gifted from the tyranny of the Immortals. Apparently, they even fought in the Great War that split the nation into four parts. If Valentina was one of them...

I puffed out my chest, trying to look big; I'd heard that was effective against dangerous animals in a book somewhere. "She isn't a spy."

Looking into his eyes was the same way with all demi-demons: all it left me with was a primal, instinctual urge to flee that made my heart stamp in fear.

But I refused to let it show.

"How do you know?" Jacques said, narrowing his eyes at me.

25

"Because I've known her since I was a kid. The main goal of the Rebellion is to get rid of the hierarchy that separates the castes. Why would she jeopardize her post now?"

His hand flashed out like a bullet. On the ground, the metallic taste of blood filled my mouth as if I'd laid my lips over a rusted pipe. I was left reeling as he stood over me, daring me to defy him again. He'd hit me for proving him wrong just as much as he'd struck me for my defiance. Out of the corner of my eye, I noticed Valentina slipping away, but I refused to acknowledge her for fear of releasing my Master on her again. I pushed myself up onto one knee and held out my hand, palm up.

Master's fingers skimmed my palm.

I was forgiven.

"Now clean up that blood. It's disgusting."

I kept my eyes averted as he left the room. It was odd. He was a half-demon so naturally, he ate people like me, but because of his OCD he had an aversion to blood. Then, like an image carried through the mist, I remembered scores of gruesomely disfigured bodies strung up by their toes, the blood draining into a hole in the floor to be collected in a basin that would need to be emptied later. And I saw a pair of gnashing fangs stripping a bone clean, human skin caught in his pearly-white teeth.

At least, I thought, *he is not a messy eater.*

There was shuffling behind me. Jacques didn't shuffle—he was inhumanly graceful. But I was running on paranoia right about now. I stood and whirled, my Gift charged and ready to go.

It was Tiara.

While Valentina had the Gift of pyrokinesis, Tiara had the Gift of light refraction. I remember once telling her that if the old man gave her any trouble, to bend the light around herself until she disappeared and then run. The normally talkative girl was hushed up now, her fear apparent.

I would put her fears at ease.

"Tiara?" I held out a hand to her. "Are you alright?"

"I-I-I'm s-s-scared..." she mumbled, wringing her dress in her hands.

I dropped to one knee once again so that we were at eye level. I gazed into those familiar brown orbs, willing her to look at me. Her whole body shook as she finally stared back. She was like a sister to me. And as the oldest sibling, it was my job to protect and console her.

"Don't worry, Tiara. I won't let him hurt you."

"Bu-but he hurt you. How can you help me i-i-if you can't—"

Tears ran down her face. I pulled her into a tight hug, holding her as shudders wracked her body. Her tiny, frail arms wrapped around me, holding on for dear life. Waiting until her sobs turned to sniffles before pulling away to wipe her face on my shirt was my best antidote. I gave her the brightest smile that I could manage, waiting until she smiled back before I continued.

"Everything's going to be all right."

"Wh-wha-what about T-T-Tina?"

Tina. It was a name that Tiara gave Valentina when she was a kid missing her two front teeth and could not fully pronounce *Valentina*. Thinking of that reminded me that it was crucial for us to stick together as a family. If I was the older sister, Valentina was our trustworthy aunt. I smoothed back a stubborn piece of her hair that refused to stay down and sent calming vibes through Tiara.

"You don't worry about that. I'll take care of her too. You just go to your room and stay out of sight. And remember—"

"If he catches me, use my Gift. I *have* to protect myself. You can handle yourself."

"Good girl." I patted her shoulder before standing at my full height. "Go on, now. I've got some business to take care of."

There was curiosity and fear in her eyes. But she flitted away at my waving hand. Mechanical, alone, I cleaned the blood from the floor with bleach from under the kitchen sink, and then put out the small flame smoldering in the corner. My shirt had blood on it from my mouth; I'd have to change it. I went to my room where Valentina was waiting, her right arm dangling next to her.

Her amber eye was glassy and unfocused, her skin now baby pink and clammy. The tall forty-year-old waved me forward, then turned in on herself. She buried her face in a pillow that I handed her. Doing my best to ignore her scream, I popped her arm back into place. Inspecting the deep gash on her arm unveiled that it would need stitches. I went to get needle and thread from the supply closet down the hall before grabbing a bottle of vodka from the kitchen and heading back to Tina. She was adjusting the bandage over her eye, something she did when she was nervous.

There was a small branding on her neck of a hawk rising from the sun. She moved her head and her hair covered it. Was that what this was all about? Her neck

28

glittered for a moment like a rainbow. I squinted at the glamour, wincing as the Mark disappeared.

Weird.

I held out the bottle. "Drink this."

When she refused, I shoved it in her hands and demanded that she drink.

She obliged, tipping back her head to guzzle half the bottle. I took the rest of the alcohol and poured it over the open wound. She cursed, "Stars above!" Then I took the needle and thread and began stitching her arm. She winced every now and then but kept quiet for the most part. She was always quiet—always kept to herself. When I imagined her, she always appeared the same: a broad woman, shoulders thrown back, hands raised in challenge.

Valentina made a noise of discomfort. I was thrown back into the rhythm of my body, forced to acknowledge the task at hand. I tried not to get stuck on the way the needle got caught on the skin, resisting. I kind of had to force it through, doing my best not to yank it. Blood made the needle wet and sticky, coating my fingers with red.

She did not deserve this.

Why did our Master believe that she was a spy?

"You have questions," she said once I was done.

I nodded vaguely, telling her that she may have been running a temperature.

"I'll be fine, girl. I've endured much worse."

A moment of hesitation and then, "Why does he think you're a spy?"

"Because I am."

Chapter Four

The Mark

"This Mark," Valentina grazed her fingers over the raised skin on her neck, "is the Mark of the Rebellion."

Observing her in that expanse of silence, I peeped what she fought to keep hidden.

On the red-brown skin of her neck was the branding and beneath her chin was a scar. The rest of her face was intriguing enough: a narrowed wise eye, an eye-patch to cover a gaping hole where her other eye once was and a broad forehead. She was built sturdy with wide hips and a frowning mouth. Her skin was smooth across her chest, like clay, but her hands were misshapen and covered with burn-marks from years of trying to perfect her Gift.

She had been through so much, had learned so much. And had fought to forget eons more. Then searched for a home and wound up here. Surely now, after all that happened, she was kidding. She wouldn't betray our family with lies.

"What do you mean?" I asked with a derisive snort. "That isn't very funny. If

Master hears you saying that…well, you'd better pray to the Creator that he doesn't take your other eye."

She harrumphed. "Then what good would I be?"

I gave her a pained smile. We both knew the answer to that.

She adjusted the eyepatch yet again. Her mouth was a straight, patient line. But her eye told a different story: it was the look of one who was faced with a dying dog and had to choose to either watch it suffer or put it down. Even her brows were lowered, furrowed, as if her mind held a great burden of mysteries. She knew something I didn't and refused to share it…Or maybe she knew that I wouldn't believe it and was sad to see its juiciness go untasted.

"Do you believe the story of our people?" she asked.

"Of course. It is the only story. Kalysma was damned and we were made slaves—"

Valentina stopped me there.

"That's where you've got it wrong," she said, her voice thick with that lilting, flowing accent that many Espanzans had.

"What do you mean? That's the story."

"No," she shook her head, "it isn't. Don't you see? It doesn't make much sense that her sacrifice was met with enslavement, does it?"

I shook my head. I'd never thought of it that way.

"Exactly!" She breathed the word as if to spark a flame of knowledge, staring at me with a maddened gleam in her eye. "Only the Rebels know the true story."

I snorted. That was total horse dung. Everyone knew the story of our Makers.

The Creator was tired of working in his fields alone. He commissioned Kalysma to help him. Instead, she lazily created us to help him rework the fields of the Garden of Eden. When we poisoned our Master's food with our hands, he grew angry, and flung us from the garden. We made our home on Zuora, and were captured by the Creator's children, the Immortals. We were always slaves and nothing more.

Nothing would change that.

"You see," Valentina began, "the descendants of Kalysma were given something else: the hidden ability to kill an Immortal."

I sucked in a sharp breath. Impossible! No one had killed an Immortal in all the years that they had ruled us.

"What do you know of the walls—of our world?"

There were three walls: Wall Seinaru, separating Amoria and Sidra, Wall Bella, separating Sidra and Espanza, and Wall Kotsbar, separating Espanza and Maeora. And these walls were every bit holy, beautiful and precious to the Immortals as much as they were glass prisons for the Gifted. But this was common knowledge. She must've meant the story behind them.

"That they were made by the Creator for the Immortals."

"True. But do you know what's beneath the walls?"

"No." I blinked at her. "Just dirt, I suppose."

"Foolish girl!" She gave me a withering look. "It's the key to an uprising."

I refused to shrink before her might. "What are you talking about?"

"Why do you think the Rebels sneak away and are never to be seen unless they will it? Why do you think they never get caught? Why do you think they appear everywhere in the country at a moment's notice?"

"I don't know," I said dryly. "Maybe they're fast runners."

"It's because the key to finding them is to go *underground*," she said. She braced a hand on my arm, gazing at me fervently. "I plan to go there tonight. Come with me!"

I shook my head without hesitation. It was too late to wake Tiara; she'd never make the trip. Besides, I had a plan. I would do it the legal way. Plus, that way we'd have papers proving our freedom to any who questioned it.

"You know, you were meant for more than this—we all were. You could be more than a monster. You could fight for a better future!" At my look, she snorted. "Come now, you don't want to end up a slave for the rest of your life."

I sniffed. "I won't be."

"Are you telling me that you're truly happy here?"

My eyes narrowed. "Of course not. But it's life."

It was a lie. This was not living. But I was afraid to let anyone know my plans until everything was final. Not even Tiara knew—*yet*.

This world was dirty, wicked, bruised, and life with my Master was suffocating and dark. There were not many jobs for the Gifted outside of the Rebellion unless you made it to Amoria. But with paperwork, we could get some form of assistance, however long it lasted. With Valentina's route, if we were not caught by Slave Catchers, our only other option was to make it to one of Master's many safehouses. He hadn't been since about a year after Tiara made it to us and he always kept it stocked with provisions—I was counting on this for when I made my escape.

"Well, without the Rebellion you'd be a fugitive with no home. What would your parents want for you?"

I saw the slender waist, red hair and freckled, tan face of my mother, the ebony skin, black fade and horn-rimmed glasses that made up my father. When the Rebellion needed them, they ran. They hid me and always promised to make a better life for us in a place that didn't exist—and if it did, they didn't have the balls or the resources to find it and take me with them. The image of them bleeding out on the floor entered my mind, their hands stretched towards one another, a deep red gash across each of their throats, a ribbon of blood weeping out. When they died, I did away with our attackers and ran.

I'd had to be strong for only a moment, but the iron in my heart remained.

"My parents were cowards," I whispered. "I'm nothing like them."

"Your parents fought for something, however briefly, and died with secrets that even I do not know," she pleaded. She glanced around the room, free of possessions or marks that I lived here, that I mattered or even existed. "You must know that we can offer you more than *this*."

I hedged. What could I say to make her drop this? I would not risk losing Tiara just because I got a bit impatient. I could wait a few more hours…I would have to. And just like that, I knew what my argument would be.

"I will not make a killer out of Tiara," I growled, sounding more monster than woman.

"That's what this is about?" Valentina blinked incredulously. "You're worried about the child's innocence?"

"What else would there be to worry about?"

"She will kill someday, whether for her Master or for freedom." Valentina shook her head with wide, disbelieving eyes. "You can't save her from that." She paused for a moment. "Do you remember what I told you?"

"No."

"Yes, you do."

"No, I'm saying that I don't believe it."

"You listen and listen well," she warned. "Mother does not take kindly to disrespect. No one is damned. All Gifted make it to the Great Beyond. Whether she kills in this life—"

"No..."

"Or the next—"

"No!"

"It is not something that is up to you."

"Yes, well I can delay it, however long that is."

"That is a coward's life!" Valentina snapped, grabbing my shoulders. I flinched. She pushed me back against the bed, staring into my eyes. I was breathing hard, my heart slamming in my chest, remembering, panicking, fighting to not scream. "You would forsake her," she cried, shaking me, "for your own security?!"

"I am saving her!"

"This is insanity!" At my glare, she shook her head. Her eyes closed off; I knew that if I didn't go with her then, our relationship would have lost something forever. It was almost enough to make me want to go—almost. "Pity...with your Gift, you

35

would have made an excellent Rebel."

As I walked Valentina to the door, her bag clenched in her tight red fist, I suddenly realized what she reminded me of: a fire blazing against the currents of the wind, refusing to be blown out. Nothing could knock her down—not I, nor Master, nor the ruler of this very planet.

She gave me one last pitying look and said, "I really hope that you find your way someday, girl. Tell Tiara that I said goodbye."

Then, with a whisper of smoke, she fled.

Chapter Five

Set Apart This Dream

I walked to the room where my Master resided, chest in hand.

Bright screens lined the walls with speakers and headsets flanking them, pulsing with a soft, sky-blue glow. Charts swathed the remainder of space, cream white paper running with blue, red and green veins of cities and territories, each colored with tacks. Each tack marked a safe house that he owned. Instead of expanding this one territory here in Sidra, he'd chosen multiple properties throughout Amoria, Sidra, Espanza and Maeora. His reasons for needing sixteen properties (four in each country, one in each direction) was partly because of his OCD, but mostly because people didn't take kindly to the disappearances that seemed to pop up whenever he was around—and maybe a few people once in a while wouldn't be that bad but he was, to put it bluntly, a binge eater.

Believe it or not, that's how he got his nickname.

The organized chaos of the three-walled room was familiar but quite surreal. A chill crept through me as I felt a pair of sharp eyes land on me. My eyes lowered just slightly, the action more out of unease than respect.

My eyes flicked up, daring to appraise him.

I remember when I was a child, I likened his skin to the chalk-white of bones, which was washed out by the burgundy of his shirt and the black of his pants today. His full, pink mouth, so used to rounding with hurled insults, was a momentary line, giving nothing away. His eyes were two burning embers trapped at the core of stars, full of heat and promises of freshly erected planets. In my earlier years of knowing him, I imagined him as a snake charmer, playing a flute as a long, black body uncoiled from a basket—now I knew that *he* was the stealthy serpent that twisted, ruined and consumed. When he moved there was nary a whisper, just a disobedient horned shadow stretching the length of the room, sometimes behind him, sometimes at his side, sometimes in another room dancing to the shaky gasps of the Zuora taking her last breaths. When he talked, all the life in the room seemed to bleed out. Sometimes he sat so still that dust collected on his frame and could go for days without eating but when he ate, he hunted in the city and sometimes you could hear the screams even from here.

When I first met him, I thought him quite beautiful. But then he slowly revealed the monster beneath the mask, and I found myself terrified and utterly exhilarated by him. But that quickly gave way to exhaustion and loathing. But I never forgot what he was. I never forgot what he was capable of.

He's dangerous, I reminded myself. *Proceed with caution.*

"Valentina is in the front yard retrieving roses," he said, "correcting your mistake."

He was an animal. Wild, stormy eyes. A primal snarl on his face. Wholly uncontainable. But then I blinked and he looked passive again, almost bored. Most would take his calmness as a reason for celebration, but his moods changed like the weather, gifting you daisies with a sweet, secretive smile one day and cracking you with a lightning-fast fist to the jaw the next.

Which shall I get after this news, I wonder...?

"I don't think she'll be back in time for dinner."

He rose swiftly from his chair. He thoughtlessly waved a hand over the screens, not looking as they went black. He approached me. His shadow was gone, probably sniffing out his missing slave, no doubt. I tried not to look afraid. But I was, very much so. He could smell my fear and delighted in it. A smirk tilted his pink mouth up and I thought, *It is better that he is amused than angry.*

"Did she cook anything?"

"Soup, I believe," I replied.

"Good, good."

It's now or never.

"Master?"

"Yes, Marve?"

"I'd like to buy back my name...both Sakinah's and mine."

He stared at me. Then he glanced down at the chest in my shaking hands. My grip tightened around it.

"I'm listening."

I blew out a relieved puff of air. "The law dictates that it's two-hundred-and-fifty drachmas for a slave's freedom. I have five-hundred-and-one. That's enough for Tiara and I to walk, right?"

He blinked.

"Right?" I squeaked.

"Let me see."

This is going too well, I thought as I handed him the chest. *Why isn't he stopping me?*

He walked back to the computer desk and set down the chest. He opened it slowly, carefully, as if it were a ticking bomb. He reached into the chest and pulled out a drachma. He put it in his mouth, bit down.

I stared.

He did this with each coin before setting it carefully on the desk. When he was done, he chose to count them three more times. I held stock still, refusing to bounce from foot to foot, to disturb his quiet, unusual calm. Finally, he stood, wiped his hands on his pants and loomed over me. The drachmas sat on the desk, staring at me from across the room as if to cry, *SAVE ME!*

"I'm afraid I have some bad news for you," he said.

My stomach dropped, an ice-cold feeling in my gut.

"It *is* two-hundred-and-fifty drachmas for your freedom."

I swallowed.

"In Amoria." I stared into his eyes, refusing to cry in defeat, but wanting to curse at the light in his eyes. He was enjoying this. "We live in Sidra. In Sidra, it is five-hundred drachmas to buy back your name. *Marve.*"

"What?" I stammered. "N-no, that's impossible. You *told* me that it was two-hundred-and-fifty drachmas!"

"You asked me after a fight. That was while we were in Espanza. Here in Sidra, it's double that," he said carefully, making sure I understood every word.

"Okay," I swallowed. "I am requesting that you give Sakinah back her name."

"I will do no such thing!" he petulantly snapped with a purse of his lips.

"Why?!"

"You both owe me. Those sweets that I give you are not free. We have to pay for the flour, the sugar, the cinnamon—not to forget the gas bill! On top of that, you owe me for your room and clothes."

"But-but—"

"And—"

"I've paid with labor. You keep practically all the money from my fights. I take a *teensy-weensy* portion of the money! That has to count for something!"

"Tiara doesn't."

"But I'm paying *for* her!"

"I'm afraid it doesn't work like that," he said, a small smile on his lips.

"That's not fair."

"Let me see now," he continued, "that's one-hundred for room and board, seventy-five for food and then there's the fifty for me counting the money. In total you have accumulated three-hundred."

I shattered like glass shards—but there was no wind to scatter me. I sat there before him like a pile of rubble, unable to call out his deception for what it was. He'd *lied* to me. But then I remembered the times where he claimed more than I could give and realized that he was not above deception, which was the least of his misdeeds. Oh, skies, how I trembled.

"So either way, you're still short." Now a smirk danced on his lips, a mean, cruel look in his eyes. "Neither of you will be going anywhere today."

I contemplated suicide in that moment.

Maybe death will be peaceful, I thought. *I would live amongst the stars, make my bed in the sagging moon, drag the sun across my chest when I felt lonely. And I would see Da and Mar. I've missed them. They would be proud that I made it—that I had not given in and been defiled by the Immortals, that I had lived this long. I would know love once more.*

"Okay," I brokenly whispered, swallowing my pride as I moved to retrieve my chest and three stacks of the coins.

"No."

"Excuse me?" I paused.

"I'll hang onto those," he said, shoving past me to snatch up the chest and the coins.

And I just knew that I would never see those coins—or freedom—ever again.

"Marve?" he whispered.

I turned. His mouth neared mine, his breath that of the trembling petals of roses and the blood of men. He reached out and touched a spindle of hair that curled against my forehead, a dark look entering his eyes. I heard his voice in my head, speaking through our bond, saying something that he only said when he had too

42

much wine, *Oh, how I adore you.* His hand fell onto my chest possessively as he stroked my breast beneath my shirt. *You are mine. You won't ever go from me. If you try—*

"I'll kill you." The words were so soft, so sweet, that they denied themselves—or they would have if he had not wanted to possess me so.

I knew without knowing that my times of evading his advances were drawing to a close—and I'd just drawn them nearer.

Tears stung my eyes, the pressure pushing against the back of my eyes heavier than a battering ram, my throat burning as if I'd swallowed a beaker of acid. I couldn't tell you everything that I was feeling, for even I did not completely understand my own emotions in that moment. But everything in me was telling me to fight, *to run.* I knew then that freedom was not something that I could buy—it was something that I had to steal as if it were never my own. I told myself in the moments after that I would fight and run, stealing not just myself but Tiara as well—or die trying.

"I'm having company today. Tell Tiara to stay out of sight. You will be serving the courses. Start off with appetizers and wine before we get to the full meal."

It wasn't a Sunday. He must've really been stressing out to drink on a Tuesday. My back straightened as a smile graced my lips. I felt a hysterical laugh bubbling up in my throat and fought to keep it contained.

Good Mother, he doesn't know the hell he has unleashed.

"Whatever you wish, Master."

If he was suspicious, he didn't show it.

One of the screens behind him flickered on, showing the front door, where two figures stood. I eyed it for a fraction of a second.

"Go!"

He jingled the coins in his hand. I didn't even look at them or the chest. With my mind made up, I turned and left the room.

Chapter Six

The Golden Immortal

I pushed the door open.

A drop-dead gorgeous woman walked in, wearing a dark purple peplum dress and matching high heels. Her skin was a pale, creamy yellow, the coolness of her steel-grey eyes enhanced by the diamond-cutter sharpness of her jaw. Her full lips were only matched by the fullness of her derrière, accented by her wide hips and large, sloping chest. Her hair was pulled up into a ponytail that bounced as she took each purposeful step. I imagined her as a lazy, fat cat playing with its own tail, used to everything being handed over, used to winning only because the other side never failed to concede.

It was safe to say that her beauty and entitlement made me instantly hate her.

She was flanked by a man more beautiful than her—even more beautiful than Master. He was the most perfect specimen I had ever seen. For the first time, I understood why people said that beauty could steal one's breath.

"Jacques," a lightened voice said, breathless like that of a lover, "my old friend."

He wore a black sweater, the thick fabric doing nothing to hide the hard lines of his chest and stomach, the planes of which flexed as he raised his right hand and flicked Jacques's nose with a sardonic grin. The other male got hard almost instantly, with no need to shuffle, and came forward with arms outstretched. This mystery man's black, velvety hair was slicked back with gel, framing a lean, sharp jaw and narrow forehead. His dark eyes danced with varied flecks of bright browns and even brighter golds, smoldering like molten lava as his eyes found mine. His skin was somewhere between a medium olive and light tawny with golden undertones, like the color of crushed oak mixed with a sticky, golden sap. The colors swirled under the surface of his skin as he passed under the light. A frown settled on his dark, handsome cupid's bow of a mouth.

Oh, the secrets you could tell, I thought, enraptured.

His eyes landed on my face. I bit my lip, reaching up a hand to touch my blushing cheeks, only to find that my skin was not smooth, but rough and ridged. His lip curled, his eyes narrowed, and his nose wrinkled. I had to stop myself from sneering as I saw the obvious disgust on his face. The look on his face was practiced and I knew that he must have slaves like me at his beck and call.

Blushing in angry embarrassment, I raised my glamour.

"Dory!"

Jacques brushed past me and swept the other man into his arms in one movement. He pressed kiss after kiss to his cheeks. It was over the top, but I knew that it was as much a compliment as a greeting. There was a small grapple as the

46

man tried to free himself, but Jacques held tight a moment longer and I was once again reminded of how important it was to teach people consent while they were young—although I guess with demons, it didn't matter since they always managed to *take*. I wondered if my Master had ever used this man in the way he used me—after all, he usually didn't touch anyone but me.

The woman sighed impatiently. Jacques huffed and yanked his face away from the golden man as if burned, blushing that space-black. He took the woman's hand and pressed a kiss to it as if he was being dragged underwater. Then he yanked his head up after nearly two seconds of contact before hugging her daintily.

"Megumi," he curtly said.

Damn perv.

I ripped my eyes away and moved aside so that they could take their seats at the dining room table. I went to the kitchen to get them something to drink and when I came back Jacques was sitting at the head of the table. I served them wine, red grapes and edam cheese before giving them the soup that Valentina made. As I was passing, the golden man reached out and grabbed my arm.

I briefly saw the glint of something sharp and dangerous at his waist—a dagger.

I turned to face him, mesmerized yet again.

"What is your name?"

So beautiful, I thought, staring into his eyes. They were like dancing embers rising into the night sky. I wanted to get lost in them—in him.

"My name...?" I became putty in his hands. I wanted to give him my actual name, but it wasn't worth the beating. "Marve."

47

"Marve," he said, tasting my name as if it were a fine bottle of champagne and not the name of a slave. "A beautiful name for a beautiful girl."

His other hand weaved through the air like the wand of a wizard, casting a spell on me that I couldn't ever quite shake in all the years that I knew him. He leveled a gaze at me, his eyes conveying a message that I was too naïve to decipher. But then his lips tilted up in a secret smirk meant just for me and a fire ignited in my stomach, kindling a heat just south of there. He suddenly looked to the gorgeous woman, a mask solidifying on his face as he traded conversation with her, which she—leaning across the table to expose her cleavage more—was all too happy to oblige.

I blushed and ducked my head. As if somehow remembering where he was, he let me go with a small shove and busied himself with the platter. My own master gave me a look and I took that as my cue to leave.

"How long have you had her?" the female's voice asked.

"Going on twelve years."

"How old is she?" asked the man.

"Twenty-one."

"Is she for sale?"

My heart skidded to a stop in my chest. This man was not like the others. He made me nervous, yes, but also...excited?

But it wasn't like he could do anything to me that my current Master had not done to me already.

"No."

"Come on," the man drawled, and I could imagine him shaking his head, a

48

small smile on his face. "Name your price."

I heard my Master growl.

That shut him up.

But then Jacques's voice turned playful as he said, "Maybe you can convince me to reconsider."

Dorian laughed, but I could tell that I was the only one who knew he was afraid.

I swallowed in fear. Days sitting by the tub, washing him, and then the moments that felt like years in that room, sliced through my mind like a blade. I closed my eyes and counted to ten.

I'm safe here, I thought, which was more of a wish than an affirmation.

They chatted for a few minutes about normal things: the castes, how many slaves they had, new hobbies that had kept them busy in the past fifteen years. I knew that the last time they'd seen each other had been before I'd joined Master Faux eleven years ago—or else I would have remembered them. But it was when the woman brought up the Rebels that I really listened. I opened my door just a smidgen and peeked down the hall where the dining room was. The golden man had his back to me. Next to him was the woman of Amorian descent, her voice silky yet cunning like my liege's. And then there was my Master, his lank body folded neatly in the chair.

"The Rebels are becoming more persistent," said the woman.

"Yes, Mimi, they are," Lord Faux replied indignantly. "But don't worry—I've got a plan…"

"Do tell!" Megumi exclaimed.

"Oh, but that would ruin all the fun!" he laughed. "Have you had any trouble with them?"

"A bit. But that's what makes the Gifted so wonderful: they're easily replaced." She seemed to think for a second. "Still, they *are* disgusting…I've never met animals so inclined to obey."

I shuddered. Some part of me knew that she was right but the rest of me didn't care.

Here, I was accepted for what I was: a monster.

Jacques snorted. "Tell me about it. They honestly believe that nonsense about the daughter of the Creator giving them life and powers."

"I admire it," said the man, and he sounded like he was frowning.

"Oh, lighten up, dear!" Megumi cried, clinking her glass against Jacques'. "They're just slaves!"

"Right," he said, but something about his tone bothered me, as if he were holding back—as if he were hiding something.

Was he a Rebel sympathizer?

"*Alors, dites-moi, Monsieur Boyd,*" said Jacques, "what brings you here?"

"The Rebels invaded my home, stole a lot of valuable objects, too. It's almost like they were looking for something. What, I can't imagine."

"That's the second time this month!" exclaimed Megumi. "Damn. What are they looking for?"

"I have no idea," Dorian replied. "All I know is that they leave death in their wake. They killed nine of my staff members. That's nine less than I need."

"As big as your manor is," said Megumi, "I bet you need lots more to uphold it."

"I'm running two hundred strong. It'll be fine."

Mimi stroked her hand up his arm as if raking her claws down the back of a slave. "If you want, I can trade you. I've been looking for a new pet. Although I may need some *convincing*."

There was flirtation in her voice. I knew that she just offered to please him. And somehow, we were the ones who were pathetic? But I couldn't deny my ecstasy when he declined with a firm, handsome 'no.'

Megumi made a disappointed noise in the back of her throat.

"I really came to ask—" Dorian paused and I took a step further out my room, wanting to hear the full extent of what he had to say, "—do you still possess the Book of—"

"What are you doing out here?" Master snapped.

I panicked and took a few steps away from the door. My Master got up, in full battle mode, and went in the opposite direction of my room. Relieved, I paused before wondering who he uncovered—a Rebel spy, perhaps? I had regular sight and hearing, so I couldn't detect what my liege did. But then I heard something fall, a curse and another crash and knew that he'd caught someone spying, for which the penalty was death. Then he reappeared, carrying a girl kicking and screaming—a thin, brown figure.

It was Tiara!

Chapter Seven

RUN!

I was supposed to warn her!

She was fighting with all her might, poor thing. He lifted her small body and slammed her on the table. I kept waiting for Tiara to bend the light around her, to disappear, *but she didn't!* Her screams rang in my ears. I don't know what part of me reacted first—my brain or my heart. All I know is that I was running back into the hallway, swift but none too silent. My powers lit up with an audible *zzzttt* that raced throughout the room.

I sent a pulse of electricity through the room. My master usually brushed off petty attacks like this but this time, he flinched. Good.

I wanted to see him suffer.

I grabbed Master's shoulder and whirled him around. *Crash!* My fist collided with his jaw. He stared at me in shock, frozen for a moment or two. That was all the time I needed. I grabbed Tiara and ran for the door. I told her to refract and push her light outwards. She did as instructed—but not before I saw the tears streaming down her small, dark and frightened face. Feeling overwhelmed, I tried to picture her as a

53

blue jay flapping its wings, carrying itself off on a current of magnolia-scented wind—

I couldn't.

"Run, Tiara, run!"

She took off into the woods, her form flickering back and forth between the seen and the shielding light. I was not far behind her. My Master roared ragefully and I heard something behind me snap. I didn't look back—only forward. The forest grew tighter and tighter around me as my anxiety began to rise.

My knees buckled—the adrenaline was wearing off. Still, I ran. I pumped my arms in exertion, pushing myself to go longer. I heard another snap of twigs underfoot as my Master ran after me. He would eventually catch my scent and then catch me.

No, he won't, said my inner self. *Just keep running. Let the wind guide you. Let the forest become a part of you.*

I charged my powers up for a second time, watching as dark storm clouds rolled in above me. I lifted my hand and then brought it down as if I were slamming it into *his* face. Lightning rained from the sky, striking a tree about five yards behind me. The tree fell with a mighty boom. That would buy me enough time to find a hiding spot.

I could feel him all around me, his scent in my nose, filling me. I knew without knowing that he was close. He could have easily caught me, but that wasn't his style. The reason he hadn't wrestled me to the forest floor was the same reason that he allowed me (only me) to question him: I was special to him. I was not only his pet

54

but the replacement for his long-lost love.

And he liked to see me fight him. My existence was erotic to him, better than any raunchy photo.

I found a sturdy tree whose limbs stretched like the arms of a giant. I began to climb, digging my nails into the trunk to pull myself up. A bit of bark dug into my bare feet, drawing blood and a soft hiss from me. I climbed higher and higher, until the sky was in reach and the ground looked like a bad dream. But Jacques raced right past me, headed straight for Tiara.

I heard her scream as he caught her, ringing through the forest, in my head, resonating throughout my heart, echoing one word: *"MARVE!"*

I shook my head, hiding deeper between the tree's branches. I closed my eyes and prayed to the Creator that she was okay. Opening my eyes revealed Master passing under my tree, dragging Tiara by the neck. Her head hung at an odd angle and even though I hated to admit it, I knew that she was dead. I held my breath, totally immobile, not wanting to draw any attention to myself.

Dorian suddenly appeared at Jacques's side.

"Return her to me and the reward will be far more than you can imagine."

Return her.

Return *me*.

I was his property, nothing more. Dorian nodded. I was suddenly more aware of my breasts rising and falling, my heart threatening to burst out of my cardboard chest.

Dorian paced back and forth underneath my tree. Jacques retreated back into the mansion; Dorian stopped. Then he looked up in the tree that I was in, as if he could *see* me. Instead of calling for Jacques, he simply extended his hand, one finger raised. On the underside of that finger was the same raised branding that was on Valentina's neck: the hawk snatching up the sun. That Mark!

Oh, my fair Goddess!

Dorian was part of the Rebellion.

Chapter Eight

You Can't Hide

I debated on the safest option. After all, he could've been trying to trick me. I mean, the same way Valentina hid her Mark was the same way he could have made his.

But Marks couldn't be made except by the people who formed the bond…

So how did he get it…?

Suddenly, I felt a small wisp of power snap back on like a television slowly crackling to life. I gathered magic in my hands and feet before launching myself from the tree. I reached out, grappling at a branch. But then a portal opened and a hand reached towards me. I jerked back but it was too late.

"Gotcha!"

That was how I found myself on the forest floor, pinned beneath the Golden Immortal. My head cracked against a branch. I bit down on my tongue to withhold my scream. I told myself that it was because of this and not his proximity that my heart thudded to a halt in my chest before picking up double time. But then he placed one finger on my lips, glancing at the mansion all bug-eyed.

Chomp!

"Ow-ow-ow!"

I yanked one arm free and slammed it into his nose.

"Fuck!"

I wriggled away. I glanced at the tree, wanting to hoist myself up, but I just couldn't stay up there any longer. My body was aching and tired from the run. My bones clacked beneath my skin as my legs banged together. But I didn't care because this was my chance—I'd make myself run until I got sick and *keep running*. I stood on wobbly feet and turned.

"That was brave, what you did back there for your friend."

In an instant, his voice changed him to someone vulnerable yet brave, self-reproachful yet understanding—all existing, all colliding, to reveal the man beneath the monster. He didn't sound like an Immortal in that moment. I looked at Dorian standing there, smiling at me as if we were two good friends, as if he wasn't a master of many and I wasn't a slave. He took a step forward. I raised my fists as my heart stamped a song…of fear, yes, but also likeness.

I wanted to trust him.

"I'm not going to hurt you." He raised the hand with the Mark, flashing it at me. "I'm on your side."

"Don't come any closer!"

My powers were all tapped out. I was basically a lamb alone with a wolf. He backed up a few steps, probably to give me enough room to calm myself down. I broke down into tears, falling to my knees. Sobs wracked my frame as I realized just

58

how much danger I put Tiara and myself in. It hurt to breathe, to think, to live. As I dragged in a ragged breath, my ribs screamed in protest.

It was my fault that she was dead.

"Relax…Everything's gonna be all right," he said, taking a few steps forward.

My head snapped up as I bore my teeth in an angry, regretful snarl. I told him to take me back and claim his reward, but then remembered something vital: *I was a Champion!* So I lunged, clawing at his eyes. When he blocked me, I reached for the dagger strapped to his waist and quickly held it to his throat. Even in that moment, I found him undeniably attractive, the proximity of his body exhilarating me, driving me to act recklessly.

"I don't want that…and neither do you." He inched a bit closer. "I want to help you."

"Really?" I said, voice cracking as I looked at his warm, open face. Still, I took more than a few steps back.

He was beautiful *and* kind—something that the world I lived in lacked.

Maybe that was why I chose to trust him, why I chose to believe in good.

I took his outstretched hand, ignoring the jolt that zinged through me when we touched.

He pulled me close, raising his other hand to push my hair back.

"Don't be alarmed," he said, his voice gentle and persistent at the same time. "You may feel a little different."

Then he kissed me.

Chapter Nine

Tastes Like Candy—No, Like Brandy

The contact was brief but undeniably sweet. His lips were warm, firm but still impossibly soft. He tasted like coke and rum, an oddly candied flavor. Smelled nectarous and gentle, like heather, but also with the wet, intense heat of a brewery. He was intoxicating, but only for a split second, long enough to feel the fleeting mix of euphoria, calm and an almost drugged high, but short enough to only hint at the quenching of desire. It was a reminder of days sneaking into the liquor stores with Tina, sipping on brandy and chardonnay, giggling profusely as we discussed in which way we would punish those that didn't help us dismantle the regime, me peeking out of the corner of my eye for my master fearfully, Valentina with an indoctrinating glow surrounding her form, as if the liquor were not liquor at all, but a baptismal water, and our sins were being purified and purged from our very bodies.

Just as soon as the kiss began, it was over.

My shoulders slumped and my vision went dark. I floated under the blanket of a persistent darkness that dragged me deep into my subconscious. I dreamt a memory, one where Jacques had shown me what had destroyed hope in him—what had ruined both his life and mine.

...My eye throbbed, already beginning to swell where he'd struck me.

I'd been sixteen at the time.

"What are these?"

"Photos. Of friends that once were."

...

The last featured Master, always stuck at the delicate age of twenty-two, sprawled on the hood of a red pickup truck. Stretched next to him was the same blonde that made a debut in almost every photo. His slender body seemed to beckon from the picture, his odd violet eyes directed at the camera, his mouth twisted in what I could already tell was his signature wanton smirk. Master's hand was caught in the other's hair, a tiny smile gracing his full, pouty lips. Behind them, the sun cast a golden hue on everything, the sky a backdrop of red, orange and pink hues.

Even then, I remember thinking that an angel-blood and a demi-demon were an odd pair.

I picked up the photo and turned it around so that it was facing him. Master glanced down once, eyes flashing back up before I could even catch my breath. I looked into his black orbs. There wasn't a flicker of emotion—no pain, no sadness, no regret...just blackness with hints of red, like blood mixed in with a vat of ink.

...

"His name was Grant."

"What happened to Grant?" his name left a sweet, saccharine taste in my mouth, and I'd be lying if I said that I didn't want to taste it—taste him—over and over again.

"He decided that there were other things worth living for." Master shrugged again, eyes never leaving mine. "So he left."

...

"Were you his in the way that I am yours?"

"Only when it was of convenience to him... Being an angel blood, Grant claimed he wasn't really that kind of guy."

...

"Look, Marve, once you're a part of the world, it won't let you go. Once you see it, you'll wish you were blind. I never really felt much for other people and I knew that it should bother me but it didn't. You are burdened with emotions. It is my duty to rid you of them."

...

"But why?" I asked, clutching the photo. "Why are you giving me a memory of your most precious person?"

"I want you to remember what happens when you fall in love."

I was awakened by my rumbling stomach. I heard a laugh coming from the front of something with an engine that purred so softly, it was nearly silent. I opened my eyes to find myself in a luxurious car. Wait. Why was I in a car in the first place? Then it all came rushing back.

I'd overheard them talking about the Rebellion. Tiara got caught spying. We ran. Tiara was caught.

Oh, Goddess…Tiara.

Tears slipped down my cheeks. Dorian turned around and gave me a wicked grin. It quickly turned into a frown when he saw that I was crying.

"What's wrong?"

I shook my head eyes burning. *Oh, Tiara,* I thought, *you were too good for this world.*

"I know you're a little shaken up right now, but…we're passing through the southernmost border."

We were leaving to go where—the Southern Isles, perhaps?

"You're sneaking me out?" I sniffled, wiping my face on my sleeve.

"Of course…I…I couldn't just leave you there."

I was a little suspicious but I had no choice but to trust him—after all, he had saved my life.

"License, please."

Dorian dug into his pocket and pulled out a gold coin. The man shined his flashlight on it, probably debating on whether or not to let us through. Then he snatched it, grunted "Have a nice day," and we were off. I looked out the window at the starlit sky. It was beautiful, full of alabaster and turquoise, shimmering silvers and glimmering golds.

I remembered his lips pressed to mine, the thoughts that entered my head (thoughts that weren't mine) and wondered…How did he do that? I touched my lips, my face warming as I smiled. He was actually way cuter than Jacques.

"I was just trying to make things easier for you." Dorian said when he saw me touching my mouth. "If you made noise, Jacques would have heard you. I would never force myself on anyone, but I couldn't think of another way. I'm sorry."

Crossing my arms, I did my best to settle down.

"Where are you taking me?"

He did not answer, but instead threw me a backpack. In it was a manila folder. Inside I found my birth certificate, a bunch of paperwork, a key, and a map like the one in Jacques's computer room, only this one was highlighted with multicolored sharpies instead of incorporating tacks. I glanced at the photo of my mother, father, and myself in the Isles. I couldn't have been older than three, my face split wide in a grin and my chubby arms waving as my father hoisted me high into the air, my mother kissing my cheek.

"Where did you get this?" I asked, finding my voice.

"We've been watching you for a while. You haven't lost a fight in the Ring of Death. You hold your own. You're brave. We need recruits like you."

"Recruits? For what?"

I wasn't sure whether to burn the picture or save it. Photos of my family were rare: we couldn't afford to be tied down to one place, lest we get caught by our pursuers. I'd been too young to understand much—

I *still* didn't understand everything.

I slipped the picture into my bra before glancing up at the back of Dorian's head. Maybe the Rebellion held the answers.

He stopped the car in the middle of a field. I got out right after he did, clinging closely to his side. I flexed my fingers, a million different outcomes flitting through my mind. I might have to fight my way out, so I had to stay vigilant. In the middle of the field was a large, dark rock. Dorian walked up to it and commanded me to put my hand on it. I did as I was told; he laid his hand over mine.

A shudder went through me as I fought to keep my breathing even. The rock glowed ruby red and then a deep cobalt. Then it shifted and parted straight down the middle, exposing a stairway beneath. I gaped at Dorian, who walked past me and down the stairs.

I cringed, but then I remembered that I was a fugitive and had nowhere else to go so I sucked it up and followed him down the stairs, only a few steps behind.

When we reached the end of the stairs, the door looming ahead, I asked where we were. Yeah, I know—I was a little late. If he was planning to bring me to his secret dungeon and torture me to death, I was already as good as dead.

"The Southern Isles are guarded by magic. This entryway takes you to the Rebellion's underground hideout. You would need a higher up Rebel to take you through the barrier and into the Southern Isles. A lot of Rebels come directly from there and when they're done with their mission, they check in here before returning home. If Madam V didn't want to see you, I'd at least *try* to take you out there but since she does…"

I tried to imagine this Madam V and saw nothing but darkness. Who was she and did she have my best interest at heart? But it was silly to question her: she was risking her life for *my* freedom—for the freedom of every Gifted slave in the Land of

66

the Three. Dorian knocked on the door, his eyes alight with mischief. I watched as a little slot opened and a pair of piercing blue eyes stared first at him then at me.

"Password!" a masculine voice barked.

"From tyranny we ran

To the underground.

Loud is our cause

Though we make no sound.

The Good Mother, we worship

And do condemn

The Great Father

For what he did to them."

The door gave a labored creak as it slid open.

"Welcome to the Rebellion."

Chapter Ten

Rebellion HQ

The underground lair was carved from stone and hardened dirt. Lights dangled above from long poles, casting an almost fairy-like glow upon the underground cavern. There was a mill where water ran, which seemed to power everything in the room; it seemed very pre-Three, which I knew was because the newest technology was only gifted to those who could afford it. There were carvings made from dirt and various dugouts in the cave with stone-chiseled signs like *Weapons Room* and *Nurse's Station*. It was organized and chaotic at the same time.

Gifted, Mortals and Immortals alike all milled about, at ease with one another in a way that I would never have thought possible. I could see the furry hair of the few that were from the icy plains of Amoria, the fishy scales of Sidra's swampiest dwellers, the whiskers of the cat-people from the jungles of Espanza and the snaky scales of those from the deserts of Maeora. They were all openly being themselves— free to live without judgement or retribution. I wanted to be like them.

I wanted to imagine them as snakes slithering through the sand, tigers pacing the jungles, wolves prowling through the night, to strip them of their sentience to make them less 'real' but I honestly couldn't imagine them as much of anything other than what society saw them as: Rebels fighting for a better life for all people. And that made me feel bad for them in an undeniably sweet way. I didn't want to get attached to anyone else. Or perhaps I should say that I didn't want to *lose* anyone else. But death was inevitable and although I didn't fear it, I knew that if I joined them, I would most likely meet an unpleasant one, as most Rebels had when they were eventually caught. But to be surrounded by this much autonomy reminded me that it was a small price to pay in order to remain…independent…?

No, that's not the word…

I turned to see Dorian watching me intently, amusement on his face as I took in the room, the people, the *F-R-E-E-D-O-M*.

"You want to join them?"

"I want to…" My magic flexed in my system as I breathed in, obviously wanting to be freed. It was hard keeping up a glamour 24/7. But would he look at me differently? "Can I…?"

He smiled, nodding.

I slowly, hesitantly, ebbed away my magic until there was no glamour left. I flexed my fingers, feeling my claws lengthen, my scales shift into place, my eyelids double as I took my true form. My magic pulsed in the background of my body, swirling in my stomach, untouched for the first time in a long time. I felt my loathing, my paranoia, my pain, my sadness, fall to the floor. I took in one unlabored breath, then another and another: not using my magic was a gift beyond measure.

69

And it was a blessing that even the Mother Goddess could not seem to grant.

It was good to be free.

There were piles of food near one side of the cave. On the other was steam rising from hot showers. I was torn considering which I wanted more. Dorian made my choice for me. His head tilted as he looked at me for a long moment, his eyes narrowed as they flicked across my form, the light falling on the chiseled features of his jaw just right, and he bit his lip in a 'fuck me' fashion. But then he seemed to remember something traumatic as he shifted from one foot to another. A fragile, disgusted look appeared on his face; for a moment, I thought it was self-deprecation, but then I realized that he only looked that way after I took my natural state.

So it must have been directed at me.

"I know you're hungry," he reminded me and in response, my stomach growled. "Go over there and get some food. I'll be back in a minute."

He took off. I couldn't help but wonder why he left so quickly. Did he not appreciate my true form? Would he rather that I look like him—as human as possible? I frowned.

I want him to like me.

But I also wanted to like *me* if that made sense.

I thought of That Look though—the look before the look—and decided to shift into my glamour form when he returned.

I made my way over to the table of food and was immediately drawn to the pies and cakes. I picked up a plate and took two Danish pastries. Then I went to the meat section and got some roasted lamb. Finally, I got a healthy bit of potatoes and veggies. Unable to resist my guilty pleasure (sweets), I bit into one of the pastries and damn near passed out again.

The fruit inside was moist and tart and sweet all at once. The crust was flaky and brittle. I loved each bite. The meat on the other hand was bitter from the salt they used to keep it fresh, but also heady and filling. The veggies on the other hand were sweet and caramelized. I wanted to slow down and cherish each bite, but it wasn't really an option since I hadn't eaten anything since the night after my last fight.

I shoveled food in my mouth. I'd thought that the meats and sweets that I'd gotten for beating Natalia in the Ring would have held me over a bit longer but that just wasn't the case. I'd been hungry all day and it was now nighttime. I was on my second round when Dorian appeared beside me.

"Marve, I'd like you to meet the commander of the Rebellion."

I knew that I looked like a total pig. I had food on my face and some of the custard from the pie was leaking down my chin. What can I say? It was too late to switch up now. I turned around, swiftly wiping my face with my sleeve.

"Valentina?"

Chapter Eleven

A Joyous Occasion

A funny feeling squirmed in my stomach—I took it to be joy. It was strange, I hadn't felt that in a long time. The older woman rushed forward and scooped me up in a bearhug. I laughed, a hysterical, disbelieving laugh, but a laugh nonetheless. It had been so long since I'd laughed without scorn. We held each other a moment longer before parting.

"What are you doing here? I thought you would have been caught and sold by now!"

"Nothing can hold me," she fiercely said. "How are you? I'm glad you decided to join us."

"I'm doing good now that I know you're safe."

"Where is Tiara?" she said, peering over my shoulder to look for the girl.

I hung my head low. "She didn't make it."

The chatter around us went silent for a second, all of us taking a moment to pay our respects to our sister in spirit.

72

"By magic we are bound and by blood we remain," I said for Tiara, remembering the quote that every Gifted had emblazoned on their heart.

"Among the stars she shall lay," Valentina finished.

I took the part of me that missed Tiara and buried it deep for the time being. I couldn't afford to be emotional right now. I had to stay focused.

"So this is the Rebellion!" I exclaimed, looking around. "This isn't what I expected."

"Let me guess. You expected rats and feces flung on the walls?"

"Something like that."

We shared a laugh.

"So if you're the leader of the Rebellion, why did you work for Jacques for so long? Why would you leave this—" I gestured all around us "—behind?"

"For the safety of my people—for *our* people. I had to get the info I needed."

I paused in recollection. All the stories she would tell me when I was a child. Of the island called Libra where all the Gifted could be free. Of a place hidden deep in Zuora where we made our stand. Of the stars that guided them, committing suicide only to deliver luck as they plummeted to the earth.

What adventures had it led to? What mysteries had been solved? What answers had been uncovered?

"And what did you find?" I asked, moving to walk beside her. "Did you get what you needed to wage this war?"

"Not enough." She waved a hand. "That's where you come in."

She walked to a section across from the Nurse's Station and touched it; a wall of dirt fell, and she stepped into the hollowed-out room without a door. The two attendants left. She made her way to a table and sank down in the chair behind it. Then she placed her chin on her interlaced fingers, staring at me. There was something sacred in the air. This was seemingly a rite of passage.

I took a cautious step forward.

"Do you know anything about Jacques Faux—anything at all?"

I knew that he hated spicy foods, but had a soft spot for anything bitter because it reminded him of flesh. I knew that he used to eat sticks of butter as a child. I knew that he loved to race in the rain because it was a challenge. I knew that he'd never been to over half of the land that he owned because he hated to travel and bought most of his estates at online auctions. I knew that he liked twenty-two rose petals— the age that Immortals became immortal—in the water for every bath and loved his water as hot as it could get. And I knew that he wouldn't want her to know any of this, that these were our secrets.

There was so much that I knew, things that I couldn't tell her.

So, I told her everything that everyone knew because it would not betray the times when he was good to me, when he told me things about himself that he would tell no one else, when he trusted me more than he trusted his paranoia.

"I know that he's a half-demon, a descendant of Mestiphopheles himself. I know that he can't die. I know that he's a diagnosed narcissistic sociopath and that he'd do anything to rule the world, and I do mean anything."

"Yes," she said, disappointment marring her face. "We know that already. Think, Marve. *Think.* There is something else you know."

74

I paused, doing as she so desperately requested.

"I know that he has feelings for a man named Grant. I know that he was the one who got away. I know that losing him changed Master—I mean, Jacques."

"He has no feelings for this man," said Valentina, "and the sooner you realize that the sooner we can get down to business."

I nodded, swallowing around the lump in my throat. To be honest, I felt embarrassed. I'd been a victim of Jacques for eleven years and I *still* believed in him?

Something was seriously wrong with me.

"Now did he ever tell you anything about the Immortals? Anything that could help us win this war?" asked Valentina. "Did he mention a weapon?"

I delved into the depths of my mind. Something fluttered by my consciousness. I latched onto it and dragged it to the forefront of my mind.

"The Immortals..." I muttered. "They are Mortal until they turn twenty-two. Do you really...?"

This was why so many did not join the Rebellion. When the Immortals were children and still Mortal, some of them—as many as the Rebellion could get to— were...*disposed of.* Rebel soldiers snuck into their bedrooms in the night and slayed them. They were rumored to take out entire hospitals, which housed some Gifted children, in order to get to them. It was inexcusable.

"We do what we need to win this war. They are conquering the world. What other weapon do we have?" Valentina asked. Then she eyed me, disgusted, and spat, "Do you feel sorry for them, Marve? After all that Jacques has done to you, would you weep for his children?"

"Of course not!" I said, without thinking.

Still, they were children. Why not steal them and raise them to fight for our cause? *But,* I realized, *that would make too much sense.*

"Now that I think about it, he did mention something called the Dagger of Truth..."

"The what?"

"The Dagger of Truth. It's a weapon that can kill any demon or their likeness. It can also make anyone believe anything the wielder says. You've really never heard of it?"

"No, and personally I don't think that would do us any good since over ninety percent of the Immortal are a subspecies of humanity. Come on, Marve. You can do this!"

Words slithered here and there, some of them useless and some of them unheard. Finally, I pieced together a bit of information that might be useful. I swallowed before uttering the words that I could make sense of: "He once mentioned that there was a way to make a Gifted an Immortal. They would retain all of their powers, with increased speed and monstrous strength."

"Yes." She leaned forward, a gleam in her good eye. "How do we accomplish such a feat?"

"I'm not sure..."

She rolled her eye and leaned—no, *sagged*—back into the chair. Her face drooped, her eyelids heavy, her mouth frowning, her brow creased in indignant disappointment. For the first time in a long time, she looked her forty years.

"If I had been with him as long, I bet he would have told me. But he never trusted me. I arrived just two years after you. Surely that means he held a little trust…" She muttered something to herself. As if suddenly remembering I was there, she straightened up, a smile on her face. "It's fine, Marve. No need to worry. I'll just send two of my best spies. They aren't young like you and are vastly superior—I'm sure they'll get the information some way or another."

"No!" I said, taking a few hurried steps towards the desk.

She smirked at me. "What could you do to help our cause?"

"I can gather intel. I'll be good at it, too. Remember the safehouse he had in the heart of Sidra—the one he always took us to? Remember how he never let us leave our room? Maybe there's something there that will help. Maybe I can go there and scrounge up some more information."

A tingle raced down my spine. His old HQ had been in Sidra: it was where he used to hold all his meetings, back when he feared us learning his information more than he feared us running away. That meant that we'd be looking in his blind spot, right under his nose. If he found us, he'd surely kill us. I paused for a moment as a certain panic made itself known.

But no…

Valentina wouldn't send me to my death.

"Very good, Marve. You're starting to think like a true Rebel." She gave me a praising smile. "You leave tomorrow."

Fear tasted sour, like the juice of a lemon on my tongue. But I wanted to earn my keep. I wanted to be of use, to be close to the woman that had become like an auntie to me in these past few years. I wondered what it would have been like if she hadn't been there to listen to me rant and rave about my Master's paranoid delusions, if she hadn't been there to rub salve into my wounds so that they would not scar, if she hadn't been there to teach me how to make pads out of old shirts when my heat came and my master had been gone from the house too long to bring us provisions.

I stood ramrod straight and nodded my head to her. Her smile grew at the action. After fixing my glamour back into place, I walked back into the cavern. Dorian waved a hand at me from across the room. I walked towards him, pretending that his smile was just for me.

"Would you be able to take me to Sidra tomorrow?" I asked politely, batting my lashes at him. "I need to get some information."

He was oblivious, but who could blame him? He was probably used to women throwing themselves at him. If I wanted to make a statement, I'd probably have to do more than talk sweetly to him.

"Damn, she's got you spying for her already? That woman doesn't waste a second."

"Can you take me or not?"

"I can," he said with a playful tilt of his head, which looked just right on his handsome face. That look offered kisses and secrets, dances and nights that were never long enough. "But what will you do for me?"

The feel of his firm lips pressed against mine careened through my head. Then naughtier thoughts made themselves known. His hands in my hair, gently tugging so that I would expose my neck. Him kissing his way down my body, nibbling on my skin as he reached down to unbutton my pants. Then him taking off his own garments to expose his—

Oh my Goddess, what was I thinking!

He tipped back his head and laughed, as if he'd heard every wicked thought in my dirty little mind. I blushed and turned away. I only looked at him once his laughter died down, and the glow had faded from his eyes.

"I'm sorry, I couldn't help it."

"Help what?"

He let go of my wrist. I hadn't even noticed when he'd grabbed it.

"I have a Gift as well. It's something I like to call Influence."

"Influence?"

"Basically, as long as I have contact with your skin, I can make you think what I want. Although there are some limitations. For one, the initial thought has to already be there subconsciously. So, if you don't want what I want to some degree, it won't work. Really, all I do is bring your greatest desire in the moment to the forefront."

I balked at him. That was problematic, to say the least. If he could read my mind, then he knew how bad I constantly wanted to kiss him. I knew that he wasn't making me want to, that I was just drawn to him, as most men and women were, but still… "So, that means that you—"

"Yeah." He gave me a smirk that didn't reach his eyes. "Do you want more?"

"What?!" I shrieked, my face red. "No! Besides," I added, "that's not what I meant."

"What?"

"I was going to ask how that was possible. You're Immortal."

"Immortals have magic," he countered.

"Yes," I added, "but not Gifts."

Everyone knew that Immortals could use runes to conjure as they pleased. The Gifted had magic to hide their different forms and summon portals—and the magic we used for our Gifts was a different magic altogether. I'd never really been taught to use magic other than to hide my form—Master said it wasn't necessary for me to learn. I think it was just to keep me under his thumb, but it didn't really matter now. Witches and wizards had been wiped out millennia ago and High Fae, faeries, were-shifters, ghouls and vampires lived apart from us, choosing to live nearer to their prey. Maybe he was Nephilim?

But those of angelic descent didn't have Gifts unless they were given angelic blood instead of born with it…And he didn't have purple eyes…

So, what was he?

"May I?" he said with extended hand. "I promise, I won't use it on you in that manner."

I want nothing more.

I shyly gave him my hand.

His fingers looped around mine. He laid a simple kiss on the back of my hand. I felt myself swooning, my breath catching in my throat before his lips met my skin, but his eyes were not glowing and there was no image. But when he let go, I allowed myself to think of kneeling before him.

My next words were more to myself rather than him. "Stop it!" I snapped.

He blinked. "I didn't do anything."

"I know—that's the problem." I rolled my eyes. "You still didn't tell me about your Gift."

"I know."

He wasn't going to tell me.

"So, what time do we leave?"

"How about tomorrow at six?" He raised his brow and damn, even *that* looked appetizing.

"In the morning?"

"Yes. Can't have you running off and changing your mind, now, can we?"

No, I thought, thinking of Valentina's smirk as she praised me. *We can't have that...*

Chapter Twelve

My Memories (Are the Unconsecrated)

That night, as I slept in one of the makeshift rooms that they opened for me, I dreamt of Jacques. His ruthless, evil face twisted in a sneer. He was the most beautiful man I'd ever known (other than Dorian, that is) and he had used and abused me in ways that most couldn't even fathom.

I had a nightmare, the same one that came and went since I was just barely of age. I was sitting on my knees by the tub, my hands clutching the sponge, the water warping them, making them ugly. There was a pale, bleach-white back before me and a calm voice commanded me to continue scrubbing. But I didn't want to. Something about it wasn't right. It felt dirty, unconsecrated, *wrong.*

I woke up in a cold sweat. I was panicking so bad that I started hyperventilating. I rushed to the small bucket in the corner and retched. I dumped out all the food that my stomach had to give and then some. I only stopped when there was a sharp ache of protest from my stomach. Dry heaving and shaking, I crawled back to my spot on the ground where the mat had been laid. I curled in tight on myself, trying to make myself small so as not to be noticed, my eyes flicking around, trying to memorize my surroundings in case I needed to escape.

Even if I was leaving in the morning, it offered comfort for my paranoid mind.

Speaking of morning, what time is it anyway?

I got my answer when Dorian appeared at the lip of the entrance, smiling broadly. The smile didn't reach his eyes and I wondered how long he waited, posted outside of my door, listening to me scream. I got up and stalked past him, looking for a place to freshen up.

After patting the walls near the Nurse's Station like I'd seen Valentina do, I nearly gave up. But then I saw a shimmering near the Weapons Room and walked towards it. Reaching out a hand, I concentrated my magic into those fingers. The wall of dirt fell away, revealing a room with a sink and a makeshift toilet.

I found a spare toothbrush still in its packaging. I began brushing vigorously. I then ran my finger through my dark red locks, trying to smooth them out a bit so that it didn't look like I got in a fight with an alley cat. When I glanced in the mirror, I felt and looked a tiny bit better. I walked out to meet Doria where he stood waiting.

"Does that happen often?" he asked, shooting me a concerned look.

"No."

"Do you want to talk about it?"

"No."

"You sure? It'll help put your mind at ease."

"No."

"Do you know any other words besides no?"

I paused, a hint of a smile gracing my lips that I hoped he didn't see. We walked in silence after that. Up the stairs and out of the underground tunnel we went. He took us to a clearing, thumbed a small black remote I hadn't noticed and took a few steps back. A jet appeared, glowing a shiny, metallic silver. It was sleek, with strong curves and sharp edges—a beautiful piece of technology.

I raised a brow at him.

"It's the only way to fly."

We boarded the jet. I strapped myself in, denying Dorian's insistent hands that demanded he do it for me. We both sat back in our seats. A translucent screen appeared before him. He tapped a few icons, put in the address of the safehouse and then we were off. I sank back in my chair as he served himself a bottle of brandy.

"Its six in the morning!" I exclaimed, watching as he downed one glass before starting another. Normally, slaves wouldn't be so outspoken around an Immortal.

But I was a Champion.

"It's five o clock somewhere."

We made it to Sidra in half an hour. Flying over the Wall Seinaru, seeing the tiny people milling about, seemed almost unreal. I remembered the story of how the walls were constructed: the Immortals offered up Gifted children to the Creator, thrusting them to the sky. A hand swept down from the heavens, snatching them up. The next morning, the walls were just *there*. If you stood by a wall and turned your head left, sometimes you could see a pair of terrified blue orbs. If you turned right, you could see a brown mouth opened in a mangled scream.

I remembered my first time passing through the walls with Jacques instead of using a portal like I had with my parents—I can still remember the pleading whispers that followed me to the Ring of Death.

When we landed, Dorian pushed a button on the remote that turned on the cloak setting. I walked with him through the mangled streets of Sidra.

It was a nightmare.

People limped here and there, sagging under the weight of their sorrows as their homes sagged under the weight of the sky. Their eyes were hollow pools of darkness, having seen the most consuming parts of the world. Hunger made their stomachs large and bulbous.

These were the Mortals that chose not to integrate themselves with the rest of society. Not working with the top caste had its setbacks, even for nonmagical folk. They stared at us in fear and wonder. They could sense the magic rippling off us as we passed. I made sure to stick close to Dorian, not wanting to get left behind. Not only had my enslavement taken place here but I had also grown up here. I knew how that fear turned these people violent, causing them to tear and bite at the skin of anyone with a drop of magic in their veins.

Children drank from dirty cups. Mothers sat on steps, their bellies round with pregnancy. Husbands were in the front of their yards, chopping firewood. Lift. Bring the axe down. It got stuck. Struggle. Pull. Lift.

The cycle repeats.

I admired their resilience. But like I said before, I knew them. My parents had ushered me to school, afraid to let me ride the bus alone. I remembered them talking to the staff in hushed tones, begging for them to protect me and nodding solemnly when the faculty said they would. They did not, of course, and often took part in my torment. I was a monster to them. Actually, I was worse—I was a monster that would not yield. I think that's why I thought myself lucky to be taken in by my [former] master and why my world was rocked when he turned out to be an even greater threat than the people that I knew here.

"So where is this safehouse?" Dorian asked, snapping me out of my thoughts.

"Just a short walk from here. It's not far," I said, taking a few steps forward.

I looked up at the sun shining down on me. But without my parents by my side, even the light could not warm me. I looked to the left and saw my father and mother chasing me down the street, looked to the right and saw them pushing me on the swing set. There was a creak as the memory faded and the wind whistled through the holes in the braided chain.

There was no room for happy memories here.

Chapter Thirteen

This Silence Is Deafening

Dorian estimated that it would probably take us a few days to look around the house and get info on Jacques. I gave it two max. We searched through each room, starting in the slave room, where Tiara, Valentina and I normally slept. There was one big bed for all of us. I spotted a hole in the wall above the lamp, which I knew had a shorted fuse, where Tiara had shot a rubber bullet playing a Mortal game called Cowboys & Indians. I never wanted to be a cowboy, seeing as the native people were so similar to the Gifted people, but Tiara was always happy to be in a position of power.

I used to always try to warn her of two things: power without planning was foolish. And power without control was cowardice. But she, either too young or too corrupt, grinned and fled to corners of the room, never truly caring.

Dorian poked his head in the room. "Come here real quick," he said with a secretive, cheesy grin. "I want to show you something."

I followed him into Jacques' room. We passed the faded couch, which was once a vibrant red but was now a washed out pink. There was a throne-like chair, its sleek, curved edges a light gold that matched Dorian's skin, the headrest a darker gold stained from the oil of Master's hair. I turned away. We squeezed through a slim doorway and into Jacques's room, its large, king-sized mattress seeming to take up most of the room. Momentarily caught in a memory, I saw a sly finger curl and uncurl, bidding me to come forward. I turned away and a very important piece of technology caught my eye.

I made my way over to the computer lying open on Jacques's desk. The screen glowed in the dim light of the room, the pops of bubbles emitting from the small screensaver. The computer was *not* password protected. I moved the mouse to navigate past the fish-decorated screensaver and to the man's history: it featured essays on Word, a few games of online poker and searches for clubs that had something called *In The Flesh*, which, if I recalled, was a game involving cannibalism that was really popular pre-Three and post-USA. But the jarring thing was that he'd been on YouTube which was, to sum it up, bad.

It was very, very bad.

"I'm going to teach you how to hack a computer—" Dorian leaned over my shoulder, his strong hand on the back of the chair as he used his other to pull out a flash drive, "—using this."

I obediently took the external hard drive from him, our fingers touching. A zip raced along my spine. I immediately dropped his gaze and connected the drive. He told me what to click or type in order to begin searching through not only the files that were still on the computer but also the ones that'd been deleted or closed. An hour into it and I couldn't find a trace of anything, which meant that I wasn't exactly sure if he'd uploaded the file from *this* computer.

"Damn, he's good!" Dorian punched the table. I jumped. He apologized. "The guy is paranoid, I'll give him that. *And* a genius."

"How?" I wondered aloud. "He doesn't even have a password on his computer...?"

"Yes, but it's obvious, isn't it?" He quirked a brow. I did not answer. He touched the mouse, keeping the screen on. "He wipes the computers every time he uses them. That way no one will know what he's done. And then he looks up things that would seem like him, but don't detail *everything*, in order to throw us off his trail." He tapped his forehead, nodding and smiling conspiratorially.

I made a face. "I don't think it's that deep..."

After another quick sweep of the room to confirm that this was his only computer, I resumed my seat in front of the desktop.

Just as I'd sat down, Dorian's burner phone buzzed in his pocket, startling me. I jumped, almost knocking over the lamp. I caught it and emitted a small sigh of relief.

Dorian showed me the phone, snorting and rolling his eyes.

Are you almost done?

I took the phone, drafting and deleting messages. It was easy to get the hang of texting on the phone. It was rather similar to the phones my parents used when I was a child, just more advanced. The buttons lit up as my fingers flew across the keyboard. I showed Dorian the text. He laughed and gestured in a 'send it at your own risk' way.

Champion...

I hit send.

After we'd finished looking through the computer, we proceeded. Dorian told

89

me that he hoped that the half-demon was still logged into his Textile account: an offline database that could hold a range of encrypted files. I found out that was not the case. I quickly opened the necessary programs on the drive and waited for about thirty minutes while it searched through computer and tried to find a password to Textile.

I wonder why Textile is protected and not the computer as a whole...

I was given my answer in seconds.

Under Dorian's instruction, I logged in quickly, effortlessly, my fingers flying across the keyboard as if it were a piano. Once I was logged in, I took a quick glance through the history and found video upon video of profiling on Immortals and Gifted genealogy, demons and the occult, along with videos that were borderline pornographic. There were also more than a few videos in Jacques's search history that gave tips on how to manipulate your magic to leave a mark on their mind once your Mark, the magical branding, had been destroyed. Man, it wasn't hard to guess what was on his mind. I glanced through his internet history to find searches like 'what's the most tender part of the human body?' and 'sodomy & YOU.' Along with searches like 'how to clean meat *without* getting blood on your clothes.'

"Damn, Jacques. You have it bad..."

The phone pinged. I snatched up the phone, my hands shaking. I didn't know if his plans were for me or for Grant, his long-lost love...and I didn't want to know. But I knew now that there was no going back. The man was beyond twisted—he was sick.

Did you find it yet?

90

No! I texted before turning back to the computer.

I went to Jacques's recent uploads and sure enough, there was a video. It showed a tall, thin woman strapped to the table, her eyes sunken into her head like small pits, her ribs sticking out and her body shaking as she tried to wriggle free. Jacques's pale hand picked up a mallet and brought it down on her knee. She screamed. There was a black light flowing from his hand, pumping dark magic into the woman. A dribble of snot slid from her nose as her eyes glazed over.

I did not envy her. No one would.

I looked through the grainy video, which was obviously shot on a cellphone. There were exactly nine views, for which I praised Kalysma. I looked through the other videos, which showed Jacques running all kinds of experiments on her, even going as far as to make her shift into her Gifted form as he peeled her scales from her body with a scalpel. I felt nauseated. Before I could see any more, I removed it and every other video.

After I was done, I went to an encrypted file on the drive. Dorian instructed me on how to carefully get rid of the encryption and open the 'special file' that he'd created. As I uploaded it to the computer, even I had to admit that it was a work of art. The Fallback—a virus of Dorian's invention—was uploaded in ten minutes. Astonishingly, we really didn't have to wait long.

A dragon appeared on the screen and spit flames. Once it faded, a bunch of antivirus software opened up on the screen, trying to save the contents. This took care of everything by wiping the computer. Dorian took the SD card as a trophy.

After that, a black line ran down the middle of the screen and smoke poured from the desktop computer. The screen stared back at me, its face slashed in half.

Dorian slapped his hand on my back. "Great job! Your first mission as a Rebel is complete. Tiara would be proud! Hell, your *parents* would be proud."

I couldn't even think her name without tearing up. Her death was so unjust, so savage. She didn't deserve to go out the way she did. I couldn't help but feel that if I hadn't interfered, she would still be here. And that was something that I would have to live with for the rest of my life.

"What do we do now?" I asked mechanically, trying to shut off my emotions.

"I guess we go to sleep. We'll reconvene tomorrow. We just have to search the rest of the house and then we're done."

I decided to take a shower, wanting to wash the blood off my body. I thought that maybe it would help me feel saner. I walked back over to the set of chests-of-drawers in Jacques's room, which was the room Dorian was using, and pulled out one of Jacques's old dress shirts. When Dorian wasn't looking, I brought it to my nose, inhaling. It smelled sour like him.

Then I went to the slave room, stripped down and went into the adjoined bathroom. Like a robot, all mechanical movements and disjointed limbs, I turned on the hot water until it was scalding. I went to the closet to grab the necessary provisions before dragging myself into the shower.

I washed slowly but vigorously, scrubbing my skin until it was raw and red. Then I took the shampoo and washed my hair, my nails scratching my scalp in the most satisfying of ways. I got out of the shower, toweled off and then went to my room. While wading through the carnage, I attempted to run a comb through my hair, but it snapped in half under my efforts, and I wound up giving up. I loved my hair, but damn—could it put up a fight!

In the room, I rearranged things. It made it a bit more manageable. I went into the drawer and pulled out a dress that was meant for Tiara.

And I just went *numb*.

My emotions crashed to a standstill in my chest before they could even start. I stared at the dress, aquamarine, her favorite color. I felt almost as if I were awash at sea, and gripped the fabric in my hands as if it were an anchor. The waves of my guilt and depression tossed me back and forth.

I quickly ripped open the dresser, stuffed the dress inside and slammed the drawer closed.

"My fault…" My lips moved, numb. "It's all my fault…"

My fist arced out, sinking into my gut. I held onto the pain with both hands, refusing to let myself feel anything else. My breath came out in an uneasy shudder, then another, and another. Chills racked my frail body. Without my friend, I was falling apart, fracturing into a million pieces, like a glass vase as it met the floor.

"Forgive me, Tiara. I've failed you."

SHUT IT OUT—

SHUT IT OUT—

SHUT IT OUT—

SILENCE.

Chapter Fourteen

Always Inside Me

I woke up in a panic with open scratches all down my arms. After the dream of Dorian, I was pulled into a nightmare. It was about Jacques. He'd turned into a thousand little bugs, biting and gnawing, invading all else. The more I scratched, the deeper he burrowed.

He's inside of me.

He'll always be inside of me.

"Here," Dorian said the next day as he sat in the chair next to me, "give me your hand."

He gently picked up my hand, his long fingers soft and warm, enveloping mine in an embrace. My heart pounded through my chest harder, spreading liquid fire through my veins. His eyes glowed; the hand that was wrapped around mine glowed as well. I heard his voice in my head, commanding me to be calm. I obliged, relaxing in my seat.

He can't hurt you anymore.

94

"He can't hurt me anymore."

I'm here for you.

"You're here for me."

The Rebellion will keep you safe.

"The Rebellion will keep me safe."

"Good."

"Okay," I sighed, my eyelids lowering as I calmly slouched in my seat. "I'm okay."

"I want you to learn how to use runes. You're going to need it for future plans for the Rebellion."

"Runes...? What are those exactly?"

He looked baffled before a look of understanding crossed his face.

"Runes are magical symbols that can make certain things happen—it all depends on what you draw." At my look, he explained his understanding: "Demons can't use runes, but they can manipulate others into using them for their own gain."

"Wait a sec." I paused, thinking back to a question he asked Jacques at his mansion. "Does this have anything to do with that book you're looking for?"

He kissed my forehead. "You're a genius."

I blushed. "I mean, if you say so..."

"Now that I've explained *that*," he said, eyes darting away, "we can search the rest of the house."

We started in the attic, working our way through box after endless box. Finally, I encountered the last, one that was carefully hidden, buried behind the others and mountains of items so thick and heavy, it almost made me want to give up searching—*almost*—which I'm sure was the intent. There was a haphazard symbol on it, one that looked like a lightning bolt with a feather. I called Dorian over. He kneeled next to me, pulled out a pen and drew over it. The rune, which I'm sure an older slave placed there, slid off the box.

We glanced at each other. Jacques must not have counted on someone who could use rune magic coming up here. It looked so easy when he did it, but I also knew that Dorian was exceptionally strong. I opened the box to see a menial photo album sitting there, covered in dust but otherwise untouched. I pulled it out and set it in my lap.

"Why would he have a rune on a box with *this* in it?" Dorian asked.

"It's obviously very important," I said with an all-knowing sniff, but really, I was just as clueless as he was.

I touched the rune and immediately felt a zing of magic zip through me. Oddly enough, it felt...familiar. I held one finger on the rune, wondering whose magic it was that I'd felt. But I couldn't place it.

Dorian sat down next to me, his leg brushing against mine. I scooted over discreetly, not wanting to feel lust in that moment since I needed to concentrate. We opened the book to see a picture of a small, helpless baby. It was totally normal looking—pale skin, fat, wrinkly hands and tiny feet—except for one thing: it's eyes.

Its eyes were two windows into a black abyss. Red was sprinkled there, swirling like a vat of lava, and the child's tiny fists were balled up. The story told through its eyes said that the child needed nourishment that it could not find on this planet—it needed a soul, which was most easily consumed through the flesh. The woman holding the child looked absolutely spent, her eyes drooping and yellow. Her stomach was still sagging, and one could easily make out black, spidery veins spreading all across her body and face.

"Well at least we know he wasn't an ugly baby," Dorian laughed, nudging me.

I nodded shakily.

The page flipped and the same woman stood in a pasture of wilted flowers, the gleam of dark magic in her eyes. There were animals there, their bodies misshapen, their ribs poking out and their eyes sunken in. Her arms were spread wide as if warning off some malignant force—no, not warning—*welcoming*. A young boy stood beside the woman whose crazy smirk matched hers. There was a deadness in his eyes that made the woman almost seem…*safe?* It was obvious that Jacques's entire family was insane.

"Okay, so we know that he was always crazy," Dorian offered, smiling crookedly, but that same confident humor was gone. He looked…*afraid.*

The third picture was of two women, both with long brown hair and matching grey eyes, although one wore a crown of gold, the other of silver. I thought they were either twins or very close in age. The slightly shorter one looked crazy, yes, but not totally evil…or maybe she knew how to mask it? I slid the picture out of the book and looked at the back. *Fleur, Queen of France, and Celeste, Queen of Wales, circa. 1799.* Most Mortals would wonder how they took a picture when cameras were 'invented' in 1816, but demons had been using them a full century before that.

Dorian was deathly quiet. I glanced over at him. The golden undertones were gone from his skin, replaced by a fear stricken white.

I put the picture back before flipping to the next.

The next was of a younger Jacques in a tux. He stood in front of a large house just slightly too small to be a mansion, a devilish smirk on his face. There was a girl next to him, her black tresses bound up in a single French braid, her eyes wide-set and a demonic crimson. She was frowning. She was in a long lacey dress and I couldn't believe what I was seeing.

I looked on the back: *Jacques & Elmire Faux – The Wedding.*

"This is a joke, right?" I snorted.

"What? What is it?"

He read the inscription. "He was *married*?!"

"No."

"It looks like it."

"No."

"How do you know?"

Because I know everything about Jacques and if he was married, I would know.

I grumbled a little something under my breath.

"Maybe it meant that he was at someone else's wedding?"

"Maybe…"

"Funny. This Elmire chick almost looks like she could be his sister."

They both had the same pasty white skin…but it couldn't be. She looked so…*normal*. I mean despite the unearthly beauty and the red eyes, she had a certain *sanity* to her that he and the rest of his family lacked. But she looked so sad, like she was trapped, and Jacques had a way of doing that to people—trapping them in an infinite loop of sorrow. I put the picture back into the photo album and turned the page.

The next picture was of a man with dark black hair pulled up in a ponytail and dark, red-flecked irises; he was the spitting image of Jacques, the only thing setting them apart being this man's devilish goatee. The picture after that was of a man that I had come to familiarize with in just a short span of time: Grant. After that, the album was full of pictures of Grant, full of happy memories of a happy couple—sort of. Then the pictures of Grant just stopped. As Dorian continued flipping pages, I zoned out for a moment, trying to remember happier days with Jacques, but they were all tainted.

"Oh, sh—!" Dorian jumped, knocking the book out of my hands and across the attic floor.

"What!" I startled. "What is it?"

I got up, carefully grabbed the book and held to my chest. I looked to Dorian for guidance, who stared at the wall, his face closed off. But his eyes betrayed him: they were filled with pure terror. I didn't know what I'd find: a scarred back, a dead Mortal, or perhaps a pentagram?

The last picture was of Jacques sitting at a table, an assortment of meats before him, his mouth marred with blood.

I immediately shut the book. There was not a doubt in my mind as to what he was eating in that picture: human flesh. Normally, he would not let his appearance become so sullied, but only I knew how monstrous he could become when his innate hunger took over. I shuddered, but the memory stayed locked in my mind, partially because it was crucial that I remember one thing.

He's a monster. He's not capable of real love.

And I suddenly realized who's magic that rune was, even if it did have Jacques's family crest on it—

Valentina's.

I would never come back up here again.

Chapter Fifteen

They Lied

It was now our third day in the safe house. Valentina was getting restless. Dorian's phone was ringing off the hook, buzzing every thirty minutes or so. She was pissed, which made me want to stay gone longer. I knew what people were like when they were angry. I knew the damage they could cause, both intentional and unintentional.

We were currently listening to Lyson-S on the ancient radio, her voice floating through the speakers. Apparently, Lyon-S was a half-Gifted, half-Immortal singer who imbued magic into her songs. She was able to make you feel what she felt. This was a song about immortality, which was supposed to be sung from the point of view of someone who was fully Gifted. But apparently, she couldn't find anyone daring enough to sing the song.

So, she sang it herself.

Think of it as the Gifted version of Billie Holiday's *Strange Fruit*. According to Dorian, the Rebellion even played it at their rallies. The rallies were held to incite people to fight back against the Immortals. Even the Mortals were known to act out once the song came on.

It went like this:

"What's the price of living forever?

So lonely but always free.

Condemned to walk, a common drifter,

Feet never touching the street.

As I recall, you were destructive…

My poison, my drug, my disease.

I even stayed when you said you'd save us,

For that lie, blood washed in the stream.

You stand on the corner, a righteous pariah.

You never practiced what you preached…

Here I stand, a phrase you don't remember.

You sink and walk right past me…"

"What is this song called?" I asked.

He pulled out a pack of cigarettes.

"Mentiti Sunt," Dorian said, speaking Latin.

"They Lied…"

He lit the cigarette, the tip burning with its small flame. Smoke floating up to the ceiling. He dragged in a long breath before speaking again: "You'd never expect someone who is from both worlds to be so outspoken." Dorian rolled his neck back to rest his head on the back of the chair. "It's insane."

"It's brave."

He blew out a breath, sounding tired. "Maybe…"

I felt tired, too. Tired and broken and full of so much rage. I wanted this war to be over. I wanted us to be free, to have fair jobs, to get fair pay, to pay the same price for houses, to have the same kinds of insurance, to be afforded the same opportunities in life.

Most of all, I didn't want to be seen as a monster, a Rebel, a thug. I wanted to be a woman. I didn't want to be dangerous.

I wanted to be beautiful.

Chapter Sixteen

Why Do I Miss Him?

Dorian packed up his stuff and told me to do the same. I thought of the Rebellion's unforgiving yet fearless leader and the hard, unfeeling ground, and begged him to let us stay the night. It was only our third day in the safe house. Surely there was *something* we could do together before it was time to go back. He promised that we would sleep here tonight and then head back in the morning.

I took off my clothes and put on my old master's shirt. Its scent filled me back up. I wanted love from a man that was incapable of giving it. Did that make me crazy? Or did that make me desperate?

I wanted to live. I wanted to be free. And I wanted to be whole again equally so. The last people I loved this fiercely were gone. The last people I loved with this much passion died.

Before I knew it, I was shaking, my hands and legs going numb. I couldn't even stand without falling. I sank back down on the edge of my bed, trying to fight off the thoughts of my former master's darker side.

It was no use. He invaded my brain, my heart, my soul. There was no point in fighting it anymore. I was confused. Sometimes I thought of the evening baths and hated his guts, others I thought of the days of grooming and wanted to love every part of him.

Something was seriously wrong with me.

I had a dream that I was sitting with Master Jacques, his face drawn and his eyes dull. I looked to him for guidance and was met with silence. In the dream, he picked up a large book and set it on the table. He opened it to a certain page, one that had been marked, and began chanting. My heart beat wildly in my chest as his chants grew louder and more frenzied.

Then he just stopped.

He pushed away from the table, his eyes glowing red. Horns sprouted from his head and his canines grew in length, sharpening to delicate points. His skin was an unnatural black that glittered like diamonds. Even the darkness bred light. I called out for him to stop, to tell me what he just did, but he kept right on walking, ignoring every word. I looked down at the book and saw a picture of a girl, her breasts unbound, and her head thrown back as she chanted. A portal swirled in the background, a pair of red eyes blinking from within it.

What did it mean?

I woke up. I didn't puke, but I was still shaking and nauseous. My ears rang and I gripped my head, dizzy. Things got fuzzy. The ringing in my ears reverberated throughout my body, echoing within my very soul. I fought to keep my head, to stay sane. Dorian appeared at my door. I didn't realize I'd been crying until he brushed the tears away with the pad of his thumb.

Why was he touching me so openly?

I told myself that he didn't know me. And yet I leaned into the touch, nuzzling my nose into his palm. He was warm and safe, beautiful and kind, loving yet strong, closed off but somehow still vulnerable.

I would let him ruin me, if only he never let go.

"What's wrong?"

I shook my head. "Nothing."

"You know," he said, taking my hand in his and tracing odd patterns on my palms, "it helps if you talk about it."

"There's nothing to talk about."

"I'm up—"

"You're always up." I paused, realization dawning on me. "Do you *ever* sleep?"

"I only sleep around two to three hours a night."

"Yet you seem fine," I said, noting his chipper mood and upped energy.

"We're both up."

"So?"

"So, let's talk about it."

He sat on my bed. I jumped, but he only wrapped an innocent arm around my shoulder. I knew not to fear him, yet my body reacted that way after thinking of more painful subjects. It was all thanks to Jacques, of course. Still, I wanted it to be different, less guarded...*safe.*

"The dreams started a while back, but now that I'm out of the mansion, they're different…"

So, I told him. I told him about the nightmares. Dorian frowned as I explained to him that I missed my Master even if he did abuse me. I admitted that I felt like nothing without him, for he gave me a purpose: to strive for perfection.

But I didn't tell him why I had the dreams. I didn't tell him about how they were all too real. The nights kneeling by the tub, washing Jacques. Or the days where he would force me to touch him, how he made me promise that I loved him—that I would never leave him the way Grant did—before he fed me. How I almost started to believe the lie.

I thought of my skinny, slanted features, my sharp jawline, my crooked nose and my flat, starved chest. I wasn't attractive by any sense of the word, but men like Jacques ate me up. Honestly, in this state I could be mistaken for a guy. Most of the Lords and Ladies in Sidra didn't want to send their men to Jacques because they knew they wouldn't get them back. He sodomized them and then he ate them. I guess that meant that I was lucky to even be alive.

But I didn't want to be.

I wanted to tell Dorian, but I was *scared.* I had a chance with him. I had a chance to be stronger, braver, *better.*

Not damaged.

"Do you miss the beatings?"

I picked at a splinter in the wooden bedframe. Pulled. It got stuck under my nail. I winced, focusing on the pain. My life was simply that—pain.

I let loose a shuddery breath, replied, "It's what I deserved."

"Don't you see, Marve? You don't deserve that. No one deserves that."

I picked at the wood under my nail. "You're an Immortal. You have slaves just like he did. So how am I supposed to trust you?"

"I pay my staff. They aren't slaves. They can leave whenever they want."

Thinking back to the conversation between him, Jacques and Megumi, I yanked it free, tossed it aside. "I don't believe you."

"It's true." He placed a hand under my chin, made me face him, and when I angled my gaze towards the ceiling, he moved his head into my vision. I sighed and looked at him to see him staring at me patiently. "One day I'll show you. If you want, that is."

See how life could have been? See another side of the coin? See proof that he's a good man?

"Sounds like a plan."

"We need to work on getting you well first. I'm going to talk to Valentina about getting someone to train you. Maybe Jaxon or Rhea or Armeria, although Armeria can only train you at night…"

"Is she a vampire?"

"No. Its, um…its best if I let her tell you."

I pursed my lips, blinking slowly, and nodded. "Okay…"

"It's actually a funny story."

"How so—?"

"Like I said…" He wouldn't meet my eyes. "I'd have to let her tell you."

Chapter Seventeen

The Bazaar

"So, you mean to tell me," Valentina ground out, rubbing the bridge of her nose, "that you didn't find *anything* that could help?"

I wanted to tell her about my dream but seeing her so angry made me nervous. What if I was wrong? What if Jacques showed me the dream to manipulate me? What if he had the book and she sent me back to get it?

Dorian ran through a list of alternative options.

Valentina listened silently for a long time, not saying anything, her eyes trained on me. I could practically hear her thoughts stirring around in her head, the word that defined her rigid features: *weak*. She was not just disappointed in me.

I *bothered* her.

"I know that you're not exactly ready to face Jacques yet." At my flinch, her eyes widened in that way that said she was trying to avoid rolling them. Then, after a long moment, said, "I'm going to send you on a special mission. I'm sending you, Dorian, Rhea, Armeria and Jaxon. Do you think you can handle it?"

"I don't know what we're doing...?" I mumbled.

"Why he favored you is a mystery..." she grumbled, just loud enough for me to hear.

My heart slammed to a standstill in my chest, and when it did resume its rhythm, its beat was hollow. My eyes stung, my throat thickening in a way that made it hard to swallow. But I refused to cry in front of her...

Dorian reached out to touch my shoulder, but Valentina glared at him. He retracted his hand.

I felt like I was alone on a deserted island, watching the ship of my future sail away. I reached out a hand, wanting to catch it, wanting to wade into the water and swim to it if I could, but the waters pulled at the bank of sand at my feet, pulled at *me*, threatening to wash me away.

To hide my shaking hands, I put them behind my back. My teeth ground together, holding in my scream of frustration and heartache. Was this how she treated all Rebels or was I special?

The Mark on Valentina's neck reappeared with a sparkly glow. It took me a moment to realize that she was calling the other Rebels she had mentioned. My back stiffened, the tears in my eyes fleeing as quickly as they came. My hands tightened into fists as I placed them at my sides. A cocky smirk appeared on my face, the same one that I wore in the arenas.

I am a Champion. A Champion!

In minutes, three Rebels filed in.

One was short, stocky, and had curves for days. Her skin was a deep cocoa brown, her afro bobbed as she cruised into the room, throwing up a peace sign as she sing-songed, "Buenos dias, Señora V!" A small, pretty blonde girl floated in behind her who couldn't have been older than eleven, a long, flowery dress on her form, her azure eyes blinking over first at me, then at Valentina as she said, her voice pealing like trill of bells, "Hello, Madam V!" Last to come in was a large heavyset man, as tall as he was wide, his dark eyes finding mine and searching them, then his mouth tilting up before he turned to Valentina and nodded silently.

"Ah, the Triple Threat!" Valentina chirped back and as the light flickered across her form, I noticed her same red undertones tinted in the skin of the Afro-Latina girl and the same shape of their nose, the color of their eyes. Were they related? She didn't seem to show her any special favoritism as she flicked a hand. "You know the drill."

They nodded before glancing at Dorian and me.

"I know that you normally work *alone*," Valentina addressed Dorian, "but since you wouldn't shut up about working with Marve, I thought I'd give you your chance."

Dorian's eyes darted away from mine, red dusting his cheeks, making him look like a bashful schoolboy. It was cute. I could tell that Valentina found it nauseating though.

I smiled shyly.

He tilted his chin up, confidence seeping out of his very pores, and asked, "You ready for this?"

I imagined his strong body splayed over mine, his pants around his ankles, his mouth on my neck, and shuddered. But I knew that looked weird. So, I rolled my shoulders back, cracked my neck and let my Glamor fall away. My bones ground against one another as my body straightened just slightly. My scales slid into place, my teeth becoming more jagged, lengthening and hardening as my eyes glowed. Dorian shuddered and looked away. But my feelings weren't hurt this time. The others looked different with these eyes—*meatier*. I gnashed my teeth, grinning when Rhea gave me the universal look of respect.

"Somebody's got *scaaalessss!*" she cried, her Espanzan accent thick like Valentina's.

"As you can see, my niece can be very spirited. She's next to lead the Rebellion. Respect her like you respect me," Valentina eyed me, "and you're set for life."

I nodded, trying to match the energy. "Cool."

"Why are you still standing here?" Valentina had already turned back to a stack of papers. *"Go!"*

I turned around, but everyone had left but Dorian. He rolled his eyes at Valentina when he thought she wasn't looking, but she grunted, "Get out of here, Sparkles, before I kick your ass!" With precision that would normally have been impossible for someone her age, she threw a stapler at him. He yelped as he batted it away and speed-walked towards the entrance to the dugout.

"Where did they all go?" I asked, standing at his side.

"To the jet."

***

Rhea bumped into an Immortal man and he cursed, dropping his bags. She apologized in a scatter-brained way, immediately dropping to her knees to help him pick up his stuff. He eyed her, trying to decide what she was, how he should go about this. Her hands shook as she picked up a black suit. So quick that I wasn't sure if I saw what I saw, she slipped her bandana off her arm and into the bag, beneath the suit. She averted her gaze as she handed it back to him.

Assuming her to be Gifted, as I had, he snatched his things and left. "You're lucky I don't report you to your Master, girl!" he spat.

"Thank you, sir."

He harrumphed and stalked off. His shoulder bumped into me. Not wanting any of his trouble, I immediately apologized. His eyes swam over me for an eternity. I froze, ice-cold filling my veins and a nervous burn in my stomach. But then he turned and stalked off. Before I could sigh in relief, Rhea was pinning me with a daring look. She held up a snazzy gold watch with a triumphant grin.

My eyes widened. That was dangerous—and smooth.

"Five drachmas says you can't do the same."

"I don't have a bandana," I whispered back.

"You don't need one." She leaned in as if to kiss my cheek, her lips brushing my ear. "I planted a bug in his bag—that's what they're for. That lover of yours sowed listening devices into the seams."

My eyes got even bigger.

113

"Five drachmas," she wagered again, waggling her brows at me.

My head tilted up. This would be a simple feat for a Champion. Easy money.

"You know you can't sell that," I said. "You don't have papers."

She snorted. "You let me worry about that."

This next exchange happened in seconds: She swaggered over to a stand huddled off to the side, leaning on it as if to get some shade. The wrist with her Mark sparkled. She dropped the watch onto the wooden counter. A man in a kufi, wearing all silver and a long thobe, dropped eight drachmas down, one by one, as if he had literally dropped them—except he didn't snatch them back up. He swiped up the watch. Rhea took the drachmas, glamoured her Mark and kept it moving.

Easy enough.

I lowered my gaze, trampling through the bazaar. Vendors shouted things at Immortals, cursing at Gifted children with scarred feet and dirty hands to keep it moving, unless they had money and papers, that is. I reached into my back pocket, feeling for the papers Jacques gave me when we signed our agreement, but came back empty. Of course! I'd left him behind.

Even if I *had* remembered to grab them, they were useless now—the Mark on them had long since faded. I had broken our contract.

I bumped into a woman, her yellow, cat-like eyes watching me closely as she steadied herself. A crate full of samosas and plantains jostled in her arms. A long tiger's tail flicked behind her. I cursed and then immediately apologized to the Gifted woman. Her mouth curved down, covering a fang, as she asked me where she knew me from.

"You don't know me," I said, dropping her gaze.

"I'm sure I do," the Espanzan girl said, tilting her head.

"No, you don't."

Her eyes flicked over me. This was bad. This was very, *very* bad. If she identified me, I was as good as dead. Then the Slave Catchers would see that there was an unchaperoned Gifted here (which was a stupid phrase for it considering you could come here as long as you had papers, present Master/Mistress or not) and come after me. I flexed my fingers. I would fight my way out if I had to. I'd killed before. I'd kill aga—

"Whoa!" a voice shouted.

Most people didn't turn. But I did—and so did the girl. Dorian stumbled back, glaring at a boy from the Southern Isles, who had the same armored body as me. My heart softened at the kinship. The boy, who couldn't have been but a few years younger than me, puffed out his chest, slamming it into Dorian's. The other man didn't stumble back, but instead sent an unhesitant right hook into his jaw. The shouting intensified.

My eyes darted around for Jaxon, Rhea or Armeria, but I didn't see them. They wouldn't make it in time! I turned to the Espanzan girl, snatched the crate she was carrying, and placed it on the ground. Casting one more wide-eyed gaze around the bazaar, I stood on it. I took a deep breath, knowing that this would mean my death, the end of the great Champion Marve of the Lightning Fists, and raised my voice.

"I have fought!" I cried.

"What?!" shouted an old Mortal man, his back hunched and his hands wrinkled with age. His brown eyes twinkled in the pits of his black face. "Speak up!"

"I HAVE FOUGHT! I HAVE YELLED! I HAVE DIED A THOUSAND TIMES! I HAVE ENLISTED THE HELP OF MANY OF MY PEOPLE! I HAVE SENT MANY TO THE STARS! I HAVE FORSAKEN THE OATH OF THE GOOD MOTHER AND BOWED AT THE FEET OF MEN! FOR WHAT?!"

But for the most part, people didn't care. Some Gifted children stopped to stare, pointing, cheesy grins on their face as they chanted, "Champion! Champion! Champion!" But most people didn't bat a lash. The world had seen people tired of the struggle, but that didn't mean that *it* was tired.

So, I sang, loud, clear, bold, true. I sang for the stars. I sang for Tiara. I sang for my people.

"What's the price of living forever?

So lonely but always free."

Someone stopped, nudging the person next to them. Then they leaned in close, whispering as they afforded me another glance. I was dead meat. But I didn't care. I had to save Dorian.

Because he'd saved me.

"Condemned to walk, a common drifter,

Feet never touching the street.

As I recall, you were destructive...

My poison, my drug, my disease."

Dorian's head popped up, awash in a sea of bodies. The people were clamoring now that they recognized the song. They knew what it meant. It meant that freedom was near. It meant that we were here to save them.

An Immortal shouted for a Slave Catcher as she marched up to the crate and kicked it from under my feet. I tumbled to the ground. She raised her foot, slamming it into my nose. I stared up at her, bloodied, and sang as loud as I could.

"I even stayed when you said you'd save us,

For that lie, blood washed in the stream."

"Wait!" she shouted. "I know you!"

I grinned, blood dribbling from my nose, running into my mouth. "Do you, sister?"

"I am *not* your sister!"

"You stand on the corner, a righteous pariah.

You never practiced what you preached...

Here I stand, a phrase you don't remember.

You sink and walk right past me..."

People had stopped, staring. I glanced over at Dorian, who was seconds from rolling around on the ground with the boy from the Isles. There weren't any Slave Catcher's near...yet. A few Immortals rolled their eyes but continued shopping. I really needed to make a scene...to save someone I barely knew.

I stood—and lunged at the Immortal. I clung to her silken robes and gold amulet, trying to make her see that she—*they*—were killing us! They were taking our lives in cold blood, beating us, calling us all kinds of things and for what—because we were born looking different than them?!

Why?!

What gave them the audacity to think that their lives were worth more? Their religion had been tampered with! They force-fed us ours! And for what?!

Why?!

Her pale white skin gleamed as she stumbled back. One of her rings slid off her finger as I clasped her hand in mine. I shook as memories overtook me.

I stood in the kitchen as my old master watched me, his hands braced on the doorframe. His shirt was open, fluttering from the air of the A/C. It was then that I noticed his nipples, rosy, pink and blossoming on his chest. He stared at me, a dark look in his eyes and a devilish smirk on his face. He moved slowly, one hand moving to reach into his pants, playing with himself as he eyed me, the other hand moving out to—?

He crooked a finger at me.

Valentina leaned over the stove, stirring a pot, shifting her weight to one leg, groaning in pain as she did so. Tiara sat at the table in the dining room, playing with a doll, still too new to have peeped by Master's cunning just yet, looking up at me curiously as I froze in terror. I clutched a fistful of rose petals in my fingers, hand shaking, shaking, shaking—why was I always shaking?

"Do you see this?!" the Immortal woman shouted. "She's hurting me!"

But I wasn't. I clung to her, but I hadn't advanced violently. She wished violence upon me before I ever had her. I tried to hand her back her ring. She flinched, tears streaming down her face, as she screamed for help, weaponizing her tears (her privilege) in the hopes it would get me killed.

I saw myself kneeling at the feet of my Master, his black magic flooding my veins like some type of foreign pathogen. My head whipped back. I screamed. He bit into my neck, ripping the Mark from my skin. I'd made a deal with the devil. I'd sold myself out—for what?

A nice bed and food.

I was gonna die, I was gonna die, I was gonna die—

"Calm all that down, lady!" a Gifted man yelled back. It was the one that had been fighting Dorian. Now he was standing there, filming on a beat-up phone. "She ain't do nothin' to you!"

"She hurt me!" The Immortal Lady insisted. "You!" she snatched up a child, who could have been Immortal or Gifted or Mortal—who knows? "You saw it!"

The child began to cry.

I saw myself sitting at his feet, his hand coiled in my hair. The fire snapped and crackled before us as he tipped his head back with a sigh. I opened my eyes, staring into the flames. The pages of The Revenant stared back at me, eaten by the fire as they turned to blackened ash. He chanted my name. This was what I lived for.

Not a deity on another astral plane.

But for him.

"Man, don't do the baby like that!" shouted the Gifted man.

The fires of a thousand stars gleamed in my eyes as I stared into the Immortal's eyes, cursing her to a fiery pit. "Let that child go."

"You're not worth my time, you damn beast!" she spat back, snatching away from me, then patting the curls of the blonde child. "Come now, child. I'll buy you a new dress."

The child smiled and followed the older woman, but not before throwing me a disgusted look.

"Thank you, Mistress," I whispered, watching them walk away.

Some people stared at me in shock and revulsion, but most looked away. Finally, minutes later, after everything had died down—after I had become another beast kneeling at the feet of false gods—the Gifted girl from before found me. She snatched me up. Under my feet were crushed plantains, smashed samosas and—now that I noticed it—many (now useless) dates.

"You owe me!" She growled, fisting my shirt. She yanked me forward— and then suddenly let me go, her eyes widening. She backed up a step, holding up her hands. "I don't want any trouble."

"What do ya mean?" I growled. "Don't you wanna fight?"

"I ain't finna throw hands with a Champion," she muttered, "even though it would be an honor."

I hadn't even charged up my Gift. How did she know who I was?

"May Kalysma bless you, sister," she whispered before slipping into the cracks of the ground.

"What the f—"

Had I imagined this entire encounter? And the people milled around me, refusing to stare or even glance my way. And something about it proved to me that this all had indeed happened

"Let's go!" Dorian's hand clamped on my shoulder, pulling me away from the spot where I'd frozen. I stumbled back. He took off running. "Come on!"

The Gifted children still chanted "Champion! Champion! Champion!" But no one gave a crud enough to pause and look or see a legend in their midst. Because a beast—Champion or not—was still a beast at the end of the day. I handed the ring to one of the children, then turned and took off running. My world had already been ruined by Immortal greed, and money couldn't buy my way out of the predicament I was in now, but maybe money could give these kids a fighting chance—

Not to end up in the same place I was now.

Chapter Eighteen

Truly a Champion

"She did what?!"

Valentina was fuming. Her face was splotchy red, her eyes practically jumping out of her skull. I flinched, but no one seemed quite so scared except me. I told myself that it was because she was angry, and not because I feared being thrown out, that I was afraid. But deep down, I knew it wasn't true. I wanted to make her proud and earn my keep, but all I seemed to do was fuck up.

"But she *saved* me," Dorian insisted, eyes locked on Valentina. His hand twitched at his side. I knew that he was trying to use his Gift, which I still hadn't figured out why he had. But that wasn't at the front of my mind. Besides, it wasn't like he had used it against me. He steeled his shoulders and tilted his chin up and I knew that even though he couldn't use magic to make her see reason, he was going to win this argument: his confidence alone was reason enough to believe him. "She's a loyal asset. Why else would she risk recapture—and her life—just to save me? And her speech wasn't all that bad, either."

"Mm."

"Without her distraction," a golden-haired, white woman volunteered, "we wouldn't have gotten our intel."

"Isn't that what *Dorian* was doing?" she asked.

Oh, fuck. That's why he was fighting? It was staged?!

"Perhaps. But how do we know it would've worked?" she asked. "It wasn't garnering *that* much attention. But when she sang...? They all listened."

Armeria. She'd told me about her curse that afternoon as we were flying back. I hadn't realized that it took effect as soon as the sun hit the ground. She was a child by day, a woman by night. Apparently, she had tried to have her Gift stripped from her body forcibly by a witch known as the Gift Gouger. She was known for gobbling up magic in some horrendous ways, her bargains for curing people of their Gift for Immortal approval far from fair.

"Play it again."

Armeria set the record player on the desk. That was the whole reason I hadn't seen her. She had been in the jet, recording everything that was said with the mics that Dorian had sowed into in the seams of the cloth. The crew was now wearing all new purple bandanas. It was badass, for real. I asked Valentina when I'd get my own, but she said that her plans for me were all too delicate and that I wouldn't need one.

"You recognize that girl from the Isles?" asked one Immortal to another.

"No. Who is she?" said the second, a younger-sounding man-child.

"That's the Champion. They call her Champion Marve of the Lightning Fists."

I hummed in satisfaction. Even coming from the dirty mouths of Immortals, my name still sounded like a prize.

Rhea snorted, "I prefer Skelly." Everyone stopped, staring at her. "You know? Skelly?" At our blank looks, she raised a brow. "Like Skeleton? The kid's a walking pile of bones!"

I would've laughed had it not been so insulting. Like, really? Did she have to go there? I wasn't skinny by choice!

Valentina gave her a sharp look and Rhea stopped sniggering. "Maybe we should consider one another's circumstance before we start throwing jokes. Not all of us can be blessed with such *full figures*."

Oof. Was that a fat joke? Tina must have been in a really bad mood. Rhea rolled her eyes before putting a stick of gum into her mouth and under her breath, cursed, *"Puta..."*

"¿Quién?" Valentina hissed back. Then said in English, for us all to hear, "Don't get slick with me, girl. Keep playing. Niece or not, you're still replaceable."

The bubble Rhea was blowing popped. She started spewing apologies, but not before she threw me a look that could set houses ablaze. The curse had been meant for me, it seemed. I saw heat dancing across her fingertips and flames simmering in her palms and realized that she had the same power as Valentina. Just because they had the same power didn't mean they were related, but she had called Rhea her niece twice now, so it had to be true.

For some reason, I'd never imagined that Valentina had family, let alone family that was half-Immortal, half-Gifted. It was astounding, really.

124

Armeria paled but continued to play the tape.

"How much do you think she's worth?" the second voice said.

"Fifty, maybe sixty million drachmas."

"Damn!" the second voice cursed. *"Who does she belong to?"*

"The Binge Eater."

"The half-demon *Binge Eater—as in the grandson of* the *Mestiphopheles Binge Eater?"*

"The very same." The first voice was clearly grinning.

"Aw, nah. I'm not getting into bed with fallen angels. You hear about the last joker they skinned who crossed 'em?"

"It was just business. Besides, it wouldn't be crossing." The first Master, who I now recognized as the Master that Rhea bumped into, sounded too eager to be talking about turning over an intelligent being with feelings over to a monster. *"It'd be handing over a prized possession. He'd be indebted to us!"*

"He skinned him—alive. And then he cut him up into little pieces and served him to his family—while he ate with them. Does that really sound like the kind of man you want to do business with?"

"Every monster has a chain. If he crossed us, he'll be bringing down the wrath of Eastern Sidra on himself. Does he sound that stupid to you?"

"Nigga," said the Immortal, *"you sound stupid. Who do you know that can protect you from the literal devil and his grandson? Do you not remember that the Binge Eater once ruled the Land of the Three—before it was what it is now. Back then, it was just the Empire. He had half of Europe in his pocket, too. And—"*

125

"But he doesn't have those connections anymore."

"What connections do you have?" the Immortal asked the first, obviously unintelligent Immortal.

"I know the Golden Immortal."

The tape cut off. Everyone turned to stare at Dorian. I blinked, looking at all of them, wondering what they knew that I didn't. But then I remembered. Dorian was the Golden Immortal. Did he really hold that much sway amongst the Immortals?

Dorian looked downright nervous. He glanced around and then his eyes settled on me. They seemed to soften and harden at the same time. He looked like he was hiding something, although what I couldn't imagine. For some reason, my lips tingled as I remembered our kiss.

I wanted to taste him again.

"So what?" Dorian asked, finally locking eyes with Valentina. "What do we do now? They're not going to stop looking for her. She's too well known."

"She was in her Armored State at the bazaar—" Valentina's eyes cut to me "—weren't you, Marve?"

"Yes?" I squeaked.

Rhea guffawed. "She's not built for this, *Tia*. Look at her!"

They looked at me. I stared back at them, my eyes probably too wide for my head, a draft floating from my mouth. But then I realized—

I had no alternatives. It was either this or Jacques. This or be used for the rest of my life. Him—

Or turn myself into a weapon, become a living storm—

126

Not wear Champion Marve as a mask, but to *become* Champion Marve of the Lightning Fists.

"I'm in."

***

They debated over how to proceed. Jaxon, Dorian and Armeria were for training me or at least gauging what stage my powers were at now and going from there. Rhea and Valentina were all for throwing me out into the wild and seeing how I fared.

You can guess what I was for.

They argued for what felt like hours. The longer I stood there, the longer I felt my mind retreating farther and farther into my body. I didn't want to die. I didn't want to be a weapon. No matter how much I didn't want to be useless, I was tired of fighting for everyone else.

Who was going to fight for me?

"I've got you," Dorian said when I swayed. He held me steady. "You know you don't have to do this," he offered.

I leaned my head on the shoulder, not realizing the intimacy of the action. His arm wrapped around my shoulders, hugging me to him. His hand blazed trails of fire wherever he touched.

"I want to."

No, I don't.

"You keep fighting all these wars, soon you're gonna burn out."

"Wise words, old man."

He shrugged. "I've seen it happen too many times."

He was still holding me. We seemed to realize this at the same time. He let me go and took a step back, his hands twitching at their sides, wanting to reach back out. I knew this because I wanted to do the same thing. Strange, this lust that bound us, this want that drove us, this desire that hurried our hearts.

"Are you two done?" Valentina barked.

I blushed, nodding. Good thing I was still in my Armored State. It was hard to see the blood rushing to my cheeks when I looked like this.

"I'm sending you two on a mission to blow a hospital tomorrow. Hopefully then, we'll know if your powers are worth anything anymore. If they are, we can talk about getting you in contact with these Immortals. Maybe we can pay them off, stop them from turning you in?"

"Why would you need to know if her powers are good to save her?" Dorian asked incredulously.

"If she's not worth saving," Valentina was staring into the depths of my soul, "then why go through the trouble?"

"Oh-ho-ho, that's cold-hearted, even for you!" Rhea laughed.

"No," Dorian snapped, "it's a bitch move. We don't do that to family."

"What do you care? You gonna run off with her? You gonna start a family?" Valentina snapped. "A little happy friggin' family—a beast and an Immortal! How rich!"

"That's a low blow, Tina," I whispered, shocked at her cruelty, "even for you."

"I did everything to get you out!" Valentina snapped, the woman I knew and loved gone from her eyes, having fled from her to give heed to her now apparent dissatisfaction. "EVERYTHING! And you were so ungrateful. Now I send you on a simple mission and you stir up trouble. You're turning out to be more trouble than you're worth! I knew your parents. They were good people. I'm saving you as a favor to them. I've looked out for you *for them*. But you're standing over there, looking all mopey and frightened like a deer in a forest—what am I supposed to do with that? How can I make a Rebel out of a child?!"

My thoughts ground to a standstill in my head. My mouth opened, closed, as I panicked. She leaned back in her seat, annoyed as her fingers strayed to her eyepatch. She invested a lot in me. I'd lost her an eye…and I wouldn't allow myself to take another thing from her.

Ever again.

"Let me make it up to you."

"I'm listening."

Chapter Nineteen

A Not-So-Bright Idea

I said that I wanted to make it up to her! I mentally urged myself to go faster. *This is NOT what I had in mind.*

"Really bright idea, asshole!" I cried at the man running behind me. "Bait the Slave Catchers and see if I'll turn into a living storm, eh?"

"Well, what'd you expect!" Dorian yelled back, his words garbled as his teeth gnashed at the magically-enhanced rope around his wrists. "You think I was just gonna let you shoot some bolts at *me*?!"

"Maybe next time! But—"

"Oh, shut it, you two!" A third, more feminine but still slightly husky voice snapped. "You two bicker like an old married couple!"

I could feel electricity stirring in my belly, refusing to move from that one spot, as if afraid to be stolen from my form if it moved when I did. The woman leaned against the tree next to Dorian to catch her breath, her eyes two pools of amber, her afro bouncing as she worked off the rope around her ankles. Flames sparked to life in her palms as she went at it with her fingers, trying feebly to undo the knots before our pursuers got closer. The ropes were magically enhanced and could not be burned or cut; the only way to get them off was to untie each thread, and whoever wound them must've been a sailor in another life. I tried not to stare at her, but her skin, tinged a few shades darker than Valentina's, held a distracting glow that left me at a loss for words.

I turned only to stare down the barrel of a loaded gun.

"Ah!"

She left her spot by the tree, slipping through the darkness. My body tensed. The magic inside me swirled faster, faster, faster, but still not strong enough to be brought out. I tried to grab hold of it, but it slipped through my fingers like water. The man, dressed in the grey uniform of a Slave Catcher, cocked the gun, and I knew from previous run-ins with Catchers that the bullets were coated with demon blood. It would make me a slave to the demon's command. This also meant that there was a demon on standby.

Human Slave Catchers, I could understand, since they held no blood to make them kin to the Gifted. But how a magic-user—no matter how many lavish prizes they were given—came to work for the Immortals, selling others into slavery for the profit of demons and the Eternal Ones, I'll never know.

"Don't think about it, hottie," he chided as I reached inside myself, my eyes glowing as I searched for my powers. "You make one wrong move and I'll put a bullet through that pretty little skull of yours."

I snorted. "Far from it."

I dropped my Glamor. My bones shifted, reforming, changing, making me into something that was old and new, something *other*. I saw my green eyes reflected in his, my pupils slit like a crocodile's, my teeth razor sharp like my nails. My body was hot, so I opened my mouth, releasing heat. He stumbled back a step, his face screwing in shock and disgust.

Right into Rhea's ember-covered blade. My new ally smirked at me as his head caught flame. I glared back at her. The runes on her dagger faded as she wiped the blood on her pants before sliding it into its sheath with its brothers and sisters. Her fingers curled and the flames doused. The Slave Catcher's glassy brown eyes stared up at the sky, the human's face pale, clammy and bloated like an egg that had been fried too long, only not nearly as appetizing.

"Dude!" I hissed.

"What?" she asked innocently, batting her lashes at me. "I just saved your life."

"He was *mine!*" I hissed, reaching out to shove her.

Her eyes narrowed at me. "The point was for you to use your powers. If you weren't going to use them, we wouldn't have come on this stupid side mission." She growled at me. "And what was *your* plan, breathing on him with that hot ass breath?"

"It's how I release heat!"

"Funny," she sneered, "I just sweat."

"I'm from the Isles. I have the genetic makeup of a crocodile. We don't sweat."

Even as I explained, I knew that she didn't care. As if my looks didn't set me apart enough, so did the differences that you couldn't really see. All because of my genetics. That was her Immortal-half talking, making her think she was better than

132

me—because she didn't have any outward markings that indicated that she was not borne purely of the master race. My hands tightened into fists, shaking. The audacity.

She imitated heavy breaths. "What ya gonna do? Blow on me?"

I glared at her. "You are such a frigging bitch!"

She recoiled. "Excuse me?"

"You heard me. You're Valentina's niece," I whispered back, "so if you wanted a better gig, then you shouldn't have decided to tag along."

"Actually," Dorian's rich, tenor voice said, "I invited her."

"What?!" I snapped back, just as Rhea said, "You're lucky I said yes, Skelly."

"How many times do I have to tell you?" I said, whirling back on her. "My name is Marve!"

"That's the name your Master gave you," Rhea said, "you are—"

"Enough!" Dorian shouted before glancing over his shoulder. "In case you haven't noticed, we have six—no wait—" he shot a look at the one on the ground, "—*five* highly skilled Slave Catchers chasing us, along with a demon in the back of their van, and a bomb that could go off at any minute!" He glanced at the backpack which housed the bomb, which wasn't really a threat since *I* had the detonator. "Unless you two dunderheads want to get caught and go back to Jacques—" I flinched "—then I suggest you hustle and get to this hospital *now!*"

"So-o-ory!" Rhea sarcastically drawled with a roll of her eyes. "Let's go!"

"That was totally my idea!" I volunteered as we took off again.

And it was. I'd originally planned to make it to the border and steal away all the Gifted babies being born in the hospital, but once we found out that the Immortals planned to sell the children to demons to be consumed (their flesh was soft like veal to demons, as Jacques told me once) and had already Marked them, we decided to just spare them the future capture and blow the whole place up. But *somebody* (*Rhea*) decided to flirt with one of the Slave Catchers while she was on break, and had accidently let slip that we had a bomb, warning her to leave if she wanted to go on a date in the future, which caused the other woman to sound the alarm and attempt to turn us in.

"If you had just kept it in your pants!" I angrily whispered to Rhea as another bullet whizzed past.

My powers rolled over in my stomach like a cat on a sofa.

"Is this really the time?!" Dorian snapped in the background.

"Ayudame, Sparkles—" Rhea whisper-yelled back, "—and tell your girlfriend to chill!"

I paused as Dorian blushed. Girlfriend? He had told her that I was his girlfriend? I knew that we were more than friends, but I had no idea that he felt that way about me. I thought we were avoiding labels.

Pretty sure friends don't totally wanna fuck each other the way you two do, a voice said in the back of my mind.

He glanced at me nervously and said, "She's not my girlfriend."

Disappointment coursed through me. *Ouch.*

"Oh!" Rhea rolled her eyes again. "Then why were you two sucking face while I was talking to Gretchen?"

"Gretchen?" I whispered in disgust. "Of all the people there, you chose a chick

134

named *Gretchen*?"

"It was either Gretchen or—oh!" she ducked before replying: "Are you really one to talk, Skelly?"

"It's Marve!" I looked at her like she was an idiot and slowly sounded it out: "Mm-are-vh!"

"Get down!"

Dorian grabbed my wrist and yanked me to the ground. My powers moved to the spot that he touched, my wrist pulsing where my second set of veins—the set that carried my magic—bounced like a second heartbeat. I knew that we had an extra organ (a small sack) attached to our stomach's which held our magic, and that veins carried them throughout our bodies. But it still astounded me how different Gifted were from other magic-folk—and humans. We were literally built different. But it was as if I was somehow lacking an essential part of what made me Gifted—like I wasn't breathing air, but carbon dioxide.

No, I realized, *if it were air, I wouldn't feel it. It moves like water behind a dam—it's there, but unreachable...*

Dorian hissed as a jolt raced from my body to his. But then he suddenly stared at me and moved closer. My magic revved the nearer he came. When he had touched my shoulder, it flowed from my stomach to the spot where our skin met, a dog at the heels of its master. I knew that it would come forth if I were in mortal danger, but even tricking my mind didn't work.

"So," he said.

"So," I grunted, my breath like a steel wall erected to keep him out.

135

"You think you can use your powers for me?" he asked, his cool, minty breath blowing across my face. His gold-and-brown-flecked black orbs blinked at me and as a warmth stirred in my stomach, I blinked back at him slowly, knowing then and there that I could do anything, would *be* anything, if only he would look at me like that for the rest of my life. "I only need a spark."

"Okay."

I took my hands back, closing me eyes. He touched my face, his hands warm, like the small flames that I'd seen Rhea conjure a thousand times since I met her earlier in the evening, now too weak to do so. It was all riding on me.

Is it because of his Gift? I asked myself. *Is that why I can finally breathe around him?*

I gathered magic in my palms.

Or is it something else?

My eyes opened and I saw the five Slave Catchers split off into two groups, three going to the left, two to the right, the right side missing one part that made them whole, which allowed them to function as a unit.

He tilted my face up, stared into my eyes, his eyes cold and detached. He was a scientist right then, not my partner, not my friend. I felt those walls that I erected around my mind fracture just a crack, letting through a small stream of water. His hand traveled down, cupping my neck the way *his* hand did every time he fucked my mouth.

The magic spun underneath my skin, stronger now, surer of itself. I felt my mind heaving under the pressure of having to be what everyone wanted me to be.

Why did my heart mend and rebreak—beating for others, but going silent for me?

Why?

Another gap was parted through the dam in my head. More water was flowing, faster now, stronger. I heard a dark laugh coil around the forest, there and gone in seconds. My heart quickened in my chest. I felt panic touch my brow as my anxiety rose, a beast come to steal me away.

The spark stuttered on my hands, dying just a bit. Dorian turned my face to his, leaned forward and kissed me. I felt fire *everywhere.* The contact was brief, but just enough to amp me up. The spark crackled to life yet again. I grabbed onto it and held it steady before commanding it past the trees and towards the group coming up on our right.

They were easier to take down, seeing that they were missing a member. Electricity zipped through the air, there and gone in seconds. There was a crackle, a boom. They flew back, a hole in each of their chests. They twitched for only a moment before going still. Their eyes were glassy, empty, dead.

I did not have time to wonder if they had children, wives, husbands, families to mourn. All I could think was: *I've got to live...Live, damn it! Live!*

I concentrated on the electricity that coursed through their dead brains, both theirs and mine, and *pulled.* I pulled it out for all I had left in me was waning fast. Then I concentrated on the life sparking through the other three headed my way.

Zap!

One fell, smoke pouring from his form, his body twitching, then still.

Zap!

137

I missed.

I faltered for a moment. The woman took advantage of that. She ducked low. I shouted in terror for my friend and the stranger with me. They both stumbled back. I did not.

I reached out. Quick as a jackrabbit, I grabbed the gun and wrenched it from her fingers. I turned it on her.

Pop!

Down she went.

I pulled the trigger after aiming again. Smoke poured from the barrel, but instead of a bullet firing forward, there was blowback. The gun had jammed. I fell back, gasping, crying, wishing that my two companions had not depleted their magic stores and could help.

FLOOOMMM!

A great wall of fire flew forward. The last person fell back, clawing at their head, now engulfed in flames. Rhea winced and dropped to her knees before her.

"Where did you come from?!" I screamed at Rhea. "I totally had them!"

"No," she winced, "you didn't."

She gasped in and out, in and out, in and out, then out, out, out, then…nothing. Dorian ran over to her and wrapped his hands around her neck tenderly. He breathed in for her, his skin glowing blue with the color of his magic.

But she lay still like the dead. *Not like the dead,* I told myself.

She was dead.

Chapter Twenty

Thoughts of You Consume

But then Rhea gasped and coughed, and I knew that everything was right with the world. How had this enigmatic Afro-Latina woman already engrained herself into my daily pattern, already become an essential part of my life? How had this war against the Immortals changed me—made every interaction, every life, necessary, lovely, vital?

"Rhea?" I whispered, crawling on my hands and knees over to her.

"Yes?"

"This was my plan," I chucked the words, "don't forget."

"Don't worry," she tossed them back just as strongly, "I won't."

"Come on, you two," Dorian said, "let's go blow this damn thing."

***

I told myself that it was either them or me. There was a trueness to it. They would grow to be Gifted Slaves who would one day fight to kill people like me. So it was really something I liked to call the Us vs Us vs Them Conundrum.

We blew up the hospital, children and all. As I watched it burn, I felt a deep satisfaction, and there was no wrongness to murdering children, only a misplaced wrongness at the lack of guilt. I did not know when I changed—when it became this. But now that it had, I knew that I had to see this war to the end.

For Tiara.

For my parents.

Even for Rhea.

And Valentina.

For Dorian.

For me.

***

Dorian's hand touched my own, but there was wrongness to it, a lack of warmth. And suddenly the dam broke. All the water, the memories, the years of abuse, came rushing forth, fighting to be heard, acknowledged, relived. *"Ah!"* I heard, only realizing later that the noise came from me, as I pitched forward. Dorian stumbled away, staring at me as I crumbled into glass shards.

A hiccup yanked from my throat. Tears gushed down my face, staining my fists as they gripped the dirt beneath me. I didn't disassociate as I'd hoped. Instead, I was left to face every grueling moment of my trauma. And it *hurt,* as if I'd been tied to a stake and set aflame, the tendrils of fire eating away at my skin, the smoke filling my lungs, choking me—no, not even that little.

It felt as if the magic was being ripped from my very body.

I felt a hand reach out and cup my own. I looked up through bleary eyes, dragging forth breath after merciless breath, each intake of air stabbing me from the inside out. I saw a pair of black eyes staring at me, only the color in them swam with concern. He looked at me as if he had no idea what I was going through, yet sympathized with me, as if he, too, had been wounded emotionally, but only by watching the emotional scars be ripped open within *me*.

But it wasn't any easier.

And I was *not* okay.

As the world spun around me, my silent tears stayed trapped behind my eyes. I was relieved that my secret fragility stayed intact, but also hurt. Hurt that he was okay with being a murderer. Hurt that I was, too. Hurt that we both believed that this war wouldn't change us and had not cared when it had.

What happened to the woman who would protect Tiara, one of her own, at all costs? Tiara, who had no one. Tiara, who was goodness and light. And no matter how much I tried to convince myself, the children from the hospital were nothing to me—empty faces, un-whispered promises. But at least I knew Tiara's story.

Her parents were Mortal. They had sold her to Jacques when she was six, when her Gift had emerged. Just like many of those children in that hospital probably had.

But we were family...bound by magic.

Then again, so were Dorian and I, Rhea and Valentina, Blue Eyes and those children that died today and all the countless children who I'd murdered in the arena. Because even if we were fully grown, we were starved—if not physically, then mentally. Unallowed to grow, to become who we were truly meant to be, to reach our full potential. All of us.

But then I thought of Jacques. I thought of what I risked by fighting. And I didn't care—at least, not enough to fight for anyone but myself.

Because I didn't really care about anyone as long as *I* could remain free.

Which was awful.

And the final thing that tore me into a thousand little pieces, like an imperfect paper crane, the thing that influenced all my relationships going forward, was Jacques. He was the reason I gave up time and time again. And he was the reason I couldn't quit, why I'd always keep running. And he was the reason that I couldn't love anyone else more than I loved myself.

After all, Dorian claimed to care, but would rather believe falsities rather than face the fact that some messed up stuff had happened to me before we'd even met. But he was just a man.

And men were far weaker than women.

Chapter Twenty-One

I Want You to Stay

"Again!"

I charged. My Gift flurried around my body, chirping like a thousand small birds. My lightning-coiled fist pulled back then shot forward. Dorian dodged the punch. I threw another, clipping his ear. The other Rebels that I'd come to know stood in the corner, but it was not their approval that I wanted to earn. Valentina nodded as I sprung on my hand, kicking out.

Dorian stumbled, just a bit too much to be real, and I suddenly realized that he was faking it. He was overexaggerating this fight in order to make me look good. And he was fighting back just enough to keep from looking suspicious.

After the bombing of the hospital a week ago, Valentina ordered me to be trained by Dorian. She said that we had to work to make me stronger, to increase my physical and magical stamina. Rhea said that it was obvious that I had some form of PTSD and that it came loose when I thought of fighting. What she didn't know was that there was another problem at the root of my dilemma.

143

Tiara... My mind whispered. *I'm so sorry.*

Because without anyone to protect, I found myself useless.

I heard a dark voice whispering in my ear, easing and creaking like the wind through the bowels of a boat. And that boat was awash on choppy waters, the smell of salty sea in the air. I was the ship. The water was my declining mental state. But what exactly was the wind?

What threatened to topple me over?

My powers fizzed and died out and I stumbled to make it seem intentional.

What *he* did to me, what he took from me, had ruined me somehow.

And I didn't know how to fix it.

Dorian wrapped his arms around my torso and slammed me on the ground. His fingers grabbed my arms, pinning me. His head flew down, his lips stopping to hover just above my ear.

"You okay?" he whispered.

I tapped the ground.

His hands tightened on my wrists.

"I'm fine," I whispered back, closing my eyes.

His body was tight against mine, matching my tension. He shifted and I felt the length of him, stiff against my thigh, and wondered if he was tense for a different reason. His lips pressed into the back of my ear. I froze. He took in a quick, steadying breath. Let it out with one word: "Live."

Before I could think to respond, to turn my head and kiss him back or fight or fling him off me, he rolled away.

"Very good," Valentina clapped. "Very good indeed."

Valentina turned to leave.

Dorian didn't touch me until she'd left. Then he grabbed my wrist and kissed my palm. I told myself that he was just funneling his magic through my second set of veins as quickly as possible and not flirting. But his Influence ramped through my body in seconds, calming me, reminding me that I was safe.

"Thank you," I murmured.

He winked at me. But that cocky look quickly turned to alarm when I swayed. He caught me before I fell.

"Are you okay?" he asked again.

But his voice was muffled, as if he were speaking through glass. My eyes felt heavy and each second of blinking felt like an eternity. I felt my legs sweep out from under me, Dorian's scent of heather and brandy surrounding me with comforting thoughts as he pulled me close to his chest. He waved everyone else off.

"Relax, guys!" he snapped when they surrounded us. "She just needs rest."

"Yes," I mumbled, "rest."

But it felt like I'd already been sleeping for an eternity.

***

He stepped in my path again. "Wait!"

"Stop."

"But—"

"Enough!"

My throat was tight and when I yelled, it hurt. I could feel the tears pulsing against the backs of my eyes, like two great hands, always pushing. I wanted to

curse, to throw up my hands and say 'fuck it all!' But the truth was, I didn't know

how to kill an Immortal any better than he did...And I didn't know how to love

anyone without loving them violently.

But the way he looked at me also made me want to stay.

"I'll tell you where the book is." The words were bitter and as soon as they left

my mouth, I regretted saying them. "I'll tell you and then you can go."

"But—"

"Go!"

"What if I don't want to leave?" he quietly asked, looking down. "What if I

want to stay, broken bits and all?"

I fell forward into his arms, shaking but without tears. I raged against my

parents among the stars. I raged against my old life and my old family. I knew that

I'd give anything to go back to those days, to rewrite history and grow up with my

parents. Even if that meant not knowing Tiara? *a voice asked. And I wanted to say*

no, but I knew that it wasn't the truth. I raged against what would have happened to

me if I'd stayed. Lastly, I raged against the broken shell of a girl that I'd become.

I was tired of fighting. Tired of losing. Tired of life.

I startled awake. Dorian was sitting there in the cave, staring at me. His eyes

looked troubled, stubble on his jawline, teeth clenched.

I immediately panicked.

"What is it?" I asked. Adrenaline made me sit up straight, glancing around the

cave. We were in the Rebel hideout, in the room that they'd reserved for us. "What's wrong?"

"I want you to be calm when I tell you this." He glanced over me. "May I?"

I nodded, immediately feeling more tired as I realized just how much that dream had taken out of me.

He crawled over to me on his hands and knees. Then he reached out, gently picking me up. His hands touched my forehead where my hair made its widows peak. He looked at me, waited for my nod, then combed his fingers gently through my hair. My body hummed in response. He wasn't Influencing me, but instead using touch to comfort. And somehow, I liked it better. Even though he was not feeding me magic, which I'd been drained of by Jacques, he was still feeding my soul. He pulled me close, his chest rumbling as he hummed low, singing a song I'd never heard before.

"That's pretty."

"Thanks. I wrote it for a band I used to be in."

"Hmm…" I didn't really care in that moment. "Nice."

"Valentina wants us to talk to her about something you said."

"Okay."

"While you were asleep," he said, having to repeat it a few times for me to catch what he said.

"While I was asleep?" I raised a brow. "Why would I need to vouch for anything I said while asleep?"

"You mentioned something vital to the mission."

"About?"

"About the book that we're looking for."

"Book?"

"The book?"

"The book?" I paused and the memory slammed to the forefront of my mind. "Oh!"

"Why didn't you tell me?" he sounded hurt.

"I didn't want to worry you."

"Do you know something?" he asked. When I stared at him in horror, he threw up his hands. "I'm sorry. I have to ask!"

I told him about the dream. He said nothing for a long moment. And then?

He laughed.

"You silly girl!" He shook his head. "That's it!"

"Um...yeah?"

I was confused.

"You may have just solved all our problems and you don't even know it!" he grinned at me—a mad, unassuming grin. "I love you!"

"Um what?"

"Not like that!" He immediately countered, waving his hands. "I meant, you know, in the way—"

"Right."

"Ya'mean?" he asked.

"Yeah." I nodded. When he looked like he didn't believe me, I blushed and said, "Of course. Totally."

148

No matter how much I wished for another way.

"But..."

He set me down before leaning his head in, his nose skimming my cheek. I gasped. His lips touched where his nose had, just light enough to not be a kiss. I held as still as possible, refusing to deny him yet refusing to breath him in. He gave me a look that said he was fighting the same urges. He dared to breathe in my space and I stiffened in response to the hungry look that entered his eyes.

"Roses...Perfect..." he rumbled, his voice deeper than it was before.

I wanted him right then and there—damn who heard. I bit my lip, blushing. All his control snapped; he melded his lips to mine. He tugged on my bottom lip with his teeth and I felt electricity jolt through my body, igniting me. I gasped and he deepened the kiss, his tongue quickly slipping into my mouth, tracing the planes and crevices there.

I moaned into his mouth. He braced his hand on my back, getting closer. Our bodies fit together like a lock and key, so perfect, so right.

I pulled away this time, not wanting to let these sensations muddle my focus. I had a job to do and it was about time that I got my head in the game. He frowned at me, silently asking why I stopped. Feeling my resolve waning, I stumbled to my feet and walked through the rebel sanctuary. He followed me silently and I tried to pretend that I didn't feel the hurt radiating off him.

Some Immortals paused to greet us before hurrying about their day. Some Gifted girls gave Dorian the eye. I moved a bit closer, silently telling them that he was off limits. But was he really mine? Did a few stolen kisses mean less to him than

149

it did to me?

We went to the lip of the dugout where Valentina was. She was currently sitting there, her hand splayed on the table, playing with a knife as she quickly stabbed between each finger. She was moving so fast that I could not follow her with my eyes. I decided to mess with her. Snuck next to the table and said, "Boo!"

She jumped, driving the knife into her finger. She cursed, raising the finger to her mouth and sucking on it. I grinned back at her. She never was this easy to scare at Jacques's mansion. Maybe she was on edge, on guard for some reason or another.

"Hey, Tina!" I said, giving her my most innocent look. "Whatcha doin'?"

"You tell me," she hissed, placing her chin on her hands, "you're the one who's been keeping secrets."

"I didn't forget—I just got a little side-tracked."

"I've seen the way you two look at each other." She paused for emphasis, giving us a stern look that was all business. "That won't be a problem, will it?"

She picked up that knife once more. It wasn't a threat but a promise. I shuddered. She was serious.

"No, it won't be a problem." Dorian stepped forward to stand next to me. "I believe that we have a new lead."

"Oh?" She smirked at us, a wicked gleam in her eye. "And what is that?"

I chimed in, telling her about the dream that I had. I didn't skip over any details but she still wanted me to repeat it multiple times. I broke down the room, what the book looked like, even what our former Master was wearing.

"This is interesting…" She mused, her palms flat on the table. "This could change the tide in our favor. But who to send?"

This time, Dorian was the one eager to please.

"Send us."

Valentina and I looked at Dorian incredulously.

"What?"

"Send Marve and me. She knows that place like the back of her hand. And I'm good friends with Jacques. It'll be easier than sending someone who doesn't have a clue how all this works. So, send us."

She paused, contemplating his request. I bounced on the balls of my feet, the adrenaline already coursing through my veins. Surprisingly, fear didn't immediately set in. Dorian was literally bouncing up and down, full of whatever energy that drove him to act so reckless. Finally, Valentina looked me square in the eye. At her answer, my heart pounded in my ears like water, rushing all around me, preparing to sweep me away.

"You leave at dawn."

Chapter Twenty-Two

The Progression of Darkness

I had another nightmare that night, lying next to Dorian in that little cave. Valentina refused to let us leave the hideout to sleep somewhere more…comfortable. She said that she wanted to make sure we didn't chicken out. I didn't blame her. This would be tough for the both of us, seeing as we both had relationships with Jacques.

My nightmares had progressed to where I wasn't just by the tub.

This time I had a towel in my hand, scraping it along the inside of his leg carefully but quickly. He told me to slow down, as if he were savoring every moment. His skin was ice, his constantly decaying flesh always morphing between white and black, his body trembling…but his breath? His breath was a branding seared into my skin, always commanding, never asking, never offering consent. I was avoiding what I knew was inevitably coming. He leaned back, spreading his naked legs.

That was when I heard a voice. I glanced up and saw Valentina standing there, watching us. She didn't look angry or even horny like Master did. But she didn't look afraid like me, either. Honestly, she looked like she could care less. But why didn't she intervene?

I was shaken awake by Dorian, who had a concerned look on his face. His hair was wild and spiky around his head. I stared up at him in wonder and amazement, dazed. I blinked and his hair was in the same slicked back style that it normally was. I touched my head.

"Do you want to talk about it?"

"No."

It was my burden to bear.

I had absolutely no idea how Dorian knew that the sun had assumed its throne in the sky, since we were underground. But he knew. He took me out the cavern and into the main part of the cave. We then walked to another cavern on the opposite end of the food. He touched the wall and a doorway appeared, this one with a tiny sign in front of it that said *Weapons Room*.

At first, I thought that my fists were the only weapon I needed, but then I beheld the glorious, glittering instruments of death and I wanted them all.

I ran over to a bunch of holsters. Dorian buckled one around my waist, then one around his. He explained each weapon to me as if I didn't already know. My Master had trained me to use the basics. I skipped over the mallet, past the pike and the quarterstaff, past the club, scythe and mace, to go to the gleaming knives. Even if my Master had not trained me, I still had the basic instinct to wield a blade: after all, men had their swords and girls had their daggers.

They called to something darker in me, the part that wanted to drive a knife into his gut. There was something so intimate about pressing your knees on someone's arms, pushing your full weight down on their chest and then driving the tip of the blade into their heart. These wouldn't kill Jacques, but they would do a fair amount of damage. I grabbed about four daggers of various length and size. My favorite was this curved blade etched with golden runes.

"What do these mean?" I asked, holding it out Dorian.

He took it. Our hands briefly touched. We locked eyes. He looked at the blade. I stamped down the hurt that shone in my lowered gaze.

I didn't want his pity.

"This rune," he said, tracing his finger along a chaotic mark, "is a rune for a quick death. This rune," he touched one that was more graceful and elegant, "gives the wielder speed and stealth. We'll need it for this mission. This rune," he touched one that was drawn messily, probably in haste, "is a rune of protection. If you have this blade on you, nothing can hurt you."

"Pft. Fat chance."

He handed the blade back, careful not to touch me again.

I looked down at the dagger and saw my reflection. My skin was rough and bumpy with spikes running over my chest, arms, legs and back. I stared at my own reflection, for the first time in my life believing the words that Jacques hammered into my head. I wasn't merely ugly—I was a monster.

"Are you afraid of me?" I asked, looking up at Dorian.

He didn't look away. He looked monsters like me in the face every day. Was I just another beast to him?

"You might want to stay in your Armored State for when we confront Jacques," he said with finality.

I wanted to lift the glamour against his instruction, to be the version of me that he found attractive. I wanted to be beautiful. *But he must love me for me,* I finally realized. I let my brown, spiky skin do the talking as I wiped the blade on my shirt. Dorian avoided my eyes as he picked up his own scimitar.

I silently slid the dagger into the holster. Our relationship was complicated. But it was nothing that we couldn't fix. After the mission, I would confront him about it. After the mission, I would decide as to whether I wanted to take the chance of falling for him or not.

I turned around and was met with the sight of an archery set as elegant as the man we were going to hunt down. The bow was pitch black with red runes running down the curve of its side. The slew of arrows next to it had tiny runes etched into the wood. The head of the arrows glowed with an unnatural light.

I want it, I thought.

I walked to it and picked up the bow. It was the perfect weight. I then picked up the arrows, slung them over my shoulder, then walked back to join Dorian at the entrance of the room.

"Be careful with those," he warned me.

"Why?" I said, knocking one arrow and aiming it.

"Those are ash arrows. One shot with those and you'll make any magic user incapacitated."

"What's so special about ash arrows? What are they?"

"They're made from the dust of faeries. Getting shot with one will make you—

"

He stopped because I aimed at his pants. He looked positively livid. I grinned, putting the arrow back in its quiver.

"You're cute when you're mad," I said as a fire spiked below, bopping his nose with a grin.

"Don't play like that," he warned.

"What are you gonna do?" I smirked at him. "Spank me?"

If he was shocked by my words, he didn't show it. A wicked gleam entered his eyes. The smirk on my face widened into a full-fledged grin and he look satisfied.

"Just watch what you're doing, little one."

I followed him out of the cave and up the stairs.

I'm ready, I told myself, although deep down I knew that there was no convincing myself. *Ready to kill a demon.*

Chapter Twenty-Three

Tiara

We made it to his car in record time. Passing through the wall was a piece of cake since we had plenty of drachmas. When I asked him where he kept getting the gold coins, he told me to stay focused on the mission. I mean, I knew that he was Immortal and owned half of Amoria, but he wasn't in his territory and I didn't see a coin purse on him. Maybe he used portals?

We passed the sandy dunes that Maeora was known for, the blazing sun beating down on us like a war drum. The lines above the sand seemed to pulsate from the sun's radiation, the false sun's rays touching this land more than most. I spotted a Weeper slithering through the sand, the bottom half of its body a tail, its yellow eyes following us through the pounding heat in what could only be thirst. Since the water around Maeora was all oceanic, they didn't have much to drink. Ever since the Great Change, freshwater was scarce among the locals and had to be shipped from Espanza, where it was purified; the only other place to get it was Amoria, when the snow melted and the two rivers that ran from Amoria to Espanza and from Sidra to the tip of Maeora were easy flowing.

We then traveled through the jungles of Espanza. Yellowish-green eyes followed us as men and women leapt through the trees, their bodies twisting in a paramount of shapes. The road passing between the Walls and the lands was long, which meant that there was also only one port of entry to travel through—unless you flew, of course. A child waved as we passed, her face totally normal other than the large whiskers; when she turned, I saw a thick orange-and-black striped tail flicking around behind her. I saw two Slave Catchers approaching behind her and before I could see any more, I looked away.

When we finally made it to the swamps of Sidra, I felt my heart stutter. A pair of large, beady eyes blinked up at me as we passed before disappearing into the murky water. I remembered that the varying lands and climates solely surrounded the Rings of Death—everything else was cities of concrete and glass. I would often wonder why they put the magically-climate-controlled Rings so close to the Walls before regretfully realizing that they don't want slaves running away.

Immortals were not only cruel, but systematic, too.

I tried to look around the swamps, towards the cities beyond it, which housed the Immortals and their Gifted slaves, remembering the time when I saw the land for what it was. I tried to run away once and had made it close to the Wall only to find that not all land was a swamp. In fact, most of it was a sea of concrete. My Master's land was somewhere between this, tucked away in a corner of a forest where the swamp began, conveniently close to the arena. I'd gotten caught because I hadn't known where to run to, since back then I had been blindfolded before being brought to the Ring every time without fail.

One day, I thought, gazing far off as Dorian and I turned deeper into Sidra, *one day I will see Amoria.*

The closer we got, the more on edge we both became. Dorian bounced his leg, talking faster and faster. The manic speech was hard to understand but I nodded and agreed at certain parts, trying to at least seem like I was following what he was saying. Finally, he paused to look at me. His face was solemn, his breath an omen.

"If I tell you to run, to leave me behind, you must do so without question."

I sucked in a breath of air. What was he talking about? How could I leave him? He made me feel things that I was too afraid to feel on my own. He made me soar past the sun into the stars, made me want to be a better woman.

How could I ever leave something like that behind?

"I mean it, Marve. If I say so, you have to turn and run."

"I'm not a runner," I said just as solemnly, "I'm a fighter."

It was true. Every time Jacques attacked one of my friends, my family, I fought back. I was afraid of him, yes, but I didn't let that fear hold me back. He needed to be stopped. And I would be the one to stop him.

"You need to understand." He fought back some nameless emotion, but it shone clear and true in his eyes. "You—you—"

"What?" I searched his face. "I what?"

His gaze closed off as quickly as it had opened to let me inside. I had failed whatever unspoken test he'd dared to voice. "I—I mean, *we* can't lose you...ya know, because you're vital to the mission."

What did that mean? He couldn't lose me. Why? Because I was so important to the Rebellion? Because he wanted me to satisfy a passing fancy?

"All right," I sighed, dropping his gaze. "I'll run if I have to."

"Good girl." He patted my arm. "I'm just glad that you're safe."

Not for long, I thought as we approached the wooded enclosure that was Jacques's land.

"I guess we'll have to walk from here," Dorian said, pulling over.

He reached past me into the glove compartment and pulled out a small bottle of whiskey. He downed that in a few gulps. I briefly wondered if he was an alcoholic. But then I dismissed the silly thought. After all, I'd only seen him drink a few times.

"All right!" He said, pumping his fist in the air. "Let's do this!"

Despite his loud mantra, we walked slowly and quietly through the forest. The same trees that seemed to curl around me before bent out of the way to let us pass. I filtered electricity through my system, lighting our way with a soft purple glow. After a while, Dorian seemed to get irritated by his own impatience. He knocked my feet out from under me.

I gazed into his eyes, surprise on my face.

He gave me That Look, as if he wanted to kiss me again. It was weird to me, totally foreign in fact. I could kiss him a thousand times and it still wouldn't be enough. He stole the air in my lungs each day and gave me life in return.

Was it because he was my first kiss? Was it because he was my first everything?

I could only imagine what it would be like if we had actual sex.

He drew a rune with his finger. Just like that, a portal opened. He carried me through it—and on the other side was Jacques's mansion. From what Jacques taught me as a child, I knew that runes worked if there wasn't magic already in place protecting the land. It was like an electric fence. Once you were outside the fence, you could use as much magic as you wanted to get from place to place or to cast any incantation. The runes guarding the walls were the reason that we had to drive or fly from place to place. One could take down the barriers here, but you had to be stronger than whoever put them up, and since they were made by a former slave under Jacques's influence…we didn't stand a chance in hell bringing them down.

Unless we killed him, that is.

"How did you—?"

"Magic is a very powerful thing, Marve."

"Can you teach me how?"

He set me on my feet.

"Someday."

The wind shifted, blowing towards the large house. And the later seemed to expand, to breathe, almost as if it were alive. Jacques's unwanted advances weren't the only reason this mansion never felt like home: this place reeked of supernatural danger, wrongness plaguing you, each of your senses screaming at you to run far, far away. I could feel in my gut that something was going to go wrong. It was in the way the air danced along the back of my neck, making the tiny bristles there stand on end. But I didn't care. I wanted revenge for a dead friend.

For Tiara.

But most of all for the part of me that ceased to exist.

My bones *clickety-clacked* as I trudged up to the house. With shaking hands, I pulled out the key that Dorian gave me the day I escaped and slid it into the lock. Freezing, listening for what felt like an eternity. I could hear the spirits of dead slaves turning over in the rose garden, but not his eminence. I turned my wrist and the key moved with it.

With a click that resonated like thousands of agonized cries, the door was unlocked. I shook as I eased it open. And suddenly I was a child again, sneaking into my parents room after a bad dream to watch them sleep without waking them because I was too afraid to ask if I could spend the rest of the night in their bed, craving another's warmth. Was cautious but still floating through the cool, crippling haze of my nightmare. I didn't want to be alone, to die alone, to make my journey to the stars *alone.*

As if sensing this, Dorian grabbed my shoulders and spun me around, not wasting a second of our precious time.

He smashed his lips against mine. His kiss was desperate and angry—not at me, but for what fate had dealt us. And my heart stopped as I realized the truth that had been obvious to everyone but me: he didn't expect us to make it out alive. He reached up to lightly tug on my hair. I moaned, pushing up against him. He wasn't hard like I expected, which made me realize what this kiss was about.

He was saying goodbye.

And suddenly, I knew that he volunteered us, knowing *he* would probably kill us, just because he believed death was a better outcome than living our lives in fear.

He was the bravest, dumbest man I'd ever met. And I'd never felt so deeply tied to another person.

I pulled away as tears suddenly streamed down my face. He wiped them away, but they wouldn't stop. I reached out to him, needing him to hold me, to tell me that everything was all right, to tell me that we would survive this. He denied me this solace. I stepped through the door with bleary eyes.

I went into the place that had come to feel so foreign, so wrong. Jacques's black magic permeated the house, thickening the air with its seductive evil. I walked through the dimly lit halls, passing up the room that was given to me out of obligation, but was never truly mine. I went down one hall, past the trophy room and the bathroom then up the stairs. I could feel Dorian following me, feel the spark between us, but refused to acknowledge him for fear of giving us away.

Before I faced my old demons, I had to find that book.

I could feel its darkness calling to me, whispering to the deepest, vilest parts of my soul. I felt the pull strengthen as I passed a room that I had never been permitted to enter before. Could it really be that easy? I pushed open the door and stopped. Somehow, after all the horrors I had beheld while under Jacques's rule, I was still shocked by the lack of fucks this man gave.

Standing there, her long, crinkly black hair unbound and floating around her head, was Tiara. Magic made her stand upright, but her eyes were cold, lifeless. Her dark skin was thin and dry, stretched across her bones like a poorly applied adhesive. Her head was thrown forward as if she were praying, her hands clasped before her. There was a barrier of dark magic around her, preserving her body, holding her in the position.

His savagery knew no bounds. Unchecked, he had taken Tiara's lifeless body and stuffed her like an animal. Then he used his magic to make sure that she never rotted. I knew that the bodies of the Gifted could be used in practically any manner if they were not burned. I wondered what happened to the bodies of my parents and suddenly, the feeling that I could not register before came upon me like a hurricane.

My magic pushed from my body, pulsing throughout the room as an enraged scream came from my throat. I threw myself forward, reaching out to touch her cheeks. She was so cold...I'd never known her to be anything but warm and beautiful. I felt a hand on my shoulder and spun around to see Dorian standing behind me, shaking his head.

"Quiet!" he hissed, looking like the poster child for stealth. "Let's keep looking!"

I wanted to snap at him, but I couldn't as I realized that I was just redirecting my anger. If he didn't care about my feelings, he would have left me here to die like her. He cared.

I was just feeling sensitive.

My bottom lip wobbling, whispered, "But Tiara?"

"We'll come back for her. I promise! But we *have* to *go!*"

He grabbed my arm and practically had to yank me from the room. I resisted for only a moment, realizing that he was right. I couldn't afford to be distracted. But what of my friend? Her soul could not pass to the stars if she was here.

I walked to the next door to the left. I felt another kind of magic—something darker, older—behind this door. I was scared to see what I'd find here. I knew that he'd left her there for me to find. It made me wonder if I'd find my parents in the next room, since he'd bought the house that was once my home when they died. But the magic here was long forgotten.

There were no Gifted here.

"Murderer," it called, beckoning me forward.

"Freak," it said, stroking one clawed finger down my spine.

There, sitting on a pedestal, was the Book of Beginnings. It called to me, whispering things that appealed to my black heart. Dorian didn't seem to be affected like I was, giving me a nudge to grab it and go. I approached the stand, staring down at it in wonder. It hissed at me.

"What a dirty thing you are. Won't you take me for your own? Won't you show me your new home?"

"I will," I breathed, reaching out.

My hands closed around it. I lifted it slowly, feeling its soft, worn edges. I turned around.

"What are you doing?" a silk-smooth voice whispered.

Oh, Mother, I thought as my eyes appraised the speaker, *what am I to do now?*

Chapter Twenty-Four

Marve

"Marve," he said, his eyes blinking red and black.

A chill trickled down my spine, like a skeleton dragging itself from the grave. There was a fracture, a tempo within me, going *ba-dump* again and again. My breath wheezed to a halt in my chest, at a total standstill, as he rummaged around my thoughts like a thief in the night. I smelled his scent of saltwater, of the Black Sea, and felt his demonic presence wrap around me like a vine ensnaring around a tree, entangling himself in my limbs, cutting off sunlight, the only sustenance I had, in order to bloom. My hand twitched, wanting to reach for the blade and drive it through my own heart, but then I thought of my parents waiting for me in the stars and I knew that I would have to confess, to tell them why I'd forsaken the name they originally gave me and took the one he [originally] forced upon me.

He raised a brow, and I could see the angry bull behind his calm exterior. He was waiting for my response. Even after I'd left him, he expected total submission and civility.

166

"Master," I said, inclining my head.

I don't know what it was about him. In his presence, without anyone who needed my protection, I was weak, a cowering bitch before her sharp-tongued master. It was just the roles that we had fallen into, I guess. Then Dorian's fingers skimmed my arm, pulling me back into reality. I pulled the Book close to my chest, staring back at *him*.

"Give me the Book," Jacques said, holding out a hand.

That's when it hit me.

He knew that I'd come back. Not for the Book, it seemed, but for him. He knew that I needed him in my own way, knew it and used it against me.

"Come on, Marve," Dorian urged, tugging on my arm. "We have to go."

But I couldn't.

I was frozen.

I could feel my mind fracturing the longer I stood there, succumbing to his influence. I felt Dorian take my hand, felt his magic push against the walls of my mind, trying to force me to remain calm, strong, resolute. But Jacques was a virus, overloading my brain. I felt a trickle of blood dribble from my nose. I swayed.

Jacques licked his lips. "You are mine, pet."

His voice was straining, caught between lust and patience. And I knew that if I stayed, he would take all I had to give, use me till I shriveled up to a husk, and then consume me. I would die if I gave in to him. I would be raped and murdered. Of course, he would take his time with me. Only when my soul could no longer bleed light for his darkness to consume—only then would he kill me.

167

I may have been suicidal but that didn't mean I wanted to go out like that. I wanted to die on my own terms. And I didn't want to be put down like an animal.

I handed the Book to Dorian.

I gathered electricity around my person, made it as big and bright as it could possibly be. I watched the look on my old master's face change from impassive to livid. He lunged at me but for once, I was faster. I knew this like a card being dealt for my hand, only *I'd* stacked the deck against *him*. I pulled out the rune-covered dagger from my holster, brandishing it at him. I waited until he was on top of me before plunging it into his side.

He didn't even flinch.

The wound began to stitch itself closed around the dagger, his black blood bubbling up around the hilt, swaying this way and that, refusing to spill.

I tore the dagger from his side, sheathing it. If that didn't work, then I would try the arrows. I twisted away from him, flipping into the air as I knocked an arrow. I aimed straight for his putrid heart.

Breathe in...breathe out. In...out. In...

I released.

Strong and true, my arrow hit its mark.

He paused, gripping the arrow. Black veins crawled up and down his skin, spreading from the spot the arrow hit. I was reminded of the image of his mother as she held him as a baby and was repulsed: all he did was destroy. I looked to Dorian. He seemed torn between letting me battle my demons and getting us to safety. I nodded at Dorian, who nodded back solemnly.

168

Today was not the day.

Dorian drew a rune and a portal appeared. I walked towards it, throwing one last look at Jacques. He had completely changed forms. His skin was the blackest of blacks, his eyes were a ruby red and horns the shade of night springing out of his head. He bared his fangs at me, a primal hatred in his eyes.

I shuddered.

It was not a pretty sight to behold.

"I'll find you." His voice was deep and guttural. "I'll find you and when I do, you'll pay dearly for this."

Fear raked its nasty claws down my spine. I stepped through the portal. I heard his ominous laugh as he yanked out the arrow, leaving the speared tip in his chest. Then he turned and tossed the arrow towards me. I didn't have time to duck, to run through the portal—anything.

The portal began to close behind me.

Chapter Twenty-Five

Dorian

Dorian reached out at the last second and yanked me through the dimensional opening.

We came out at the rock, the entrance to the Rebel HQ. I put my hand on the rock and Dorian put his hand over mine. I felt a tremor rock me from within, a heat bubbling in my core as a groan rumbled in Dorian's chest. The rock glowed and it was my first time noticing a tiny rune under our hands. It split apart, and we went down the stairs. I kept my eyes locked ahead, refusing to look at him and see his eyes judging or that damned smirk of faux confidence on his mouth. But when he leaned forward to hold the door open, his face seemed moodier, more serious…darker.

The door swung shut behind us and it felt as if we may never leave again…

"What's with you?" I snorted even though inside I was tremoring for a new reason. "Who died?"

The smirk came round although it was tinged with the bitterness of anxiety. But seeing anything close to a smile on his handsome face was enough for me. I grinned back.

We entered the cave with the Book in hand. Dorian went straight for Valentina's tiny office, carrying the Book of Beginnings away from his chest carefully, as if it would rear up and attack. I stood out in the hall, waiting. I could tell that they'd already dismissed my presence, assuming I'd leave. But that was fine. I'd wait my turn.

"I can't keep lying to her," Dorian's voice said, sounding defeated.

"She's broken enough as it is!" Valentina hissed back and her voice was full of scorn. "The last thing she needs is for her parents to come back from the grave!"

"But she should know the truth. It's time to tell her."

"No!" I could imagine her leaning across the table, that steely look in her eyes. "It will ruin everything."

"Then when is the right time?" He said softly and then, an afterthought: "I've fallen in love with her."

I paused, replaying his words over and over in my head. He's fallen in love with someone. Me? I was the only one he'd been around these past few days, so it had to be. But why keep it a secret?

Why deceive me further?

"Don't tell her. She'll only grow to hate you."

"But maybe she'll understand. Then she'll help us—"

"HA!" Valentina's laugh shook the entire cave. "She lived with a demon! He abused and manipulated her in ways that would disgust even you, Dorian. If she finds out that we plan to raise a demon with *her* as the sacrifice, we're screwed! We can't *tell* her! We must keep this between us. On the day of the blood moon, we will raise Akiva and raze the earth. Understand?"

I felt like an idiot. I never asked what they planned to do with the Book. And I never asked why I had to be the one to get it. But now I knew. What I'd known before all of this—something that seemed to escape Valentina—was that demons could not be manipulated, and they could *not* be trusted. They were devious, cunning creatures that fed on chaos. Raising one would kill us all—not just the Immortals she misguidedly vowed to annihilate.

I mean, what did she plan to do? Attach reigns and guide the damn thing? And Mestiphopheles was the worst of the worst—the First of Them. Even if we were descended from The Forsaken, none of us had strong enough powers to stop him—and we had *nothing* that he could ever want. This was a suicide mission!

She would get all of us killed!

"I told you to get close to her. To make *her* fall for *you*—not the other way around. Do you know what this means? The mission is compromised—because of *you*." She paused then said in a voice that would have been kind if not for *what* was uttered: "You're our best smuggler. With you alone, half our slaves are offered better lives in freer countries. Don't let your feelings get in the way of your higher purpose."

"I don't have a purpose without her."

"Then you're of no use to me." Valentina snorted in disgust. "Get your priorities straight, Boyd. I'll see you tomorrow morning."

There I was, eavesdropping, when Dorian left the cave, his face twisted in

172

anger. He ran right into me. I stumbled but he caught me around the waist, his hands lingering before he let me go. I took one look at him—

And I ran.

"Marve!"

Out of the underground hideout, past the entrance, to the field. I didn't know where I was headed, just that I couldn't stand to be there any longer. When I couldn't find my way back and didn't know which direction civilization was, I stopped. With angry tears of betrayal streaming down my face, I glanced around in panic. Great, now I was going to get caught by Slave Catchers!

"Marve!"

"No!" I yelled.

Well, really, wheezed. My voice was gone. I'd done all that running and had nothing to show for it. I hadn't even thrown him off my trail—just winded myself. I gasped, not crying anymore but now craving the air that I'd been denied since the moment I left him.

"Did you hear any of that?"

I stared at him. And then giggled. The laugh bubbled past my lips like a hot spring. He glared at me. But I couldn't help it. What an asinine question.

"Damn, stupid walls!" Dorian threw up his hands. Then he fixed me with this complex look before facing the ground, fists balled up, quietly admitting, "I never meant to hurt you."

"Ha!" I wasn't laughing anymore but now glaring wholeheartedly. "This is like some f'd up tragedy!"

"It doesn't have to be."

"You make me crazy!" Throwing up my hands, amended, "I mean, I'm *not* crazy—but you make me *feel* crazy! And I don't know who to trust! You and Valentina have led me down this rabbit hole and-and-and...I just want out." Tears burned my eyes again. "I can't believe I let myself get so wrapped in-in-in-in the thought of you—of us! And you were the *only part*. You were the only part of my life that I could chance, the only part that I could bank on because you were the only part that made absolute sense. Do you know what that *feels* like?"

Thunder crackled overhead. He didn't respond.

"Well?"

"I've been too reckless when it comes to you!" He ran a hand through his slicked back hair. "I need to get my head in the game. I need to—"

I slapped him.

There was my initial shock and revulsion at being the one to cause him harm. But it was overshadowed by undeniable rage. He stared at me, his face cracking open in a way that said this wasn't his first time getting hit. A tiny piece of my glass heart fractured. But it was swallowed by the black of everything else.

"Okay," he mumbled, "I deserved that. But you have to understand, I didn't mean to hurt you. I was never on board with any of this. I just wanted to get you out of the fighting pits—and the Rebellion offers the best protection available. Before we got you out, Valentina promised me—she *promised me*—that you wouldn't have to go on any missions. She said that we could take you back home to the Southern Isles. But this is all about revenge. God damn it! I should have known she wouldn't—"

174

I placed one finger over his lips. He paused in his tirade, looking down at me like he wasn't sure whether to turn and run or stay and fight it out. I moved my hand to hold the side of his face, a stolen touch, a forbidden gesture. *This could be the last time that I touch him,* I thought, realizing that the blood moon was close at hand.

Then we'd all be dead.

His anger soothed itself. I smiled through the pain of all the lies, the secrets, the deception, and took his hand.

I stood up on my tippy toes, breathing in his scent, more flowery than alcoholic today. My nose skimmed his cheek. He stiffened, clearly unsure. Then, in a move of finality, I pressed my lips against his, stealing his air for the first time. He gasped, his head tilting just slightly, his lips panting against my own, and I hated how well we fit together, our bodies gluing like some kind of mold, our hearts beating as one, our veins pulsing with fire. The kiss told me all I needed to know.

We were enemies. And we would stay estranged until I could trust him again— but I knew that our chances of surviving this together as a couple were slim to none. I'd been such an *idiot!* He never really cared about me—he and Valentina had just used me for their own gain!

But maybe, I thought, *I can use him without getting my heart broken.*

And to do that, I would need to know as much as possible. I would need to reopen old wounds, to investigate my parents' death, to peer into Valentina's lies, to see through his deception. I pulled away, staring him in the eye.

"Let's go," I said, trying to communicate with my eyes that we were not safe here. "Explain everything to me at the safehouse."

We were in the safehouse from before, sitting across from one another at the island. A thick, awkward silence hung between us. There were so many words left unsaid. I wanted to tell him that I loved him back, but truthfully, I was too afraid, too broken, to feel that for him. The glassy sky above us would one day break and fall in shards around us.

I just knew it.

Dorian took my hands across the table. That familiar tingle raced to-and-fro on my spine. His gaze was deeper than the ocean, his eyes containing multitudes of caution, love, and fear at once. That was what was silly about Immortals—they lived forever yet they lived in fear all the time: fear of falling, fear of losing it all, even—it seemed—fear of dying.

We Gifted had a saying: "To live fearlessly is to love exposed and unhindered. Bonds cannot hold my heart and the sea cannot contain my love. I will follow you to the stars and meet you there on that great astral plane."

As Gifted, we had much to fear but we never let it show. To acknowledge and expose our fear was to welcome death. Life was too harsh for us to want to live forever. But to die young was to admit defeat. That was not an option.

Consequently, we lived boldly and recklessly, unafraid and with no excuses.

"Start from the beginning."

"First off, everything you know is a lie."

He proceeded to tell me the 'truth.' Apparently, Cato and Kalysma were both angels of Light. And the idea that one of them was married to Sam and was thrown from the Garden? *That was a lie, too.* They were both pure beings with the best of intentions. The only thing that was true was the fact that it involved the Creator, Kalysma and Cato.

You see, Cato and Kalysma were angels, servants of the Creator. They one day asked for a prize to be given to the worthiest of humans. Cato chose immortality for the descendants bearing his mark, for it was what the angels were. Kalysma chose a unique gift for a human and each of the ones born under her sign. They found the human, a mortal woman named Alice, and bestowed upon her the breath of the Creator. She could breathe this breath into the people around her but could only give one gift per person; no one realized then that the two could come together and make one that was two halves of each.

"What was the point of lying?" I asked him, leaning forward in my seat. "What was the point after all these years?"

"Why did the slave owners use their religious books to enslave Gifted all those years ago?" He asked, shrugging. "To keep them oppressed. Think about it—if you believed that your god was a slave, then what would that make you? What could you do against fate's grand design?"

I wanted to believe that we were Nephilim—sisters to the Immortals. But I feared that no one knew the true story other than the angels themselves. Nephilim. Demons. Either way, we were inbred just like the Immortals. I didn't believe this story any more than I believed the original.

Maybe it was not meant to be known.

Still, I smiled and nodded, agreed, and complied.

Why does it matter? I wondered. *Why must we be defined?*

"And Valentina is no better," Dorian continued, shaking his head. "She was planning to work alongside Jacques for as long as it took for her to secure power, using you as a bargaining chip. Once she got what she needed, she was going to double cross him and kill him—and possibly you, if it came to that. She wants to wipe the planet clean and rule what's left, just like Jacques. Which is why neither of them can have this."

He pulled out the Book of Beginnings.

"Hello, sweet thing," it whispered to me, always the seductress. *"It's been ages since you've held me. Won't you open me? Won't you use me? Won't you kill for me?"*

I shuddered at the thought of using something so powerful, so sinister. Dorian was absolutely right. If this book fell into the wrong hands, who knows what kind of havoc they would wreak?

Still, I wondered why *I* had to be the sacrifice. It wasn't an answer that I wanted but needed. When I asked Dorian, he said that Valentina had looked into my past and that my blood was special. Something to do with Alice. What, I couldn't imagine. Knowing this did not put me at ease. I would probably be hunted my entire life. But if the book was gone, that was one less reason for me to be on anyone's hit list.

Which left us with one option.

Chapter Twenty-Six

So, We Buried It

No matter how many times we tried, the book would *not* burn. (We wound up catching the island on fire *twice* but that was a problem for another day.) Dorian tried ripping it to shreds, but it was like it was protected by some otherworldly force: the seams wouldn't budge. In all reality, there was no point in trying any of this because it wasn't just covered in incantation—it was forged by God's Breath. I suggested trying a rune—just as blood calls to blood, magic calls to magic. But it was no use— no rune would stick to the book, sliding off its cover like water on plastic.

That's when it hit me: maybe we could bury it.

Dorian grabbed a shovel from the shed behind the house. He took me deep into the woods, book in hand. I couldn't carry the book, for I was weak-willed, and the book had a powerful influence over me. Apparently, it had that effect on those with confliction in their hearts. Dorian was of sound mind, body, and spirit so he managed just fine.

The fact that this house was near a forest, just like Jacques's main mansion, did not escape me. In fact, the one on the other side of Sidra looked almost exactly like it, except this one was smaller. But I digress.

I hadn't even noticed that Dorian stopped until I ran into the back of him. The breath whooshed out of my lungs and when I sucked in for air, my lungs were filled with the scent of him, all male. My head swam, my vision blurred, and I was filled with a fleeting sense of euphoria.

"Are you ready for this?" He said, staring at me as if he too had felt that brief connection.

I shook off the feeling.

"I'm ready."

He took the shovel and drove it into the ground. I watched his muscles flex as he pulled up a mound of dirt. He dug up a hole about eight feet deep. Sweat dripped from his forehead as he drove the shovel into the ground once more and let it sit there. It was like a knife to my heart.

Watching him work, watching an Immortal slave away for the safety of me, a Gifted, left me disoriented. Why would he go this far for me? Did he not realize that Jacques and the Rebellion would come looking for it, for both of us?

"Before you do this," I said, stopping him as he picked up the book, "I need to know why."

He blinked back at me. "Why what?"

I paused. Did he not know what I meant? Or did he not want to speak it aloud, for fear that what we were doing would finally become real?

"Why would you go so far for me? Stealing the book, angering the Rebellion, burying it for me when you could use it yourself…Why?"

He looked at me for a long moment, sizing me up. I shifted under his dark gaze. I had somehow offended him.

"We talked about this," he said, raising a brow, "remember?"

And he was doing it again—talking to me like I was a kid. It hurt. Reminded me of days with Jacques, when I would be talked down to like an idiot and handled as such.

I nodded. He rolled his eyes at me. I glared, ignoring the tiny smile on his face, the bit of hope there for something more.

"Then you know why." He paused for a moment. "It's not good to ask questions you know the answer to."

"Maybe I don't believe the answer, maybe that's why I'm asking—for confirmation."

"Then you truly are a fool."

He dropped the book into the hole. He took his time burying it, shoveling dirt back into the hole as if we had all the time in the world. With every tip of the shovel, I felt as if a piece of me was being buried with it. He was so reckless, so careless, so beautiful, so relentless, so perfect in his rejection of fate. How could I become like him?

"You need to let go of the past," Dorian said, snapping me out of my reverie.

I jumped. "What?"

"You look haunted," he replied, giving me that all-knowing look once more. "I know what it's like, to hang on to things even when they cease to have meaning. I've been there. It's not a good place to be. You need to pull yourself out that hole before it buries you."

"What do you know of it?!" I snapped, suddenly feeling defensive. I knew that he was trying to help, to get through to me, but every time he got close, I pushed away. The response was automatic—a reflex. "You don't know me so just stop!"

"I know you better than you think."

I was reminded that the Rebellion had been watching me since I was a child. But that didn't mean they knew the inner workings of my heart. No one did—not even me.

"Please stop," I whispered, clutching my heart, trying to drive out the pain, the confliction there. "You're hurting me."

"The truth always hurts, but that doesn't make it less true. The lies you tell yourself before you go to sleep at night, that's what's really destroying you. You need to let go before you're consumed."

How many nights had I stayed up thinking the same thing? How many days had I walked in the same circles, trying to let go of the only thing keeping me alive? I was addicted to sadness, to pain, to self-loathing.

How ironic was it that the one to kill me, to bury me in unhappiness, was me?

Dorian came forward, taking each step slow as if I were a wounded animal rearing to attack. He laid one hand on my cheek, rubbing it with his thumb. My eyes closed involuntarily as I favored his skin on mine.

He was like a drug to me.

And drugs did nothing but destroy.

182

Chapter Twenty-Seven

My Path, My Decision

Which path was mine?

Sadness, heartbreak, misery—that was all I knew. My parents were murdered just days after my sixth birthday. Jacques took me in and kept me under his cruel thumb until the day I left. Yet I never dared to dream for more. I thought that I was cursed since the day I was born, that I was marked for a destiny of solitude and anger.

Happiness was a far-out island that I had to swim to. The waters of my depression were black and deep, threatening to pull me under at a moment's notice. Dorian was the promise for something more…but what happened when he grew tired of me? What happened when he realized that I was worth absolutely nothing, that I had a curse laid upon my very soul, staining my existence? What happened when that glassy sky shattered into a million pieces, that thing that kept the darkness at bay, only to pierce us both with its sharpness?

Maybe I should just kill myself to save us both the heartache.

Despite what would be fair or reasonable, Jacques wasn't a monster by choice—he was born that way. And I loved him for it—for treating me the way that I deserved to be treated. I wasn't worthy of love. That was why everything I wanted was always snatched out from under me.

And I was broken beyond repair.

"Good Mother, forgive me."

In the night, between restless sleeplessness and a sort of heavy exhaustion, I threw up on myself. It was all over my shirtfront, staining it a dark yellow and brown. I couldn't remember what I'd eaten that day or if I'd eaten at all. It was a good thing that I hadn't slept in Jacques's old shirt, that I had slept in my clothes. Despite myself, I'd felt the sickness coming earlier in the day and couldn't bear ruining the part of him that I still had left.

A dark shadow slipped through the walls and stood over me. I screamed. He'd finally come for me. I was as good as dead. But then I remembered that Dorian was in the house and, forgetting that we were now enemies and thinking I could alert him to the malevolent presence before it was too late, I screamed again.

"Why are you screaming?!" A deep voice matched my volume, tone for tone— and it *certainly* wasn't Jacques.

I squinted in the dark. A light flipped on. Dorian stood over me, his face a mixture of annoyance and amusement.

"Dorian?" I said, my heart speeding up for a whole new reason.

I surveyed him. There were bags under his eyes, dark and heavy. His eyes had lost that sheen that they had when I'd first met him. He smelled heavily like alcohol. I took comfort in that. We both had our demons.

But that didn't mean I would let him get off easy—not after all the misery he'd caused me. There was no way to let bygones be bygones. And there was no way that I would surrender my heart to him—ever.

"What are *you* doing up?" I hissed, glancing at the clock on the nightstand next to my bed. It was close to three in the morning. "And why do you smell like—"

"Hennessy?" He asked, raising an eyebrow. "It keeps me vigilant."

I snorted. "Fat chance."

He just stared at me, his vision swimming from dilated pupils to normal.

"Dorian, if I ask you something, you have to promise to be honest."

"Sure. What's up?"

"Are you drunk?"

"A little," he said with a burp.

"And do you often drink like this?"

"Yes."

"Are you an alcoholic?"

He rolled his eyes. "Of course not. I can stop any time I want."

"Isn't that what an alcoholic would say?"

He scowled, seemingly not at me, but himself. I paused for a moment. Maybe he was right. But something about this seemed habitual, as if he'd done it a thousand times.

"You were screaming again," he reminded me as I sat up in bed.

"Again?" I asked, rubbing my forehead.

I had a headache coming.

"You scream in your sleep almost every night," he said factually, looking so indifferent to my struggles. "And then you puke your guts out."

That's when I realized that he wasn't indifferent—he was *used* to it.

"How the hell would you know!" I snapped, glaring at him. "What the fuck are you doing watching me?"

"I pay attention to everything you do." He said quietly. "How I feel about you—it fascinates me. I've never felt like this before."

The pain in his eyes made me pause.

"And how is that?" I said, anger fleeing just as quickly as it came. "How do I make you feel?"

"I would go to war for you. I'd die for you. I'd let you break me, let you use me, let you abuse me if you wanted...I'd do anything for you. Anything you want and more."

Something inside of me shut down at his words. That was how I felt about Jacques—that and so much more. Despite that, I still ran.

"Do you have a death wish?" I snarled, trying to make him see the worst part of me, that I wasn't good, that I wasn't the one for him. "You're just going to die like everyone else that loved me."

"That's a risk I'm willing to take."

I shook my head. Maybe I wasn't the only suicidal one in the room, on this planet. I sighed and looked down at my fingernails, bitten down to the stub.

"Why are you up anyway?" I asked.

"I stay up every night just in case he comes back for you. I don't want him to

187

take you. I don't want to lose you."

"I was never yours to begin with."

"Perhaps…" He said, breathing heavily through his nose. "It's not like it matters anyway—you'll have to face him eventually."

I shuddered at the thought. My former master would most likely kill me on sight. For I'd slighted him in the worst of ways: I didn't love him unconditionally.

It shouldn't have mattered that he held no feelings for me. If he was my god, I should love him no matter what. I should follow his every command.

But I couldn't.

I served the Creator.

I served the Good Mother.

I served myself.

And maybe that wasn't so bad.

"You've lost weight," Dorian said, snapping me out of my reverie. "You don't look so good."

I went to the bathroom and looked in the mirror. What looked back at me haunted my soul. My once-auburn hair, which used to hold a certain sheen, was now dull and lifeless. My cheeks, so full of red lifeblood hours ago, were now ashen and gaunt. There were bags under my eyes. My skin clung to the bones beneath it.

Even when I was with Jacques, I never looked *this* bad.

And suddenly I knew. Jacques's demonic presence had ruined me. My body had not only revolted, but also become dependent on the pain. Without him, my body turned on itself. With or without him, I would drown in this pit.

With or without him, I would die.

I tore the shirt off my body and stuffed it into the bathroom trash—there was no saving it now. I felt my body and cringed; I was all sharp edges, not a curve in sight. There also wasn't a spike in sight—I'd perfected my glamour. Dorian appeared next to me, his gaze travelling to my bra and lingering there. I didn't want to cover myself, turning to stare at him, the embers in my gaze combating the infernos in his—and losing.

I decided to think while I brushed my teeth. No doubt, my breath was rancid. I usually auto piloted through these rituals, for they reminded me of Jacques, his need for cleanliness and my own need for control. And I suddenly realized that I needed to get over Jacques *and* him before this obsession killed me…or before I killed myself.

Like a neurotoxin injected directly into my bloodstream, the result of showing my demons was paralytic, maybe even detrimental. I loved violently. And my depression was destructive.

Dorian was suddenly by my side, holding my hand. His hand was beautiful, warm, safe. I laid my head on his shoulder. He moved to wrap his arms around me. That's when I really started crying.

I'd done this to myself.

After a second of this, Dorian swept my legs from under me, curling me up in his arms. He carried me to my bedroom and sat on the edge of my bed, just holding me. I clung to him, burying my nose in his shirt and breathing him in. It was going to be hard hating him. But I couldn't forgive this betrayal.

I *had* to stay strong.

I moved my head from his shoulder, staring him in the eye. He looked back at me in a nonjudgmental way. I leaned my forehead against his, just staying like that for a moment or two. Finally, he lifted his hand to smooth down my matted hair. If I wasn't so sad, I would have smiled.

"Dorian," I whispered after a long moment, "I need you..."

His eyes brightened, hopeful.

"I need you to use your Gift again, to Influence me..."

"Is that all I'm good for?" he chuckled regretfully.

His hand turned a soft, warm blue. He pressed his fingers to the side of my head, his magic coursing through my veins, making me feel like everything was at least bearable. The chaotic storm in my head quieted to gentle raindrops. He sang under his breath, a song about dragons, magic, and the will to live for all eternity. I hummed in the back of my throat and when I swallowed, the spit hurt going down, but I felt more whole than I had in a long while.

"Now smile."

I frowned at him.

"Come on!" He tickled me with a goofy grin on his face. "Smile."

I couldn't help but laugh at his face. He looked so silly. He stuck out his tongue at me. That had me smiling. And the smile stayed there even after he straightened his face.

"You have such a beautiful smile," he said honestly. "I wish I could see it more."

I grinned at him. Despite our differences, he somehow still made me happy—

and I cursed myself for it. It was like the depression was there, but it was just an afterthought. I knew that I shouldn't base my happiness off one person. But I couldn't help it.

I still wanted him to be happy with me. I still wanted him to be proud of me. I still wanted him to love me.

And some part of me still wanted to love him back.

Man, I realized, *I suck at being an enemy.*

His mouth was now a hairsbreadth away. I made the first move. My lips crashed against his, rough and insistent. He kissed me back, his kiss gentle and sweet. I let myself get lost in him, let myself be all right, let myself feel a fraction of what he felt for me.

And for just a moment, I was alive again.

He parted from me. We both breathed heavy. That's when his eyes changed, from loving worship to defiant guilt. I wanted to kiss him again, to lose myself until there was no way back. But it was clear that he needed to tell me something.

"Why'd you stop?" I asked, fisting my hands into his shirt.

I wasn't done using you, said a darker part of me.

"I don't want you to hate me."

He set me on the bed.

He ran a golden hand through his hair. That's when I noticed that he used something we magic users liked to call alchemic gel. Combine the gel with magic and run it through your hair with your fingers and you could have any style you wanted. The color wouldn't change, but the strand thickness could be manipulated. A few strands stuck out, showing that his hair was actually spiky beneath it. I ran a hand through his hair.

It stuck up in every direction, which I adored.

(Curse him for being so cute!)

But then he gave me a guilty, pitying look and I snapped out of it, watching his every move.

"How much do you remember about the day your parents died?"

I'd lied before. I remembered "Everything," I answered.

I was standing on my father's feet as he spun us around the room. My mother was singing a Gaelic song, her red hair standing around her head like a living flame. I was laughing, wishing on the inside that we were Immortal, that we didn't have to run to keep from becoming enslaved by people who thought of themselves as gods. Then suddenly the door was being broken down and there were men everywhere, with guns and knives. They slaughtered the only family that I knew and left me standing there, alone and afraid.

I screamed for my Mar and Da to come back, for them to save me the heartache of being an orphan. But they didn't. They lay on the floor in a pool of blood, their lifeless eyes staring up at me helplessly. Then suddenly I was exploding, electricity flying from my body in all directions. I glowed with power and made vengeance my new name.

My arm shot out. Electricity flew across the room like a dagger. It hit the first two square in the chest. One by one they dropped like flies, twitching as my power coursed its way through their bodies. The other three ran. I pursued but my skinny, childish legs only took me so far.

They got away.

I would never forget that day. Or the days after, when I alternated between eating what food was left in the pantry and lying with their corpses. I brushed Mar's hair; I cleaned Danri's glasses the way I'd watched him do hundreds of times. I remember even pouring my magic into my fingertips at one point, attempting to reanimate them. Only I hadn't been taught that in school. So, their bodies began to burn from the inside out. I ran out of the house, sitting at the swing set, rocking back and forth as the flames rose into the night. Jacques found me a couple of days later and...

The rest was history.

Wow, I'd totally forgotten about that. So, I had burned them. Which means that as long as they hadn't killed any Gifted, they'd made it to the stars...

I wanted to cry at the revelation.

"Well, what if I told you that I knew who killed your parents?" Dorian said, bringing me back to the present.

"I'd say you were lying." I narrowed my eyes. "Because you weren't there, right?"

"I wasn't. But Valentina was."

My heart ground to a stop in my chest. I stared at him. What was he trying to say?

"Your mother could give someone life with a mere thought. Your father could take it just as easily. They were the strongest Gifted that Valentina had ever seen.

193

She wanted them to rejoin the Rebellion in the Southern Isles where they met. They refused, claiming that they left the war, the Rebellion, behind to start a new life as Mortals. They swore to never use their powers again. They planned to take you to Libra once you were old enough. Valentina stopped them at every chance she got. She liquidated their assets and killed anyone willing to help them. The Flame of Life and The Black Death got exactly what they'd wanted—a Mortal life and a Mortal death."

I remembered that well. My father and mother would tell me of a magical place where we could live free, where we could be ourselves without fearing retribution. That was Libra.

"Valentina ordered the hit on your parents."

"No. She wouldn't do that."

"She said that if they wouldn't join us, then they didn't deserve to live. She ordered the hit. I'm sorry for not telling you sooner."

Valentina killed my parents? She was the reason that I was alone, that I'd lived with Jacques all those miserable years? She was the reason that I was so unhappy now?

It was her fault...?

Her fault!

I stood, grabbing my holster. I reached for one of the daggers, took its gleaming sharpness into my hand, watching my reflection clear as day in it. I saw my mixed brown skin, caught between the white of my mother's and the dark brown of my father's. I saw the almond shape of my father's brown orbs but the green of my mother's eyes. I saw my father's strong jaw, my mother's round forehead. I was my parent's children. But they didn't believe in revenge.

Now it was all I could think about.

But then I looked into Dorian eyes and my anger was redirected. And just like that I hated him all over again. My anger was now hot and bubbling like acid in the pit of my stomach, swelling up to surround my heart.

I curled my other hand into a fist and slammed it into his chest, snarling at him. I wanted to plunge the dagger into his side, but I couldn't. Despite our enemy status, I didn't know if Gifted-Immortals could die—and I didn't want to see him die.

At least, not by my hand.

"Was it real?" I whispered as he crumpled upon the ground.

"What?" he wheezed.

"Was any of it real?" I spat, raising my foot above his face. "Did you love me?"

"I still do," he whispered, opening his eyes.

His face was so soft, so full of love and care and attention. And I just *broke*. The blade fell onto the bed with a thump. I dropped onto my knees next to the bed and curled my arms around my midsection as a wave of betrayal and hurt swamped over me. I wanted to scream, to cry, to scatter in the wind.

I wanted to join my parents in the stars.

"I'm sorry," Dorian whispered, shuffling towards me.

"I hate you," I whispered.

"What?"

"I *hate* you! Dammit! I hate you, I hate you, I hate you, *I HATE YOU!*"

"Marve…" he whispered, his voice broken as he took a faltering step forward.

I held up one finger. He froze. I turned my hand, pointing at him.

"There's nothing you can say. You knew about this and you hid it from me."

"I just found out right before we left. She had been planning to use you from the beginning. She joined Jacques's work force so that she could watch you, to see what you'd become."

An angry, bitter laugh—between a guffaw and a cackle—tore from my throat. I wanted to kill him but caring about him held me back.

Dang it!

Jacques *was* right—my emotions *did* make me weak.

"Was she satisfied?" I asked, wanting to know if there was anyone on this planet who thought I could defend myself.

His reply cut and repaired simultaneously: "Yes." He laid his hand over mine, as if his next words were the worst he could possibly say, but they were just an extension of his former. "That's why she wants to use you—so that you'll become the greatest weapon: a sword in her scabbard, fighting for world domination. She doesn't want to free the Gifted or make the Immortals pay for what they did. She wants to be higher than all of that, higher up than the Creator himself."

She was no better than Jacques.

"Let me guess." I snorted, giving him a look that meant business. "She wanted you to get close to me."

"Not exactly," he hedged, rubbing the back of his neck. "She wanted me to convince you to join the Rebellion. I did that. After that, I was supposed to leave you alone. But I couldn't—"

"Because you were *so* in love with me," I interrupted, batting my lashes at him.

Just like that, I hated him all over again.

He just stared at me.

"As fun as this little chat has been, I really do need to get some shut eye," I said, crawling onto the bed and burrowing under the covers.

"Marve," he whispered, still on the floor, "you're scaring me."

I rolled onto my side, facing the wall.

"Please talk to me." When I didn't answer, I heard him sigh. "I'll stay here— just in case."

"How long do you think it'll be?"

"Until I'm sure that you're safe."

"Not that!" I rolled my eyes even though he couldn't see. I knew that he couldn't have known what I meant. But I was mad at him. "How long do you think it'll be until she realizes that the Book is missing?"

"Well, I used magic to create a duplicate, so I give it a day or two before she catches on."

But we both knew that evading the Rebellion couldn't possibly be *that* easy.

Chapter Twenty-Eight

I Feel It Running Through My Veins

Dorian woke me up early in the morning, telling me to dress for battle. I showered and got dressed in under thirty minutes. I was decked out in all black. I put on the belt that held all the knives. I left the bow and arrows behind.

I was ready to become the hero I'd always needed.

Dorian and I ate cereal in silence. There was nothing that I wanted more than to know what to say to him. A lot had come out last night. Dorian told me that now I needed to do two things: forgive and learn how to love again. I rolled my eyes at the heinous thought.

Easier said than done.

Dorian set his spoon and bowl in the sink. "We're training today."

"Training?" I asked, raising one inquisitive eyebrow. "Training for what?"

"You know, using your magic—or your fists, if that's what suits you. You don't know how to use runes. You haven't really used your Gift since you left. You need to train. If the Rebellion catches wind of our location, you're screwed. And if Jacques catches up to you, you're as good as dead. That's why you've always gotta be on the lookout for opps."

When I asked what that was, he said they were an older term for enemies.

"I hadn't thought of that." I paused, weighing the pros and cons. "To be totally honest, I don't really use my Gift outside of the arena."

"Why?" He reached out to trace a finger along my arm; my electricity crackled to life at the touch. "You have a beautiful Gift. You're a living storm."

Stupid Gift—can't turn on for me, but it'll listen to him!

"Well, thanks, I guess..." I blushed, looking away to examine a spot on the wall.

"Do you know anywhere we can train?"

"Yes."

I promptly got up from the table. Dorian was just a few steps behind. I took him to the living room, where the uncomfortable chairs sat, and a painting hung. I walked up to the painting, tracing my index finger along the frame. It slid over a ridge and voila!

The door was open.

We walked down the corridor into the hovel beneath. We pushed open the door and stepped into the arena. It was big enough to easily fit one hundred people, maybe more. We had magic to thank for that. Dorian brushed past me, careful not to touch me as he took his place on one side of the arena.

"If you're not prepared to kill me," Dorian said, facing me, "then you're not prepared to win."

"Funny," I replied with a smirk, "I knew a man who used to say the exact same thing."

There was no countdown, no premonition. He just came at me full force. I shrouded myself in electricity, bathing the arena in blinding light. I heard Dorian curse and knew that he couldn't see me. I gathered electricity around my fists and, following the sound of his voice, hurled a series of electrified hits at him.

He dodged all of them—all except one. I cracked him in the jaw, not pulling any punches. He flew back, a blackened mark on his cheek where our skin collided. He didn't fall, I'd give him that. He came at me, using his superior weight to topple me.

His knees were on my arms. His head was bent forward, as if he were trying to see the soul trapped beneath my gaze. He reached out, laid a hand on my cheek. I suddenly had thoughts about giving up, about failing, about losing this fight. I put up a mental shield, brick by brick, and kept him from burrowing any further.

I was unprepared for what he did next, though.

He gazed deeply into my eyes, the brown and gold in his eyes flickering like an abandoned light. I stopped struggling. He leaned closer, his face completely blank. That's when I remembered what I was here to do. I exploded electricity around me, effectively throwing him off me.

I pulled one of the large daggers from my holster. Dorian was slower to get up this time but nonetheless, he got up. I stalked towards him slowly, savoring each step that brought me closer to victory. Dorian stood there, ready for me, and it took me a moment to remember that he needed physical contact to use his Gift: he was virtually powerless without it. I was on him in a matter of seconds, my blade at his throat as I pinned him with my gaze.

I don't know how he did it. One second, he was beneath me and the next he was behind me, twisting my left arm, my dominant arm, behind my back. My parents had raised me to use my right arm, but I'd be lying if I said it was naturally stronger than my left, and without them, I had fallen out of practice. I dropped the blade. His breath ghosted on my neck. There was something about his closeness that turned me on.

He picked up the knife before tucking and rolling away from me. I removed a second dagger from its holster. This was the one with the runes. I threw it at him; it barely clipped his ear. A drip of blood fell from his ear, but the wound stitched itself closed almost immediately.

I picked out another one before lobbing it at him. He didn't even slow down when the dagger embedded itself in his shoulder. He just gripped its hilt and tore it from his shoulder. There was blood. How was he totally calm while injured?

"You're not prepared to kill me, Marve."

I blanched. *Of course, I am!*

But then, I really gave it some thought.

Even after all I knew, after all he'd done, I still could not truly wound him. Even after every instinct screamed at me to put him down, I still thought twice. That was when I realized that I'd somehow grown to care for him, just a little.

I dropped to my knees, bowing my head. Dorian stopped in front of me. I was unprepared for his next action: he sunk to his knees before me, dropping the blade in the process. I didn't realize that I was shaking until he wrapped his arms around me. My voice shook as I asked him why I couldn't do it.

201

Why couldn't I kill him?

"You're more human than you realize," Dorian said, rubbing my back.

All these years, I'd been raised to be a monster. Killing was in my blood. But when faced with the one who put my entire existence to shame, I hesitated.

What was wrong with me?

"You're not ready to fight. Maybe in a year or so. But not now."

Dorian said nothing when I pulled away. He just watched me silently, a thousand answers to the millions of questions in my eyes. I picked up each blade, sheathing them in my holster. After that, I made my way back through the corridor. Just like before, Dorian was one step behind me.

I went to my room and pulled out the picture of Jacques and Grant from my discarded pants. Jacques stared back at me, a small smile on his face. I'd given him everything and came up empty-handed. It'd gotten me nowhere. How was I to move on from that?

"You need to let him go," Dorian said from behind me.

I jumped, whirling around. I hid the picture behind my back. It wasn't that I didn't want him to know that I'd been looking at it—it was because I didn't want him to see it period. It was my photo—my memory.

It was the last bit of *him* that I had left.

A demented, hateful, possessive love like that—it was hard to forget.

I didn't realize that I'd been crying until Dorian made his way over to me, wiping my cheeks with his sleeves. I buried my face in his neck, breathing him in. It was a small luxury, one that I shouldn't be allowed, but a comfort still. I didn't know what was wrong with me. I needed to let him go yet I held fast with both hands.

I loved him with my entire being.

I wanted him to love me with my entire heart.

I held on to those first few months of being with him, the months when he showed me kindness, with my entire soul.

"I know how you feel," Dorian said, pulling away to look me in the eye. "I felt that way about my parents for years—even after they died."

"You were happy that your parents died?"

I couldn't imagine such a thing—my parents were my entire world before Jacques.

Shadows walked in his eyes.

"My relationship with my mother and father was complicated at best. Once I gained my inheritance, I left. I was in Paris when I got the news that they'd died."

"I thought Immortals couldn't die."

He said nothing.

I held onto this bit of information. So, there *was* a way to kill Immortals? This was *huge*!

I mentally prayed to the Good Mother, thanking her for this tiny piece of knowledge.

"Why is it that you didn't use your Gift for all the time that you were free?" Dorian asked, parting from me.

"It's tied to my emotions. The more broken I feel..."

Nothing else needed to be said.

"And now?"

"Now what?"

"How do you feel now?" Dorian asked, reading my face.

I feigned a smile. "It doesn't hurt as bad. It's bearable. I can finally breathe again."

It was because of him. Dorian had showed me that I had a lot to offer, more than being a slave ever got me. I wasn't perfect but I was still better than the trash Jacques made me out to be. I was learning to live after years of being dead inside. It's like the depression was still there but it was more in the background, a lingering afterthought in a flurry of manic love.

Not that I loved Dorian.

I took the blades to the living room. While walking there, I gathered the necessary supplies. I wanted to sit in the golden, throne-like chair that was reserved for my old master, but as I neared it, I felt his strong, murky presence. Shuddering, I turned and sat in the chair reserved for Valentina. I cleaned and sharpened each blades individually with care and precision. As I dragged the sharpening stone across the blade, I thought of driving it into her skull.

Zing! Went the blade.

One strike for the parents you took from me.

Zing!

One strike for all the lies.

Zing!

One strike for the girl I used to be.

Zing!

One strike for the girl who died.

Zing!

One strike for the rage, slowly brewing in my heart.

Zing!

One strike for the reborn me, making a new start.

He asked me to play tag with him in the street. But I worried that the Rebellion's spies were lurking, either them or Jacques. He made a face. I glared at him, saying that we didn't have time for things like that—we were being hunted. And he got an attitude—*with me.*

"No wonder you're depressed," he snapped, "you don't do anything but sit with your thoughts."

I flinched. My hand twitched, wanting to shield my face. It was the first time he'd ever truly gotten angry with me. Delicately, as if I might shatter into a million pieces, Dorian grabbed my wrist, which I then noticed was trembling. I wanted to jerk away, seeing Jacques in his form, but then, as I focused, I saw Dorian again.

Dorian, who wanted me more than his calling, his empire, his life.

Dorian, who loved me.

Dorian wouldn't hurt me.

The look in his eyes was sad and understanding all at once.

"I'm not going to hit you," he sighed.

I said nothing.

"I'm sorry for raising my voice, babe. I really am."

"…"

"I want us to do something together. *Anything.* I just want to spend some time with you outside of this house. I know that this is where you and your parents were before they were killed. It's doing strange things to you. Every time I look into your eyes, I see a piece of you dying."

"I can't. This place is the last thing I have left of them."

"Please try." He gave me a pleading stare that I'd never seen on his face before. "For me?"

But no matter how enticing he looked, no matter how beautiful he appeared, I knew that he was a lying snake and that I would never fall for those charms again.

Chapter Twenty-Nine

Our Beating Hearts, Twisting Bodies and Mingled Magic

"Today's gonna be a good day," I said to myself when I woke up that morning.

And I was right.

Even though I'd begun to wonder how we'd managed to stay in the same safe house for just under a week, Dorian assured me that Jacques had no cameras on his properties. I remembered that Jacques once told me that with today's technology, someone could easily hack into them and watch his every move, so he did without. But then again, what did those monitors in the three-walled room survey? Part of me was paranoid that he'd changed his mind, that he was watching us right now, but then Dorian kissed me, and I forgot for a little while.

Before I did anything, I went to the closet and reached into a hidden compartment above the clothes rack. There was a small statue there. I set it down on the floor before sitting before it, legs crossed. I wasn't sure whether I should pray to it, but finally decided that it was all right. After all, I wasn't sure if I could trust Dorian or his story about Kalysma. So as far as I was concerned, she reigned

207

supreme.

I closed my eyes, reaching out to hold the statue. The black goddess stared back at me, her face fierce, her hair a wild mane around her head. I closed my eyes, repeating a few basic prayers in my head. My Gift flickered to life, traveling from the vat in my stomach and circulating throughout my body. Religion gave me a sense of purpose and, I realized, power.

When I opened my eyes, the statue was glowing. I wondered why it would do that—unless the stories were true. This was proof that the Goddess was indeed that—a goddess. But then I thought back to Dorian's words. I flipped the statue upside down. There was a small compartment in the bottom. I slid it open to see a pair of batteries.

I closed it. There had to be an explanation for that. I mean, it's not like it was only reacting because I had powers of electricity, right? She had to be real. The Goddess gave us life—and she could take it away if she heard such blasphemy.

Suddenly the powers I felt died out. I tried to tap into them again but was unsuccessful. I got up and carefully placed the small statue back in the closet. Despite what most Mortals thought, it wasn't the statue that I worshipped. It was what the statue represented. It was kind of like Christians and their rosaries. It was just a symbol for something—or someone—far more real.

I showered and dressed in a green velvet dress and matching flats. Just wearing bright colors and looking nice made me feel more positive about the day. I came to the kitchen to see Dorian at the table, scattered pieces of paper with runes on them thrown around. His hair was looking extra wild today, sticking up every way. He looked so cute that I couldn't help but blush as I took the seat across from him.

"I need to ask you something," Dorian said, not looking up from the device that he was fiddling with. It was a small black thing no bigger than my pinky nail, with a tiny slit in the side. Dorian slipped something inside the slit, something that glowed with a blue light—the color of his magic, of his soul. "I need you to refrain from getting offended when I ask you. It's just a matter of science, you see."

"Anything."

"Are you a virgin?"

"WHAT?!"

"Of course, your magic will be diluted," he continued. He didn't eye me up the way he had before. In fact, he seemed intent on staying as still as possible while he rambled on. "But what to do while—"

"Dorian!"

He jumped.

"What in the constellations are you talking about?"

"Well, I was thinking last night…" He seemed bashful now that he knew I was following what he was saying. "Jacques is looking for your hiding place—my coordinates have told me so. He's hunting through each territory with a vengeance. It's only a matter of time before he finds you."

I shuddered.

And if he found me…

"I can hide you with magic all I want, but he's a half-demon. He can still *smell* you. So that got me thinking—what if I change your scent?"

"There's no conceivable way to do that."

"To conceive, there is."

I paused, for we were treading on dangerous grounds now.

"What are you getting at, Dorian?"

"Okay." He took a deep breath and gazed deep into my eyes. "If I were to take your virginity, a piece of my soul would become yours and vice versa. Your scent would change. Maybe that's all you need to evade him until we get you to a safer location."

I didn't blush this time, for I could see the opportunity. I eyed his dress shirt, noticing the top two buttons open, and the gel not in his hair, making it stick up in all directions, some pieces falling on his forehead, framing his soft, feminine face, and the way his jeans hugged his hips. He'd done this on purpose, looked this good today, to show me what I could have—to entice me. And I wanted him badly. Maybe some lingering influence remained from his Gift. Maybe I was just merely a woman reacting to the presence of a man. Maybe we were meant to find each other in the night and become one. *gag*

Maybe this was fate.

"Of course, there are drawbacks."

"Of course," I said, using my last few moments to savor the idea. "And they are?"

"Since a piece of your soul is gone, your magic will act...*different*. It won't be as strong. Not for a good while."

I thought back to the way my magic had been acting since I'd been so depressed.

"Pft. That's not a problem."

I mean, I had been kissing him since the day I met him, so sex couldn't be *that* different. Then again, I would be going farther with him than I had anyone else. He was my first kiss, my second real friend and my third savior. But what if it got weird?

Not like it matters, I suddenly realized. *It's just sleeping with the enemy.*

"Does it have to be right now?" I asked, pressing my thighs together. "I need some time to…prepare."

"Take all the time you need."

That's when it really did get weird. How were we supposed to interact in the moments leading up to this? I pushed away from the table and stood up. My knees were wobbly, but I managed to play it off. He avoided looking at me, probably to spare me the awkwardness.

"I just realized…"

He looked at me through his lashes. "Yes, darling?"

"You're totally shy!" I grinned.

He bit his lip, not saying anything for a long moment. "I'm not used to having to chase."

"Meaning?"

"Women usually make the first move with me."

"So, you can't flirt?" I asked, raising a brow, trying not to grin.

"There's no need."

Look at me, he seemed to radiate.

"I mean, you're sexy as hell," I said, "but aren't you a top?"

He shrugged. "I'm not even sure I know what that means…"

I pursed my lips, trying not to laugh. "So, your entire life, women just flocked to you?"

"Pretty much."

"I don't understand."

"You don't have to," he replied, touching the counter. "Try not to overthink it. I promise you, it's not that complicated."

"Have you always been this cute?" I asked.

"I used to be fat," he admitted, blushing. "But I took care of myself."

I tried to imagine it but couldn't picture it. "I can't see that."

"Most women can't. They only see what they have before them."

"Is it gonna hurt?" I asked.

"The first time is supposed to hurt for Mortal women, but I'm not sure about Gifted women. For Immortal women, their hymens constantly heal itself, so for them, yes."

"Ouch," I muttered. A jealous thought crossed my mind. "How many?"

He dropped my gaze. "You don't wanna know."

"Yes, I do."

He rattled off a number. I covered my mouth as my eyes widened.

"All Immortal?" I asked once I'd recovered.

"Mostly," he said, "but I will admit, my first was not."

212

"How in the hell...?" I breathed. "That's like, an obscene number of people."

He shrugged. "I'm sure to someone your age, it is."

"All women?" I asked.

He bit his lip, trying not to smirk, a secretive, coy smile at best.

"I mean, I don't normally endorse prostitution but damn, at least tell me they paid you. Cause you don't need to be packing all of *that*—" I looked down "—and not get paid."

He shifted in his seat, his mouth twitching as he rubbed his thumbs against his forefingers. I felt the change in his magic almost immediately. My comment had fucked with him, so I knew that he hadn't told a lot of people this. I touched his hand.

"I'm sorry. I was kidding. It's totally cool. I mean, whoever you sleep with, however many people...it doesn't matter. I like you for you."

"It's not that. It's just...you don't know how true that statement is."

"I don't understand."

"Never mind..." he shook his head.

"Do you have any kids...?" I asked.

"None that I know of..." he shrugged. "I would never elect for a woman to have the surgery that allows them to have children."

"Surgery?"

"I'll tell you about it later. Let's just say...there's a reason you rarely see Immortal women pregnant..."

A fearful shudder tingled down my spine.

213

That's when it suddenly hit me: I missed the company of other people. We'd been in this house for Goddess knows how long, just the two of us. I missed the sun. I missed the air and the hustle and bustle of the city. With Jacques I'd usually been inside, but at least I had Tiara (Kalysma rest her soul) and Valentina.

I got a handful of drachmas from Dorian before walking outside. Even from the porch of the house, I could feel the pull of the Book of Beginnings. It called to the monster inside, the self-loathing part of me that ate away at what was left of my frayed soul.

How was I to move past that and heal?

I walked down the winding road that led into the city—or what was left of it. All the continent was covered in it—glass and concrete—you couldn't escape it no matter where you went; the only place that didn't was the Isles and I hadn't been since I was a toddler. I suddenly craved something that made me frown: an endless ocean, the salty spray of the sea whipping around my head, filling my lungs, flaxen sand beneath my feet, and the possibility to dive into the water, to never resurface, to lose myself to it and get lost in my own freedom—and I knew that the sea was not only evil and a reminder of Jacques, but also a piece of me, too.

And suddenly I remembered walking into a sea as powerful as any god, the ocean deep and dark, calling to me in the middle of the night, the white sand shifting under my bare feet, as I contemplated walking into the ocean and never coming back—but then two chocolate-colored hands wrapped around my childish legs and hoisted me into their arms, and I reached out a hand for the waves, and cried when they did not come for me.

214

Was I just always sad?

I blinked and suddenly I was in the middle of the street, my glamor still raised, with Immortals and their slaves walking past me but not speaking, although one Amorian with silver hair and yellow wolfy eyes stared at me as if to ask if I was all right. Steeling my shoulders, I walked until I made it to a tavern.

Its wood was old-looking, sagging, the sky above dreary like an afternoon of tea and small talk, but its door looked welcoming enough. The inside wasn't much better, with a bar with wooden stools, a karaoke machine, two loudspeakers next to the door (I couldn't place the song, but it spoke of love not having to choose) and pathetic looking Mortal men spread around, a girl in each of their laps, sometimes more than one, and I knew that these were ladies of the night and that these had to be Slave Catchers off-duty—after all, who else could afford to rent another's body and not have the aged agelessness of an Immortal.

I reached into my purse and pulled out a drachma. Sauntering forward and praying to Kalysma that I looked like I belonged here, I handed the drachma to the man behind it. He handed me a large lager of beer.

In old societies, someone my age would have barely been old enough to drink. But this was the 22nd century! People did as they pleased. I picked up the lager, eyeing it for a moment before bringing it to my lips.

I sipped at it slowly, hating the bitter, earthy taste of the yellow, frothy liquid, but loving the warm, tingly feeling that it brought me. Since alcohol was rare here and money to buy it was even rarer, there weren't many people here. I huddled in on myself, trying to keep that warmth that was spreading across my stomach, seeping

215

into my bones. The stool next to me groaned under the weight of another person. I looked over to see Dorian sitting next to me, glaring at my lager, glaring at *me*.

What did I do?

"What in the Creator's grand design are you doing?"

"Drinking." I looked back at him. "What are *you* doing?"

"Stopping you from making the worst mistake of your life. Why would you think that *this*—" he shot the lager a glare "—would be the answer to your problems?"

I paused before giving him my answer: *"You did."*

"What?" He looked as if he might haul off and smack me.

I flinched. Then thought back to that time on the plane. He seemed so much calmer when he had a drink in his hand. Maybe it would work for me, too. Maybe—

"Stop it!" He snatched away the drink and when I tried to grab it from him, he let it go. It fell to the wooden floor with a clatter, shattering into a thousand little glass shards. I gaped but he looked smug, saying with his eyes, *That was all you.* "You can't talk your way out of this, Marve. And—" he held up a hand, "—you can't convince me."

"Are you drunk?" I blurted, then immediately slapped my hands over my mouth.

Yeah, great idea. Let's piss him off further. Gosh, do I want him to hit me?

The bartender looked ready to fight. But dorian sent him a look so fearsome that the larger, broader man immediately backed down. Dorian grabbed the man's bare arm roughly across the counter, his eyes glowing with a faint blue light. I could practically see the images flying through the Mortal man's eyes, the pain, the terror, the death that Dorian promised him in that touch. The glow faded and the man trembled as his eyes darted all around, anywhere but Dorian's gaze, where a threat of violence made its bed.

"If you give her one more drink," Dorian said quietly, his face a mask of death, "I will cut of your balls and feed them to you myself. Do I make myself clear?"

The bald, bearded man nodded once. Dorian gave him four drachmas. The man gave him a bottle of jack.

"What the literal fuck!" I glared at him. "Are you serious?! I can't drink but you—"

"It's too late for me!" Dorian snapped back, throwing me a much more PG-13 version of the glare he just gave the bartender. "There's still a part of you left—a part of you that we can save."

That's when I realized that he had his demons. The fast talking, the arrogance, the swagger in his step, it was all a mask to hide one thing: he was broken beyond repair. But I didn't know how he got that way.

Maybe we weren't so different...Maybe he had his reasons...I laid one hand over his. He moved his from under mine, shadows creeping in his gaze.

Dorian tipped back his head and drank deeply from the bottle. Those shadows in his eyes became brighter, more violent, but his posture eased forward until he was hunched over the bottle. This bottle was the epicenter of his existence, the thing keeping him together. He reminded me of a broken toy, glued together by naïve dreams of justice for all and a bit of alcohol. What did he see in me that made him

217

ward me off?

But that answer was also obvious in every move he made around me: he saw a spark, a light in the dark, something beautiful.

And he looked at me like that—like he saw beauty and not a ravaged piece of meat rubbed raw. But then I thought of the looks of pure disgust and loathing he'd give me and thought, *At least, sometimes he did.* I watched him as he took another swig, then another. I reached out to him, but I passed right through him.

Magic. Even now, he used magic to keep me at bay.

He betrayed me.

But I guess that's what happened when I decided to trust him. I opened myself up to his love but exposed myself to his pain. If he managed to hurt me again, I'd surely die. But maybe before that, I could live and love and just be free from the troubles that burdened me.

So, I opened myself to the knife at my throat and prayed that he didn't apply pressure.

"You wanna dance?"

He nodded.

I grabbed his hand and pulled him to the small bit of space between tables. He put his hands on my waist and pulled me close. I could feel his heart beating in tangent with my own, his soul intertwining with mine. I laid my head on his shoulder. He was warm and safe and mine if I would just give him the chance.

The music above us was by Lyon-S—I recognized her voice. Her tone was sultry and sugary, dangerous, and maddening, all at once. She spoke to the deepest part of me, dragging the goodness in me to the surface and exposing it for all to see.

"I am you,

You are I.

I'm just a girl,

You're just a guy.

But there's a pool,

An ocean between us,

I wade in the water,

It only needs trust."

Dorian was still holding that bottle behind my back, but he didn't need it anymore—he had me. I pulled his arms from my waist and grabbed the bottle. I took one swig, needing an ounce of liquid courage before I did what I did.

"You fill my mind,

You make me suicide,

You make me see the truth

In the starry sky.

What is this feeling?

Am I falling in love?

You must be an angel,

Sent from above."

The lyrics were twisted in a sense but very much true. The only difference—even now—was that Dorian didn't make me suicide. In fact, he pulled me farther from the ledge every day. Maybe she didn't mean literal suicide. But what? What could that possibly mean?

"In my mirror,

I see you.

My hands are cold,

Turning blue.

Your heart's a fire,

That's nothing new.

Warm myself up,

And cut you loose."

Most minds were like any other muscle. If they went to waste, they would rot and stink like a piece of meat left out in the sun. But if someone took the time to train them, it could do wonders. My mind was kind of like a rubber band—pull too tight and it would snap. But if I stretched it far enough, trained it, it would do my bidding. Which meant I could train my mind not to need him or anyone else—*ever again.*

"You make me feel like I'm worth it.

You make me feel like I'm deservin'.

You make me feel like the moon,

Push and pull, gravitate towards you."

It was true. Dorian made me feel like this every single day. I could feel myself trusting him, could feel myself falling for him. If he pushed too hard, I might pull away. But if he gave too little, I might not take him seriously—or even go back to hating him. It wasn't fair to him—not a bit—but it was just how I operated.

"This is the song without a chorus.

I wrote it just for us.

Take it slow, baby,

Don't rush.

I'm so drunk, darlin',

Off your love."

That's when I noticed that he was watching me intensely, his gaze a black furnace filled with brown-and-gold embers; I let it warm me. He licked his lips, a primal look taking over his eyes. I froze. One of his hands went north to my hair, entangling in my crinkly, nappy red locks; his other travelled to my hips, pulling me closer.

A shudder traveled through me at the proximity. The sounds of music and glasses clinking faded into nothing. It was just us, the air around us and the passion in our hearts. His eyes hooded, taking those embers with him as he leaned his head forward. His breath washed over me, smelling of spearmint and jack.

"Marve…" He breathed, sounding dominating and surrendering all at once. "I want you."

"And no one else," I whispered.

I traced my hands from his shoulders to his arms, thick and roped with muscle. He was slender but built—wiry, I think the word was. The way he looked at me, the way he touched me, the way he said my name—I might just end up falling in love with him.

"Let's get out of here," he grunted, his words a request and a command. But he must have noticed the latter when I did because he added, "Only if you're ready."

"I'm ready, bae..." I whispered, kissing him once, softly. "I want you, too."

Shadows crossed his face. "Even after all I've done?"

I swallowed. "I could say the same to you."

"You've done nothing wrong," he quipped.

Yes, I have, I thought, *I've mistreated you more times than I can count.*

And I didn't just mean the using him part. I meant always snapping at him. I meant asking him to use his Gift on me to make myself feel better, feeding off his magic and his presence to keep myself sane—and alive. At the end of the day, I was not better than Jacques. But I truly did want him.

And, I told myself, feeling him shift, *he's mine for the taking.*

He reached out his hand to the left of us, briefly separating our bodies. I whimpered at the lack of contact, at the lack of *him,* and he chuckled. The tip of his fingers began to glow as he traced a rune in the air. It gleamed softly. He grabbed my hand, led me through the portal that appeared.

We stepped into his room. It had been a while since I'd last been in here and it had changed drastically. Scattered on the walls, covering at least two completely, were sketches—*of me.* Some were complete and some were half done, as if he'd started and had gotten frustrated and quit. There were some of me smiling, some of me frowning, some of me glaring and some of me sleeping.

The shading around the ones of me sleeping were dark and haunted. My face was twisted up as if I were in pain in some sketches, tears streaming down my cheeks in others. There was never one of me in peace while I was asleep, which I instantly regretted. Sleep was a time to wind down, to drop the day's troubles at the door. But it looked like my troubles were amplified.

I turned to Dorian to see him staring at me, watching my every move, gauging my reaction. I almost gave up on seeing any in my natural form until I saw the one on the wall above the computer, which was directly across from his bed. My face was twisted in an angry snarl, my clawed hand raised and my spikes gleaming. I looked fierce—like the warrior of the Southern Isles that my parents had been too afraid to let me be. If the truer Rebels had their way, I'd have no need to be ashamed—I would look like that all the time.

I looked at Dorian to see his uncomfortable avoidance give way to a look of appreciation.

"Why do you look away from me when I take my true form?" I asked, letting a part of the glamour fall away, showing my inhuman eyes watching him.

But he looked. His brows were lifted, his eyes wide, his mouth hanging open in shock. No, not shock...*Awareness*. I leaned forward, smelled his scent change. I felt him thicken against my outer thigh and realized.

Good Mother! This form turns him on!

"I kind of have a thing for girls from the Southern Isles...But I didn't want to see you as just another girl from the Isles. I mean, I've never been in a relationship with any of the girls that I've been with except Mimi—"

"Mimi?" I paused and then unwillingly thought back to the first time I saw him at Jacques's mansion, to the woman with the massive cup size. Then I thought of my flat brown chest. We were practically opposites! Why did he pick me? "I don't

223

understand."

"Marve," he said carefully, "you are exactly what I want in a woman. Strong. Fierce. And just a bit broken. You're utter perfection."

"So, I'm a project to you?"

"No. I just want to show you the love that you deserve. Is that a crime?" He frowned. "You're a wild thing—a beast at your core—"

"Beast? So now we're using racial slurs?"

"—and I will not let you suffer while we're together."

"I'm not yours."

His lips tilted up. "For now."

"..."

"I didn't mean to offend you. I just thought since we were both Gifted, we could use that word with one another. I do it with Rhea all the time. But I'll stop if you want me to."

"I get it. I just…can't believe you of all people called me that…"

His lips were suddenly at my jugular, kissing my pulse. "You're angry. That's good. Making up is the better part of fighting."

My heartbeat jumped in my chest. And then the words he first said when I saw the pictures registered. *My true form doesn't repulse him? It's exactly what he wants?!*

I let the rest of my glamour fall away, felt my bones shifting as my spikes slid into place, felt my teeth changing shape, felt my claws lengthening. Feeling empowered, bold, I raked one claw down his arm, fighting a grin when blood

224

swelled to the surface. He shuddered. Sure enough, he hardened even further.

"Why would you keep this from me?" I asked quietly, trying not to smirk or frown for fear of scaring him off.

"When I was young, my father had an older family friend. She was…like you. She saw me as a man when no one else did. My father walked in on us once, killed her right then and there, beat me until I wet myself. I felt so scared, so ashamed, so disgusted with myself…I just—"

"He traumatized you," I stated, frowning when his eyes dropped to the ground.

"I was told that I needed to be with an Immortal. Someone…*like me*. Being a half-breed, it was imperative that I marry up. When I started dating Megumi, I thought my parents would be proud of me. But she was a poor Immortal—a rarity among our kind. She wasn't smart or strong, but she was wicked. I began to realize that I only dated her to get back at my parents. I broke it off time and time again, but she always weaseled her way back in." He brushed a hand across my spikes, his eyes glimmering with fear and wonder. "I was afraid to want someone like you. So, I hid it. I ran from it. I buried it."

I could see that this made him uncomfortable even now. I slid the glamour back into place, but then he raised his hand to touch my cheek.

"Please, stay the way you were. I want to see you—the real you. I'm not a teenager anymore—I can take it."

I let the glamour fall away like a coat to the floor. He breathed in sharply, staring at my hard lines. Part of me felt weird that he was comparing me to a cougar that he knew. But his beauty made it hard to hold a grudge. I glanced back at the walls and he looked at me warily, obviously trying to understand what I was feeling when I looked at the drawings.

I smiled softly at him, silently telling him that I appreciated each piece of art that he'd crafted around me. He pressed his hand against my cheek, pulling me forward as he laid a sweet kiss on my mouth. He pulled away, asking with his eyes if this was okay. In answer, I leaned forward. I traced my tongue along the shell of his ear.

I laughed as he growled, so primal, so male. This time he kissed me roughly, his mouth more urgent, his hands more persistent. He hooked his fingers under my dress and pulled it over my head. I reached out and tugged off his shirt, admiring the planes of his stomach. I traced one finger down his chest, stopping at the v of his hips.

He suddenly grabbed my hand, stopping me from exploring further.

"Do you know what you're getting into?"

"No. But I know you—the real you."

He choked on his own spit.

I may have been confidence and hard steel on the outside, but inside, I was a bundle of nerves that coiled in my stomach, making it tighten. I'd never let this happen, gone this far. What if it went badly or what if he thought of me as a "pet" as my old master did? How should I proceed? Where did my legs go? Was I supposed to lie face up or face down?

I decided to take a chapter from my old master's book and feigned confidence.

"This is nothing I haven't done before."

A blatant lie, but it worked.

His eyes narrowed and he picked me up, gently laying me on the bed. He paused for a second, reaching in his pockets and coming out empty. Then he came to lay next to me, hooking one finger in my bra and removing it in one swift movement. It was clear that he'd done this before. But I wasn't one to give in or let up, especially now, when the stakes were so high.

My breasts sprang free. Dorian palmed my chest. The sensations were odd but welcome—until I remembered things that I didn't want to. Why did I have to remember now? Why did this have to be a thing?

"Please…" I whispered. "Don't…"

"Did you say something?" he paused in his ministrations, tweaking my nipple between his fingers.

"I don't like that. Please stop."

And he stopped.

It was weird but it made me happy. And I respected and thanked him for it. Never had I been listened to in an instance such as this. He did not strike me or tell me to be quiet or even ignore me and continue. He just…*stopped.*

Did that make him weak?

And did that make me weak for respecting him for it?

All I had left on were my underwear. It suddenly hit me full force what I was doing, what I was *about* to do with him. But that was overshadowed by what I wanted, by the weight of my attraction to him. I would lie with a man for the first time in my life and rebel against all those dark thoughts in my head that told me I wasn't pretty enough.

Because he made me feel beautiful.

Chapter Thirty

When It All Goes Up in Flames

When Dorian left the next day, I decided to do something for myself.

I slipped out of the dirty sheets, took a shower and got dressed in the simplest clothes that I could find: a hoodie and some jeans. I pulled my hair up into a messy bun. I also applied some lip gloss. I wanted to blend in with the crowd. But I knew that if I didn't do a little something to enhance my look, I would come off as suspicious.

I looked in the mirror and nodded.

I looked normal.

I walked into Dorian's room to see a box sitting there wrapped neatly in a bow. It had my name scrawled in capital letters on the tag. I opened it to see nothing but an old-world phone. I understood the message almost immediately. He'd be there if I truly needed him.

But me, being young and infatuated, could not resist falling into his gravity.

Yes, I invited him.

I left a voice message to entice him, suggesting the craziest thing that I would ever think of—clubbing. I waited another hour, but he didn't reply. I called one of the emergency contacts, his right-hand in the Rebellion: Rhea. She came to pick me up and took us to Hector Lane, her dark brown afro bobbing as she bopped to a song on the radio. Maybe we could be friends...

"What are you staring at, Skelly?" she asked, not looking at me.

"Aaand the moment is dead! Thank you for that. It was getting a bit too cramped in here anyway."

She laughed.

Her scrap metal junk of a car gave one final growl of protest before stopping completely.

It died. No surprise there.

"How've you been, Rhea?"

"Better than you, I'm sure," she said with a shrug and a lazy grin.

That was as smart-alecky as her comments got that evening. I eyed the woman next to me. She was gorgeous, short but built thick, curves everywhere. Insecurely, I worried that Dorian knew her in a more intimate manner. After all, he seemed to 'know' everyone.

"How well do you know Dorian?"

"Mutual friends." She chuckled then added, "Your memory sucks, Skelly."

I decided not to press the matter. And asked an even more dangerous question.

"How do I know that I shouldn't kill you?" I asked.

She seemed trustworthy enough. The other woman turned to look at me, her golden eyes alight with fire, and said, "You don't." I got out of the car.

"It's okay, Rhea," I said as she hopped out the car before kicking it with her tiny foot. "The club's not too far away, see?"

Sure enough, the light of the club blazed bright and true. *Justice.* No name fit other than this. After all, it was one of the clubs owned by the Archangel, Raphael. He set many religions on their way and now that he'd Fallen, he made his home here on Zuora.

We walked the rest of the way up the hill and to the entrance of the club. Unlike the clubs that I'd seen on TV, there was no line. I raised a brow at Rhea.

"Trust me," she faithfully assured me, "it's lit."

Yeah, I thought as I beheld the inside of the club, *as lit as a sprinkler.*

An elderly, black Mortal couple was doing the cha-cha slide in the middle of the floor. The old woman, with her hair falling in her face, gazed up at her lover adoringly. I prayed that Dorian and I looked at each other like that when I got that age. The black man smiled down at her without a care in the world, his eyes twinkling.

"Oh, Ernest, I can't stand it when you look at me like that," she crooned, leaning her head on his chest.

"Eliza," he murmured, "you'll always be my girl."

"You make me feel like a teenager every time I dance with you!" she squealed, touching her cheeks excitedly. "I love you."

He kissed the top of her head. "Right back at ya."

A faded picture of the owner, the Archangel, was hung on the wall, his arms spread wide and his bare chest glistening with sweat. Rhea led me to a small door in the back. She knocked twice and a huge man standing at seven feet squeezed through the door. His rich brown skin and golden teeth glistened as he beamed at us.

"Password?"

"Micha Slays."

"Right this way, ladies." He moved away from the door to gesture with his hand. As we passed him, he grinned and said, "Enjoy yourselves, okay?"

"Thanks!" I chirped, only sensing the menace in his tone in my memories.

We stepped through the opening, which seemed to stretch to let us through. Here there were nearly a hundred bodies, all squished together as they grinded on the dance floor. There was a long bar squeezed into one of the walls. And above us, dancing, slithering, grinding and quaking, were women inside glass cages, their bare breasts and asses pressed against the glass. One woman fondled herself and just like that, I remembered.

We hadn't used protection last night.

Rhea yelled something over the blast of the music, and I quickly forgot about my dilemma. After all, I was sure that I couldn't get pregnant off one night of fucking…or the day after. The trustworthy Rebel grabbed my hand and towed me to the bar, where a sparkling woman covered in nothing but glitter leaned over the counter. I tried to ignore the way she squeezed towards us, her eyes beckoning. This was not something that I was used to.

I let out a nervous laugh. If Master were to see me here now, he'd tow me away in seconds. That was the one thing that I appreciated about him: he always made modesty a priority.

"What can I get you, sugar?"

I frowned. Sugar? Was she coming on to me?

Rhea elbowed her way next to me and asked for two margaritas. I hopped onto one of the stools next to the counter. A man bumped into Rhea, throwing her small body against mine. I caught her and held her upright as I glared daggers at the man. He turned and looked at me, winking.

"Asshole!" I yelled over the music, but he didn't seem to hear me.

"Don't worry about it!" Rhea yelled to me, cupping her hands around her mouth. "People are always doing stuff like that here! Don't let it bother you!"

"And you *like* coming here?" I yelled back.

She shrugged. "Believe it or not, tonight is pretty tame."

I took the moment to survey her. Her brown skin was even darker than my father's and her golden eyes were like two pools of liquid honey. She wore a black dress with white crosses on it, a leather jacket, combat boots and black choker with a silver cross and chains. Even her cat-like pupils were stunningly beautiful. If I had to guess, I'd say that she was from the jungles of Espanza. When she snapped and a flame appeared in her palm, I looked away, the gesture reminding me of Valentina.

I have to trust her.

She picked up the dainty drink that the bartender had set before her and drank deeply.

"With enough of these in your system, you won't care either." She turned to the bartender. "Take care of my girl."

233

The bartender set the drink before me, which was way bigger than Rhea's. Rhea stopped me before I could grab it, pulled out a vial, and poured it over the glass. Her eyes gleamed wickedly.

"For the full experience."

Don't trust her, a voice told me.

But I didn't listen.

I picked up the large glass filled with a red alcoholic-slushie mixture and a single pink umbrella. It looked cute—harmless. I took a sip. It didn't taste bad, either: sweet, sticky red syrup only barely overcome by the smooth bitterness of alcohol. I threw back my head and guzzled the last of the drink.

My head swam as I straightened. I'd moved too fast.

"Can I get two more of these?" I said to the bartender.

She nodded eagerly and brought me what I asked for. I drank both in quick succession. Despite cooking the meal, I hadn't eaten earlier. And I promise, I wasn't trying to get drunk. I know—the faster you drink, the harder the alcohol hits you. Like I said, I was *not* trying to get drunk.

I was trying to get totally wasted.

But the more I drank, the more I thought about the two men that had integrated their way into my life. I thought of Dorian's hands on my hips—but then some unwelcome thoughts of my old master's fingers fisting my hair entered my mind. And I suddenly realized that everything that brought me here had been a part of something bigger. Maybe *I* was a part of something bigger. Maybe I was destined to rise above, and like a phoenix in the ashes, cheat death.

"You know what I think?" I told Rhea.

But she was gone—she'd disappeared in the crowd.

"Great! Now I've gotta go find her!"

I sloppily jumped from my stool.

The world rocked and sloshed. I straightened up. For a moment, everything seemed too close, then too far away. There was a heat in my belly from the alcohol, but it was different from lust or nervousness—thicker, somehow. I tried to count how many drinks I'd had by counting on my fingers but got stuck on how funny my fingers looked. They were so *tiny*! This made me laugh.

I stumbled through the crowd, eyeing every face. I didn't see her. I was overtaken by the urge to urinate, so I made my way towards the bathroom. The walls in the bathroom were stained with smut and piss. I made it to the toilet, sighing in relief. Suddenly, someone banged on the door.

"Someone's in here!" I yelled, blinking slowly.

That pounding reverberated through the room.

I flushed, then pulled up my underwear and jeans. Whoever was out there wasn't leaving anytime soon. I washed my hands before yanking the door open.

"Hey, buddy! What's your problem?!"

"Darling," he said in a smooth, clear voice. "There you are."

A scream ripped from my throat. My powers exploded around me. He reached out one pale hand, the nail on his pointer finger long and black, and pressed it against my cheek. A swell of blood rose where his nail met my jaw. I raised an electricity-infused hand and karate chopped his head, watching with pride as he stumbled, his eyes dazed for one precious moment. I pushed past him and sprinted for the door. But he was everywhere, invading my senses in a vicious assault.

The world closed in around me. Jacques's scent filled my lungs, clogged my veins. I couldn't see, gods dammit! I couldn't—

And then there was the cool night air around me. The sweat was plastered to my skin, making my clothes stick to my frame. Sweating was a new sensation, one that only happened when I was in my glamoured form, like now. My eyes cut through the darkness. The world teetered, slurred and then stilled. I raced to Rhea's car to find her leaning on the hood, smoking.

"Let's go, let's go, let's go!" I screamed.

"What's the rush, Marve?" She asked me, giggling.

"We don't have all day! We've gotta go!"

"S'is okay, love. S'is okay," she slurred.

She leaped in the front seat and jammed her key into the ignition. But it didn't start. I leaped out and lifted the hood. I poured electricity from my body into the car. It roared to life.

"Start it now!" I cried, running to the passenger side.

And that stupid woman sped off without me!

"Sorry!" She leaned out the window. "Too slow!"

I heard Jacques's laugh behind me. I pulled out my cellphone and dialed the one man who could save me.

"I need your help!"

***

When we got home, Dorian changed the locks. Our little issue from this morning was not at the forefront of my mind, but it didn't mean that I didn't care. When I told Dorian about seeing Jacques, he cursed. That's when he told me that Jacques wasn't the only one hunting me down—the Rebellion had thugs all over the place, waiting for the opportune moment to strike. "Trust no one but Rhea," he told me. A heaviness settled on my heart.

If Dorian got hurt because of me...

Dorian's stomach rumbled and he eyed me from across the room. I didn't feel like cooking, but my years from being with Jacques taught me to always keep moving. I moved the chicken into bags, beat it, made homemade seasoning for the green beans using onion powder, salt and Ranch packets. I cooked dinner in record time, setting the cordon bleu before Dorian with pride. He asked me how I knew that cordon bleu was his favorite. I shrugged. I didn't even know that. I just wanted to try something different for him.

I sprinkled some more salt on my green beans before shoveling a forkful into my mouth.

"Mm..."

While we were eating, we discussed different places that we could go to evade the two parties hunting us. He mentioned his manor. As badly as I wanted to see Dorian's childhood home, I really didn't want to put his territory in danger. Dorian took my hand across the table. The ache that resounded in my heart was dull but still there, nonetheless.

"I need to keep you safe." His voice was a low rumble. "I'd give up everything as long as you're okay."

From day one, he'd protected me—and since then, he *always* stuck his neck out to save my skin.

I swallowed the bite in my mouth. He was truly too good for me.

"Thank you, Dorian." I whispered, gazing deeply into his eyes. "I don't know what I would do without you."

"When the time comes, I need you to trust me wholeheartedly."

I nodded vigorously. He'd done so much for me already. How could I not trust him?

When we were done eating, I did the dishes before taking a shower. I let the hot water soothe me, rolling my shoulders to ease the tension there. When I got out, I asked to borrow one of Dorian's shirts. He gave me the oversized T-shirt willingly. I put it on before crawling into Dorian's bed.

I curled into his side. Dorian reached out and pulled the scrunchie from my hair, making my hair fall around my face like a curtain. He brushed the hair out of my face, gazing deeply into my eyes. I was unprepared for his urgent kiss or his hands that roughly grabbed my waist and yanked me forward. I kissed him back, tasting the bittersweet of his tongue.

I laid my head on his chest before drifting off to sleep. I felt his arms around me, and I knew that I was safe. I didn't dream of Jacques or Tiara, but I didn't dream of Dorian, either.

I didn't dream at all.

As a result, the haze of sleep was dark, peaceful and totally welcome. And I was grateful for it.

In many ways, Dorian was my savior.

Chapter Thirty-One

How Deep Are These Waters?

Time passed in the blink of an eye. I'd wanted to relocate to a new safehouse but admitted that I was worried about moving too soon when our trail was so hot. What if one of our pursuers saw us leave? When I walked through the streets, I sometimes saw Jacques's face, but I knew that if it were him, he would have made his move by now. Dorian assured me that we were still going to go to the party with the Immortals and find the two Immortals who recognized me, but he didn't tell me *how* we were going to take care of it. But I knew from our last conversation that I *had* to trust him.

Everything he was doing was for me—for *us*.

On the night of the party, we practiced dances. We pre-planned how we'd walk in. We rehearsed how fast to move if problems were to arise and we had to leave. I didn't expect things to go to complete crap, but I didn't want to hope too much, either. I now stood in my bra and panties before Rhea.

To be honest, I didn't like being naked in front of other people. It was scary. It made me think all kinds of mean thoughts about myself, made me think that they were thinking sinfully of me, that I would become their 'pet' for the day. But she was a girl. Girls didn't do stuff like that to other girls, right?

I told myself that I'd be fine.

"So which dress should I wear?"

I held up two dresses: one was a silky purple number with intricate petal-like folds, while the other was a red sheath dress with a long slit up the side that exposed my right leg. Dorian had them stitched along with some clothes for himself; apparently, he didn't like wearing Jacques's clothes. Rhea, clad in skinny jeans and a blue sweatshirt, answered immediately.

"I like the purple one," she said, a spark of envy in her eyes. "It makes a statement."

"And that statement would be...?" I raised an eyebrow.

"That despite what the Immortals try to force-feed you, you are beautiful and truly one-of-a-kind."

"Aw, thanks."

She held up a hand. "I'm not saying that. The dress is."

I made a kissy face at her, momentarily forgetting my terror. "If I didn't know any better, I'd say you had a crush on me."

She scratched her cheek, blushing. "Yeah, yeah—don't let it get to your head. Besides, I'm leaning towards men right now anyways."

I shrugged. "Doesn't mean you can't find me attractive."

Her eyes touched the top of her head. "You're really fishing for a compliment, aren't you, Marve?"

I smiled. "Perhaps. Or maybe I'm just messing with you."

"You don't wanna mess with me," she said, "I'll break your heart."

"Not like that," I said, somehow looking up at the 5'3" woman. "I meant that I was kidding."

"Dios mios," she spat. "Are you sure you speak English?"

My head cocked to the side. "Why are you always so hostile around me?"

She didn't answer.

I strapped on my sheath to the middle of my leg, right above my knee. I slid one of my many daggers into the sheath. Then I slid the dress over my head and down my body. Rhea fluffed the folds, her hands lingering on the folds that could conceal a vast armada.

I couldn't really blame her.

It was a beautiful dress and I felt beautiful in it.

I held my head a little taller. And the darkness ebbed away another fraction.

Rhea came up behind me. I sat down in front of the mirror. I was in Dorian's (formerly-Jacques's) room since my room had no mirrors. To be honest, it was kinda weird that Jacques designed the rooms like that. Yes, he was conceited—but was he really that insecure that he didn't want anyone to admire their own beauty?

He wanted us to believe that we were ugly.

He wanted to tear us down.

He wanted to break us.

I was constantly feeling defeated but not totally broken. He'd cracked the shell

242

of my armor, but his arrow had missed the strong woman beneath. Now look at me. I was going to a party to dance with the Immortals. I was a snake hidden in the grove.

I'd left Jacques behind. Together, Dorian and I left the Rebellion behind. Now we'd gone rogue. It was dangerous, Rhea had reminded me this morning—a decision that left us with too many enemies and too little allies. But it was also an opportunity, one that we couldn't let slip by.

At this party that Megumi was throwing, we could find friends. I glanced at the sun/hawk branding on Rhea's neck and shuddered. Friends outside of the Rebellion.

Rhea pulled me back to the present as she ran a comb through my hair.

"So do you know the people at this party?" She said in her thick Espanzan accent.

Where Maeoran accents were heavy and kind of like grunts, Espanzan accents were sexy and discreet. Listening to Rhea talk was like listening to Aretha Franklin sing a love song: haunting and seductive.

"I know of them," I answered.

"I wish I could go…"

"Who says you can't?" I met her gaze in the mirror. "You can wear the other dress. You *can* go."

"Oh, no!" She shook her head vehemently. "I wasn't invited."

"*I'm* inviting you right now." I turned to look at her full on. "Why won't you come? Then at least I'd know one person there."

"First off, you don't know me." Her golden eyes met mine as she looked at me through the mirror. "*Segundo*, my face is too well known. I'm part of the Rebellion,

243

remember?"

"I was, too!" I defended.

"Yeah, for like a week," she insisted, rolling her eyes. "I get that you mean well but it's not happening. Just because you and Dorian left doesn't mean that I can too. We all have our priorities."

"But—"

"She's not going."

I jumped. There was Dorian, a look in his eyes that demanded respect. Rhea smirked at me in the mirror in a look that said *"Gotcha!"* I wasn't one to kneel. I lifted my chin a fraction higher.

"And why is that?"

"We're on a mission," Dorian replied definitively. "You don't need any distractions. Besides, she's not an undercover agent like me. The Immortals know who she is. If she goes, she'll be killed."

He left no room for discussion.

"What about me?" I asked, staring at him in the mirror. "They know my face from the Ring. Don't you care if something happens to me?"

"Aren't you usually in your natural form?" Rhea asked, raising a brow.

"How do you know that?"

"Dorian would tape your matches and play them for the other Rebels."

I saw Dorian's face. He was embarrassed. I was too scared to ask why.

"He wanted us to see what an asset you'd be," Rhea finished.

Now I was confused. I thought the Rebellion had wanted to recruit me since I was young. If that was so, they wouldn't have to watch me.

"Why would you need to do that?"

"Valentina still correlated with the Rebellion while working with Jacques," Rhea said with a sigh. "She was worried that you might become a problem if we pulled you out too early."

I snorted. "A problem?"

"Enough, Rhea."

"Why would she think I'd be a problem?"

"Well—"

"*Enough*, Rhea!"

"No." I shook my head. "I want to know why."

"She knew what Jacques was doing to you and she was afraid that you might be in love with him," Dorian reluctantly mumbled.

My thoughts ran to a standstill. His words echoed in my head. *She knew what Jacques was doing to you. In love with him.*

She knew...

She knew...?

She knew!

"She knew?" I repeated back.

Rhea shook her head. "She just told us that she thought you might be compromised. She didn't tell us why."

"She knew and she didn't do anything?" I choked on the words.

"What happened?" Rhea asked, staring at me in the mirror.

245

I shook my head as my mouth wired shut. I was trembling with rage. She knew that he molested me, and she did nothing to help?! I knew that Tiara didn't know she wasn't even allowed in his part of the mansion. But Valentina…?

I thought of her as an aunt—*idolized her*—and she did nothing to stop it?!

I took this piece of information and buried it deep. I couldn't use it now. I refused to let it ruin this night. I fixed a smile on my face as I thought of happier things: Dorian's face when sunlight reflected off his skin. Tiara's smile when we would sneak into the kitchen, sprinkling sugar on ice and munching on it happily. My parents' laughter as they spun around in the kitchen, my mother's singing floating through my head.

I saw Dorian's frown as he left to suit up. He looked angry—like he couldn't protect me. Like it hurt him to see me hurt. I knew that if he'd been in the mansion with Jacques and I, he would have broken the other man's hand before he let him touch me.

And it made me happy to know that he cared.

I turned back around to face the mirror. Rhea got to work on my hair, pulling it into an elaborate working of braids. She reached out to grab the small, jeweled crown that sat atop the dresser, a gift from Dorian. I watched her work with inexperienced eyes, trying to follow her movements.

That's why it was good to have another black woman working on my hair. She knew how to do all the styles and how to work with my grade of hair. I thought of my mother as she plaited my hair in front of the bathroom mirror and smiled—the first genuine smile in what felt like forever. Mar always lovingly said that I had her color hair, but my father's grade, which I was always proud of, because it meant I was a little bit of everything.

She placed the crown atop my head. I looked like a princess. But I didn't merely look the part—I felt it, too. The point of this entire outfit was to look like— no, to *become* one of *them*—an Immortal. I was far from immortal, as mortal as they come, but *they* didn't know that.

And being on the arm of one of the wealthiest Immortals north of Sidra was a huge advantage. Dorian had over half of Amoria doing his bidding. Smuggling Gifted out of the northern territories and into the Southern Isles was his specialty.

This was his first time taking a Gifted into his territory as his guest, where Megumi was throwing a party. Megumi was originally from the southside of Amoria but had moved north to 'scout for new territory.' Personally, I think she moved to be closer to Dorian. After all, he was stunning and had personality to boot. And I'd be lying if I said it didn't make me a little jealous.

After all, she could spend eternity with him, while I could only give him a few good years that would pass in the blink of an eye.

I kept my insecurities to myself, but I knew one thing: I was going to make him remember me.

Now that my hair was out of my face, Rhea went to work on my makeup. The dresser was littered with foundation, concealer, mascara—you know, the works. But she bypassed all of that. She grabbed a tube of gold, glittering gloss and spread it across my lips. Then she put on some eyeshadow that was also gold and glittery, matching my crown. She finished the look my adding a light coat of blush.

"I'd add mascara, but your eyelashes are already long enough. Any longer and they'd drag on the floor."

"Rhea," I gaped, "are you jealous?"

"Stop flirting with me, you whore," she cracked a grin, only half-serious.

I looked in the mirror. My makeup was simple but elegant—it was like I'd tried but not too hard. The gold crown that adorned my head had a jewel in the center literally made from starlight, which was clear with a glow on the inside that changed colors depending on the light. Rhea handed me some gold bangles, and I realized that the purpose of this was to set off the sparkly look—even my dress had golden sparkles in it. But why?

"Wow."

I turned around. There was Dorian in a tuxedo that sharpened every angle of his rigid body. His golden skin glowed with magic and the gold-and-brown flecks in his eyes swam with an almost possessive adulation as he appraised me. That look—it could set worlds on fire. That's when I realized the second reason for this look. It was to tell the world tonight that I was his and his alone.

His eyes raked up and down my body as though he liked what he saw, too. I stood up, gathering the folds of my dress in my hands, and glided over to him. I'd practiced my walk too, wanting to appear as smooth and graceful as any Immortal. I'd say that I passed. Dorian placed a hand under my chin.

"You're beautiful," he said, looking at me the way he would before he kissed me.

I tried to sound confident. "You're not half bad yourself."

248

Instead, my voice was a little hoarse. But who could blame me? The man was stunning.

"I'm not gonna front," Rhea said, nodding. "You two look like a major power couple. I wasn't sure about you at first, Marve. I mean, Dorian had been working alongside the Rebellion since he got his inheritance. It was weird that he just cut all ties with our cause. But now...? I can see it."

"Thanks..." I mumbled, blushing.

A part of me had still thought he left it behind for himself...Not me. But hearing her say it aloud made me blush even harder. I'd *changed* him, maybe not in every way, but in the important ones.

And he'd changed me, too.

"You're my queen," Dorian said, his eyes ripping off my dress and devouring me. "Never forget that."

I nodded, at a loss for words.

"You ready to go?"

I nodded again.

"All right. The car's outside." He turned to Rhea. "Thank you for helping."

"It was nothing," she replied.

He reached into his pocket and pulled out four gold drachmas. He placed them in Rhea's palm. She looked down at them as if they were nothing. It was odd, seeing a half-Immortal half-Gifted pay another who was also half-and-half for something other than a fight that their slaves had gotten into. But based on what Rhea said, she didn't have slaves, and if Dorian was to be believed, neither did he.

Her golden eyes twinkled with a thousand secrets. I wanted to know them all.

Dorian took my hand and helped me to the car.

The gravel was rough on my feet but not unwelcome. It was common for Gifted to go without shoes and he'd warned me that I had to hide the fact that I had not donned them tonight. When we were first enslaved, the Immortals took our shoes and made us walk to our new houses while they rode in fancy cars. We turned it on them and made it a symbol of pride—to go without shoes was to be a part of a special club. I wore none tonight—a symbol of my defiance. It was now July, the middle of summer. I took in the night air, still and quiet as usual—dead. If this were the Old World, there would be grass and more wildlife other than the few birds that had survived the Great Heat—but since it was not, there was nothing but gravel and concrete. Hopefully there would be more wildlife up north.

The sky still had a touch of light when we got into the car. Dorian and I sat in the backseat. A man sat up front—a chauffeur, I realized.

"Where to this evening, Boyd, sir?"

"Take us to the country of lights. Take us to the party."

One may call to question how we could travel across the American continent so quickly. Here's how: each country was connected by invisible portals. Travel to one wall and you reached the next portal. These portals were only usable if you had someone with Immortal ancestry with you. This is why the Gifted had such trouble running away. I once heard about a Gifted person that hacked off their master's arm and tried to cross the barriers that way but alas, the Immortal had to be living and willing. That's what made the Rebellion's alliance with the select Immortals so fantastic—we had a taste of true freedom.

The Gifted could live without masters but were forbidden from most jobs—unless you could keep them without higher education. We could work but had to pay a 'fee' for the upkeep of the Walls. With food and other necessities, we had to pay higher taxes. And we had to wear special armbands that marked us as what we were. If we were caught by Slave Catchers, the government would do nothing to intervene. At least, with Masters, we were guaranteed food, water, heat and shelter. And in school, we were taught a separate regimen than Immortal and Mortal children.

In school, Gifted children were taught that we were all 'within and without.' We were taught to be ashamed, how to hide our looks. And we were taught how to use first aid without modern technology, how to kindle fires and set tables. It was all geared towards enslavement. It wasn't unusual for classmates to go missing or to show up with bruises where the Mortal children had jumped them. Even in their adolescence, Mortals and Immortals had a sort of alliance.

And the few Gifted that penetrated these circles became spies, watchdogs for their masters. They told the authorities when and if someone was planning to leave. They told if anyone was thinking of staging a coup. And they were rewarded. A thick slice of pound cake went a long way in the eyes of one without sugar.

That's why some Gifted fought for the Immortals.

We neared Wall Seinaru. I thought of the cat-like woman and wondered if she had changed at all since I'd last seen her.

The party was smack dab in the middle of Amoria, the northernmost country on this continent. I didn't know much of the other continents other than Africa, which

Dorian told me was untouched by magic. Something about that made little sense since he owned land there and Immortals generally kept their territory aflame with magic. Then again, this house was unprotected so maybe he was telling the truth. I wondered what it was like to be the richest man out of an entire country like Dorian.

It must be nice—nice but lonely, for no one was your equal.

Jacques owned a good deal of Sidra, but I knew that he didn't own as much as Dorian. At least we had him beat in that prospect.

"What's Amoria like?" I asked Dorian, peering out the window as we passed the murky swamp.

"It's very cold. It's usually covered in snow but right now, the snow has melted, so the forest is very temperate. Gifted people there have thick hair, like fur."

"Where's your fur, wolf-man?" I asked, tracing a finger across his leg.

He laughed.

I remembered a conversation that Dorian and I had a month ago. Not only had Dorian allowed Megumi to move onto his land fifty years ago, but he'd also gifted her with forty 'workers' to begin her empire. I guess he saw something in her, something that he liked, something that appealed to his Immortal half. It was now 2120 and she still hadn't left. Did he allow her to stay because he had feelings for her?

Was that it? Was this his way of giving up on me? He was going to take me there, show me what I was missing for choosing not to be with him...

My heart couldn't take it.

Dorian rested his hand on my knee. I pulled out of the intrusive, insecure

252

thoughts. It was me wearing his crown. It was me that he went to sleep with and woke up next to every morning. And it was me that he loved, *not her.*

"Now what will you do while we're here?"

"Stay quiet. Keep by your side. Only speak when spoken to."

"The trick here, when the abuse happens, is to think of something funny. It's easier to pretend that you're in a movie—that these aren't other conscious, intelligent creatures being tormented by our kind, but actors. Pretend to watch through a lens. That way they can see the amusement in your eyes."

"I can't imagine…How can I find this funny? I'm one of them."

"You *were* one of them."

"…"

"Do you understand?"

"I'll always be Gifted. You can't take that away from me. No one can."

"Just play pretend," he sighed. "Fix a mask on your face. What's that Mortal saying…? Fake it till the cows come home?"

I said nothing.

"Have you ever been to one of these parties before?"

"Only one. It came to an *abrupt* end."

This was after my old Master helped himself to one of the slaves of Mistress Amator. The two were still good friends to this day. But she rarely visited and even then, she always left her male help behind.

We passed through one checkpoint to get to Amoria. We made our way up the driveway to a house that was pretty enough, but rather lackluster. Even my old master's place was more elegant than this. Dorian took my hand and helped me out of the car. We stopped at the front door and checked in before heading inside.

Only when we stepped inside did I realize that I had it all wrong.

High vaulted ceilings rose to make the big house seem even more spacious. The walls were a deep indigo with black trim. The entrance hall seemed to stretch for miles on end. Dorian placed his hand on the small of my back, leading me through the foyer and down a hall into a huge ballroom. Immortals stood around with two Gifted slaves per Master or Mistress.

I looked around, suddenly realizing that we were the only ones without slaves. I was suddenly greeted with a horrifying thought: was I to play the slave?! Dorian moved his hand to place it on my waist, pulling me close.

No, I realized, *of course not. He wouldn't hold me so intimately if that were the case. Thank Kalysma!*

I looked up at him, but he looked straight forward, his back erect and his eyes dancing in amusement. I was afraid to see what he saw. After all, he said to feign amusement when someone was being abused.

I followed his line of sight and my stomach rolled over with nausea.

A Gifted slave stood with his back to me, his hands raised as if lifting a great weight. In the air, another Gifted slave floated, her hair twitching around her head like green tentacles. She was stark naked, her eyes screwed shut as if she were in pain. Her breasts rose and fell as she heaved breath after agonizing breath. Masters and Mistresses stood around her, gawking and laughing while their slaves stood in the background, avoiding all eye contact.

I knew what they were thinking because I had immediately fallen into that role: *I hope I'm not next.*

Dorian led me to one Master. He nudged the man, who had a large potbelly and a thick brown-and-grey mustache. His voice lowered as if he didn't want me to hear but I heard Dorian address the man as Grayson.

What was he saying?

The man laughed and told us that this slave, who he called a "damned thing," had spilled a drink on her mistress. So, he got his slave to trap her in what he called a "sphere of pain." He said it as if it were commonplace.

And I suddenly remembered him—he was the same Immortal that had bet against Jacques in the Ring of Death—the one that sent Natalia to her final resting place. I felt angered and saddened by this realization. He had not changed since then, seeming no closer to death nor redemption.

It shouldn't be commonplace to strip someone of their dignity, to humiliate them.

I tried to smile but could not.

These people weren't people—these were monsters. And tonight, Dorian was one of them. Dorian slapped the mustachio man on the back and grinned. This time I forced a smile on my face. It hurt but damn it, I had to fit in.

Or else I'd be discovered and killed...or worse, reclaimed.

I glanced around to see if Jacques was there. I couldn't see him, but my paranoia was vivid—it demanded that I check twice. I looked around one more time. There were at least a hundred people here but even in this sea of faces, to me he would always stand out.

I didn't see him.

Dorian and I silently slinked away from the small crowd that was forming. Dorian took me to a table filled with shrimp, lobster tail and mussels. I picked up one of the platters with shrimp and cocktail sauce. I swirled the shrimp in the cocktail sauce for a moment, beating down the thoughts that said it was like blood, only thicker.

I wasn't a slave anymore—I didn't have to step into the Ring of Death ever again.

I ate a few shrimps, just barely keeping them down. It made me sick, knowing that they were doing that just a few feet away. But I'd be okay. I picked up a glass of chardonnay, sipping at it tentatively. Dorian downed three glasses of champagne, his eyes losing focus, his cheeks becoming flushed.

Maybe this was why he drank. Maybe it was too hard for him to be what everyone expected him to be. Maybe he felt guilty.

A familiar man found Dorian, wearing a flashy three-piece suit. His teeth gleamed with gold as he grinned. I remembered my father once saying that whatever man wears gold in this life, will not see gold in the next. Did that hold true for the Immortals as well—for any of the magic folk? He gripped Dorian's hand for a long moment before glancing at me. Dorian stumbled, but his eyes hardened, sobering, when he recognized him.

"Well, well, well!" The man grinned. "If it isn't my favorite brother from Amoria! How's it going, Golden Immortal?"

"It'd be fine if you'd stay off my case," Dorian ground through a fake smile.

"Come now." The white Immortal's eyes flashed dangerously, and I wondered what Dorian was going to say to get him to leave me alone, to let me go. "It's just business."

"Speaking of business," Dorian looked over him, "I have a proposition."

"I'm listening."

"Come with me," Dorian put his hand on his shoulder, "away from listening ears."

The Immortal cut a glance at me. "And prying eyes?"

"The ones who'll know," Dorian's fingers tightened, "are those who need to."

He didn't deliberate. "Well, all right."

I stood there, watching, waiting to see if he'd need me. For what felt like hours, I waited for any kind of confirmation that the man took the bait. When Dorian finally found his way back to me, the man had made his way across the room. He tightened his belt. He and Dorian locked eyes for a tense moment, and I wondered again if he could be bought off. But then he raised his glass, nodded, and looked away. I blew out a breath.

"Is that it?"

"He won't be saying anything."

I grinned. "So, we're good then?"

"For now." He paused. "There is one other potential problem."

My stomach writhed. Of course. It couldn't be *that* easy. "What is it?"

Everyone turned to stare at another spectacle. I was almost afraid to look.

257

Megumi was covered in a crème-colored body suit that clung to her curves. Diamonds covered her chest, but you could tell from the arch of the material that she had it going on. She wore a pair of matching heels. And around her neck hung a necklace that gleamed with a prismatic color: starlight.

Dorian watched her every step, his eyes trained on her as if she were a panther slinking through the brush. I elbowed him in the stomach. He coughed. She made her way over to us, her eyes switching between Dorian and I as if sizing us up. I was unprepared when she threw herself into Dorian's arms, planting a kiss square on his mouth. He stumbled back but she held on tight, digging her claws into his shoulders. When she finally decided to release him, she looked me dead in the eye, a challenging gleam in her gaze.

I wanted to throttle her. No, I wanted more than that. I wanted to pull out the dagger from its sheath and drive it into her wicked, slutty heart. Her catty eyes gleamed with that of a thousand glittering knives.

Dorian took a handkerchief out of his pocket. Wiped his mouth before spitting into it. The he held out the handkerchief. "Want your gum back?"

She was not amused.

He stepped away, taking my hand in his.

Megumi frowned for a fraction of a second before smiling. But I could see the anger, the humiliation in her eyes.

That's right, lady. He chose me.

"How are you doing, Megumi?" I asked, forcing her to acknowledge me.

"I'm sorry." She smirked at me. "Who are you?"

258

"This is my girl," Dorian said, wrapping his arm around my waist. "She's from Espanza."

She raised a brow. "Let me say this loud and slow, in a way that you'll understand: *Él es mío.*"

"Not hardly," Dorian interjected. "We had a thing once but that was a long time ago. We've both moved on, right, Megumi?"

She pouted, jutting out her bottom lip. "Don't be that way, baby."

Electricity crackled up and down my spine, heating my flesh. I had to fight to keep it contained. But it was as if she'd lit a flame under my skin, flaying me to a crisp of jealousy. I had no choice but to react. Dorian squeezed my waist, silently telling me to calm down.

"Come now, Dory," she purred, giving him a sultry look. "You know you miss this."

Her hands twined around his shoulders. He removed them and took a step back, towards me. I tried not to leap for joy when he reached for my hand.

"I think he's made his decision…"

"Do you wanna go, bitch?" she snapped back.

I threw my head back and guffawed. (Definitely not my most ladylike moment.) "I bet I can take you."

She eyed me up and down. I reached up to adjust my crown. Her eyes narrowed at the movement.

"You gave her starlight!" She turned to gape at Dorian. "That was our thing."

My heart stopped in my chest. *Their thing?*

His face paled. "Stop. I said we could be friends. Let's keep it that way."

"Dorian..." Her lip wobbled in a sudden display of sadness. I could see her pain but felt no sympathy. "You don't mean that."

"I do." He took a step back. "We're not good for each other."

"But we're perfect together."

"You're doing great on your own."

My heart paused in my chest. I hated hearing him compliment her.

But she wouldn't give up without a fight. Her eyes flashed. "You're mine. And I'm your—"

"Megumi," his voice was low, "this is embarrassing."

I barked out a laugh. The other woman stood there in shock. Dorian took my hand and led me away.

It wasn't until we were at the edge of the ballroom that she retorted: "I know who you are. I know who's looking for you."

A roll of panic befell me. I grabbed my head as it suddenly started to ache, like a thousand gongs were banging in my head. Dorian watched me carefully, waiting until we were back in the hallway to scoop me into his arms. I leaned my head on his chest. He held me tighter, taking me outside.

A black car pulled around, that same driver from before in the front seat.

"This was a bad idea. We should never have come here."

Dorian gently placed me in the car. Then he ran around to the other side and got in. The car sped off without a word from Dorian.

Even the driver sensed his urgency.

I looked at the shadows dancing along Dorian's face. We passed under a light. I saw him clearly. Then we passed under a bridge and the darkness overtook him once more. I reached out in the dark and he took my hand.

"Dorian?"

He turned to me silently, his eyes graver than sin.

"Kiss me."

He reached out and pulled my head towards his. He combed his fingers through my hair, undoing the braids and letting my hair fall in loose waves around my face. I leaned forward. His mouth brushed mine once. Our breath mingled in the space between us.

And then he was kissing me with an animalistic ferocity, his lips rough and urgent against mine. All I saw was him and his ex, kissing. And suddenly I was angry because he had to have kept in contact with her—why else would she have reacted so strongly to him? He traced his tongue along my bottom lip. I refused to grant him access, keeping my mouth firmly shut, but my lips were still puckered.

He growled. I shuddered as a moan of want left me. He picked me up and placed me on his lap, me straddling him as I felt his want through the folds of my dress.

Nausea hit me again and my body rolled as if I were on the choppy waves of the sea. I got off his lap, holding as still as possible. The nausea subsided slightly, enough for me to raise my head to look at him. He was watching me. I managed to muster a weak smile, one that he returned.

"Are you still having those nightmares?"

I shook my head. He already knew that, of course. But neither of us knew what it meant.

"Megumi recognized you." He looked angry, his golden face turning a deep red as his sharp jaw flexed. "She knew who you were from the moment she saw you. She knows you're Gifted. She knows who you belong to."

"Used to."

"What?"

"She knows who I *used* to belong to. I am no one's now."

"Not even mine?" Dorian asked, looking at me imploringly.

I looked away. The night sky was beautiful, stars gleaming in every direction I looked. The crescent moon sat highest in the sky, its beautiful face round and open for all to see.

I do not belong to you, I wanted to say. *I am not a product that you bought. I am not a slave that you claimed. I am my own. I am free.*

But I knew that he would take it the wrong way, so I kept my mouth shut.

I thought back to Megumi kissing him. As soon as I saw it in my mind's eye, my blood started to boil. It was time to face facts.

I'd given him my body. I'd given him part of my soul. I wanted him—all of him. I knew that now.

So why couldn't I say it?

Maybe I should keep my options open, I thought, knowing that he was doing the same. But then I realized, *I have none.*

I leaned over, resting my head on his shoulder. He sighed. Then he linked an arm around my shoulders. I smiled to myself. I hadn't lost him yet.

He was mine for the time being.

But then darker, more depressing thoughts came in. I let myself mope.

The party was a total bust. We have no allies. We got scared and ran like cowards. Of course, it should have been obvious that we would come out with nothing. What was the point of even going?

Dorian squeezed my shoulder, his face tender as he stared out the window. And it suddenly hit me: he was throwing me in Jacques's face. He knew that Megumi would report back to him, knew that this batch of Immortals would not yield any assistance and knew that showing me off was as much to tease Jacques as it was to ignite Mimi. I didn't understand why the two meant so much to Dorian, why he would go so far just to prove that he had what they didn't.

How deep was their relationship, really? How well did the three truly know each other? If they'd all hooked up, I wanted to know. If Jacques had courted Dorian and given him the chance to walk away, I wanted to know. If he simply wanted him and Dorian was a frigging tease, I wanted to know. I didn't like being kept in the dark.

It drove me wild.

You're complicated, I thought, *and you hold your secrets close to your chest.*

I thought of the pale man, realizing that he would be enraged knowing that I was so close, yet so far.

I have my secrets, too.

Chapter Thirty-Two

The Last One Standing

I walked through the near-empty streets of Sidra two days later. I should have known that something bad would happen—nothing good ever comes from strolling around a dark street at midnight. An old Mortal man sat on the corner, mumbling to himself. I reached into my pocket and pulled out two drachmas. I put them into the tin cup sitting next to him. I briefly wondered why Dorian never let me leave the house without [at least] a few drachmas on hand.

Was it out of necessity or paranoia?

I walked past a hookah shop before stopping in front of a rundown pawnshop. Inside, silver and gold gleamed like stars and boxes were lined up neatly in brown-stained corners. Graffiti decorated one-fourth of the main wall. On closer inspection, if I tilted my head just right, I realized that it was a hawk snatching up a gelatinous blob that looked like the sun.

Now where had I seen that before?

"You like my artwork, precious?"

I jumped about a foot in the air, my powers kicking on with a jolting *crack!* I whirled around to see two young women standing at the corner, making their way towards me with matching sneers on their faces. I heard rather than saw the *creak-creak-swish, creak-creak-swish* of their butterfly knives flipping opening in succession. Caught off guard, I backed away until my back hit the wall. One girl laughed.

They were dressed in all black. I thought back to that graffiti on the wall. Where had I seen it?

"See that spot right there?" The first girl pointed at the hawk on the wall. "That means it's our territory."

"It's the sidewalk," I said bravely, ignoring the gleaming blades in their hands in favor of my own weapon, my own power. "What makes this spot more yours than mine?"

"Ooh, you hear that, Gina?"

"Yeah, Bree?" said the second girl.

"The kid's got balls."

They both had matching brandings on their necks. When the first stepped into a patch of moonlight, I noticed a thick scar running from her forehead to her bottom lip. I frowned, wondering who she played slice and dice with. The girl glared at me, knowing that her scar was exactly what I was staring at. I didn't budge as my gaze locked with hers.

If she wanted me, she could have me. But I couldn't promise that she would walk away in one piece...or at all for that matter.

"You got a staring problem, precious?"

"No but judging from the looks of your scar," I tapped my cheek, "I'd say someone got you good."

"Excuse me, precious?"

"Look, honey." Gina gave me a warning look. "Bad mouthing ain't gonna get you nowhere but face down in the gutter, ya digs?"

"I'd rather be face down than stuck looking at Scar over here. But at least she's still got her health, eh, Mufasa?"

"I'm gonna make you wish you were never born, precious," said Bree.

"You suicidal or something?" Gina eyed me.

I was. But I wanted a good fight. And I wanted to go out on my terms.

Bree turned, her dark face still harsh with what I perceived to be anger. Her Espanzan companion's (Gina) sneer fell away and I saw one corner of Bree's mouth turn down. I suddenly realized that Bree couldn't un-scowl; her face was stuck just like that. The need to release my powers grew with every passing second. I shifted, uncomfortable. Bree's scowl deepened and for a second, I thought that maybe she *could* change her face.

To something uglier, that is.

I saw the thick hair on Bree's arms and legs, the bear-like set of her eyes, and realized that she was Amorian. I was willing to bet that she was a Gifted person from Dorian's territory. I briefly wondered if he knew her or if he'd brought her into the Rebellion himself. Maybe if I told her that I knew him, they'd let me go. Then again, they'd *have* to know that, or they wouldn't be after me.

With a roar, the first girl charged at me. I spun and my foot landed in her gut, bringing her to a temporary halt. She grunted but kept on coming, her friend falling behind to flank her. I paused to listen to her racing heart, wanting a good fight. Before I realized what was happening, Bree had me pinned, her switchblade digging into the bottom lid of my left eye.

I kept stock still. I didn't want that blade going any deeper.

"You know how much you and Sparkles are worth?" Bree whispered in my ear. "2.4 million drachmas a piece. They didn't say you had to come back in one piece though. Now where should I start?" Her blade found its way to my tongue before she brought it to my ears. "Changed my mind. I wanna hear you scream."

"Make it quick, Bree," complained Gina. "I gotta see Jaxon in thirty."

Bree turned to answer.

My head flew forward, ramming Bree. The girl rolled off me with a groan, clutching her bloody nose. Her friend watched from the sidelines, eyes darting between the two of us as she obviously tried to find an opening. My fist flew out, crashing into Bree's face with a delicious crunch. Her head went flying back, blood spurting from her already-injured nose.

"Gotcha!" I giggled.

I knew that I was a bit of my old master in that moment, a bit of a sadist. You couldn't sleep among beasts without becoming one. Still, it surprised me even then at the thrill that jolted through me at causing another pain. I felt a heat in my stomach and a throb between my legs. I was my master's girl all right.

"You little runt!"

Bree came at me again, fists flying. Her fighting was muddled with anger, and it was way too easy to dodge her swings. I caught her fist in my own before sending my knee up to ram into her solar plexus. She crumpled with a whimper, but I recognized a façade when I saw one. I skirted away, jumping on the balls of my feet, mouth open to release the heat rising inside of me. My powers crackled onto a higher level, making the lights around us flicker on and off.

Both girls either didn't notice or didn't care as they made their way forward, their faces both set with bloodlust.

My hand raised and a great purple mass of swirling energy crackled between my fingertips. Bree stumbled back, her scar illuminated by the flickering lamplight overhead. Gina froze, her eyes blown wide as she stared at the electricity with awe. My hand flew out, the electric ball flying through the air as if it were nothing more than a dodgeball. It hit the scarred thug square in the chest with a sizzling pop, lighting up the air and exploding in sparks that sent her flying.

Gina started running.

Bree fell to the ground, blood spraying the concrete. I moved forward, my Gift leaving as quickly as it came. I stood over her, revealing myself to be predator rather than prey.

"You're still alive?" I grinned when she groaned. "Don't worry, girl."

I raised my hands high. The lightning came forth instantly, the perfect weapon. It crackled in the air, making my hair swish around my head as my veins hummed with this newfound power. The cut under my eye burned and I was going to pay her back for it tenfold. As the air crackled, I could feel every spark as if it were a piece of me.

Not as if, I mentally amended. *It is. I. Am. Power.*

"I'm going to make you wish you were never born."

With a cackle, I brought the arrow-shaped bolt down on her head.

***

I took in a deep breath, smelling the funk of the city: barley, oil and cigarette smoke. I also caught another scent of Earl Grey tea—the scent of my prey. I ignored the third and final scent—the scent of feces as Bree released her bowels. The dead was never a smell that I liked. But there wasn't time to linger on that—not when a fresh kill was so close.

"By magic we are bound and by blood we remain," I rushed out. "Among the stars you shall lay."

I set a quick jolt of electricity towards her body, waiting until I saw smoke begin to rise before I took off.

I chased after the other girl. She was fast, weaving in and out of alleyways. I got her cornered in a dead-end alley. I took my steps slow, taking my time. Electricity crackled around my body, making the air sing with power.

To my surprise, Gina disappeared in a pillar of black smoke. I took a tentative step forward, feeling the gravel under my feet. I smelled her before I saw her. I turned just as her fist collided with my face. I stumbled but did not fall.

Gina disappeared again, this time falling from the sky. I expected it this time as I'd realized that her Gift was teleportation. I exploded my electricity in all directions. She spazzed above me, falling on top of me. I pushed her off me before standing

271

over her.

I drove my foot first into her gut and then into her face. I stomped on her upper body, driving her into the ground. One thing's for sure: she didn't get back up. I nudged her over onto her side with my foot. She was breathing but barely; I could tell that I'd broken at least two of her ribs.

Her mouth opened once then twice. I powered down so that I could hear her without the crackle of electricity. Blood streamed in a steady flow from her nose and mouth. Her cracked lips moved but produced no sound. I got down on my hands and knees, pressing my ear to her mouth.

"The Rebellion sends its regards."

She drove her knife into my side one time then pulled it out. Red streamed everywhere, staining my shirt and pants. She smiled weakly and shuddered her last breath.

I crackled electricity on one finger. It was weak but just the spark I needed. I set her body aflame just like I had Bree's. The sickly-sweet smell of burning flesh was familiar but unwelcome.

I didn't want to kill my own kind—I wanted us to prosper.

A pain sliced through my side as the wound pulsed and throbbed. Blood gushed between shaking fingers.

How would I get home?

Chapter Thirty-Three

Will I Ever Be Free?

The face of the homeless Mortal man that I'd given the drachma to appeared over mine.

"What happen'd ter ya?" he asked, eyes darting over my body.

"Please…" I couldn't raise my hand. "Help."

"Ya got sum'n for me?"

My eyelids fluttered closed. I felt my body being lifted. He asked me which hospital I wanted to go to—the one people went to when they get shot, which is usually where people died at, or the good one that was farther away. I groaned.

"No…no…'spitals…"

"Then where d'ya wanna go?" he grunted, placing me in his shopping cart.

My magic thrummed through me. I felt my tie with Dorian tighten my heart, strengthening it. My pulse slowed just slightly. But I'd already lost so much blood. The Mortal man stared at me as my Glamor flickered on then off.

"Please," I chocked on each word, as my head threatened to give way to unconsciousness. "Home."

"Imma need a ticket fer the bus."

His fingers skimmed my heavy pockets. I was powerless to stop him as he took my drachmas. He gave a triumphant 'huzzah' and dumped me out of the cart. I crashed to the pavement. Before he left, he pulled out my phone and hit speed dial. Then he tossed down the phone.

"It's yer boyfriend," he mumbled then trudged off.

"Hello?" Dorian asked. "Marve? Is that you?"

My lids lowered again, staying shut because they were too heavy for me to lift. The darkness behind my eyes was suddenly pierced by light outside of them. I was no longer drawing on the electricity around me. I felt the magic of a portal opening, tugging at mine, locking onto my location and pulling.

I gave in to the dark.

***

When Dorian got me on the other side of the portal, he immediately drew a healing rune just above my ribcage. I hissed as its heat made its way through my skin, closing it. He made me eat kidneys and egg yolks raw. Yuck. But I was in position to complain. When I told Dorian what happened, he was far from pleased. Frantic, he insisted that we get out of town immediately. Despite my victory, I was baffled.

"What's wrong?"

"The Rebellion knows that we've abandoned them. We know too much…Now that you've managed to kill one of them—"

He began opening drawers and stuffing the contents into a small duffel.

"For the record, there were two of them."

He shot me a dark look.

"Okay, okay...I get it," I mumbled. "I messed up."

"I've been fighting alongside them for years. There's no way you won that easily." He paused to shake his head. "It's just not possible."

Ouch.

"Maybe I'm just that good, *Sparkles*," I sniffed, crossing my arms.

"You don't understand." He turned and I shrunk back from the urgency of his gaze. "I trained those girls myself. Once word gets back to Valentina that you killed them, they'll bring the whole pack after us."

"But—"

Ring! Ring! Ring!

I dug my phone out of my pocket. Dorian had gotten it for me a while back, a sign that he trusted me. I didn't really use it except to contact Rhea when I needed her help. I wanted to make more friends but it was hard when I was on the run. I answered and was immediately met with the sound of a relieved sigh.

"Hello?"

"Megumi told me that she saw you at the party—said you were with that boy. She said she went over the camera footage from her house." His voice was as emotionless as ever. *"She even sent me a picture. Facial recognition confirmed that it's you, Marve."*

There was no room to feel panicked or defeated. I felt numb. My hands shook, my body swayed, but emotionally, I was dead.

Of course, he found me, I thought. *I am his property, and we still have a slight Bond despite him removing the Mark from my flesh. After all, Bonds take a long time of separation to fade from the soul, and even longer for the soul to heal from the loss.*

Suddenly I was nine years old again, kneeling before him, magic coursing through my veins as he made me repeat the sacred vow.

"Will you die for me?"

"Yes."

"Will you wipe away your past and take the name I give you?"

"Yes."

"Marve. Your electricity is blue when it's at its strongest. Your powers, your body, your soul—they are now mine. I will mold you into the perfect partner, the perfect weapon, and together we will rule the world"

Without warning, he bit into my neck and swallowed the blood that immediately swelled to the surface. I screamed. He pulled away from me, staring at my face as it contorted with pain. My body began to burn, and I knew that in some way, he'd thrown me into the lake of fire. My vision blurred and suddenly there stood a monster before me, its skin as black as the eons of space, horns sprouting from its head, its eyes bloodred and its teeth flashing like the headlights of a car right before it ran you over.

I wanted to run away but I couldn't—I felt so weak.

I felt him twist a hand in my hair, either holding me still or, even then, exposing his intent to use me in the worst of ways. He dug his finger—no, claw—into his palm.

Then he pressed that palm into my wound. My body burned hotter somehow and I knew that I was damned. He said something, something that my ears instantly rejected, something that I forgot. Then he pulled me into his arms and pressed his fangs against my neck.

I tried to twist away but I was helpless.

Rrriiippp!

He tore the skin from my neck. I didn't get to see what the Mark that bound us together appeared like, but I used to imagine that it was the Mark of his House—a lightning bolt and a single feather. He was a descendant of Mestiphopheles, after all. He threw back his head and swallowed. Tears leaked down my cheeks and all I could think was that this was wrong, and sick, and vile.

He was a monster—and I'd just made a deal with the grandson of the devil.

Gone was the man that had shown me kindness and beauty and the utmost respect. When I looked into his eyes at that moment, I saw a damned thing, a creature born of darkness, a demon.

Oh, what a fool I was.

"Kalysma," I weakly begged, "take it back."

But I was met with silence.

Silence. She was always silent. Was she truly the Mother of the Gifted? Did she even care what happened to me? Was she even watching or had she already grown bored of the tragedy that was I?

But I wasn't that scared little girl anymore. I was a woman. I saw Dorian watching me, his eyes worried. And I wasn't so innocent, either.

"It took me a while to pinpoint your location. I should have realized why I was getting bills for one of my properties. It was very clever of you to hide in one of my safe houses. I raised you well." I could hear the smirk in his snake-like voice. *"When I returned home and saw one of my maps missing, I should've immediately guessed that you'd been hiding there."*

"How did you get this number?"

"That doesn't matter." A lengthy pause. *"I'm coming to get you."*

The phone clicked dead. I glanced at Dorian, clawing for air. He laid a hand on my arm.

"We need to leave," I wheezed, "now."

***

I packed all my clothes into a matching duffle. Dorian insisted that I wouldn't need them where we were going. I ignored him. My lover stood in the doorway, watching me. I glanced at my old master's shirt and, finally, decided to leave it behind. Dorian made a noise of pride at that. I still ignored him, trying to focus on keeping my own breathing even.

I put on my holster and pocketed all my knives. I buckled the sheath for my arrows onto my back. I took one last look at the room before I walked outside. Dorian reached into his pocket and pulled out a small black device no bigger than my pinky nail. I instantly recognized it as the device that he was fiddling with all those weeks ago.

"What is that?" I asked as he stuck it to the front door.

"A bomb."

I took a few steps back.

"Don't worry. I designed it and I put my magic into it. It'll only go off once Jacques opens the door."

"Oh! That's...neat?"

We piled into the car, throwing our duffels into the back seat. I texted Rhea an encoded message before putting the phone back in my pocket.

A sea so black, a night so dark.

I knew that she would understand. I also knew that he hadn't tracked the phone—we hadn't talked long enough.

Rhea texted me back.

We drove for a good hour. I dozed off to sleep. I felt Dorian's presence and, like a warm blanket, that made me feel safe. But still that darkness was at the edge of my mind, creeping in like the unforgiving bleak that was night.

Will we make it? I wondered. *Will I ever be free of him?*

Chapter Thirty-Four

Am I A Formality?

I looked at the expanse in wonder. My eyes took in the large trees and were eager for the world beyond them. I gazed in awe at the bushes carved into scenes from *The Bible* and *The Revenant*: David and Goliath along with Cato and Kalysma kneeling. There was also a hedge cutout of a flame, which was the symbol for the flaming stars in the sky, lighting our way to the place Beyond. Feeling sentimental, I kneeled before it, kissing the ground. Dorian kneeled next to me, his hand clutched in my own. I searched for words and found none.

Finally, we both stood.

Dorian was the first to speak: "If I didn't know any better, I'd say this place had gotten bigger."

"Do you think the Rebellion are hiding around here?" I asked.

"I'll do a perimeter check."

He took off.

The wind changed directions.

Dorian came charging, hot on the pursuit of a large man. When the man was within reach, Dorian caught him by the throat. The man squirmed, gasping for breath. I noticed a tattoo of a dragon twisting around his neck. As Dorian began pummeling the poor guy, I briefly asked myself why a Rebel spy would have the tattoo of a dragon and not a hawk.

"Whale blubber!" The man cried between punches. "Please, Boyd, sir, I said whale blubber!"

"Wait," I held up a hand just as Dorian came to my side, "did he just call you his master?"

Dorian took a long, searching look at the man. He surveyed the dragon tattoo before looking past the blood on his face. There was no denying the authority in that look.

"Hao?" The golden man paused. "Is that you?"

***

I watched as the limping man leaned on Dorian. Blood formed stains on Hao's plainclothes, but you could tell by the way he shook his leg every now and then that he was just a bit numb. I turned to Dorian and planted a swift kiss on his check, the gravity of his readiness to defend me in my head.

He really did care.

"Whale blubber?"

"It's the safe word," Dorian explained.

There was a twinkle of lights, like a man-sized rainbow, glowing blue, red, orange, indigo and pink—a glamour. The Amorian servant disappeared. I looked up to see a great golden gate guarding the manor. Still, that was not what took my breath away—it was what flanked it.

Two mighty stone dragons were perched on pillars on opposite sides of the gate, giving the manor a regal and fearsome appearance. Each dragon had imposing red bodies and golden underbellies. Their brute heads were pointed skyward. Angry blue eyes glared up at the Heavens as the mythical beasts twisted their long bodies, their claws grasping. They looked like they would take off any second.

Boyd stopped at a facial recognition scanner. A red beam flew across his face. I heard the system checking for a glamour or imperfection. There was a buzz.

As the gates flew open in their berth to let us pass, I just barely caught the family crest. It just so happened to be a dragon head breathing flames from its gaping jaws. I tilted my head. The flames seemed to flicker before my eyes. Just below the crest was the inscription *Boyd Manor.*

"Boyd Manor is my family's estate," Dorian explained at my questioning stare. "My father was a Gifted slave fresh off the boat from Japan. My mother, his Mistress, favored him above all others and when she got pregnant, she decided to marry him. They married in secret, and she took his name before telling him to wipe all memory of him off the face of the Zuora. That was his Gift, you see. After that, she gave him everything he could ever desire and killed herself when he died."

My brain whirled with all this new information. I knew that it was illegal for Gifted and Immortals to marry one another. Their hatred for us went farther than instinct—it was engraved into their DNA—and our fear of them was just the same. But now I *knew* that there was a way for them to die. I briefly contemplated beseeching Rhea and telling her, but maybe she already knew—after all, she was half-and-half, and had probably encountered this before. Then I thought of Valentina's mission for me and questioned everything I'd ever known.

Can they?

"I thought Immortals couldn't die."

"There's a lot you don't know." He paused, eyeing me thoughtfully. "Have you ever noticed that there aren't a lot of Gifted females from the Southern Isles around?"

I paused. "Actually, yeah."

"There's a reason for that. And the history is dark."

So, he told me.

Since Immortal women's hips didn't grow as wide, it is particularly difficult and dangerous for them to give birth. And since their skin eventually thins so much from the constant aging forwards and backwards, it is very easy to break— particularly around the stomach. (This thinning only happened at this rate with women—men eventually replenished their skin cells.) Therefore, c-sections are nearly impossible without harming the child. Because of this, through the miracle of magic and science, Immortal couples have been known to buy Gifted women from the Isles and surgically strip them of their scales before applying them to the Immortal women's bellies using a magical fusion process known as New Growth, which then allows them to have children without cutting into the child.

All of this had to be done illegally [now] since even those who wrote the laws found this to be overly cruel. Many have said that Immortals were made this way because the Creator did not want them to multiply and instead have a few of them on the earth, but once this method was discovered, it quickly grew in popularity. But even faster, it was outlawed when Gifted women from the Isles were hunted to near extinction. Of course, the black market still exists and many still wish to be mothers. Immortal men had given up on having children but will do anything to make their wives happy.

The Southern Isles has been slow to repopulate but is making a recovery. Still, despite this, between the years of 2090 and 2110, there was a boom in Gifted girls born in the Isles, with around two born to every mother. I was born in that time and wondered why I didn't have a sister. But, then again, they were fighting to protect us, so I really couldn't complain. Many programs have been put in place to ensure our survival [while we are recovering.]

Still, as a Gifted woman from the Southern Isles, it was frightening to say the least.

I stopped walking, thinking it over. Gifted women had been forced to be surrogates for years, since creation. I knew that. But I didn't think they would find a way around it. It was terrifying to think of.

Maybe that was how we kill them off. Take away their means of reproduction...

Yes, it had to work. Of course, it was barbaric. But they'd given us poison and kidnapped what children we did have, so fighting dirty was the *only* way to win!

"Why are you telling me this?" I asked, refusing to look him in the eye.

"I trust you," he said faithfully, grinning at me. "The Rebellion has used low-down, dirty tactics to fight this war. And I'm sick of seeing innocent people die—on both sides—"

"Innocent? We are enslaved, Dory. You don't really think—"

"What about me? I'm not bad. I care about the Gifted, just like I care about the Immortals. I don't want to see anyone get hurt! And neither do you. If the Gifted people would just be *patient*—if they would just *wait* a little longer—then they could save up money and buy their freedom! I know so!"

"Freedom can't be bought. It must be taken." Something hit me rather suddenly. "Is that what people on your estate do—they buy back their humanity? Is that what your father did?"

He flinched. "No. But killing more people isn't the answer."

"Don't you get it? We aren't *people* to them! To the Immortals, Gifted are just animals—monsters—that don't deserve respect or dignity. For Goddess's sake, you use us like cattle! You breed with us, you beat us, you make us work for close to nothing—"

"You?!" he snarled. "What do you mean 'you?!'"

"Damn right I said you!" I hissed, glaring at him. "I tried to buy back my freedom. And do you know what Jacques did? He kept all the drachmas I'd saved up…He kept it and told me to save more, knowing good and well that he wouldn't give me another penny so long as I even thought of freedom! So how dare you—how dare you say that we can just buy back our freedom! If *your kind* had any intention of giving us *freedom*, then we wouldn't have been enslaved in the first place. There is no more waiting. It's been far too long. We must act. We must fight!"

285

His voice was quick, deathly quiet as he said, "Then why did you leave the Rebellion?"

I looked away. "I didn't know things had gotten this bad. And I didn't want to die or even fight anymore. But screw it, Dorian…This has got to stop."

He stared at me, breathing heavy, his hands balled into fists. I could see the racism in him, the self-hatred that he'd been taught from an early age. I hadn't wanted to believe that he hadn't sympathize with the other side—hell, I hadn't even considered it. And there had been a part of me that had sympathized as well. After all, I couldn't bear to murder children!

But we had to do *something!*

"I'm not a racist," Dorian sighed. "I just don't really believe that the situation is as dire as they claim. I mean, things have gotten better in the past twenty-odd years. Oppression isn't really the same thing as it used to be."

"Right. Because you live in a mansion. Because your daddy fucked an Immortal and she felt sorry for him. Tell me, how did your parents look at you? Were you not a bargaining chip?"

He flinched. "That's not fair. You can't use that against me. It's not fair."

"I'm just being honest. After all, if you're not oppressed, then why did your parents view you as an abomination. And don't say they didn't—I can see it in your eyes. Now you feel like if you spout that same stuff your dad was on, they'll accept you. Well, let me tell you—they *won't.* Your dad was a racist just like your mom— he felt bad for the people who already had everything. Just like you. And he blamed the oppressed for their disparages. Just like you. And when faced with the perils of

286

our oppression, he told you that it was better to wait than to stand up and fight. Now who does that sound like?"

Dorian said nothing for a long time. And when he did speak, it was a final spout of nonsense: "If it was like that, then why did my mother go so far for my father? Why did she take her own life when he died? Did she not love him?"

My reply was quick and ruthless: "Did she set her slaves free when she realized she loved him? Or did she give him a place above them? Just because you feel for one of the people in that position, does not mean that you sympathize with all the oppressed. The Master is always gonna have his favorite. I believe that your mother may have been in love with your father, yes, but was she in love with the plight of his people? No."

A tear streaked down Dorian's face. He looked over my shoulder off into the distance, not saying anything. And it hit me.

"Was it your father who beat you when he caught you with that Gifted woman from the Southern Isles? Or was it your mother?"

He said nothing.

"Mm. That's what I thought."

"I didn't realize," he whispered, finally looking at me. His eyes looked guilty, sad, angry—but he lacked the fight that I needed to see there. It's okay. He'd get it someday. "I'm sorry."

"I don't think you're racist," I added. "I just think you've severely misinterpreted the situation. Your misinterpretation is hurting people, but you've made amends. If you were, you wouldn't smuggle people to the Isles. I guess what

I'm trying to say is that I get it. You've done what you think is your part in your mind, but what I'm saying is that as long as there is a fight to be had, there is a fight to be had."

But could I really say that when I'd run, too? When even before I ran, I hesitated. Dorian had been on this planet far longer than me. So, it was natural that he was tired of fighting. But I realized that the difference between us was that I never used my exhaustion to justify their hatred.

And I wasn't Immortal.

"I wouldn't expect you to think otherwise, nor would I deserve it." He paused. "If you felt this way, then why are you running from Valentina. Don't you want to help her free the Gifted at all costs?"

"I want to help our cause more than anything, but summoning a demon is madness. It will kill *everyone*, Gifted included. No point in fighting for freedom if we'll all be dead."

He must've always felt this way in the back of his mind. But I could tell by the way he voiced his argument that he'd never actually said it to anyone. I wasn't sure why he did what he did for Valentina, unless he'd tried to convince her otherwise and had failed. But maybe he went so far for me purely out of love and the fact that he thought I had the power to stop what was happening.

It was kinda fucked up, but I understood his reasoning.

I thought back to the Book of Beginnings. When I asked Dorian about it, he said that it would remain safe from Jacques—he made sure of that. That's when it hit me: maybe Immortals could die from a broken heart.

We continued through the gate.

Proudly stretching across a well-cared-for lawn was Boyd Manor. Flowers of all colors decorated the yard, whipping in the wind like miniature flags. Tall trees were spread in the background, making the establishment look as if it would be swallowed by gangly limbs at any moment. The large country estate could easily host a party of five-hundred guests. I walked forward, arm in arm with the man that'd grown up in the house of dreams.

An air of royalty surrounded the manor, demanding a certain sort of respect and wonder. Light filtered through the trees, dimming with the fast-approaching nightfall and casting an unearthly glow on the property. The manor was a creamy white. Golden light seeped from the windows that circled the house. Just a hop, skip and jump away, Hao had reappeared and was walking the perimeter, a handgun strapped to his waist and a shotgun clutched in his hands.

I wondered who else was waiting for us inside.

"I take it you like my home?"

"Your house makes Jacques's look like a steaming pile of—"

Dorian threw back his head and laughed. The sun glimmered off his golden skin, sparkling in the night like my own personal set of stars. The world around me faded to insignificant sounds and colors as my powers flared up unexpectedly, making the air around us crackle with the hum of electricity. I watched the purplish electricity light up the air, making each follicle of my hair stand on end. Dorian watched me, making my heart spike.

"How does your Gift work?"

"I think it's tied with my emotions," I said, dazed.

"What set you off?"

"Something beautiful…"

As we strolled along, Dorian struck up a new conversation. Today was his first time talking about his parents in earnest. Something about it seemed caring but resentful, as if they'd had a falling out of some sort.

"Until I ran away, my parents held a firework show for me there—" Dorian thrust his arm to the yard "—every year, just for my birthday."

"They loved you."

"It was a formality."

I couldn't remember what I'd gotten for my birthday from my parents. We were always so poor—a simple cake was a huge gift. With Jacques, he granted me a day off and a book of his choosing. Most of the novels were about slavery and obeying your master. For some reason, the message stuck with me sometimes and other times seemed like lies.

I'd always had my rebellious phases.

"Have you seen fireworks before?"

"No." I shook my head. I then added grudgingly, "I was always locked away in my castle."

"Would you like to see some fireworks?"

"If we get the chance…"

A pop in my ear. A tilt of my axis. My stomach lurched and my hand automatically flew down to hold it. I paused, waiting for the nausea to pass. Dorian grabbed me, giving me a steady hand.

"You've been sick a while now. Do you think—"

"It's nothing."

As we took the few first steps, a barrier of magic flared. It felt like my body was being pulled in every direction, threatening to tear off my skin. Dorian glowed with a blue light and just like that, the magic subsided. A dark-skinned woman with black, slightly graying hair opened the door. Dorian and I quickly jogged up the remainder of the steps.

As I looked over the old woman's smooth hands and lined face, I could tell that she was probably even more beautiful when she was younger. Her dark brown eyes seemed to twinkle with a good-natured sort of mischief, making her appear years younger than she probably was. She was tall, had great posture and seemed to exude confidence. Her dark hair was pulled up in a bun with a few loose strands plastered to her face. The old woman was dressed in a standard housekeeping uniform, a dripping sponge clutched in her hands.

I could hear the air wheezing in and out of her lungs as she stood in the doorway. Light spilled behind the graceful woman, enveloping her in a golden hue. Dorian watched the woman with a love and adoration that I was immediately envious of. He pulled her into a long hug. When he pulled away, the woman was smiling.

"Cousin Yvonne!" Dorian exclaimed.

"Boyd, sir!" The elderly woman stepped aside. "Welcome home."

Chapter Thirty-Five

Set Fear on Fire

Dorian swaggered past the old woman and into the manor. I nodded my greeting then stepped past her. In those few seconds, I caught a whiff of her scent of oak and a decaying corpse and instantly saw her for what she was: a half-demon. All half-demons smelled unpleasant, with a rotten scent unique to them: Jacques smelled like the Dead Sea while this woman smelled like a corpse—it was unique to each creature. From what Jacques told me, it had something to do with their demonic souls and the dark magic rotting their human flesh. I knew that Dorian wasn't a half-demon, which meant that his mother had a brother or sister that had slept with a full-blooded demon.

I guess I never really thought of demons as having family. I always thought of them as evil, selfish, solitary creatures. That sure was something.

The maid shut the door and scurried around us. I chose to ignore the unbelieving glance she threw at me. Yvonne clapped her hands and a bustling crew of people filed in, each clad in either a modest maid outfit or a normal butler suit.

There had to be a hundred of them. Maybe even more.

"Staff, our Master has returned."

She bowed in our general direction. The rest of the staff bowed in synchronization before giving a devoted "Welcome home, my Lord!" Yvonne was all business.

"Get to work! I want this house spotless—and I mean *spotless*!"

"We have a few bags in the car," Dorian informed Yvonne before she went into complete dictator mode.

Yvonne called a few workers to unload the bags from the car. They were there and back in less than three minutes. They whisked our bags away and up the stairs to who knows where.

I took the time to look around the inside of the manor. The large room we were in branched out with shining marble floors. A stage was in the back of the room, hailed by two staircases with golden rails. The staircases led up to a multitude of thick wooden doors that stretched along a regal landing. I thought of Dorian as a boy playing hide-and-seek in these endless halls then remembered that Dorian was an only child.

What a shame…

"How many rooms are there?" I asked.

"There are two-hundred rooms here in Boyd Manor. There are three floors and one rather extensive basement. The help sleeps on the third floor. There's no need to go to the basement since it's not in good condition. My room—I mean, *our* room—is on the second floor."

"Wow…"

I stepped forward and peered farther around.

Two large mahogany doors were at one end of the hall up the staircase. The only thing significant about the mansion so far, other than its size, was the sleek, technologically advanced kitchen around corner. The front yard alone was easily the size of Jacques's safe house in Sidra and the plot of land next to it. I turned back around to see Yvonne staring at Dorian and I with some expectation and a lot of indignation.

What was her deal?

"Are you going to introduce me?" she huffed.

"This is Marve—" Dorian placed a hand on my waist and pulled me close "—my fiancée."

What? Fiancée?

I glanced at him. He gave a slight nod. I looked back at the maid and gave her a bashful smile.

"That's funny—I don't even remember getting engaged."

Dorian laughed loudly, the sound causing a few of the workers that were cleaning nearby to jump. Yvonne began laughing as well as her eyes landed on me. It was a small, teetering sound, as if she wasn't sure whether it was funny or not. Dorian gazed into my eyes for a fraction of a second, his eyes burning with a slight glow. The look caused a strange shudder to pass through me.

What was he planning?

"Isn't she funny?" Dorian grinned, giving my hand a squeeze.

"Very," Yvonne said dryly as she looked between the two of us.

"Marve, this is my cousin, Yvonne. I know you probably can't tell, but she's three years older than me."

"I never would've imagined..."

My stomach gave a sharp lurch. I reached down to grab it and groaned as a sudden heat flayed me from the inside. A bead of sweat rolled down my forehead.

These hot flashes will be the death of me.

Watching Yvonne was like watching water boil. It seemed harmless enough but once it got hot enough, it could scald.

She was about to explode.

"Yvonne, I—"

"So first you get her pregnant," Yvonne snapped, "and then you just whisk her away here. Is that it, Dorian? You know that it is forbidden for an Immortal and a Gifted to be together. Do you want to end up like Aunt Georgia?"

"What are you talking about?" I sighed. "I am *not* pregnant."

I made sure to lock eyes with the elderly woman.

She obviously wasn't in the right state of mind.

"Just so you know," I was now eyeing the other woman, searching for insanity, "we came here because we're in danger."

"Now you have her lying for you?" The old woman's eyes were sharp and scrutinizing. "Is she pregnant, or isn't she?"

"Babe," Dorian said in apology, grabbing for my hand, "let me explain."

I felt angry and humiliated, like someone had pulled the biggest prank on me. I

295

didn't know what was happening to us—to me. He had so many secrets and he only let me get so close. I wanted to know him—all of him. But I couldn't if he kept planning everything without me.

"What's going on?" I whispered, pulling away.

"Dorian called me before you came. He said that he'd gotten involved with a girl and that something had come up. What do you expect me to think? If she isn't pregnant, then what—"

"She really is in danger…But she's *not* pregnant. I didn't know what else to do," Dorian pleaded. "You tell me."

The woman stared at me for a long moment. After a second, her eyes began to glow with a bright light. When they dimmed, she gave Dorian a slight nod.

I thought back to all I'd learned today. This Aunt Georgia must be Dorian's mother. She was an Immortal with a brother who'd impregnated a demon. Their offspring could use magic and had Gifts. I added this to my brain catalogue.

It didn't make sense. Why would the Immortals feed us lies with these walking contradictions right in front of us? Was it really about power and control?

Dorian looked past the maid's shoulder, blatantly ignoring my questioning stare.

"Right…" The maid pressed her lips together, disapproval flickering across her face. She caught me looking and masked it with a *tiny* smile. "The only way to protect her is to marry her. After all, the magic that will bind you will hide you for a while—but not forever."

"Wait, *what?*" I said, staring between them. "Who's getting married?"

"In that case, we should move your wedding up. When did you say it was?"

"Wedding?" I started to panic. "What wedding?"

"We haven't picked a date," Dorian quickly said, silently shushing me.

"We don't want to rush into anything." She threw me a pointed look. "I was thinking—oh, say, next week."

She was clearly trying to scare me off.

"Next week?" I glanced between the maid and Dorian, who still wouldn't look at me. "That's a bit soon." The maid shot me a sharply accommodating look. I shrunk back. "I-I-I mean, I thought that I was supposed to meet everyone first."

"Everyone else is dead," she grinned, "so don't worry about meeting our family. If what you say is true, the date is not too early. We want to get this done as quickly as possible. After all, you can't stay here forever. I'm sure that you can understand."

I was so confused. First, she was forbidding us to see each other romantically, then she was telling us to get married? What was with this woman? They were both staring at me. I realized that they were waiting for an answer.

"I—"

"Perfect!" The other woman clapped her hands together and grinned at the both of us. "I'll start making the arrangements. Oh, Beatrice!" she crooned.

A redhead who looked no older than fourteen appeared at the older woman's side. She was clad in a standard housekeeping uniform. Her hair was in a messy ponytail and the freckles on her cheeks looked more like specks of dirt. But her smile was warm and inviting, a sharp contrast to Yvonne's ire. I instantly liked her.

297

"This is Beatrice," said Yvonne. "She's in charge of your room. Beatrice, try not to be in the way so much. What did I say about lingering?"

Beatrice bowed and slipped into the shadows. The dogmatic woman gave us another dubious look. Then the extraordinary lady, with a sharp click of shiny heels against marble floors, was gone.

"Dorian." I turned on him. "Marriage?"

"Not gonna lie, I was bluffing," he said.

His jaw tightened. I wasn't sure if he was angry, confused or passive. To me, he looked like a mixture of everything. But if this just proved anything, it was that I didn't truly know him. Not his heart or his plans.

"Dorian!" I slapped his arm. "Why would you do that?"

"It was bound to happen anyway…"

"Isn't this kind of soon?" I grounded my teeth together to avoid screaming. "I mean we hardly know each other."

"It wasn't too soon for you to sleep with me…"

I couldn't think of a response. It had been *his* idea. Now he was spinning it on me?!

"It's the 22nd century!"

"I'm just trying to protect you!"

"I don't understand how having a shotgun wedding is protecting me."

"The marriage runes that are painted on our bodies binds us in a way that even sex can't. Our souls will literally be linked. It will make us one. After we spend some time here, we'll leave and go to another safehouse. I'll send some servants to dispose of Jacques."

"No."

"Why?"

This was all kinda convenient. First, he has sex with me. Now I've gotta marry him?!

"If anyone's going to dispose of Jacques, it's gonna be me."

"What?" Imagine him snorting. "You're no match for Jacques."

"Excuse me?"

"At least, not alone." He eyed me skinny, frail body in a way he never had before: as if he didn't trust me to stand on my own. "Not in your condition."

I wanted to cry, scream or stomp off, but I wasn't a kid anymore. I was twenty-one! It was time to put on my big girl panties and buck up. But it didn't change the fact of things: he didn't think that I could handle myself. In his eyes, I was incapable of protecting myself.

So, I just had to get stronger to prove that I was ready.

"So," I forced a tiny smile, "are you going to show me around?"

"I'll have someone show you the place. There's something that I need to do."

He dashed off.

I stood in the middle of the room by myself, feeling about as lost as a giraffe in Antarctica.

Someone tapped on my shoulder.

I whirled, heart racing, to come face to face with an older black man. His face was creased with lines, like an origami paper that had been folded then unfolded time and time again, but his eyes were ageless. I smiled at him.

Hopefully he'd be nicer than Yvonne.

"I offer you my sincerest apologies, ma'am. I didn't mean to startle you. Lord Boyd has requested that I give you a tour."

"Oh, yes, that'll be fine," I murmured as I followed him towards the stairs. "Thank you."

"It's my pleasure, ma'am."

We made our way up the stairs, me marveling at the polished surfaces and old paintings, him gesturing with long, steady hands. He named a few of the men and women in the pictures, saying that Dorian painted them all when he was young. The faces on the wall ranged from happy to shocked.

"Who are these pictures of?"

"These are Lord Boyd's conquests. He would get his canvas to make them into the works of art you see here. Once the paint dried, he took them to bed."

I swallowed my jealousy. There were many men and women in these portraits. I wondered why he'd been so shy about it when I'd asked him. After all, the only ones that were even slightly homophobic were Mortals. As far as I knew, us magic-users didn't care one way or another. But then I thought back to what Jacques had told me when he told his story of him and Grant. Maybe I didn't know how far homophobia reached because I wasn't a part of the community.

And for that, I was sincerely sorry.

I looked for a portrait of Mimi and came up emptyhanded.

"Oh." I fought to make my voice cheerful, holding back a grimace as I eyed the portraits. "That's different, huh?"

"Very, ma'am. Lord Boyd did what he had to do to assume power. A lot of people wanted to take this land for their own once his parents died. Dorian made as many allies as possible, by any means necessary. He knew that if he gave up this land, it would spell doom for its inhabitants—mainly, the staff...If you ask me, he is the most sacrificial man I've ever met."

And suddenly, I was bothered. It didn't bother me when I'd thought he'd just slept with people randomly. But to know that he'd sold himself to protect people, which meant that it most likely wasn't even his own will—that people sought him out, used him even?

"There are a *lot* of pictures here," I gaped, head swimming.

The man paused on the staircase. An unnatural air seemed to blow through the manor. He didn't creak or bend. I shuddered and huddled a few steps closer. He turned to look at me down his nose, his eyes flashing with an unnatural blue—the color of his master's magic—and I knew that I'd just crossed a line.

"Is it a problem?" he asked, his voice neither Andrew's nor Dorian's.

A shiver of fear raced down my spine. But *that* wasn't what bothered me. It was the picture that I *didn't* see. But how did I say that after I'd said too much already? I shook my head and the cerulean glow faded from his black orbs.

"Why would that bother me?" I articulated as I followed him up the stairs. "He's with me now. I'm Marve of the Lightning Fists. I can protect him."

Although lately, he did more protecting *me*.

"Would it bother you," Andrew asked, "if he bedded anyone you knew?"

301

"It depends on who it was," I bit out.

We stepped around a bend. I stopped cold in my tracks, staring. Jacques stared back at me, beaming mischievously as his eyes beckoned, his hand draped over his head. He wore a robe, the silken fabric carefully placed over his nether regions. In his other hand, he held a glass of wine, his tongue sticking out of his parted lips which were stained red from the drink. I knew that look all too well and I wanted to scream but instead I looked away—and pretended to see nothing.

"Where's Megumi?" I rasped, trying and failing to catch my breath.

"What?" Andrew asked.

"Where is Megumi's portrait? I want to see it."

"There is no portrait of Megumi," Andrew replied quickly, his eyes darting away—but not before I saw the look flash in his eyes: pity, plain and true.

And I understood. I understood why he would have sex with all these men and women, why he would do what he had to do in order to keep his family and his staff safe. I knew that he appreciated the Gifted, loved us. But to go that far to save us...?

And I'd judged him. I judged him without knowing the full story. Attempted rape had taken a lot out of me, so I knew that coercion must have destroyed him from the inside out, especially since he was supposed to be this all-powerful guy. I didn't want to hear any more. But my mind still raced.

The Immortal from the bazaar, the one we saw at the party...? Was that why they'd been gone so long? Had he used him, too? And Dorian had been afraid to tell me. And I'd poked fun at him about it!

What the fuck was wrong with me?

302

And suddenly I realized just how selfish of me it was to expect him not to have any partners other than me. And I also figured out that my Master was more a part of me outside of my bloodlust—I'd adopted some of his 'love' habits, too. But then a sick, greedy feeling landed on my shoulders—and took ahold of me. I wanted to deny it but there was no reasonable way that I could.

He was mine.

And I'd come too far to go back now.

"This place is huge!" I nudged the old man, but the move felt mechanical. "Big family, huh?"

"Actually, no. It was always the help, Dorian, and his parents. Now it's just us and Dorian."

"What's with all this space?"

"This manor was originally smaller but was later expanded to also accommodate an extreme amount of additional people."

"Why?"

"When Dorian was a young boy, a war between Immortals and Gifted was on the horizon. Many from both sides flocked to the wealthiest, exceedingly powerful Immortals since they had their claws sunk into both the magical and nonmagical society. Dorian's parents were some of those few. They expanded their manor into what you see today."

"So what happened?" I was more than thirsty for information—I was parched. "Was there a war?"

"Do you think we would be here if there was?"

"Touché."

We passed a few suits of armor and another hall of paintings. Each brushstroke had its own story to tell, each smear of paint hiding another secret, each shadow upon the picture revealing another truth. Down the hall, two doors stood proudly. Andrew was indifferent as we came ever closer. I was intrigued to say the least.

"You're a nice guy." I gave a small laugh. "You're nothing like that old lady that let us in. She was scary."

"That would be my wife, ma'am."

My face burned and I began spewing apologies. The old man either didn't hear or didn't care as he walked on. When he did speak, there was a smile on his face.

"Don't worry," he said. His voice lowered. "She scares me, too."

I blinked, confused. "Who are you, exactly?"

"My name is Andrew. The woman who greeted you earlier is my life partner, Yvonne. I am the housekeeper. Yvonne is the head housemaid. It's our job to make sure that everything in the house is running smoothly."

We traveled down the hall. I glanced at a life-sized carving of a dragon. My lips turned up at the sight that was already familiar. Andrew stopped in front of the two mahogany doors that intrigued me so. The housekeeper placed his hands on the brass knobs.

"Most of our guests prefer the library." He threw me a pursed lipped glance. "I'm sure you won't mind."

Not waiting for an answer, he threw the doors open and stepped aside.

I stepped inside and felt all the air escape my lungs in one large whoosh. There, towering above me and stretching endlessly, was the largest expanse of books I'd ever seen. Shelves that reached the ceiling traveled down the room, stacked with more literature than I'd ever imagined. A small fireplace sat in the back of the spacious room. Two comfy looking armchairs rested in front of the blazing flames.

But that wasn't the best part.

My eyes widened as they settled on the painting above the hearth. In a beautiful etching of golds, reds and blues, a mighty dragon sat atop a mountain. The large beast's cerulean eyes narrowed in something akin to determination. I was taken aback by its fierceness, totally enraptured. Its red scales, which broke off into gold as I inspected its slightly exposed underside, seemed to slightly gleam from the brightness of the fire beneath the painting.

On the mighty dragon's back was a figure so dark and ominous that I was still scared even after I looked away. He was pitch black, bleeding night and shadows. He was Death. I admired the way the red sun contrasted the blue sky of the painting. The drawing of the great ball of gas illuminated the room more than the fire.

"The Boyd family believed that dragons, resolute and strong, held the key to ruling a nation. A long time ago, when Dorian's ancestors on his father's side first settled in Japan, they were to choose the symbol of their clan." As Andrew and I gazed at the painting, I imagined the dragon speaking to me as it soared through the sky. "They were fascinated by the tales of flying giants borne of fire. To them, dragons were deities that ruled the Heavens and the Zuora alike. Even though they were mortal, the family decided to emblazon a dragon on their family crest, representing power, dignity and a prosperous, eternal youth."

I was more than humbled.

I was completely awe-struck. When I asked who painted *Death and His Dragon*, Andrew told me Dorian had. It was astounding—his talent.

It reminded me of a poem I once heard called *Death*:

What does Death have against a rose?

He is jealous of her beauty,

Her strength,

Her resilience.

So he touches her petals gently,

Taking her for himself.

What does Death have against Man?

That they live in freedom.

Against an angel?

He does not want to be a slave,

Yet he admires their devotion.

What does Death have against an earthly slave?

Nothing,

For they are always delivered

To him.

Death owns none,

Yet rules all.

And sadness, grief and sorrow

Owe Death an apology,

For when Death lay dying on the battlefield,

Bleeding night and shadows,

No one came to help.

"What's the story behind it?"

"I…don't know."

Something in his voice shivered like the Earth under the weight of the sky. I paused, pondering my next moves. I felt Jacques's influence slither up and down my spine, gripping my bones. I turned, making my eyes larger, and let a smirk dance on my face. Confidence snatched hold of me. Andrew seemed to panic in those moments, and before he could run, I took a step forward, reaching out to grip his hand in mine.

"Andrew?"

"Yes," he quivered, squirming.

"You can trust me."

"I—I don't know, ma'am." He blinked at me. "I don't think he'd want me to say."

"It would please me very much," I said, my voice a hiss like a snake's. When I looked into his eyes, I saw mine glowing back at me—but mine didn't look green in their reflection, but a dazzling, glinting red. I didn't want to think where I'd seen that red before. "You can tell me what really happened. It'll stay between us."

"Lord Boyd overdosed on a mixture of cocaine and alcohol in the late 1900s. It took our family physician quite a while to revive him. When Dorian was well enough, this was what he painted."

"Wow..." I took my hand from him. He swayed, blinking slowly, the spell broken. I reached for the painting, but I was too far to touch it. "That's all that I need, Andrew."

"In that case, I'll inform Lord Boyd that you're here and don't require any more assistance."

Andrew dashed from the room.

Not once did I see him turn back, although I did notice that he rudely shoved a house cleaner out of the way in his haste, crying out "Move it!" as her only warning. I shrugged (he was probably going to report back to Yvonne) and turned back to the books. Walking past the shelves, I trailed my fingertips along the sides, feeling the strange softness of their leather spines. I walked to another section of the library and found four glass cases housing religious texts: *The Revenant, The Quran, The Bible* and *The Torah.* I checked over my shoulder before going into one of the cases. I plucked a book from its spot at random. Taking it to the fireplace, I plopped down in a chair.

The golden letters stared up at me. I slid a finger under the cover and opened the ancient masterpiece. Dust spilled out. As I got comfortable, the flames roaring in front of me warmed my skin. Thoughts of magic, dragons and Dorian consumed every stream of my consciousness.

But there was something else—a stream of visions on the horizon. The light in my eyes reflected off my hands...I felt a ripping sensation in my back, as if wings would burst forth at any moment...I lurched forward and was greeted with visions of the End.

Chapter Thirty-Six

Micha

My eyes flew open. The ground suddenly fell away—but I was held aloft by two beautiful wings. I was hovering over a city as endless as the sea. Dogs howled into the night, labored screams rose into the air and smoke filled the sky. I wasn't sure where I was but I knew one thing...

The Earth was breathing its last breath.

A woman clothed with the radiance of the sun wore the moon on her scarred, dirty feet like silk slippers. She had a crown of twelve stars squished on her head as she slinked from the shadows and into the light cast off by the flames. Her stomach was round and swollen like the infected gums of a child and I knew that she was close to giving birth. In her womb was the contradiction that pained the life of the few of us that were forced to wander this forsaken land. Her hair was like the writhing snake that crept through the Garden of Eden. Yet her voice was as beautiful as the song of praise Mestiphopheles sang before he went Dark and was cast from Heaven.

I moved to cry out to the woman named Misery, but my voice was not my own.

Suddenly, an awful roar split the sky in half. A mighty red dragon with seven heads and ten horns ripped itself from the sky, its wings beating like the angry fists of a warrior as he struck his breast. On those ten horns were seven crowns and as those horns grazed the light of the burning sun, it seemed to suck all the beauty and justice from the world. The sun winked out like a candle in the wind. The only light was the one cast from the flames that consumed the city and everything else in its path.

I could feel the thrashing child in the woman's womb. He was terrified of what was to come. The dragon moved towards the woman in a space without time, ready to devour the child as soon as he fell between his mother's legs and drew his first breath.

A man appeared. He was wrapped in a white robe of humility. On his head was a golden crown of beauteous divinity. In his hand was a sword with a hilt shaped like a lion's head, its silver mouth agape and emerald teeth gleaming like stars. The man struck the mighty dragon with the very edge of the sword and the great winged serpent fell upon the Earth with a cataclysmic roar and was dead. Very suddenly, I was compelled to look at the street.

There was a group of people dancing around the fire and singing praises to the cloaked man. Not too far from them, a group of angry men and women tore at the clothes and flesh of a preacher, not noticing their lord and savior, who watched them with sadness and pity. The man thrust out a hand and the rioting people fell dead. Then the man opened his palms and the people around the fire fell silent. The man opened his arms to embrace them and together, he and the people ascended up into

311

Paradise.

I turned around to come face-to-face with an angel. He had six wings sprouting from his back, a halo around his head and Glory seeping from his very pores. His cloak was gray with the ash of the world. He grinned at me. Then he lifted a hand.

I fell to the ground, writhing in agony. Hisses and spits fell from my lips and I knew that I was consumed by evil. I fell to my haunches and bore my teeth at him.

"You've chosen to die for love. Only the Boyd power will save you. Though you may not remember what I say to you now, know that your decisions will decide whether you save the Gifted people, or lead them farther from freedom. Either way, this is your sixtieth try at life and you only have one more until you meet Her in the Great Beyond and face judgement. Gifted are not usually reincarnated, but She has deemed you special, the one that will take her place as the Mother—"

His head cocked towards Paradise where celestial music spilled from the sky. There was a shout. The angel beats his wings three times, took to the sky and was gone. I turned around to see the ruin, unsure if I truly was the cause of it or not. A pain ripped through me and—

"Do you like that book?"

I slammed the Bible closed, hiding a wince as I lost my train of thought. It all faded from sounds and colors to a comfortable darkness and calming silence. Dorian looked down at me expectantly, his eyes glowing in the light of the flames. The religions of old had always fascinated me, but he, like most Immortals, did not seem to really care about them.

"Yeah, it's nice," I answered.

He gave me a coy smile that I found sexy. "I never really liked books much growing up. I found them too…wordy."

Then something changed in his eyes.

"What?"

"Your eyes were glowing."

"Yeah, sure..."

He shrugged. "I guess it was just the light."

"Dorian?"

"Yes?"

"I'm not ready to settle down."

"What do you mean?"

"This feels like a bad dream."

"It's not. No matter how much you wish, it won't go away. Marve," he said carefully, "I cannot stress this enough—you're being hunted. I only want to protect you."

I saw myself atop a roof, the flames of hell staring up at me. I saw me running towards the edge as a laugh bubbled up in my throat. Then I felt myself falling, the wind whipping my hair, slapping my face as my soul came alive. I felt the pavement beneath my body then the roar of fire enveloping my skin. And I felt…*free.*

This was all too much.

"It could…possibly."

"…"

"…"

"What are you saying?"

"I mean, it's always an option."

"I'm not going to give up till you're safe."

"You wouldn't have to protect me. No one would."

"You're not suggesting—"

"You're right. I don't know what I was thinking."

"Why?"

"I'm not ready for freedom. I'm not ready for life. I'm not ready for anything except to see my parents again."

"No. Don't say that. *Please don't say that.*"

"I'm just saying—"

"Stop."

"But—"

"Stop."

I tried to sink into the chair but of course, Dorian wasn't having any of that. I found myself turning away as he kneeled in front of me, just a few feet from the fireplace. He took my hands in his and began to draw odd patterns on my palms. I closed my eyes as the fire began to warm my skin. I wasn't sure what felt better—his hands or the flames.

And I suddenly realized why I'd voiced these thoughts aloud. I needed him to need me. I needed to hear him say that he loved me, that he valued my presence, that he wanted me around. But he didn't. He didn't say anything for a long while. He just stared into the fireplace, his eyes wide and lost, as if he too sometimes thought of jumping into the flames.

Finally, he asked, "The library is pretty impressive, right?"

I didn't trust my voice, so I made a noncommittal noise in the back of my throat.

I tried to focus on the fire and how its warmth spread across my body. I tried to imagine how the flames looked at that very moment—a mix of red and orange, dancing haphazardly across the logs. A steel grate trapped the fire, kept it at bay. The flames took their revenge out on the bark, stripping away every piece that was still brown and leaving black, charred remains. There was a pile of grey ashes at the bottom, resting like an obedient dog at the feet of its owner.

I heard the rustle of clothes. He'd moved closer. My breaths came out in odd chatters. My chest was tight and constricted. My whole body was filled with panic. The once-holy book slipped from my fingers and fell to the floor with a jolting thump.

"Cha-ta-ha-ta-ha-ta—"

"Marve?"

I took slow, deep breaths.

"Are you all right?"

"Yes."

He took a deep breath, and I knew that whatever he had to say was important. For a second, I thought he was going to say the words that I so desperately needed to hear. But I honestly craved death so much that I denied my ears the joy of hearing it. So I spoke. I said something that I knew would hurt him to ease the hurt in my own heart.

"I can't marry someone I don't love."

"You still don't love me? After everything I've done for you—for us?"

I didn't love him. I cared about him deeply—but it wasn't true, honest love—not like what he felt for me. I wanted to love him back. I wanted to be the woman he desired—that he deserved. But right now, I was too afraid, too uncertain, to be anything more than his lover, his companion in the night.

And I was angry that I still had to mull it over, that I felt guilty for not feeling the same, that he was trying to guilt me into saying it back. I couldn't tell if I was angry with him for what he was doing or angry with myself for letting someone else have so much power over me that I could not commit to another.

"What if I told you that it would benefit us both? What if I told you that the Immortal that wanted to turn you in—the one from the party—agreed not to turn you over as long as I find someone to split my land with?"

"What? I don't understand."

"The Immortal—Kristoff—offered not to turn you in as long as I found someone to divide my land with. The bastard thinks he's slick, but I know his game. He wanted me to give half my land to Megumi, which means that she would be responsible for managing it...and protecting it. I told him that there was no way I'd do that—she's weak for an Immortal. So, I offered you." I watched him as he watched me, considering what to say. This was as much as a business deal as it was a romantic partnership. "If I marry you, you will have protection using the binding from the marriage runes. Which means that if I divide my land with you, I will be

316

able to protect you if your land is attacked."

"I still don't understand. Why would you need to divide your land?"

"He wants me to make myself vulnerable. The land will already be weak from the ties being transferred over. This leaves me open to attack. I don't know when he'll make his move. It could be a week after the transfer or ten years. All I know is that he wants Amoria for himself. Can't say I blame him, though. Rumors have been spreading that I'm not really a Master, just a sharecropper that owns the land and rents it out to Gifted families and offers them my protection." Frustration clouds his gaze, making him seem older, the lines in his face deepening. "Damn it! I should have known I couldn't keep up the lie forever. I should have known that I couldn't protect everyone."

"So let me get this straight. You buy land and give it to Gifted families—no wait—" I backtracked at his look "—you rent it out. These Gifted families are not your slaves but business partners. You just tell everyone that they are." A piece of the puzzle was still missing. "But what do you get in return?"

"Whatever they get from the land, soaps, crops, clean water—they give me a percentage of the profit."

"What percent?"

"Fifty."

"Oh." I paused, thinking. This was a lucrative deal. Anyone could find out at any time and that didn't give them much to live on. I bet he did this on purpose, to look better. The less they had, the better he looked in the eyes of other Immortals. "So, you want me to take over some of your land, leave it vulnerable,

317

and…what…?"

"If you marry me, it will nullify it. So even though the land will be yours, my magic will still take a part in protecting it. You won't really be vulnerable."

"But it will still look as though you did as he asked?"

"Exactly."

"Hm."

It was a smart plan. I had nothing to lose from it, really. I knew that Immortals used their magic to put up barriers. I was guessing that Dorian still had barriers over Megumi's land, which meant that she was still protected. Poor Dorian. His magic was stretched so thin.

No wonder his mind took a toll. And drugs and alcohol had a different effect on Immortals—it made them more productive and added a temporary boost to their powers, but the crash…I'd seen it in Jacques's days of owning more land. Now that he had less, he didn't really have a need. But still!

"My magic isn't strong either. What if you're stretched too thin?" I wanted to hold him, but stayed in place, refusing to touch him for fear of what that would mean to him. "What if they kill you?"

Immortal magic constantly held Immortal bodies in a state of reanimation. Contrary to popular belief, they did age, but their magic made them constantly age backwards at the same time it aged forward. You could see it in the lines in Dorian's face where his skin had stretched and unstretched. It was more than risky.

It was insane.

"I understand that. But if I can shield you from Jacques, for however long, until

I locate the Dagger of Truth and take him down...then it's a risk I'm willing to take. Besides—"

Dorian considered me for a second. I stared right back at him, immobilized. I could feel the Earth stop before titling so far on its axis that my head began to swim. His golden hand closed over mine, the movement so fast that I jumped. Dorian moved to stand, pulling me up with him.

My heart began to pound.

I wanted him.

Dorian's voice, hot and misty like a summer rain, brushed over my skin. I could feel pieces of me falling to the floor like glass shards and before I could grab them, I was swept away. What was he doing to me?

"Can I...kiss you?"

"I don't see why you're asking now. You never really asked before."

"I know. It's just...I knew you wanted it then. But now...I'm unsure."

I bit my lip, my lashes lowering. "It'd be my pleasure."

And I meant it.

His mouth fastened firmly over my own. The golden aristocrat's glowing eyes fell closed and took my doubt with them. I closed my eyes.

I kissed him back.

I could feel his heart against mine. I dug my fingers into his narrow shoulders but just as suddenly as the kiss started, it stopped. Dorian yanked away from me and took a deep breath. He was lust. He was confliction.

And he was mine.

"Marve…" He looked so torn that my chest ached. "You'll be the death of me."

"My thoughts exactly."

I hope to be your death, just as you are my life.

My eyes fluttered as Dorian cupped my cheek. His hands were fire on my skin. As he gazed at me, I struggled with myself. The fact that he was now tracing my bottom lip with his thumb didn't help matters, either.

"I'm in love with you," he said looking at me cautiously. "I do want to marry you. Not just because of Jacques or the Rebellion. I want a life with you."

He cradled my face and gave me one more lingering kiss. In it was a promise forged by years of unbound magic. He made my knees go weak. He made my heart race a thousand times faster, as if it would beat out of my chest. He made me feel like freedom was just in my reach—like I could be myself without judgement.

But I did not love him back.

I looked into his eyes and saw the strangeness of them—the beauty. No one had ever looked at me like that—as if he would lay down his life for me. I wanted to be wanted—no—I *needed* it. Would it be such a sin to follow his plan and marry him? Would it be so hard to love him in return?

"Think of all those lives," he reminded me. "I know that you're tired of fighting. This way, you'd still do your part, without having to kill anyone. It can be oddly fulfilling. I love helping people. And I thought—maybe that you—?"

"I do, too," I said once I could think straight.

One kiss—one kiss changed it all. Some said love could stop wars. Was it true?

"Here." He reached into his pocket. "Take this."

Encased in a glass box that sat on his palm was a small silver ring. Cut in a marquise was a blue diamond. The silver of the ring's bed circled it. Flanking the blue jewel were two white diamonds. On the inside of the band was the name *Boyd* and as Dorian slipped the ring on my finger, I felt a sudden influx of power.

My own powers called back in response. They immediately swirled from my Majik sack, rushing down the length of my body, past my arm, to my fingertips where they stayed. I wondered how they could come alive so easily and then remembered: his love. His love was enough motivation for my body to produce the hormone called Majik, which gave me the ability to use magic, and my powers grew tenfold every time he came near me. It was like sex and dopamine, only a thousand times more satisfying.

"This was my mother's." Dorian stated factually before kissing me. "Combining some of my power—" the band was blue "—and your power—" the band was now purple "—you will always be protected. When you are in your hour of need, this ring will unlock the guardian of the Boyd household."

I had no idea what that meant but I decided not to dwell on it as the ring's band went back to that silvery color. I peered at it closely. It was more whitish than most silver I'd seen and was shinier.

"This is the prettiest, shiniest silver I've ever seen!"

"It's platinum…and yes, it is something. But it doesn't compare to you."

I blushed. I just knew that my eyes were twinkling like a child's. "Wow! It's so…so…"

Beautiful.

I'd never really seen platinum like this. Among my many chores, Master had me polish his silver and keep stock of his jewels. But I never really risked retribution enough to *look*. To think, I was entrusted with something so precious…Then to be treated as an equal?

Dorian loved me.

He slid the ring onto my finger. I felt the coolness of it and its weight. I flexed my fingers but the ring, so sure of itself, did not slip or slide.

Dorian sat in the feather-soft chair in front of the fire before pulling me into his lap. I snuggled closer, breathing him in. He was my own personal drug and there was no way that I was giving him up now. We sat and talked for an hour or so, me playing with his hair and him tracing patterns on my back. I hoped that was what our lives would always be like.

"You paint really well, Dorian."

"Thank you."

I yawned. Dorian kissed my head. I almost felt like a purring cat as Dorian traced a finger along my spine.

"Sleepy?" He said, a grin in his voice.

"Mm…A bit."

He suddenly stood with me still in his arms. I squealed as he pushed open the library doors and walked through the halls past blushing maids and chuckling butlers. I could get used to this.

"Can you train me?"

He opened the door to a large room, his skin never breaking its contact with mine. It housed a massive king-sized bed with purple sheets and a golden cover—an odd color combination that somehow worked. A painting adorned the walls and as we curled up in bed, I was bombarded with want.

"Don't worry," he said, trailing kisses along my jaw. "I won't be the only one protecting you. You'll be safe."

I wanted to get up and fight back. I didn't want to wither away as some long-forgotten princess. I wanted to earn my keep. I wanted to train. I wanted to take down Valentina and Jacques myself.

But he wasn't ready to hear that.

Chapter Thirty-Seven

Kindness

The next day I was awakened by a knock at the door. I sprang up in bed, feeling the covers next to me.

Dorian was gone.

I looked around at the walls. There was a picture of a man, a woman and a child. The man had harsh lemony skin and cold brown eyes, the woman brown-skinned, her hair pulled in a black bun and her eyes an equally devastating onyx, and the boy who couldn't have been older than twelve had golden skin that was a mixture of them both, his brown-gold eyes unique and his sweetness and innocence just as purely his own.

Who were these people? The boy was Dorian—that much I was sure of—but the cruel-looking man and stoic woman…Were those his parents? Why was a picture of Dorian and his family on the wall? I looked around the room and saw two regal dressers that would have taken up my room in Sidra alone. But this wasn't Sidra.

Where was I?

The knock sounded again. This wasn't Jacques's mansion (thank the Goddess!) and it wasn't the safe house. And just like that, I remembered. I was at Dorian's manor! I covered myself with the sheets as the door creaked open. In walked that maid from before—what was her name?

Oh, that's right. Beatrice.

"I'm here to help you get ready, mem."

"Get ready? I don't need help getting ready."

"It is custom, mem. Even the Master has someone to help him. He asked me to be gentle with you." She held out an outfit bag. "He's even gone through the trouble of designing your clothes for the day."

I hesitated. Dorian had ordered her to help me get ready? Maybe it wouldn't be so bad. I stretched as my back and feet suddenly began to ache. There was no denying it.

I needed help.

I nodded at Beatrice. She hung my outfit on a little hook on the wall. I briefly wondered why I didn't hear Dorian get dressed. I asked Beatrice. She said that Lord Boyd had purposely instructed his maids to be as quiet as possible.

At my look, Beatrice told me that he had no interest in the maids. He'd been using them for years and had never taken one to bed. I sighed. This jealousy thing was getting out of hand. I really needed to get over it.

I slowly eased out of bed, already naked thanks to last night's escapades. Beatrice looked neither bashful nor disgusted at my state. She commented that I should eat a big breakfast when we went downstairs. I agreed. I was starving.

She took me to the adjoined bathroom. I was surprised to see that the bath was already full. Steam rose up from the water. I got in the tub and sunk into the water. My muscles began to relax as I soaked for a moment.

Beatrice cleared her throat. I opened my eyes, which I hadn't even noticed were closed. She watched me expectantly.

"So are you just supposed to sit there and watch me? I'm not going anywhere."

"No, mem." She blushed a little, as if embarrassed about having to explain this to me. "I'm supposed to wash you."

I sat up. Wash me? I'd never been washed before. I mean, I had washed my old master in the past. But to be on the other end of it...?

This would be interesting.

Beatrice held up a sponge that appeared from nowhere and came to me. She dipped it in the water, not too far from my private area. I scooted back to give myself more room. She went to work, scrubbing my back, my chest, my feet—my entire body. She was rough but gentle all at once, getting rid of every bit of dead skin.

I refused to let her wash me, you know, *down there*. She sighed as if in pain and handed over the sponge. I scrubbed myself before passing it back. I watched as the sponge literally evaporated into thin air. I looked at the Gifted woman in shock.

"I can control matter," she confessed.

I blinked, confused. What the hell was matter? I was too embarrassed to ask.

She read the look on my face clear enough.

"Have you been formally educated?" she asked.

I shook my head no. It was kind of true. I dropped out of school when my parents died. When Jacques found me, he didn't focus on my education. He focused on my battle training. Knowing that I enjoyed reading, he gifted me written works on my birthday, and in all the books I'd read, it had never mentioned 'matter.' Stupid and ugly, he sometimes called me.

That's how I felt at this moment.

"I am...erm...self-taught."

"You should speak to Master Boyd about this. Perhaps he can have you educated."

I didn't answer because the thought of revealing to Dorian that I wasn't smart was, well, embarrassing. I didn't even know that he'd been educated. After all, he said that he didn't like to read. Jacques had been educated at one of the best magical schools in the world—Pendragon Academy. Hell, the only reason I spoke so eloquently was from being around him. Maybe if I was educated, I would come closer to eliminating him.

I wrapped the towel that Beatrice handed me around my body. She led me to the mirror in the bedroom. I looked at myself in the mirror: my skin was crimson, rubbed raw. The only thing redder than that was my hair, its curls wild and untamed around my bony head. Beatrice returned, holding a bottle of oil. She lathered me in it, rubbing me much more gently this time.

I smelled like roses. I asked Beatrice why she picked this scent. She said that heeding a friend, Dorian told her to find something that enhanced my scent and, since I smelled like roses and spring water, she got this one.

At first, he wanted to cover my scent—now he wanted to enhance it?

Maybe that meant that we truly were safe.

Beatrice picked up the outfit off the hook. She unzipped it. I stared at the outfit in shock. It was a strapless bodysuit made of lace that was forest green in color. He wanted me to wear that?

Why?

I dressed in seconds, throwing on the suit. While dressing, I watched Beatrice watch me with pursed lips. I briefly wondered why but then realized I didn't care. Beatrice made me sit in a chair in front of the mirror. Then she went to work on my makeup.

I looked in the mirror once she was done. I didn't look like myself. My cheeks were rosy while my lips were red and plump. She did a cat-eye with eyeliner, making my green eyes appear piercing. To be honest, I didn't even look on the cusp of twenty anymore.

I looked like an elite woman.

I asked Beatrice to take off the makeup. I didn't want to look like someone else. I wanted to look like me. Beatrice did it but released a sigh that said I was being difficult again. I sighed, too.

I'd only been here one day and they were already trying to change me.

Slowly, carefully, I let go of my glamour. First appeared my slit-pupil eyes, then my scaled skin then finally the claws on my fingers.

Monsters playing dress up, I thought with a laugh.

Beatrice waved a wand over my face, removing the makeup with sonic sensors. Oh, the wonders of technology! The makeup pulsated and fell from my skin.

Beatrice left without another word. I left the room to look for Dorian. I checked the library and the kitchen, but he wasn't there. May I just add that the staff in the kitchen were doing their thing and it wasn't even eight in the morning yet. I walked through a random doorway on the first floor and found a massive dining hall.

I left the dining room to stand in the foyer, utterly lost. *Click, click, click!* I turned around at the sound of heels on marble. She grabbed my hand and pulled me into a room with a small cot pushed in the corner, a desk and a chair. On the cot sat Andrew, who was playing a handheld system, his eyes trained on the game console and the sound of little creatures crying out.

I smiled. I used to love Pokémon as a kid.

"What are your intentions with Dorian?" Yvonne asked, taking a seat in the chair.

"I'm not sure. I haven't quite figured that out myself. But I do know one thing."

"That's rich!" She paused, her eyes narrowing. "Is that why you want him? Because he's rich?"

The thought hadn't even crossed my mind.

"I say this with sincerity."

She stared into my eyes. I knew that I was being tested and I frankly didn't give a rat's ass. I wanted Dorian's happiness, his safety, his desire, but even I wasn't exactly sure what we were doing. He'd once told me that we were casual lovers. And now that he'd said he'd loved me, now that we were getting married, I saw no reason that this should change.

After all, he was the one who never really wanted to label us.

"Dorian means a lot to me, and I wouldn't risk his safety for anything."

Lame, I know, but I wasn't a poet—I'd never been good with words—especially when it came to my feelings. But she got the gist.

"So, the feelings are mutual." She smiled at me. "That's good to know."

She stared at me, and for a moment, her eyes flickered between red and black. I took a step back as I remembered what she was. I knew that she was dangerous—all demons were. She frowned at me, and I felt my powers fizz and die out. She cocked her head at me, like a bear passing a man, and I wondered if this was how I was meant to die.

There was a puff of smoke as her ghostly cackle travelled through the air.

She was gone.

"Weird old hag…"

I left Andrew to his game. Now random shudders passed through me with no sign of stopping. Beatrice flung a blanket around my shoulders as she passed. The rough fabric scratched my neck. I pulled it tighter with the sudden cold, wincing now and then but otherwise all right.

Dorian suddenly appeared in front of me, his eyes wide.

I stopped dead in my tracks, the momentary chills gone. "Are you okay?"

"Yeah, I'm fine." He paused. "Are you okay? You look a little paler than usual."

"I'm fine. Just a little under the weather is all."

"How are you liking the manor so far?"

"It's great!" I chirped a little too quickly.

He narrowed his eyes. "What's wrong?"

I wanted to say, "Everything." But I didn't want to sound ungrateful. The way I felt about him was scary. Being hunted by Jacques was scary. Being around another half-demon was scary. Everything was too much at once and I could feel myself fracturing under the weight of it all.

He frowned as my breaths became more labored. I couldn't believe it. I was having a panic attack *again*.

"Marve," Dorian touched my cheek, "you need to calm down."

A wave of peace settled over me. Dorian didn't pull away until all the fight had drained from me. Why was I so upset anyway?

"Everything's going to be okay, Marve."

"I'm going to be okay?"

"Yes. Say it with me."

"I'm going to be okay."

"Yes, good." He took my hand. "Now come on. It's time for breakfast."

I nodded and followed him to the dining room. The table was laden with a buffet of food. Brown pancakes, golden waffles, freshly sliced fruit of various colors and origins, orangish-white cheese grits, lumpy pale brown oatmeal—everything that could possibly be desired. I sat to the right of Dorian. We ate in total silence, the table stretching endlessly despite there being only two of us.

"Is this real?" I asked more than once.

"It's the country! Everything is real! Everything is grown on a farm up the road. Meat cannot be obtained, as you know. But everything else…?"

So I ate and ate until the thought crossed my mind yet again.

This manor was beautiful—magnificent even. But something about it felt so warped and it made me feel alone. I wondered what secrets its walls held. Dorian reached over to take my hand. Just like that, I forgot what I was thinking about.

I ate in silence, not realizing that he was using his Gift on me. Maybe it was better that I didn't know. After all, he had given me the perfect life. Only when we were done eating and had risen from the table did I broach the subject of my training. Dorian listened intently, not once interrupting to laugh or deny me.

"I could always train you."

I thought of me on top of him, a blade against his throat. I saw him tangling his hands in my hair, kissing me, distracting me. *Oh my...*

"That's probably not a good idea."

"Andrew can always teach you. He oversaw my training when I was a boy. I'm sure he'd be happy to help you."

I heard a snort that sounded suspiciously like a laugh from down the hall. My cheeks heated in an instant. Dorian breathed hard through his nose, clearly trying to control himself. Like him, I wanted to march down there. I knew that it was Yvonne—I could feel it in my bones.

I shook my head.

"But isn't Andrew ancient?" I asked.

Dorian smirked, using my moment of weakness to point out, well, my weakness. "Maybe this is a sign that you shouldn't fight at all."

"I want to be trained!" I said, trying not to sound like a bratty ten-year-old.

332

"Do you? Do you really?"

I pushed away from the table. I could see what he was doing. He was trying to change me, to force me to let him take care of me like he had with Megumi. But I was used to fending for myself—and I didn't need him. I huffed and stomped off.

I would show him.

I would show Valentina.

I would show Jacques.

I would show them all that I was strong.

***

Andrew sat on my chest. My arms were handcuffed behind my back. We were in a training room in the basement, which was just down the hall from the old-timey movie theatre. I struggled, trying to flip him off me. I could tell that he was trying not to laugh. I screamed in rage for what may have been the hundredth time.

"Stop struggling," Andrew instructed. "You must master your body and your mind."

"I feel like such an idiot!"

I was crying now—big, fat, ugly tears. My head began to hurt in the way it does when you cry too hard, when there's too much pressure. I closed my eyes as the room began to blur. I felt a weight come off my chest then the bite of the cuffs relieving from my wrists. I felt a body lay next to mine. I rolled over and saw Andrew lying next to me, staring at the ceiling.

"What are you doing?" I asked, wiping my face.

"It's okay to cry," he said, his voice surprisingly strong despite his age. "You just can't give up."

"I'm not giving up," I sighed.

But maybe I was so eager to confront Jacques and Valentina because I was eager for one of them to kill me. I mean, sometimes I really wanted to live. But life felt like too much at times. I formally only had a fourth-grade education, I couldn't take down the organization that killed my parents, I couldn't bring down the man that abused me. Hell, I couldn't even tell Dorian how I felt.

"I can see a great pain in you," Andrew said. "And I want you to know that it's okay to be in pain. It's okay to feel like you're not strong enough. It's okay to take a break. But you've got to remember that pain is only temporary."

I thought of slitting my wrists. It would be hard with the scales. But if I used my glamour and cut deep enough, I would be okay. I would see my parents again. I could be free.

"You're right." I rolled over to escape his prying eyes. "Pain is only temporary."

***

Dorian was waiting outside the door when I was through. My body felt normal, lighter even, but my mind was weighed down and aching. I collapsed into his arms, maybe a bit melodramatically.

"Damn. All that after an hour of training? You really suck."

I punched him in the arm, albeit without any force.

"Shut up, jerk."

"Aw..." He hoisted me into his arms. "Do you want me to give you a backrub?"

I could hear the lust in his voice.

"No way am I taking one of those from *you,* Master Boyd." I grinned cheekily. "I know how that ends."

"Does this have something to do with the fact that I lied about our engagement? You don't get it—Yvonne is super scary!"

"Not that." I batted my lashes at him, biting my lip. "You'll have me spilling all my secrets."

He stopped walking. I looked up to see that he was staring at one of the paintings, a horrified look on his face. Had I said something wrong?

"Who told you about that?" he whispered, almost to himself.

"No one." I quickly lied, already able to tell that this was a bad situation. "It was just a joke."

"Just a joke...?"

"Yes. A joke." I poked him in the side. "You know what a joke is, right?"

"A joke..." He laughed under his breath. "How could I forget myself?"

"Um...Dorian...?"

He had returned to normal. "Yes, love?"

"Never mind."

"..."

"Man, I'd kill for a drink right now."

Yes, I was trying to distract him.

"That sounds perfect. I could use a drink myself."

335

He carried me to the kitchen amid scurrying maids and resolute butlers. He snapped his fingers and one of the passing people produced a bottle of jack. I figured out two things from this: he did this often and bourbon was his preferred drink. A rather short man informed us that he would bring the drinks up to the office in a minute or two. Dorian took us to a small office with papers staked on the desk; he swiped them to the ground with barely a thought.

"Um, darling?"

"Yes?"

"Weren't those papers important?"

"They were just about my different businesses. I'm running a self-audit."

"Self -audit?"

"I donate a certain percentage of my wealth to the Rebellion's cause. But I'm still running a lot of things on the side. I do a self-audit every month. This way I can make sure that no one is funneling money out for other expenses."

"Does anyone help you?"

"Sometimes I get Yvonne and Andrew to help but I mostly do it myself." He set me down on the desk before turning to grin at the man in the doorway. "Ah, the drinks are here!"

He scooped them up and slammed the door in the other man's face. He unscrewed the top off one bottle before pouring some alcohol into each glass. I reached for one but he smacked my hand away.

"What do you think you're doing?"

"I'm drinking with you...?"

"*What?!* I'm not letting you drink! First, you're drinking a shot and the next, you're sitting in an AA meeting with only a peg-legged stripper and a box of tissues to keep you company."

"Odd flex but okay."

He downed one glass, said "Cheers!" and then downed the other. He refilled in record time. I sat there watching him, wondering if I'd made a mistake egging this on.

"What's the point in having two glasses if you're the only one drinking?"

"Right you are."

He threw one of the glasses at the wall. It shattered into a million little pieces. I took note of his pressured speech and whirling emotions. Was this what it was like being an alcoholic? I hoped to never find out. I thought about his behavior for a long time. Dorian felt uncomfortable talking about whoring out for information.

"Tell me about your life?"

"There's not much to say. I went to Pendragon Academy with Jacques in my late teens. My father was an alcoholic who beat me constantly. My mother just stood by and watched. They were happy with each other but unhappy with me. Still, I was able to charm my way into getting what I wanted."

I paused. Dorian's father beat him? Before, he made it sound like his parents were happily in love. Now it sounded like he had neither a friend nor ally in this world. I felt devastated at not understanding the breadth of his pain and he? He looked as if he expected me not to believe him already.

"I've got the scars on my back to prove it," he volunteered.

He unbuttoned his shirt before taking it off gently, hesitantly. He began to turn, and I realized that I'd never seen his back. I was too busy looking at his face. Too busy ravishing him. I instantly felt guilty at the sight of the canvas before me.

Slashes zigzagged across his back. I reached out to run my finger along one starting at his collarbone and disappearing into his pants. What monster would do this to him—to a child?

He set the brandy and cup on the ground.

"I said that my parents were in love—I never said that they loved me. I wanted to be a drummer in a band growing up. My parents didn't support the decision and reminded me of it constantly. I would sneak down to the wine cellar and drink wine from our stores. When my parents died, I threw myself into my work, trying to see if I could live up to my father's expectations—if I could build the empire that my parents worked so hard to garner. I couldn't do it, Marve, so I told Yvonne to run my empire while I took time off to work with my friends to start a band. After forming the River Styx, I realized that the record company thought that I wasn't pale enough to start a band and that I wasn't black enough to be a rapper. I gave up and came home, finding solitude in the strangest places. Smuggling Gifted into the Southern Isles, training them with the Rebellion—that was what made me happy."

More importantly, it's what other people could expect and accept of you.

I didn't say anything for a long time. I just leaned forward and pressed my lips to his back. I kissed every scar, hoping to show that I accepted him no matter what, that I would never hurt him like that, that I was here for him. He turned around, took one long look at me and pounced. I removed his clothes gently as he tore at mine. He tore my poor bodysuit to shreds, sitting between my legs, grinding his hips against mine.

I let him take over, rubbing my hand across his chest, cradling his face, kissing him as softly as possible without losing myself in the sensations. He yanked off my panties—soft scraps of lace—before dropping his own pants and boxers. He dove inside of me with no hesitation, thrusting his hips flush against mine. I swirled my magic around us, enveloping us in our own electric haven. He pounded into me like no tomorrow, claiming what was his, asserting his dominance.

And I let him. I gave him all I had to give. That's when I realized that I was trying to make love while he was simply messing me. It was okay. After all, it was his body, his moment, his life.

Besides, could you truly make love without *being* in love?

He came inside me with a soft wail of pleasure. Shudders racked my body as his seed filled me, leaking out onto the table. Dorian got dressed in record time before using the last shreds of my bodysuit to wipe me and the table down. I sat there in my bra and nothing else, trying to decide what to do next.

Dorian picked me up and set me on his lap. He wrapped his arms around me, squeezing me tight. I snuggled into his chest, loving the feel of his warm embrace. I didn't realize that I'd dozed off until I felt the soft warmth of the bed beneath me. Dorian slid into bed next to me, holding me close, spilling all his huge secrets into my tiny, open palms.

I went back to sleep, unaware that he was making a vow, promising that neither of us would get hurt like that again. I had a dream that I'd told him that I loved him, that I'd been able to commit. I didn't realize that I'd said it aloud in my sleep or that Dorian heard me.

And I didn't get to see him smile.

Chapter Thirty-Eight

A Raid

The next day was as eventful as they get. Dorian was gone again when I woke up, but a note was on the side table, telling me that he loved me but had business to take care of. It was strange, reading those words in his elegant script, which was almost feminine: *I love you.* I could hear it a thousand times and I'd still want to hear it agains

Beatrice got me up and scrubbed me down like yesterday. I had to keep from snapping at her when she did my chest since it was so tender. She dressed me in loose clothes—a cobalt blue chiffon dress and a pair of flats.

I asked her if Dorian had designed the clothes this time. She reluctantly told me that he did not, but he had picked them out. I felt good knowing that he wanted to take care of me. Beatrice didn't try to put makeup on me but handed me a thing of lip balm. She doused me in oils again, making my skin look shiny and, despite my weight, healthy.

I went to the table just as they were bringing out breakfast. I ate some cream of wheat and jelly-covered toast. I glanced at the head seat, wishing that Dorian were with me. But then I realized that if he were, he wouldn't get any work done. Then we wouldn't have anywhere to live.

I borrowed a notebook from Yvonne, took the map that Dorian gave me when he took me from Jacques and wrote down all the safehouses that I could find. I wanted to leave here to keep Dorian's territory safe. But, even though this was a difficult adjustment, I actually needed this kind of stability and careful attention.

I stared at the notebook for a long time, debating.

Did I want to leave this simple life behind?

After a while, I began doodling in the notebook, drawing stick figures of Dorian on top of a dragon or me and Tiara in the foyer. I wished that she could see me now, see what I'd been given. I could see her running through the halls, me teaching her how to read, her gorging on the food at the table. She'd be so happy here. I just knew it.

Crash!

I went to the top of the stairs to see two men standing in the foyer, masks covering their faces and a dagger in each hand. I recognized them as soldiers from the Rebellion. Panic blossomed, making my heart slam against my ribcage. Dorian came out of the kitchen, stumbling drunk. I glanced between him and the Rebel soldiers, comparing the difference.

He wouldn't make it up the stairs in time.

"Dorian, look—"

A hand clamped down on my mouth. I kicked and scratched as terror took over my senses. Whoever was holding me backed up from the stairs and towards my bedroom. Fuck, I knew what that meant. I bit down on their hand, drawing blood.

"Damn it, Marve, it's me!"

I turned around to see Andrew standing there, blood dripping from his hand. The old man quickly led me to the bedroom that I shared with Dorian. He went to one of the walls, pushed against it. A fraction of the wall moved to reveal a stairway. Terror made my heart rage, threatening to beat out of my chest.

"Andrew, what's happening?"

"Rebels are attacking the estate. It's my job to make sure that you're safe." He gestured to the stairway. "Now get going. Just keep walking and you'll make it to a safe room."

Fear seized my heart. But I wasn't concerned with my own safety.

"But what about Dorian? Will he be okay?"

"He can handle himself. Just know that the longer you stand here arguing with me, the less time I have to protect him."

"I can help! I can—"

A crash sounded. I jumped. Andrew shoved me towards the stairway. I thought of Dorian and the way he'd protected me. Was it selfish of me to take up his time, to deny him his protection, to—

"Would you just go?!" Andrew snapped.

I took a few steps down the stairwell. The door closed behind me and I was left in darkness. That was how I felt when I wasn't with Dorian—like I was lost in darkness, unable to find my way out. My powers crackled to life, illuminating the area around me in a purple glow. I made my way down to the bottom of the stairwell only to find Beatrice and Yvonne there.

"Are you all right, mem?" Beatrice said, rushing to my side.

She laid a hand on my cheek. Her hand felt cool to the touch. She touched my other cheek and then my forehead. Her eyes swam with concern. I swayed and she helped me sit on the floor next to Yvonne.

"She's running a temperature. What should I do?"

"Make sure that she doesn't leave this room." Yvonne stood, powerful and strong. "I'm going back into the wreckage."

"Wait…" I moved to stand but swayed on unsteady feet, which I fought to hide. "I'm going with you."

"No," Yvonne sighed, "you're not."

"What about Dorian?! What if he needs me—needs my powers? I can fight!"

"Dorian will kill us all for letting you leave."

I had to bite my tongue before I cussed her out.

"I'm not weak."

"Tell me, child. Why do you have such a need to prove yourself?"

I had no answer. Was that what I looked like—like I had something to prove? It wasn't validation that I needed, it was the man fighting in the foyer for all of us, his power, his touch, his love. Still, I had to show that I was strong enough to live without him, even if it wasn't necessarily true. I sighed and leaned back, laying my head on the wall next to me.

"Go without me," I said, eyeing her up and down. "But if something happens to my fiancé, I'm holding you responsible."

She grinned devilishly at me, her fangs jutting out. "I wouldn't have it any other way."

She went up a stairwell and into the battle ahead. I don't know how long we sat there, waiting. My head swam and I felt sick to the stomach. It wasn't the fever that was killing me, it was the constant fear of losing him. Beatrice watched me like a falcon, her eyes never leaving me.

"Tell me about him. You've known him longer than I have."

"Who, mem?"

"Who else?" I snapped, then softened my tone. "I'm sorry."

"I don't think it's my place. Just ask him when you see him."

"I have asked him. I just want to make sure that I remember him, that I do him justice. In case…" I trailed off, tears brimming in my eyes.

"You've gotten to know him better than any of us, even more than his cousin. He loves you, mem. I don't think you need to remember him. He wouldn't die on us now. He has too much to live for."

I smiled and leaned my head on her shoulder. I sang to myself under my breath, trying to keep calm. The room was soundproof so I couldn't hear a thing that was going on upstairs. It was a blessing and a curse. I wanted information, wanted to know if he needed help, but at least I didn't jump at every clash and bang.

The door opened and I cowered in fear. Who was it? Beatrice moved to stand in front of me, ready to defend me until the very end.

345

"What's the safe word?" Beatrice barked.

The light in her hands twisted and turned, never staying on just one form, sometimes a hammer, then a sword, then a pistol. What a fantastic Gift. Every weapon known to man was at her disposal, power in her very fingertips. I huddled a bit closer to her, clinging to her plainclothes, knowing that Kalysma sent her to me for not only servitude, but protection.

"Whale blubber!" he called.

He stumbled into the light. I almost fainted from relief. I got up and ran into his arms, almost knocking us both over. There was blood running down his face, so I kissed him where it was dry. He had a nasty head wound and his shirt was torn, but otherwise he looked to be all right. As soon as I thought it, the wound stitched itself closed.

"Dorian, don't ever do that again!" I said in between kisses.

"I'm fine," he said with a small smile, hugging me.

"I told you it would be all right, mem," Beatrice added from the corner.

I ignored her. "What happened?"

"Rebel soldiers attacked the manor. They'd been hiding in the trees, waiting for us to get here. The only reason they didn't attack sooner was because they were waiting to see if we had any other allies."

I sighed. Maybe it was a good thing that we hadn't recruited anyone at Megumi's party. I still blamed her for a lot of our woes—she told both the Rebellion and Jacques about our status.

"You seem a little better, a little more…?"

"Sober?" He asked with a wink.

"Yes."

"Nothing's more sobering than a good fight."

"What about Yvonne and Andrew? Are they okay?"

"They're doing okay. Yvonne was hit with an ash arrow, which slowed down her healing process, but didn't kill her—good thing they didn't have the Dagger of Truth or we'd be in serious trouble. Andrew tripped and broke his hip. Crazy old man. I told him after the last invasion not to fight."

"They both just love you, baby," I cooed, reaching out to stroke his face.

He turned his head and kissed my palm. A jolt went down my spine. He pulled me close. I swooned when he planted a warm kiss on my mouth.

"I'm so glad you're okay." I hugged him tight. "I don't know what I'd do if anything happened to you."

His eyes sparked with hope. I knew what he was waiting to hear. But I wasn't ready to surrender my heart just yet. I mean, we had so much ahead of us. Anything could happen in the next few days, let alone the next few months.

I laid my head on his shoulder, softly humming to myself. He seemed to sag a bit more against me, as if my lack of affection had burdened him somehow. Beatrice opened the hidden door that was at the end of the stairway. I led him up into our room. Beatrice made sure that there was nothing that we needed before she left.

Dorian took my hand and led me to the bed. He sat down. I took a seat next to him, embracing his essence, his warmth, his beauty. I decided to grab provisions and clean his wound. I moved from the room to the bathroom, grabbing what I needed

347

before sinking into the bed next to him. I put peroxide on a cotton swab and went to wiping down his head and face. The blood had seeped into his burgundy shirt, turning it black, so I tugged the first few buttons open.

He stared at the wall pointedly. I got another swab and dabbed at the blood on his collarbone. His body seemed to heat under my touch and he squirmed whenever my hands met his skin. I fought the urge to smile. He was definitely going to be okay. It wasn't until I had almost cleaned him entirely that he grabbed my hands, shaking, and stared at me with worry and fear.

"I need to tell you something."

Ah, man.

"Remember how we buried the Book of Beginnings?"

"Yes."

"I told them where it was."

"I'm sorry." I blinked, confused. "You did what?"

"Please don't make me say it again." He looked at me imploringly but gave up at my blank, unassuming stare. "I gave the Rebellion the Book."

A million different possibilities went through my head. They could use it to stage an all-out war against the Immortals that opposed them. Countless Gifted would die. The few Immortals, like Dorian once was, that stood with them would lose everything. And where would that leave us? More importantly, where would that leave the future generations?

Would there even be a future?

"Why?"

"Their messenger said they'd kill you one way or another. They said they knew you were here and that if I didn't give them the Book, they would eventually find you and kill you or hand you over to Jacques. I know about your situation. I know that he beat on you and I...I just couldn't give you up. I couldn't make you go through that—not again."

I picked up his hand and placed a kiss on his palm the same way he did earlier. He looked into my eyes and all I saw there was a man in love trying to save his woman. I reached out, grabbed his face and planted a kiss square on his mouth. His lips trembled as he whispered "I'm sorry. I'm so sorry," under his breath. I parted from him only when he stopped apologizing.

"You didn't do anything wrong. You protected me."

His eyes shone with wonder and gratefulness, as if I'd somehow saved him.

"I love you," he said with such conviction.

My throat swelled.

Say it, you coward.

I kissed him again and said, "I know, Dorian. I know..."

He parted from me, his gaze only partly occupied.

"So what was in that book that was so special anyway? I mean, that thing was creepy. I'm kind of glad it's gone."

"Runes," he said solemnly.

"That's all?"

"These weren't just any runes. They were runes that the Creator used to craft the entire universe. These are runes that were used by Mestiphopheles himself to bring down the heavens. They were runes that gave any human, Mortal or Immortal, the power to take enslave the entire world. Don't you get it, woman? These were world-altering, god-making runes!"

"Okay, I get it!" I paused, biting my lip worriedly. Dorian flicked his thumb across my bottom lip, commanding it from my mouth. I blushed, but I did not forget my question. "If it did all that, why did Jacques have it?"

"It is passed on from descendants of Mestiphopheles, from father to son. Jacques was a direct descendant. We'd need to get it from him and then summon a demon to use it."

"Then why does the Rebellion want it? I mean, they can't use it anyway."

"I overheard Valentina talking about it once. If you draw a pentagram, you can summon any demon of your choosing. The stronger the artifacts in the pentagram, the stronger the demon."

And I knew that if the request was big enough, they'd have to do something for the demon in return.

"So...?"

"So if they summoned Jacques, or worse, Mestipho himself, the demon in the pentagram would have to do one thing for them. That's how magic like this works. They could strip away every Immortal on the planet with a single word. Hell, they could destroy the planet with a single word!"

"Well, if it does all that, why hasn't Jacques used it yet?"

"He can only use it when he's been summoned. No pentagram, no magic. No magic, no rune. No rune, no spell."

"So basically, this just gave them the single most power in the world."

"The most power in this universe." I cursed and he paused. "I don't know what we're gonna do now."

An idea hit me full force.

"I know exactly what we're gonna do." It was crazy. But it just might work. "Dorian, when do you think they're gonna use the book?"

"Tomorrow's a blood moon. I guarantee they'll use it then."

"We're going to steal the book back and destroy it."

"How do you plan to do that?"

"A demon made it and a demon will destroy it."

"What demon?"

"Yvonne's a half-demon, isn't she?"

"Yeah but we can't use her. We need all the magic we can get. We'd need a full-blooded demon."

"What about her mother?"

"She'd never work with us. The woman is pure evil and holds no allegiance to anyone but herself...not even Mestipho can get her on his team. Maybe Abaddon will help us?"

"If he's anything like Jacques, he'll want something in return."

Just like that, we had two goals for tomorrow: retrieve the Book of Beginnings and destroy it.

I prayed to the Mother Goddess that this would go over well. Because if it didn't, we may very well destroy life as we know it. The very air chilled, as if it knew our plans. I leaned against Dorian, hoping to steal some of his warmth. This had to work.

Because if it didn't, we wouldn't get a second chance.

Chapter Thirty-Nine

Let's Do Battle, Moose

The next day, Dorian was there with me, head propped up on his fist, just watching me. I blinked up at him, smiling. He prolonged his kiss, a promise there, but also an apology.

"I forgot to tell you, there's some business that I have to attend to today before we get started on anything drastic."

My mood instantly soured. I wondered if he'd done this on purpose, kissed me to get me in a good mood just to let me down. Everyone in my life had let me down. But then I realized that it simply wasn't that deep. Yet it didn't stop the pain lancing through my heart or withhold the knife sticking out of my chest. I inhaled around the pain.

"I want to spend the day with you." Tears welled in my eyes. "This could be our last time together."

"I know. But I have to take care of things here in case things go south." He planted a kiss on the soft spot behind my ear, my weak point. "Can you ever forgive me?"

"I don't understand. Why can't we be together?"

"What will all the Gifted in my territory do if something happens to me?" He looked away, his face crumpling as if he were in pain. "I couldn't live with myself if they were enslaved."

I reached out, tangled my hands in his hair. My mouth came to his jugular, kissing the vein in his neck. He groaned, shuddering. I kissed towards his lips, my hands travelling down his body slowly, an invitation. But he suddenly snapped his eyes shut and rolled across the bed, away from me.

"Let me just say," he whispered, leaning over to kiss my cheek, "that I'm really, *really* sorry."

"Mhm."

Beatrice came into the room, his outfit in hand. He got dressed in seconds. He didn't look at me before he left, his face strong, determined. I watched him leave, praying to Kalysma that I would see him again.

I couldn't lose him.

Not when things had finally stated to go right.

I took a shower, tears streaming down my face, mixing with the water. I wanted to tell him that I loved him before things got super crazy. But it was too late now. Beatrice lathered me with oils after I got out before dressing me in a blue dress that matched Dorian's magic, a blue jacket and blue flats. I reached out, picking up a golden hair pin from the box she opened and putting it in my hair.

Before I forgot, I went to the desk and picked up the heat modifier (an ingenious invention by Dorian to help me adjust to Amoria's colder months) before placing it on my neck. Beatrice led me downstairs to the dining room where sandwiches, sodas, chips and cookies were waiting. I must have slept in because it was now high noon.

I ate most of my food by myself. Pale white bread with a green, sour cucumber spread wedged between the two slices and slim, yellowish-white potato crisps that Beatrice called chips. I took a sip of the brown bubbly soda, getting foam on my upper lip. Beatrice was nearby but I still felt alone. I licked my upper lip clean. I wanted Dorian to be with me forever and ever.

This isn't normal, hissed a voice in my ear. *For Kalysma's sake, give the man a breather.*

Beatrice was watching me, not saying a word.

"Why don't you eat with me, Beatrice?"

"It's not my place, mem."

"I could use the company."

Beatrice sat down but did not touch the food. She shifted and it didn't take a rocket scientist to tell that she was uncomfortable. I grabbed a plate and set a pimento cheese sandwich on it, then a few apple slices before placing a can of lemon-lime soda before her. She glanced at me. I nodded encouragingly.

She ate slowly at first but as the minutes passed, she became more at ease and ate quicker, seemingly famished. I smiled. With those crumbs on her face, she suddenly appeared pretty in a childish sort of way.

"How old are you, Beatrice?"

"Nineteen."

"Have you lived here all your life?"

"Yes. My parents sent me here when I was just a baby. They were one of the few Scots to survive the Great Change."

"What do you mean?"

"The Scottish and Irish...Other than the ones in The Land of the Three, there are none left."

"Oh my Goddess."

I had not known that.

"I'm Irish, you know," I admitted, staring at her for validation, "on my Mar's side."

She smiled back.

"We're the same, you and I."

She nodded. But I did not mean ancestry. I meant by magic. We were both Gifted, both descendants of the Good Mother Kalysma. We were family.

I took her plate and saw her cringe, either guilty or still hungry. I made a mental note to talk to Dorian about how much and how often he fed the help here. If I played my cards right, Beatrice could become a great ally and possibly even a friend. I felt safe around her. But more than that, I felt that I could trust her.

I hoped that placing faith in her was not a mistake.

Beatrice glanced around the room, obviously checking to see if anyone saw her eating. I piled some grapes on her plate. She ate these quickly, happily and a bit guiltily, giving a reluctant smile with each bite. When she was done, to put her mind at ease, I grabbed her plate and set it next to mine so that it looked like I'd eaten the food and not her. I ate some crumb cake with raisins before belching loudly.

Beatrice stared at me with wide eyes. Then burst into a fit of girlish giggles. It was an undeniably sweet moment, one that I wouldn't have gotten away with had Dorian been there. I smiled at her and told her that this would be our secret. She smiled quickly before standing and coming to my side, glancing over her shoulder with a happy, secretive look in her eyes.

When I was done, two women came and got my plates. Beatrice informed me that the car was ready. I stood up from the table, taking one last look beyond the stairs where Dorian was. Beatrice draped a jacket over my shoulders, wishing me a happy hunting season. I went out to the car and got in. The driver took me to the border of Amoria.

We didn't cross it and instead careened west at the last possible turn. We drove to a small cluster of buildings near the docks where the water began. I looked at the passing water, wondering what lay beyond. Was there really a land where I could live without persecution, the place where my parents once promised to take me? I snorted. It was a child's dream, an impossible fantasy. One thing's for sure: a place like that couldn't exist and even if it did, it wouldn't last.

We stopped in the middle of a field. There was a lake there, stretching as far as the eye could see. There were fish swimming about and I knew from talking to Dorian that it was usually frozen. I took off my blue jacket, then my dress before kicking off my flats. I glanced around, making sure that there were no Immortals or Gifted to report back to them. After all, I wasn't in Dorian's territory anymore.

I saw the driver assembling a gun in the front seat. He got out of the car, looking through the scope at the land around us. With a removal of my glamour, I shed my underwear and bra before diving into the lake.

"Brrr!"

It was freezing!

I felt my body become weighed down with the cold. I reached up onto my neck and clicked on the heat modifier. I heard a small hum in my ears as heat spread through my pores. I took in a deep breath before going underwater. I could see that a lot of aquatic animals saw me as just another animal. That was good.

Being Gifted had its advantages after all.

I saw a large trout swimming about, wading in the water near its eggs. There was a larger fish swimming towards it, its thoughts were clear: *Eat. Eat. Eat.* I snuck up behind it before sinking my teeth into the larger fish. It flopped around in distress. I clamped down even harder, breaking its spine, before throwing my head back and swallowing.

It slid down my throat. I swam to the surface, my inner lids closing as I took in a lungful of air. To be honest, it was getting kind of old hunting fish.

I wanted bigger prey—something that would put up more of a fight.

I heard a snort behind me.

I turned to see a moose standing there, dipping its head forward to where its antlers scraped the ground. *Perfect!* I shook the water off me, running a hand across my brown skin. It would be tough doing this naked but at least I could be in my natural form. I heard something click.

The moose and I both looked over to see Hao, the part-time driver, aim at the animal. I raised a hand. Hao lowered the gun, giving me a peculiar look. It was time that I got used to using my powers. I braced my hands in front of me, creating a barrier of magic. The moose whipped its head this way and that before lowering it, getting prepared to charge.

Thump, thump, thump went its hooves as they pounded the ground.

It crashed into the barrier—and rammed straight through it. We tumbled into the water. It put up a struggle as I locked my jaws around its neck. It gave a very inhuman scream. I let go, slapping my hands onto its backside.

It bucked.

I dug my claws into its rear.

It sunk farther into the water.

I took in a gulp of air before going underwater. I dragged the moose down with me. It fought hard, bucking and biting and screaming the whole way down. I wrapped my legs around it before pulsating a small wave of my powers from my body. The lake was alive with electricity, the air singing as fish floated to the surface.

I closed my teeth around its neck, holding on to make sure that it was dead. Then I dragged it out of the water, feeling more like an animal than a person in that moment. I threw it to the ground. Blood oozed from its sides, plastered across the front of my body and coating my teeth. I licked my lips.

Nothing better than a fresh kill.

Hao came up behind me, throwing a towel over my body. I shivered with the sudden cold, pulling the cloth tighter around me. I felt the heat modifier on my neck and sure enough, it had died. I toweled off before getting dressed in a hurry. I left the body for a bigger, hungrier animal to find. In these harsh months, it was easy to guess they needed it more than I did.

As I got into the car, Hao flipped on the heat. I shuddered, taking it all in. I knew one thing from this experience: I hadn't lost my touch.

I was ready.

Chapter Forty

To the Stars

When I got home, I took off my dress and dressed in a black hoodie, black sweats and a purple bandana to hold my hair back from my face. Hopefully, the Rebellion wouldn't look too closely for Marks. Dorian was also decked out in black, looking as good as sin. He took Hao and Yvonne with us for this mission; he tried to convince me to stay home but I refused to be left behind. I brought the bow and arrows with me, along with a dagger strapped to my waist. No one else brought weapons and I *would* have worried, but I knew that they didn't need them.

Dorian pulled out a pen and drew a rune in the air, causing a slit of concentrated magic to appear in the air, which widened. We stepped through the portal and were transported to the Rebellion HQ.

It was easy enough to get down the stairwell but something was off when we gave the pair of blue eyes behind the door the password.

"From tyranny we ran

To the underground.

Loud is our cause

Though we make no sound.

The Good Mother, we worship

And do condemn

The Great Father

For what he did to them."

"You've got a lot of nerve showing your face here," the blue eyes said before the door swung open.

A column of fire billowed from inside, careening towards us like a spinning bottle top. I caught a look at Valentina: her face was a cold mask. Her scarred hands were raised shakily as she totally committed herself to the power that was her Gift. I took a step behind Dorian, ready to let him protect me. He withdrew his pen again and drew a rune in the air.

A shield of air came up between us and the flames.

The flames inched one way, then another, trying to find an opening to burn us to smithereens. Leave it to Dorian, Master of Runes, to know exactly what to do. Yvonne disappeared in a column of smoke and then reappeared behind the wall of soldiers that stood with Valentina.

She unleashed holy hell upon them, ripping off limbs and biting out throats with her bare fangs. They clearly didn't know what was coming for them as they turned their sights on her. I would have run like hell.

Dorian drew a new rune, one for transportation. I stepped through the portal with Dorian, leaving Hao behind to deal with the chaos at the entrance. The Book of

Beginnings lay on a dais, whispering to me.

"Hello, sweet thing. It's been a while since we've been together. Are you here to take me home?"

Dorian made to move forward. I held out a hand as my eyes narrowed. This was too easy.

I knocked one arrow, aimed and released it. Flames engulfed the ash arrow before it could even make contact. Valentina appeared in front of the pedestal. There was a deep gash was on her face, but she was otherwise unharmed. I knocked another arrow and took a deep breath, ready to shoot her at a moment's notice.

Dorian held up a hand.

"Why are you doing this, V?"

"Why are you so opposed to change?" She countered, raising an eyebrow. "The Immortals have ruled for too long. It's time for the Gifted to shine." She looked at me. "Why do you stand with him? He'll just use and discard you like he does the others."

Even I was startled by my own conviction as I said, "I stand where my heart lies."

"And you," she said, ignoring me and turning back to Dorian. "Why do you waste your time trying to make a Gifted happy? You know that she'll die one day. You're just wasting both of your time. I say you leave Marve with me. Let us settle our differences."

Dorian laughed. "You're out of your mind. Don't you know that I can see through your petty disguise, Jacques?"

She frowned. I looked between Dorian and the illusive Madam V. Jacques? This was clearly Valentina. I mean, she even had the missing eye and everything.

"His magic only works if you believe it works," Dorian told me. "Believe that he can't hurt you, that he is no threat, that he is nothing to you."

I tried but I couldn't. He was once my everything. Was that really him?

I shook my head.

"Breathe him in then," Dorian said patiently, keeping his eyes on the possibly fake Valentina. "Does that smell like Valentina to you?"

I took a deep breath and instantly blanched. My old master's scent of saltwater washed over me. Like the sea, he held no sustenance.

The Glamour faded and Jacques stood before me, as beautiful as ever. But when I looked, I mean *really* looked, I realized that he was gravely ill. His normally paper white skin now had a sickly greyish tinge to it and his eyes had deep bags under them. He even appeared to have lost weight, his sharp jawbones more pronounced. He looked like he might keel over any second.

I gasped, taking a step back, instantly wondering what had happened to him. Jacques was usually so put together! Dorian read my mind.

"Demons feed off terrorization. With you, Tiara and Valentina gone, he has no one to torment. He's dying."

I slapped a hand over my mouth, feigning shock. I pretended that it was Dorian that I saw before me, letting terror and sadness reach my eyes. I heard a pitiful noise drag from my chest.

"Marve," Jacques pleaded, actual terror in his eyes, "please come home. I realize that I need you. These new slaves—they won't bow. You know that I've always loved you. Come home now and I won't punish you. I'll even increase your food rations…" His next words came out strangle, forcing them clearly to me, but not to him: "I…I need you."

He needs me.

I sheathed my arrow. Dorian looked at me, shock and fury on his face. I pulled one blade from the sheath on my waist and moved to the other side of the room, taking my place by Jacques's side. Jacques reached out and took my hand. I threaded my fingers through his, taking false comfort in the icy cold feel of his perfect skin.

"Don't you see, boy?" Jacques hissed at Dorian, a sneer appearing on his face. "No matter what you do for her, no matter how much you spend on her, no matter how many times you fuck her like the whore she is—" I flinched "—you will *never* have her heart. I can give her the one thing you're too weak to give: dominance. As a beast, she craves submission. I thank you for taking care of her this long, but until the day she dies, she will always be mine."

He turned to touch my face. I reveled in the touch, wondering why he never showed me affection in the years I'd known him. Why now? Dorian's face begged me to see reason, to come back to him. I pretended that I was now looking at another version of my self—the monster that my old master wanted me to be.

Didn't he see that it was impossible?

This was my place—this was where I belonged.

Jacques moved to stand ahead of me, asserting his dominance. I took one look at him and drove my blade into his back. He gasped and fell forward, black, inky blood seeping from the wound. I ripped out the dagger before grabbing the book and running over to Dorian. He drew a rune and we stepped through the portal it made, appearing on the other side of the entrance to the hideout.

I turned to survey Yvonne, who looked tired but unharmed. Hao was still fighting his way through a group of Rebel soldiers. But where was—

"Ah!"

I fell forward. Valentina fell on top of me, pummeling me with her fists. Pain blossomed in my nose and mouth as blood spurted free. I rolled, twisting our bodies to where I was on top of her. I looked into her eyes, saw the woman that nurtured me, and suddenly crumpled with the weight of her betrayal. I pulled out a blade.

"You will always be weak!" she hissed, smirking up at me.

I slammed the pommel into her mouth. A tooth went flying. Unsatisfied, I rammed my other fist into her face. There went another tooth. Yvonne and Dorian had joined Hao to cut down the soldiers who were making their ways towards me, trying to save her. I sheathed the dagger.

My eyes glowed as I wrapped my arms around her. I pressed a single kiss to her forehead as she struggled. "By magic we are bound—"

Her head flew forward, flying into my already injured nose. I stumbled backwards, falling off her. She lunged for me without hesitation, wrapping her hands around my throat. I gasped before going still, realizing instantly that fighting would only make it worse. But she only squeezed tighter.

The instinct to live was too strong.

I let loose a quick volley of attacks, slamming my electrified hands into her midsection. She wheezed and let go, falling to her side. She was losing her touch. I kicked away from her, knocking an arrow as I did so. I took a deep breath, focusing on the white of her remaining eye.

Please, Kalysma.

She lifted her hands, heat simmering on her palms.

Let this arrow fly true.

I released.

Blood sprayed the way it only did in movies. She screamed and clawed at her face. I heard the fighting near me stop. She was no good to them if she was blind. I set the black bow in its holster before crawling towards her.

My head began to spin. My body felt weighted down.

This was too much.

But I had to see this mission through to the end.

I sat on her chest, pressing the weight of my body through my knees and into her ribcage. Then carefully wrapped my fingers around her throat. I took a deep breath, concentrating on the storm unfurling in my stomach. When my hands began to untighten, I reminded myself that she knew what had happened to me, knew and did nothing to stop it.

I said the words that every Gifted had emblazoned on their heart: "By magic we are bound—"

"No!" she mumbled. "I still have so much to do!"

"And by blood we remain."

I didn't want to do this. I didn't want to kill her. But she left me no choice. She condemned herself the day she ordered the hit on my parents.

"Among the stars—"

"No!" she screamed, gurgling on her own blood. *"No, no, no!"*

"You shall lay!"

I felt my electricity zip from my stomach, down my arm and concentrate through my fingers, sending a strong pulse throughout her body, the strongest I'd ever made. She spasmed beneath me, her mouth falling open in a silent scream. I concentrated harder, staring into the fathomless depths of the holes where her eyes should have been.

This is your fault, I thought, an angry snarl on my beastly lips, every bit the monster that they wanted me to be. *You shouldn't have gotten greedy. You should have remembered the oath that you took. You should have wanted to protect us.*

Not rule us.

I smelled her death, right before the weight of what had happened hit me like a freight train going full speed. The stench of her bowels releasing slapped me in my face. Still, I clung to her body, shuddering as the shock ran through me. Dorian grabbed me around the middle, pulling me away. I kicked and fought, even though there was no point now.

She was gone.

Yvonne lit a match before flicking it onto her body. I watched the flames eat her, wondering how this could have happened, how I could have lost everyone in such a short amount of time. First Tiara and now my Tina...

Gone.

Blue Eyes watched behind a shield of bodies, his eyes boring into mine. I had never seen the emotion in someone's eyes before—such a blind worship for what I'd stolen from him; I wondered if my eyes had once held those same shadows. Yvonne took ahold of Hao, who'd sustained minimal damage, and appeared next to us. We slammed the door shut. My powers flared and I waited until the electricity turned into fire. I welded the door shut, trapping our enemies on the other side for the time being. Dorian drew another rune and we made it to the other side where the manor awaited us.

We stumbled into the foyer, each of us sagging against the one to the left of them. Beatrice rushed to my side, letting me lean on her. Physically I felt fine but emotionally, I was drained. We went to the stage and sat down. I sank into the wood, my limbs suddenly growing tired.

"What happened, mem? Did you get the book?"

Dorian held up the book. It sang sweet words of destruction. But thanks to my earlier altercation with Jacques, it wasn't nearly as strong. Dorian planted a kiss on my forehead. I thanked Yvonne and Hao for their help, but they waved me off.

"You're family now," Yvonne said, "and family sticks together."

My eyes brimmed with hot tears at her words.

"Beatrice," Dorian said, "take Marve upstairs. She's running a temperature. Hao, Yvonne—we will do the pentagram. We need to end this madness."

I planted my hands on my hips, looked him straight in the eye and said, "No."

"Excuse me?" He said with a long blink.

"I'm not leaving. We did all this to get this stupid book—*after* we already had it once. The least you could do is let me be here to make sure that it is properly destroyed. I know that a demon can only use it when summoned. And I know that angels are forbidden from reading from it. But we are none of that, so we'll need every eye we have to make sure this goes off without a hitch."

Yvonne nodded. "She's right."

I threw her a grateful look.

My feet ached and my back hurt. I sat on the stage again, kicked off my shoes. My feet were red, swollen, throbbing from all the running. I watched as the others got out the necessary items needed for the pentagram: a vial of blood, a blade, the Book, a sacrifice and some candles.

Don't ask me how they procured the sacrifice.

"Beatrice?" I called.

The girl appeared almost instantly. "Yes, mem?"

"Bring me a strawberry soda and some ice cream."

She bowed. She returned in under thirty seconds, balancing the food on a tray.

I grabbed my snack and opened the container. It was filled to the brim with pure white vanilla soft serve, stuffed with tantalizing chocolate chunks, giant globs of marshmallow and decadent swirls of caramel. I licked my lips, eyeing the container. My stomach growled like a dog faced with an intruder. I grabbed a spoon and began devouring the frozen treat.

Other than this afternoon, this was the first time that I'd truly eaten and felt nothing.

"Babe!" Dorian threw me a look over his shoulder. "Slow down!"

"What?" I shouted, the spoon between my lips, covered with drool and the quickly melting dessert. "This could be our last meal!"

Dorian eyed a piece of marshmallow on my chin. "You look very indecent."

I rolled my eyes, set down the container and picked up the soda. I took off the top, tipped my head back and guzzled the bottle. Yvonne stared at me in abject horror, and Andrew chuckled. I felt a turning in my stomach and I figured it meant that my food desires were quelled. Before they totally forgot the mission, I set the empty bottle to the side, dipped my finger in the ice cream, and drew the pentagram with the now-liquid substance.

"Marve!" Dorian cried with a shake of his head.

I set all the items where they needed to be before standing behind Dorian. "Well?"

"Did you really just make a pentagram out of melted ice cream?"

"I suggest you do it before it gets any runnier," I sniffed.

Dorian opened the book and began chanting. The pentagram pulsated with an unearthly light, glowing red, then blue, then finally an unholy black. A black hand reached up from the pentagram, looking like a night-black lizard's claw. The lights above our heads popped and went out. My body glowed in response to the dark magic making its way into the room, but it was still hard to see everyone.

SCRRRTCH! THUMP! SCRRRTCH! THUMP!

I heard a scream that suspiciously sounded like Beatrice. Then, suddenly, the world felt cold, lonely. There was a tremor in my mind, wanting to sever to allow something to fit where something else was lost.

The demon was trying to communicate.

"I recognize my son's stench on you," a voice said in my head. It was oddly clear but also sharp and piercing, like broken crystals in the sand. I smelled the carcass of a dead animal—not the one that we sacrificed, but the scent of this demon. *"You are the one he won't shut up about? Funny...I thought he said you were a boy."*

"Yeah, that's me," I rolled of my eyes. "But he got it wrong. I'm definitely a girl."

"I can see that."

"Marve," Dorian said, "is it speaking with you?"

"Yes," I whispered. "What do I say?"

"Ask it out for lunch!"

"I don't think a demon and I have the same taste in cuisine—"

"No! God, you're hopeless. Tell it to destroy the book!" he snapped back.

"Okay, okay! Sheesh!"

I wanted to ask what set up a tent in his ass. But then I remembered what demons did: they amplified negative feelings. For me, it was sadness, which in turn bred snark. For him, it was years of pent-up anger and the sarcasm he used at times to mask it. Did Yvonne feel anything in the wake of this evil or was she immune? I heard Andrew and Hao bickering behind me.

I picked up the book once more and faced my tormentor's father. Like Jacques, he had a flare for the dramatic. He wasn't in his human form, of course. He looked like a giant ball of sludge with black feathers sticking out from his body, bubbling and audibly popping with every breath he drew. There was one crimson eye in the center of his head (if you could call it that)—something my father would call the Evil Eye. Two lizard-like hands sat close to the ground, clenched into fists that curled, uncurling time and time again.

"Destroy this book!" I said, lifting my chin and holding out the relic.

The eye slowly separated from the body as the head of the monster extended forward. It hung over me, the beast being about ten feet tall to begin with. It stared down at the book.

"Ah, yes! The Book of God. Why would I destroy it? It holds great power."

"Be-be-because," I quivered, knowing that my plan was already failing, "if you don't, then I'll kill you."

There was a laugh in my mind—cold and sinister and lacking any feeling except outraged amusement.

"Careful, little one. You can't kill me."

"I can!" I was bluffing, of course. "I have the Dagger of Truth!"

There was an audible hiss as it slid and thumped its way closer to the pentagram.

"Send me back!" It screeched. *"I will have no alliance with someone who partakes in the slaying of my kin!"*

"If you destroy this book, maybe I'll destroy the dagger," I offered.

I remembered how Master would barter in the bazaar or wager indecent prices for my battles. He was charming and cunning, and I needed to be him in that moment. I didn't really have it. No one had seen the dagger in years. But maybe I could bluff my way into achieving my goals.

I turned around and swiped the empty bottle before he could see. With a glimmer of light and a bit of magic, it looked like a regular seraph blade. I turned back around, twirling the 'dagger' in my hand.

"See?"

"I will not destroy the book until you destroy the dagger!" Abaddon hissed, sounding annoyed.

"Very well."

I picked up my runed dagger from my belt. Then I pressed it to the pretend dagger and drew a rune that I saw Dorian draw a thousand times. The fake dagger melted into a puddle of nothing, oozing down my fingertips. I wiped my hand on my pants. Then I faced the demon for the third time.

"Foolish girl. Do you know what you've done?"

I smirked. "I have an idea."

"As penance for your sacrifice, I will destroy the book. But first, I will need a drop of your blood. The book must be fed before it can be destroyed."

"All right…?"

I swiped my blade across the inside of my hand. A well of blood streamed across my palm. I then reached out and touched the Book with that same hand. The Book of Beginnings drank greedily, murmuring its thanks to me. I sighed as a bundle of energy slowly ebbed from my system.

The demon took the Book in its folds. *"Satisfied?"* the demon asked, and it took me a sec to realize that he was talking to the book and not me.

"Yes, Master," said the Book.

"Good," he responded before shifting into a human form.

I sucked in a sharp breath, memories flooding back.

He looked just like Jacques, with a well-groomed goatee and brown slicked back hair. My heart slammed to a painful halt in my chest. I knew that he wasn't Jacques, but the similarities were my undoing. He even had that same dimple above his right eyebrow. His eyes were two flames of black, his scent that of cologne on a dirty body. His plain white skin was just as beautiful as his son's and his shoulders were twice as broad. But there was also something less feminine about him than with Jacques.

He lifted the book to his lips.

"Goodbye," he said.

Then he traced his tongue along the spine. The book seemed to shudder in pleasure before crying out in pain. One by one, cracks appeared in the spine. Then the pages drifted to the floor. The cover and the pages then turned to ash.

"There," he said, "it is done."

"WHOA!" Dorian glared, "You mean to tell me that all we had to do was lick the damn thing?"

"Not necessarily," the demon smirked. "Any liquid would suffice."

"Why didn't you ask for a damn water bottle then?" my fiancé growled.

"That ruins all the fun," the demon said, eyeing me.

"Okay, man, you gotta go!" Dorian hissed, taking a step forward with balled up fists.

"Dorian," I whispered, "you can't take him!"

"The fuck I can't!" He yelled back before turning to Abaddon. "Quit making those eyes at my girl!"

Yvonne came forward. "Is this really the time?"

"Fu—"

"Okay," I said with a clap, coming towards the pentagram but not entering it, "thank you for the help! Good day to you, sir! Your son is a dick, but you probably already know that. Have a good evening. Safe travels to the fiery pits of hell. Adios!"

The demon chuckled before sinking back into the pentagram. But his eyes seemed to follow me all the way down. I turned to Dorian, who looked absolutely flabbergasted.

"What is with you?" I said, planting my hands on my hips.

"I'm just sayin'..." He shook his head, suddenly bewildered. "Ice cream, though?"

I shrugged. "It worked."

"Sorry about...*before*...with the demon—I mean Abaddon..." Dorian muttered, scratching the back of his head, "I guess I got a little carried away."

"Demons amplify negative feelings. It's how they control you. And it's totally normal."

"I can't believe we did it," he breathed; and it was then that I noticed that his voice was hoarse, his skin a sickly yellow. "I can't believe we destroyed that *stupid* book!"

"I'm just glad we got it out of the way!" I yawned. "I need a nap."

I knew that our problems were far from over. Dorian told me that they'd killed many Rebel soldiers, but Rhea was safe. She'd been away on the Southern Isles when the mission went down.

I pulled out my phone to see that I had two missing calls from her and a slew of texts, ranging from anxious to congratulatory. Funny, I never thought her capable.

U OK? I asked.

I'm GR8! She immediately texted back. *How'd it go?*

It's done.

Rhea didn't answer for a while before sending a single word: *Good.*

Wdym? I typed back.

Valentina was a bitch...the bitchiest of bitches. Like, a Mega Bitch...? Oooh, or (and I KNOW this is fucked up to say because of your 'situation') but she was a demon spawn.

I...don't feel comfortable admitting this (cause she was, like, super corrupt) but...I'm gonna miss her.

All I'm saying is...So glad she's gone.

Ok...

Hey!

Yeah?

Do you think I'd make a good leader?

Valentina was her aunt and had no children. She *was* next in line. But dragging her name through the mud literally twenty minutes after she died was fucked up. And it said a lot about her character. But I get it. There was always tension between them.

377

And in recent months, Tina was far from kind.

But then again, so was Rhea.

I swiped back: *Ask me that when you give me an answer.*

Uncomfortable, I went upstairs, powered off my phone and then laid down on my side. My chest heaved up and down as I took in a big breath. *Don't' feel it!* I whispered in my head, slamming my fists against my forehead. But the tears came anyway. Again, I took the part of me that mourned Valentina and buried it deep. She did not deserve my tears.

You keep burying things, a dark voice hissed in my ear, *and soon the ground will cave in under your feet.*

I thought of my old master, how decrepit he looked. I shuddered. I was the last witness to Jacques's tyranny. But if his words were anything to go by, he had new, braver slaves. They didn't fear him which was kind of amazing to me.

I heard the floorboards shift behind me and I knew that it was Dorian by the flowers I smelled.

"What is the Rebellion doing now that Valentina is gone?"

"I have no idea," he sighed.

I got under the covers and Dorian did the same. It was only around four in the afternoon, but I could tell that I was not the only one who felt tired. We'd won, so why did we feel so defeated?

Yvonne stopped by the room to bid us goodnight.

Dorian stared at me. "You did good today. I know that we planned for you to go to Jacques's side, but for a second, I honestly believed that you'd turned on us."

So had I.

"I'm done with that man and his sick dreams. I just want to be with you."

"I'm glad you're on my side."

I bit my lip, my texts with Rhea running through my mind. I'd never really paid attention to the way she acted or the things she said. They hurt sometimes, but this was weird, even for her. To be honest, she'd kind of always faded in the background to me and anytime I tried to bring her to the forefront, she dodged the spotlight, but not in a *shy* way. It was really weird, now that I think about it. But everyone was weird nowadays. I was wondering if this was the thing to ask so soon... But fuck it, someone had to!

"You don't think Rhea is working with the opposition, do you?"

Dorian's hand found my waist, pulling me close—not for sex, but comfort in the moments after Tina's death. "Um, no. I mean, she definitely is a snake at times, but what Immortal isn't?"

"Self-deprecating much?"

"I'm kidding. But no, she seems cool to me. Kinda funny acting at times but— wait a minute, you're paranoid!"

"Yeah...?"

He snuggled me with pride. "I've rubbed off on you!"

I grinned. "In many ways."

Dorian pecked my cheek before flicking the light off.

I felt a bit more relieved at that. I snuggled into Dorian's side, loving the feel of his arms wrapped around me. He had me in a vice grip, his hug so strong, so sure, refusing to let me go. My breathing began to slow, but just before I slept, he spoke again, the words different somehow...*off*.

But then suddenly, he began to shake, his arms tightening. "I can't get it out of my mind. I get that we planned it but seeing you standing there with him made me realize that I can't do it. I can't lose you, too."

"You won't."

"I hate this stupid war. I hate burying my lovers every time they begin to mean something to me. I hate being Immortal. I hate that you're not Immortal. I hate—" his breath choked off, stuttering in his chest. "I hate that I'm going to lose you. Maybe not to him but..."

I didn't roll over to look him in the eye. I couldn't. "The war cannot touch us here."

"Death can..." I felt his tear roll down his nose and onto my neck as he kissed me at the base of my skull. A dangerous thing to proclaim. "It takes them all..."

My magic pulsed in my veins, softly rushing at the promise I made, but knew I could not keep. "I will find a way to be with you. To stay with you. Forever. Just don't grow bored of me."

"I could never, *ever* do that." Dorian held me so tight, I thought he might squeeze the life out of me. "But I am tired of *His* games."

"Whose?"

"The Creator's."

"Dorian!" I whispered harshly. "You can't say that!"

"He hears my thoughts. Why can't I say it out loud?"

"It's different!"

"Kalysma," he whispered, "if you hear me now—"

"Dorian!"

"Save her. From death. I can't take it. Not again."

A creak whispered throughout the room, the house expanding, almost as if it were breathing. Something fell, but I couldn't be sure how. Then a stillness…like the world had stopped moving. And I felt a coldness walk along my spine. I wanted to swear at him, but why?

I rolled over, pressing a kiss to Dorian's chest, then another, and another. "I worship you," I whispered. "Why isn't that enough?"

"No—"

"I wasn't talking to you."

"These gods, with all their powers and their greatness, they would never listen to the prayers of our kind. Life is too absolute."

"Death is the only absolution."

"Love is…" he buried his nose in my hair, trembling. "Love is fire, hot, but not bad…"

"I sometimes think that you're like the sun, warm and nurturing but…sometimes you're blinding." The words came rushing out before I could stop them. "I get it now…Love is a trembling because…even when you think you've lost everything, there is always something else to lose."

And I knew it was the wrong thing to say. But I didn't know how deeply it would impact him. Not at first, it seemed. Not when the wedding was coming up and we seemed so *close* in that moment.

But it *had* affected him. And all our words had changed something in the universe, bringing out two energies that were never meant to collide, and bringing forth a darkness—

And a light.

Chapter Forty-One

Combat

I was sitting at the table that had been magicked into the foyer the next day. It had been a boring, uneventful day. All I'd done was stay in the library and sit in front of the fire. Dorian dragged me down around thirty minutes before so that we could eat dinner together. It was then that he presented me with designs for the dress.

"Do you like this one?" he asked. "Or this one?"

He showed me a pink dress with frills and puffs. It was nauseating. Then he showed me a dress that was white, elegant, but not my style. I bit my lip, debating. It was now or never. I took the pen from him and slid the notebook towards me.

"I'm going to show you what I want," I said.

"Great!" He grinned at me, then suddenly a look crossed his face and he blushed. "I don't know why, but I thought you'd want me to design it for you."

"To be honest, I'd rather design my clothes myself. Don't get me wrong, what you design is lovely. But your tastes are...not my style."

"I respect that. Thank you for letting me know." He paused. "I know Jacques

383

had you dressing like a boy. I assumed you would always want more feminine clothing."

I paused. "I actually prefer androgynous clothes. I mean, I'm grateful that you want to provide for me, of course. I just want to dress the way I want to dress." I bit my lip, pausing as my face paled, expecting him to lash out. "Is…that okay?"

"You don't need my permission to dress how you wanna. I just wish you'd told me sooner."

I grinned. "Totally."

I began to sketch what I wanted. It was silver suit of armor, with gold accents crossing the chest, arms and back. Underneath would be a black mesh shirt and a white skirt extending down the floor. Dorian suggested things, some useful, some not. I paused, wondering about the shoes. I finally decided to go without, a Gifted tradition for weddings, which we originally did not have by our own choice, seeing as we preferred multiple partners. I was compromising by giving him this and I wanted to at least look like, well, me. He jokingly suggested I wear his grandfather's watch from his mother's side. I bit my lip, wanting to say yes, but knowing that would push it a tad too far.

"It's cute," he blushed. "I'm surprised. I usually date women who like to look…like women."

Despite his words, I wasn't offended, and I glowed like the hanging moon because I knew my own worth and I understood what he meant. "Just because I want to wear armor doesn't mean that I don't want to be a woman. I think this just molds the two sides of me in a way that accepts who I am and who I was."

He paused, looking through his lashes. "I want to kiss you again."

I kissed him softly. I knew this was a big step for us. When I pulled away, I smiled shyly. "Thank you," I breathed.

His forehead touched mine. "For you...? Anything."

I reached out, playing with the hair on the nape of his neck—and saw a shadow dart up the stairs. I told him that he could change the fit of the armor. A welcome distraction on his part.

"Stay here, come up with as many designs as possible," I suggested, standing to touch his shoulder. "I'll be back."

I stood with narrowed eyes, waving off Beatrice and following the shadow up the stairs. The shadow made a right at the top of the stairs and then a left at the end of the hall. I speed walked quietly, not wanting to alert the intruder to my presence, but curious as to how they got in and what they were after. They turned down another hall, a section of the manor I'd never gone in, where suits of amour stood guard and a picture of the Good Mother—her night-black skin glowing like stars, her brownish hair surrounding her hair in fearsome, regal curls and a plethora of Gifted soldiers following the One Light down a path, the few that had already reached her kneeling at her feet to pray—loomed large and heavy. I dropped my head low, pausing before the holy picture for a fraction of a second before speeding into the room behind the figure.

When I entered the room, I was surprised to see that it was a church containing black pews with red cushions, an altar and a statue of the Good Mother pointing towards the door. The door opened and closed behind me. I glanced up at the wall behind me to see the stained glass was carved into an archway, small carvings of people surrounding it. The Mother was pointing towards the One Light, which was what guided the dead Gifted in the afterlife, leading us to the stars, to the land where we laughed, danced, sang—to home. I smiled—

But that smile quickly dissolved into a scowl when I remembered why I was so familiar with the stories that I'd nearly forgotten.

My parents taught me of our history early on, but Valentina had been the one to tell me where they now rested. I'd wanted to believe that they were in a good place, that she was right and that we all went to the same astral plane once we passed on, for the Good Mother believed that no soul was wicked. But then I thought of my teacher and wanted there to be a hell, a place where she would be held accountable for her crimes. It went against our teachings, our way of life. But I'd grown more human in my time with Dorian than I ever had under anyone else's guidance.

The figure stopped in front of the statue. Now was my chance. I raced behind it, patting my sides, but then unsure whether or not it would be good to do battle before Her. My Gift zipped throughout my room, reacting to the magic here, the sacredness of the hall, the beauty of our faith. But it wasn't until I was up on 'em that I realized they were probably just here to pray. I doubt anyone would sneak into the manor just to desecrate its church.

Realizing that it had been years since I'd been to church, I snuck up next to the person. Watching them for a prompt and receiving none, I shook my head. Many Gifted were separated from their faith when in bondage. Most of us didn't pray for fear of our lieges' retribution. I had been one of those people.

Forgive me, Mother. I have left your side for too long. Now, your house is under attack and my faith has fallen ill.

I bit into my hand, before using my finger to press down on the wound that appeared. The blood swelled. I added a bit of my magic to it before pressing my hand into the base of the statue. The blood sank into the obsidian stone, which glowed a deep shade of violet before returning to its black. The person next to me must have been truly lost, for they did not repeat my action.

"Thank you, Mother," I murmured.

I heard an intake of breath. Whoever it was had not noticed me sneak up behind them nor had they expected it to be me. I assumed it was an adoring fan from the Ring. I placed a charming smile on my face—one that my Master had me rehearse before I began fighting—and nudged their shoulder with mine.

"You must pay homage when you enter Her house."

The hood on the person shook right then left. My eyebrows furrowed. Did they fear retribution?

"It's easy."

I reached out, wrapping my fingers around their wrist, gently but also firmly. Their yellow hand shook. Their flesh was silky, soft, unblemished, so whoever they were, they were not a slave. Were they like Dorian—a hybrid? But when they moved to snatch away, my grip tightened.

"Gifted do not take kindly to disrespect. Neither does She."

The hand pulled harder. Now I was mad. They yanked again, pulling me atop them. We both tumbled to the floor. I growled, pulling back my hand as it

387

immediately tightened into a fist.

There were no candles here, just light fixtures in the ceiling. But they turned away from me. My body shuddered as the electricity rocked me. *She* was warning me. Whoever this was wasn't here on friendly terms.

I locked my hand on their narrow shoulder. Then I grabbed their hood and wrenched it back from their face. And stared.

"Let go of me!" she cried.

Mascara stained her cheeks a weakened black. Her tea-grey eyes were wide with panic. She tried to hide it, but I could smell her fear—and her eyes were a dead giveaway. I got off her and stood, placing one hand near my daggers to let her know that I would not hesitate to strike if she made a wrong move...or ran.

"What are you doing here?" I hissed, instantly remembering when I saw her at the party, when she'd turned me in.

We were not friends. Some may even dare to call us rivals. We both competed for Dorian's heart and we both knew Jacques had it out for me.

"Where is it?" she asked, raising her fists. "Hand it over!"

"Hand what over? What are you on about?"

"The book!" she hissed with a wild, paranoid glance.

I glanced at the pews. A few Gifted were sitting there with bowed heads, a young servant boy being the only one with enough gall to openly stare. When my eyes met his, he lowered his gaze and pretended to pray. The only reason I knew that he was pretending was because he was singing a song that had no praises in it.

Weird.

"What book?" I asked, blinking as I returned my gaze to Megumi.

"The Book of Beginnings," she replied flatly with a glare. "I know you have it."

"How do you know that?"

"I've been keeping in contact with your old master." She smirked at my flinch, standing a bit taller at the sight of my weakness. "Jacques told me that you killed his slave and stole his family heirloom."

My hands shook. I tried not to show it. I let go of her shoulder, yanked her to her feet and swiftly stood as I did so. *There is no book,* I thought. *But—*

"And what makes you think I'd tell you?" I asked.

"Listen, *slave,*" she spat. "I demand—"

"This is my house! I'll be the one making demands!" I angrily yell-whispered. I didn't know if I meant the church or the manor. Dorian and I weren't married yet. So, it wasn't mine. But the church meant that this was more my territory than hers. "These are hallowed grounds."

"So?" she snorted, rolling her eyes.

"So, I have the power here."

I charged up my Gift. The hair blew back from her face and her eyes widened. There was popping and crackling as electricity surged throughout the room. I raised one finger. She stumbled back a step.

"Wh-wha-what are you going to do to me?"

"That is all up to you," I replied with a daring smirk. "Remember this: it will only take one finger for me to kill you."

"HA!" She guffawed, literally throwing back her head to laugh. When her body was realigned, her eyes were narrowed, the smirk now on *her* face as she glared at me. "You can't kill me! I'm Immortal, remember?"

But I knew something she didn't.

I knew how to kill an Immortal.

Dorian had trusted me with the information, something he'd discovered when he was much younger. I'd had to recite it a few times to make sure I wouldn't forget. Of course, these rules didn't apply to demons or their offspring, so I knew I couldn't kill Jacques with it. I'd hoped that *Mimi* would be stupid enough to show her face around here. I was counting on it.

To kill her she had to want, without a shadow of a doubt, to die.

If she didn't meet this term, I couldn't kill her.

I glanced up. The five other souls in the room had abandoned their prayers, choosing instead to openly gawk at us. I fixed them with a look. Picking up their things, they trickled out of the room. The boy and his mother were the last to leave, the boy yanking against his mother's hand, begging her to let him stay, to watch the inevitable fight.

I turned to Megumi. "You're really gonna make me do this? Right here? Right now?"

"Oh," she seductively whispered, "I wouldn't have it any other way."

I smirked. This would be slow and quiet.

I was gonna make her *bleed*.

I reached down onto the sheath strapped on my leg and pulled out my favorite

390

dagger. The runes glowed as if sensing that a battle was about to take place.

She came at me first, throwing her tiny porcelain body on me. I shoved her away, twirling my blade in my hand. I circled her, taking in her posture, the weight she pushed to one leg, even her breathing.

I was going to kill her—I was sure of it.

I charged at her. I kept my balance as I drove the dagger into her ribcage. She didn't even bleed, the wound stitching itself closed as soon as it began to open.

"We made out," she said, pointing at a pew near the back, "right there."

I lunged again, this time striking her in the face. I refused to let her get to me. Anger would muddle my mind, making me misstep. A mistake was not something that I could afford. A tiny cut blossomed on her cheek and a tiny droplet of blood dripped down her face.

She knew she wasn't getting to me.

"You should have heard how he moaned, how he said my name. He said I was the best he'd ever had—that *no one* could compete. Look at you. You're just a slave! How could you ever match up to me?"

"See, bitch. That's where you're wrong. I have his heart. He's mine. He proposed to *me*."

Normally, I would have feared cursing in such a sacred place, but even the Good Mother had been known to lose her temper. I'm sure she more than understood my situation. The shorter woman shook her head, clearly in denial.

"You're just another one of his playthings, his *whore*. He'll get tired of you. Then he'll come back to me."

"As sure as I am that you have a great deal of experience spreading your legs," I hissed, swiping at her again, "I don't think that you hold a candle to me. See this?" I held up the hand with my engagement ring on it. "He gave it to me. He committed to me. He gave it all up for *me*."

She ruefully whispered, "Did he tell you that he called me?"

I pulled up short. I eyed her once more before doing a roundhouse kick to her gut. She wheezed but didn't go down. Something told me that she was telling the truth. I braced for a hard dose of reality.

"The night you left the safehouse. And again, last night. Don't you get it? You will never satisfy him."

"Because I'm inexperienced?" I hissed sarcastically, rolling my eyes.

Megumi smirked at me, and her words truly drove a stake through my heart. "Because you'll wither. And you'll die."

I snorted. "That's the best you've got? He nearly died for me. And I've seen the way he looks at you. You disgust him. But then again, I'd also be disgusted if I were a man."

"I've seen the way your eyes wander. You don't need those parts to want me."

I growled. "I appreciate beauty in all forms. Just like Dorian."

"Men like Dorian don't change. I've known him for nearly half a century. He doesn't love you. As soon as you're safe, he's going to throw you back onto the streets. Then you can go back to sucking your old Master's—"

I punched her square in the mouth.

"Say it again."

She made an obscene gesture involving her mouth and fist.

I kneed her in the stomach. She keeled over. I straddled her, fisting her hair in my hand, pulling her head back to expose her neck.

"I wonder how long it's been since Mother has seen a sacrifice in Her walls...?" I glanced at the statue, which pulsed with an excited glow. "I think seeing Immortal blood spilled will honor Her. After all, if it hadn't been for your God, She would not have been exiled and the Gifted would still be in heaven."

"Fuck you!"

I pressed my blade to her throat. She looked into my eyes, saw the conviction there, and stopped fighting. I looked into her eyes, saw the anger, the hurt, the love she still held for him. This wasn't about getting back at me. She was truly in love with my fiancé.

And that spoke to me.

"You know what?" I stood up, yanked her to her feet and shoved her towards the door. "You're not even worth my time."

She looked at me, totally disheveled, like she couldn't understand why I spared her.

I didn't fully understand it myself.

"Don't let the door hit you on the way out."

"You're pathetic!" She hissed, inching toward the door.

"Don't forget—*I* spared *your* life. And one more thing—" I threw the blade; it embedded in the wall an inch from her face, making her freeze "—you come near the manor again and I'll carve you up good, bitch."

But I'd always had problems with carrying over hatred—

And I wish I'd kept my promise.

Chapter Forty-Two

My Person, Now and Forever

Three days later, the manor was alive with the hustle and bustle of a staff with a mission. The maids cleaned with newfound vigor, repeatedly waxing the marble floors in their haste to prepare the foyer for the reception. The butlers polished the dragon statues with the utmost care. Afterwards, even the smallest caress of sunshine set off their dazzling scales. The maids set up lawn chairs in the backyard, each set made in a semicircle that mirrored the half circle of the dragons.

After that, the staff dutifully streamed white from every available surface. White ribbons streamed along the rails to the country estate. White roses were planted in the garden. White petals were strewn along the path leading to the manor.

It was odd. My old master had always preached about my purity. His hesitation of soiling it was the reason that I was a virgin when Dorian met me. My father would always sit me on his knee, tell me to keep my magic intact, to save myself till I found someone that loved me for me, a person that I felt the same about. And I hadn't listened to either of them, and yet I'd gotten everything I'd ever wanted: confidence in myself, a partner who cared, and a family.

When I thought of Tiara, almost thinking I'd seen her turning around a corner, I didn't cry, but instead smiled. We all made our journey to the Great Beyond, some sooner than others. But then I remembered that she was still in Jacques's mansion and my blood boiled.

I will free you, sister, I vowed. *It will just take time. Hopefully, I'll get the chance sooner rather than later. Only then will you find peace.*

Dorian stood in the backyard, surveying the staff as they set up the chairs and the altar. I walked up behind him, wrapping my arms loosely around his waist. He craned his neck around, glancing at me. A smirk tilted up his face and he turned to trace a finger along my cheek. I realized that my glamour was down, exposing my true form—the form that he loved me in most.

And just thinking about it made me grin.

I had an entire speech prepared in my head. I wouldn't let Megumi get a leg up on me. I wouldn't let her steal him back from me. And I wouldn't lose him to my own insecurities. I *had* to tell him how I felt.

Today.

"What're you doing?"

"Just supervising," he chuckled, still touching my cheek. "What are *you* doing?"

I wondered if I'd be too late. Shadows crossed my face as I said, "Thinking about the best person in my life."

Dorian's jaw hardened. A steely look entered his gaze, those brown-and-gold embers in his eyes dimming. His hand dropped from my face. "Are you thinking about...him?"

I raised a brow, quizzical. "I'm thinking about you."

His eyes lost that angry panic. "Oh."

"Yeah," I grinned, "oh."

He wrapped an arm around my waist. His lips found mine, his kiss as sweet as water from a summer spring. And just as warm. I smiled around his lips, tongue darting out to taste his sweetness, encapsulating ever hard line of his body, every dip of his hands in my now-present curves, every time he grunted or I panted or our souls danced with a fierceness.

This was my person.

Now. And forever.

Chapter Thirty-Four

I Do

The next day, I woke up to a soft, rapid knock at my door. I didn't move for a few minutes and finally got up from my comfy place in bed to find Beatrice and an unnamed maid running a bath for me in the adjoined bathroom.

Ah, yes, I reminded myself. *The wedding.*

I stripped down out of my silken nightgown to go to the bathroom. Beatrice and the maid helped me into the tub. I asked for the older one's name and she said that it was Alena.

Judging by her pointed ears and flickering eyes that could never stay on one shade of brown, she was of elven descent. They washed me quickly but gently, scrubbing my skin with a gentle cloth. They doused me with tonics and potions that smelled like a fistful of wildflowers. I rose from the tub slowly, mechanically, trying to keep my mind away from the one who had so readily abandoned me. I wrapped the towel around my wet hair, wincing as they dried me roughly, trying to get off all the dead skin.

They took me to the bedroom and had me stand motionless as they painted me in black and gold swirls. Some were foreign and looked to depict a magical story of some sort. Soon, every inch of my body was covered in the marriage runes, making my body glow a soft blue with their ritualistic magic. They left my face alone. As I looked at the armored dress they'd laid out in the chair for me, I knew that my outfit would cover most of the runes, save the ones on my feet.

They blow dried my hair. I winced as they ran a comb through it. I almost drew the line when Alena pulled out a pair of scissors. But she did something that I deemed fabulous. I was almost ready.

Once the paint dried, I put on my ensemble. Yvonne appeared behind me. Beatrice and Alena left silently and gracefully. Yvonne placed something in my hair, something whose cool metal washed across my face like a waterfall, and I asked what it was. She said that it was a veil.

I'd never worn one before.

I looked in the mirror.

The armor looked crisp and clean, perfectly symmetrical on my body. Even my cleavage looked more pronounced under the mesh shirt. I was actually starting to get to a healthy weight. The wedding fit was loose on my legs and tight, strong, in my chest—perfect in just about every way. I wore it with pride. Finally, Yvonne placed a rose dipped in blood the chest of the armor, a piece of paper sticking to my somewhat still-damp skin. I quickly removed it, staring down at it.

Leila Boyd, December 23rd, 2125.

I tried to imagine myself in the body of a woman, my curves ebbing and

399

flowing like water, but instead saw the moony-eyed, round, gentle face of my mother.

My skin appeared to be a deep, golden brown against its dark foreground. My hair, which was first cut in layers and then combed back in a somewhat boyish fashion, gleamed brighter than the pearls strung around my neck. I swiftly ran my hand along the smooth silk of the suit. Then, as I looked into the eyes of the girl in the mirror, the significance of this day hit me all over again.

I was marrying my best friend.

"You'll be okay, Marve," Yvonne sighed. "I know that you must be scared out of your mind right now, but Dorian is a good man. He'll take care of you."

But she misunderstood. I wasn't afraid. I was happy. Overjoyed. But also…

Actually, *YES,* I was afraid. But not of marrying Dorian. No, no…this was an ancient, primal fear, as if the hounds of hell were coming up to bite my legs and drag me away. But then I imagined Dorian standing behind me, a wedding band on his finger.

I'm ready.

***

The doors swung open. A small girl skipped down the aisle, sea thrift pinned in her hair and a simple white dress on her body; even though she was curly, blonde-haired, azure-eyed and white, she reminded me of Tiara immensely. But in her dress, Armeria looked like she fit. She twirled and threw the white roses in the air before taking her place in line just as the flowers settled.

I walked down the aisle, towards my destiny, alone. Not even music accompanied me.

That's when I saw him.

The light dusted across his golden skin as he gave his trademark smile. He was in a tailored black tux that was as dark and smooth as the night sky. His eyes shined like the stars that showed their faces only at night. His feet, like mine, were bare. In that moment, I was happy to see him accustomed to the superstitions of the lesser magical folk. If you were to ask the Gifted what would doom a marriage, they would say that to wear shoes on a wedding day was bad luck.

Where a handkerchief would normally rest, there was that same symbolic flower: a single white rose with red blood on the tip of its petals. That was an old Immortal tradition—to wear a rose dipped in the bride and groom's blood.

I trudged down the aisle, ignoring the camera that Megumi held, trained on me. She watched me with a devilish smile. I'd spared her and this was how she repaid me? I made it to Dorian. He reached out, took my hand, but there was no spark, no warmth in his touch.

I blanked out. The only thing I remember was Dorian nudging me, a bright grin on his face. He squeezed my hand and whispered that it was my part.

"I trust in the stars, in the Goddess, in this life placed in my care to honor and treasure me for all my days."

"As do I," he said, eagerly turning to face me.

"By the power vested in me, I now pronounce you husband and wife." The minister gave us both a relieved grin. "You may kiss the bride."

He gently laid his lips over mine. In his kiss, I felt the truth deeper than any emotion could go. This was my place—next to him. The kiss probably only lasted for a second or two, but when he pulled away, he breathed heavy, his eyes swimming with something hot and heavy. And I remembered that wish I made the first night Jacques beat me—

For a love grander than the constellations themselves.

The preacher told us to turn to the people. We turned to see the smiling faces of so many, some genuine and some not. The women were trying not to scowl. The men were trying not to grin too hard, shouting praises. In the background, a Gifted prayer to Kalysma floated through the speakers.

"I now introduce to you Mr. and Mrs. Dorian Boyd!"

They cheered when we both smiled.

My love, oh, my love.

Chapter Forty-Five

I Can't Help but Want You

Dorian led me to the empty dance floor. Together, we spun round and round to a love song by the famous Mortal Whitney Houston. He looked similar to when we'd first met. Strong. Confident. Oddly closed off for a reception, eyes inching towards the bar as his hands faltered on the waist.

"You can drink if you'd like," I offered, even though I knew his drinking separated us, "I know you want to."

He kissed me long and hard before going to the bar. Megumi was waiting for him there. The butlers moved about the room, offering drinks. Just like that, it was like I was at a whole other party.

The lights were bright, the music loud, as wasted couples spun around me. The place was overflowing with champagne, people acting wild in their drunken merriment. The platters overflowed with vibrant cakes, zesty finger sandwiches and everything else a party should have.

A few nonmagical humans snuck off, drunk from champagne and moonlight.

Immortals snuck after them, drunk from age. This made me wonder what I would be like if I could live forever. Would I still kill in the Ring? Would I treasure each moment? Would I have ended up with Dorian or would I have gone down my own path?

I downed four glasses of champagne, steeled my shoulders and stumbled over to Dorian. He sat next to Megumi, his hand inching up her thigh. I frowned. This was *not* the love that I had wished for—this was careless indifference. I cleared my throat. He glanced at me, then looked back at his drink, his hands coming up around the cup. Megumi stood.

"I'll give you two a minute."

She leaned over and kissed his cheek before brushing past me.

I sat next to him, unsure of what to say. But then I realized that my overthinking was standing in the way of every chance I had. I *had* to say it.

"Dorian?"

He burped. "Yes, love?"

"Why do you drink?"

He let one hand go of the cup, his head moving to rest on his fist. He looked so tired. "I don't even know anymore."

"Are you...unhappy with me?"

"Gods, no!" he cried, whirling to face me. "It's just...sometimes, when I'm supposed to be happy, I get extremely sad, and I drink. And when I drink, I am a less than honorable man. I...I'm sorry, Marve. I don't know why or...really...what's wrong with me? I just do."

"That's the nature of addiction," I nodded pensively.

And despite everything, it's not your fault.

He propped his hand on his fist, a faraway look in his eyes. I could see the memories playing in his head, the real and the alcohol-induced warped. He was losing a battle that I didn't even know he was fighting.

I leaned over, capturing his mouth with mine. I searched for nothing with this kiss, but I gave it what I had left in me. I loved him enough to try my darndest to be enough. And, I realized that I loved him enough to keep him out of the vortex that was my mental and emotional instability. Because I was truly damaged and so was he, but I wasn't so broken that I wanted to hurt him further.

"I love you, more than the stars love their bed in the sky," I whispered against his lips, my forehead barely brushing his, "I just thought you should know."

I waved Beatrice over. "Is our bed ready?"

"Yes, mem..." Her eyes darted first at me, then over her shoulder, and I was just waiting for her to say something unfortunate. "You should know..."

"Yes?"

"Someone is looking for you."

"Who?"

"Don't trust her," she whispered fiercely. "She came with him."

"Who?" I glanced around me at the dance floor. "Is Megumi back?"

"No, mem." Her nostrils flared. "I—I can't say. I've said too much. I'm sorry."

She disappeared.

Yvonne popped up behind me in a flowing lime green dress that was oddly beautiful on her dark skin. The top of it clung to her shoulders but the bottom jutted out in the complicated swirls of a rose. No doubt one of Dorian's designs. She laid a hand on my arm. I gave her a smile.

"Do you need something, Mrs. Baxter?"

"I just wanted to inform you that a Rebel is here," she whispered in my ear. "And behind her...a shadow."

Instead of slinking away, she stood by my side. Andrew walked up to stand next to her, placing a hand on her waist as both of their eyes began to glow. My eyes narrowed as I took in the room, trying to remain vigilant without alerting anyone.

A shadow darted along the floor, sniffing as it measured people. It lacked horns, but I knew who it belonged to...which meant that *he* was not far behind. *Fuck!* He'd found me.

Rhea made her way towards me, wearing a simple blue dress with a butterfly pattern and black pumps. It was a beautiful color on the Black-Hispanic woman's skin. She looked out-of-place as she elbowed her way through the crowd. Some pervert turned and whistled at her. She shot him a dark look. The man reached out to grab her and in response, she lifted her dress to expose a gun strapped to her thigh.

The man held up his hands in the universal 'I don't want any trouble' sign. Despite my pain, I laughed. Rhea punched Dorian's shoulder before glancing at me apologetically.

"Hey," she threw up a hand, "sorry I'm late."

Dorian set down his shot glass, knocking over the other glasses next to him. The bartender crossed his arms, not appreciating us distracting his best customer.

Dorian slid five drachmas across the counter. The tender offered him another bottle and with a shrug, Dorian handed him some more drachmas and took it.

Then he glanced at me and said, "I don't know what to do with this."

"You drink it...?" I asked, smiling wistfully.

> *"Too far to touch, baby,*
>
> *I let you in,*
>
> *I felt the rush, baby,*
>
> *When we kissed.*
>
> *Are you in love, baby,*
>
> *Or are you in sin?*
>
> *I've had enough, baby,*
>
> *I'm givin' in."*

His eyes searched mine for what may have been the longest moment in my entire life. Then he reached out, brushing his knuckles across my cheek. I tilted my head into the touch instinctively. And suddenly he looked at me with desperation, pain, fear.

"I've made a mistake." His lips trembled, snot dribbling down his lip. "For the past three-hundred years, I've made the worst mistakes."

I shrugged.

I waited for him to say what I desperately wanted to hear, but instead he pushed past me, stumbling towards Megumi. I didn't wait to see what happened when he reached her. I couldn't bear it.

The song switched from violins to a beat that was undeniably techno. I tried not to cringe at the overuse of synthesizers. Rhea, on the other hand, seemed right at home. She leaned against a stool, waiting for me to accept her apology. But there was still something she wasn't saying.

"Your wedding is huge." She hesitated for a still moment. "With this many people, it wouldn't be hard to hide something malicious."

Normally, this would have stood out to me. But right now, I was too preoccupied with thoughts of Dorian, to really suspect her of anything bad. Even Jacques' shadow seemed like a distant nightmare, muddled by light and love.

The synthesizers faded. The woman's smooth voice began crooning once more. The violins slowly crept back into the song. A drum counted a simple eight-count like a pulsing heartbeat.

The woman sang of love and fear and death. I clapped when the song was over.

I couldn't deny that even after it ended, the song resonated with me. I heard the DJ announce that the song was called *Heart Problems* by (you guessed it!) Lyon-S. I'd danced to her before with Dorian…The sweet memory made me ache like a cavity.

"So where were you? I didn't see you at the wedding."

"I was in the back." She injected smoothly. "I was feeling a little lightheaded earlier, so I wanted to be close to the doors."

"You should have sat down."

"I know. But Dorian asked me to keep an eye out."

"And did you?" When she asked what, I was forced to clarify: "Spot anything?"

"That's what I wanted to tell you." She leaned close, slipping a note into my hand. "That's from you-know-who."

"Valentina?" I asked, raising a brow.

How could she send notes when she's dead?

"No. *You-Know-Who!*"

"I don't know who you're talking about!" I hissed, pushing the note back into her hand. "Can't your friend wait until tomorrow? I've got a lot going on right now!"

"You don't get what I'm saying." Rhea stared at me as if astounded by how slow I was being. "You're out of time."

A shudder passed down my back. "Who sent you?"

"No one sent me. But I saw someone. And he gave me a message to deliver. He wanted to meet with you before the reception. Before he blew a hole through Wall Seinaru."

"Rhea...*who* sent you?"

"It's too late for that." She grabbed my arm. "I have to make this delivery before he kills every Rebel south of here. You took too long."

"The Rebels disbanded."

"No, we just have a new leader—me. You were right, by the way. I do make a good leader. I make the decisions that she was too weak to carry out. And I don't ever want you to think that I'm working with him. I'm not. I just can't let more innocent people get hurt because of you."

I tried to fight against her hand but she was strong—stronger than I'd ever thought possible. I glanced over at where I last saw Dorian, but he was preoccupied, whispering to Megumi. She screamed back at him, tears streaming down her face. I would have smiled, guessing that he was making his way back to me, but fear had taken over.

It couldn't be who I thought.

The shadow streaked over to me, sniffed, then suddenly shuddered in pleasure. I tried to step away. It wrapped around my ankle, trapping me in place. I tried to tug free. I nearly fell, but it was no use—his soul had found mine.

My breaths came out in short chatters. I felt a hand touch my back. I whirled around to see the last face that I wanted to see, the man that I hated with every fiber of my being. His face was sallow, his red-flecked black eyes alight with a manic craze, fangs jutting from his lips—between his Immortal form and his demonic form.

But what was the difference between an Immortal and a monster?

"Darling, I have so much to show you."

"Jacques."

"Come with me…unless you want to see your new husband lose what you crave so."

I saw his shadow quivering excitedly and the fight in me died as quickly as it came. Rhea stared into my eyes as if she were in pain, a secret in her eyes. I wanted to imagine that she didn't want to hurt me—that she didn't want anyone to get hurt. I told myself that was why she was working with him—to keep everyone safe.

Which made her one hell of a leader.

"Don't hurt him," I whispered, my mind instantly going to Dorian.

"Wouldn't dream of it," Jacques said with a roll of his eyes, leading me past the dance floor.

When Rhea moved to catch up to us, Jacques handed her a drachma.

She stared at it in confusion, looked up at him, blinked. "This wasn't a part of the deal."

He brushed her off, pulling me along. "I changed my mind."

Her eyes widened as she realized—she couldn't trust him. "You two-timing motherfucker. *Tu loco bastardo!* You told me no one would get hurt. You told me they'd all be safe!"

He flicked a wrist. She went flying into a table. He stepped us out of the front door, then turned back to look at the now-quivering woman as if she were senile. "Honey," he purred, "I'm a fucking demi-demon."

She let out an enraged scream.

He took my hand gently, a satisfied smile on his face. I was shaking, from fear or rage, even I don't know. He took me outside, wrapped an arm around my shoulder tightly, discreetly daring me to run. I sagged into him, not because I wanted to, because I was too tired to hold myself aloft any longer.

BOOM!

I looked through bleary, tear-filled eyes to see smoke spilling out the side of the manor. Orange-red flames were raging from the dancefloor, burning the manor to the ground. I heard booms shatter in the distance, smoke piling south of Amoria. Then screaming. A thousand screams—men, women, children. All hurting—all *burning*.

All compromised.

Because of me.

A shadow waded through the darkness of smoke, only barely illuminated by the kindling flames, a glowing, golden magic surrounding his form.

I knew without knowing that I would be okay. Dorian would save me. After all, I was his wife.

And what was love—what was *life*—without anticipation?

TO BE CONTINUED

Social Media Handles

Social Media Handles:

@ruquayyasajjida (Instagram)

@RuquayyaSajjida (Twitter)

@RuquayyaSajjida (Facebook)

www.ingramcontent.com/pod-product-compliance
Lightning Source LLC
Chambersburg PA
CBHW030617250626
47154CB00006B/1827